# Pocket Book of
# British Ceramic Marks

Also by J. P. Cushion
(in collaboration with W. B. Honey)

HANDBOOK OF POTTERY AND
PORCELAIN MARKS
*(fourth, revised edition)*

# Pocket Book of
# British
# Ceramic Marks

★

including
Index to Registered Designs
1842–83

★

compiled by
## J. P. CUSHION
*lately Senior Research Assistant of the*
*Department of Ceramics*
*Victoria and Albert Museum, London*

*faber and faber*
LONDON · BOSTON

First published in 1959
by Faber and Faber Limited
3 Queen Square London WCIN 3AU
as Pocket Book of English Ceramic Marks
Second edition 1965
Second impression 1967
Third impression 1969
Fourth impression 1970
Fifth impression 1972
Third enlarged edition, revised and reset 1976
This paperback edition first published in 1983
Reprinted 1986, 1988 and 1991

Printed in England by Clays Ltd, St Ives plc

A CIP record for this book is
available from the British Library

ISBN 0 571 13108 5

# Acknowledgements

The author wishes to express his gratitude to the many officers and colleagues at the Victoria and Albert Museum, numerous collectors, English Ceramic Circle members and ceramic dealers, all of whom have assisted him in the recording of elusive marks for the guidance of future seekers.

Thanks are also recorded to Mr. Murray Fieldhouse, editor of *Pottery Quarterly*, and to the members of The Craftsmen Potters Association, who have assisted him in the collection of the marks and particulars of the present-day studio potters. The author is indebted to Mr. Geoffrey Godden for information concerning the dates of nineteenth-century factories and potters.

Thanks for information concerning recently established factories, closures, take-overs etc. are due to the proprietors of *Tableware International* (formerly *Pottery Gazette and Glass Trade Review*, established 1877), and to Mr. Terence Woolliscroft of Milton, Stoke-on-Trent, who so generously carried out the research concerning the recent, and often very complicated, changes of proprietorship of many Staffordshire factories. Mr. Woolliscroft noted that by January 1972 only one hundred and forty-four factories (individual producing units) remained in the Stoke area, employing thirty-four thousand workers.

# Contents

## MARKS

# Preface: Scope and Arrangement
## of the Book

This pocket-book of ceramic marks has been produced especially to answer the requirements of the collector and dealer who has long needed such a guide when on 'pot-hunting' expeditions. In order to restrict the bulk of this volume the marks shown here have been confined to those of Great Britain and Ireland; Continental and Far Eastern marks are dealt with in the *Handbook of Pottery and Porcelain Marks*.

The marks recorded here are restricted to true factory marks and those others which by their frequent occurrence, or in other ways are of actual use in helping to identify the place and period of manufacture of a piece.

The arrangement is in alphabetical order of towns, subdivided into names of factories or owners, again alphabetically. The pottery centre of Staffordshire is treated in a separate section from the rest of England.

As far as practicable the marks are shown in facsimile (space has not permitted full-scale reproduction in all cases), the chief exception being those numerous modern marks consisting of the names or initials of the maker, or of the place of manufacture, which are reproduced by using printers' type, as has so often been done in the marks themselves on the actual wares.

The scope of this book has been extended to include many nineteenth- and twentieth-century marks not hitherto recorded, and brought right up-to-date by showing the marks of modern studio-potters.

To help the enquirer, an approximate date or period

is given for every mark together with the name of the principal proprietor where of interest, and a word or so of description of the type of ware on which the mark is generally found.

\*    \*    \*

This enlarged and revised new edition of the *Pocket Book of English Ceramic Marks*, includes that part of the Class IV Design Index which relates to pottery and porcelain (Appendix B, page 288). It is included by the kind permission of the Public Record Office and will enable readers not only to date their wares by using the tables on pages 284–287, but also to determine the name of the manufacturer or person or firm, who initially registered the design to protect it from 'piracy' for a period of three years, by consulting the Index (i.e. Appendix B).

# Historical Note and Methods
## of Marking

The practice of marking ceramic wares as a guide to the manufacturer is a very old one and was carried out by the Romans on their red-wares, but it is not until the sixteenth century in Europe that the soft-paste Italian 'Medici' porcelain appears with a fully developed factory-mark, i.e. the sketch of the dome of Florence Cathedral in underglaze blue.

It was not until 1723 that the Meissen (Dresden) factory in Saxony adopted as a regular factory-mark the crossed swords of the arms of Saxony; this mark was invariably painted in underglaze blue on the base of the article in the Chinese manner. Other European porcelain and faience factories quickly followed the lead of Meissen and in 1766 the porcelain makers of France were required by law to use a mark which had been previously registered with the police authorities.

The practice of marking was never regularized throughout the eighteenth century with the result that factories which were proud of their reputation used a recognized mark, whilst the less important factories either left their wares unmarked in the hope that they would be mistaken for those factories whose style they were copying, or alternatively, used a mark similar enough to a famous one to be mistaken for genuine. The crossed swords of Meissen were used on numerous imitations and quite openly copied on Bow, Derby, Worcester and Lowestoft.

Many of the marks encountered on ceramics are

merely those of painters or workmen and are not a sure guide to the place of manufacture even when identified, for these people were of a very nomadic nature and often worked in many different factories in the course of their career. The throwers and 'repairers' (a term used for the workers who assembled the various parts of figures, etc.) invariably used a mark scratched in the body prior to the biscuit firing. These marks when under the glaze can safely be treated as genuine, but otherwise they should be closely examined for the burr or raised edge which is unavoidable when scratching soft clay, to ensure the mark has not been ground in after firing in order to deceive.

Painters and gilders generally used one of the colours in their palette or gilt, to mark the wares upon which they worked, this information was probably solely for the benefit of the management and for purposes of payment, which was often on a piecework basis.

Not to be confused with the names of potters are those of London dealers, who during the eighteenth and nineteenth centuries had goods made and decorated to their specific orders.

The marks used on English wares were applied in several different ways, including the incising (or scratching) on the unfired clay we have mentioned above. The other marks impressed in the body at this stage are also a reliable guide and usually were names of the factory, place or proprietor, made up of printers' type and stamped in one operation.

Painting or transfer-printing under the glaze in blue (also in green after 1850) was a most common method of marking wares and may be accepted as genuine, at least as far as knowing the piece was marked at the time of manufacture.

The practice of marking by painting, transfer-printing, or stencilling over the glaze in enamel-colours, are methods which are always liable to be fraudulent, as it is possible to add these type of marks at any time after the piece has been made.

The beginner should approach all marks with caution and it is important to learn to detect the difference between the various materials, (i.e. earthenware, hard-paste porcelain, soft-paste porcelain and bone-china, etc.); this would enable him to immediately realize that a neat gold anchor on a Chelsea-type figure cannot possibly be of that factory if the body is a hard continental paste and not the soft-paste as used at Chelsea. Finally do remember that many nineteenth-century factories include the date of their establishment in their mark and those early dates do not signify that the piece in question was made at that date, and also, that grandmother, who died at the ripe old age of one hundred and one, did not necessarily acquire the piece of china she has passed down to you at her birth.

# Notes on Wares Made in Great Britain and Ireland

The English late-medieval wares are not only of great artistic interest, but historically important as the direct ancestors of the Staffordshire wares. Little is known of the places of their production, the finer specimens perhaps being made in monasteries, and though of coarse materials the jugs and pitchers are often of great beauty of form and bear simple but effective decoration.

In the fifteenth and sixteenth centuries smaller neater jugs appear with a rich copper-green glaze together with a hard red pottery with dark brown or black glaze sometimes decorated with trailed white slip or with applied pads of white clay.

A rare and distinct class of sixteenth-century English pottery comprises cisterns, stove-tiles and candle-brackets finely moulded in relief and covered with a green or yellow glaze.

English pottery tradition before the industrial period was rooted in the medieval use of lead-glazed earthenware. The sixteenth-century Cistercian pottery was the immediate forerunner of the Tickenhall and Staffordshire slip-wares, and the tradition of the last in turn gave vitality to the 'Astbury' and 'Whieldon' wares made in the same district in the eighteenth century.

The impulse towards refinement, which had been inspired by the Elers brothers (who made fine red wares in the Chinese style) and by the vogue of porcelain, also led to the making of a fine white salt-glazed stoneware in Staffordshire, where the industrializing process was finally carried through by Josiah Wedgwood. His cream-coloured ware was immediately imitated at numerous neighbouring potteries as well as at Leeds, Liverpool, Bristol, Swansea, Sunderland, Newcastle, Portobello and elsewhere, quickly securing a world-wide market.

Aside from the main English tradition are the decorative stonewares of Wedgwood, products of the neo-Classical enthusiasm.

Tin-glazed ware, largely inspired by Italian, Dutch and Chinese models, was made at London, Bristol, Liverpool, Dublin and Glasgow, but had little effect on the main current of the English tradition as represented by the wares of Staffordshire, where delftware (as this is called) was never made. English delftware was painted in high-temperature colours; overglaze enamels were used only on very rare examples and were probably the work of Dutch independent enamellers.

The seventeenth-century stoneware of Fulham, inspired at first by the Rhenish and Chinese wares, produced the isolated phenomenon of Dwight's admirable figures; that of Nottingham, though typically English, was of minor importance, reflecting latterly something of the Staffordshire style.

English porcelain of the eighteenth century is remarkable for its variety of composition. Soft-pastes of French type ware made at Chelsea, Derby and Longton Hall; soapstone pastes at Worcester, Caughley and Liverpool; and hard-paste at Plymouth and Bristol. From about 1750 onwards for several decades Derby was a most productive factory and a large proportion of the surviving English porcelain figures were made there. At Bow the use of bone-ash from 1747 heralded the type of porcelain which towards the end of the eighteenth century became and still remains the English standard

17

body; this last was a hybrid porcelain in which some part of the kaolin was replaced by bone-ash. At Nantgarw and Swansea a belated soft-paste was made in the period 1813–22.

None of the factories enjoyed royal or princely protection or subsidy and most were short-lived. Chelsea, and possibly Worcester, alone reached the standard set by the chief manufacturers of France or the many establishments supported by the rulers of small states in Germany; the porcelain of the first-named, however, ranks with the best ever made in Europe. The unsophisticated charm of Bow and Lowestoft is of a different order and typically English.

From the absence of marks, the English porcelains are difficult to identify. The chief factories were those named above, but other early manufacturers may have existed in Limehouse, Lambeth, Kentish Town, Vauxhall and Greenwich.

The ceramic art of the nineteenth century suffered no less than others from misdirected effort and mistaken enthusiasms. While the early part of the century lived largely on the artistic capital of the preceding period, the later part was chiefly occupied with the deliberate revival of former styles.

Yet in spite of unfavourable conditions the native genius of the English potters did succeed in producing wares which are both beautiful and of permanent value; the simple 'cottage china' and lustre wares of the New Hall type and its kindred earthenware; Worcester, Derby, Spode, Coalport and other porcelains which were its opulent contemporaries and successors, the charming blue-printed ware, and the entirely English brown stonewares of the Midlands and Lambeth. A singular use of glazed Parian is to be noted in the wares of Belleek in Co. Fermanagh, Ireland, where a pottery was started in 1863. Vases in naturalistic shell-forms were especially characteristic.

At the end of the century the revival of handicraft makes its appearance with **De Morgan** and the **Martin Brothers**, heralding the studio pottery of the present day.

AMESBURY (Wiltshire)
Zillwood, W., late 18th-
early 19th centuries
pottery

W.Z.
incised

ASHBY-DE-LA-ZOUCH
(Leicestershire)
Thompson, J., *c.* 1815–56
general pottery

JOSEPH THOMPSON
WOODEN BOX
POTTERY
DERBYSHIRE
impressed
and other printed marks

Wilson & Proudman
Coleorton Pottery
1835–42, general pottery

WILSON &
PROUDMAN
impressed

ASHTEAD (Surrey)
Ashtead Potters Ltd.
1926–36, earthenware

AYLBURTON (Gloucestershire)
Leach, Margaret, 1946–56
Taena Community, 1951–56
and Upton St. Leonards, Glos.
where L. A. Groves also
used mark. Studio-pottery

impressed

BARNSTAPLE (Devon)
Baron, W. L., 1899–1939
Rolle Quay Pottery
earthenware

BARON. BARNSTAPLE
incised

Brannam, Ltd., C. H.,
Litchdon Pottery, 1879–
earthenwares

C. H. BRANNAM
BARUM
incised

as from 1913–

C. H. BRANNAM LTD.
impressed

printed or impressed, 1929–

impressed, 1930–

C. H. BRANNAM
BARUM DEVON

BELPER (Derbyshire)
Belper Pottery 1809–34
stonewares
(transferred to Denby 1834)

BELPER
impressed

BENTHALL (Salop)
Pierce & Co., W., *c.* 1800–18
earthenwares

W. PIERCE & CO.

Salopian Art Pottery Co.
1882–*c.* 1912 earthenwares,

SALOPIAN
impressed

BILLINGHAM (Cleveland) and
elsewhere
Dunn, Constance, 1924–
studio-pottery

incised

21

BIRKENHEAD (Merseyside)
Della Robbia Co. Ltd.
earthenwares, *c*. 1894–1901

DELLA ROBBIA
impressed or incised

top initial that of decorator

BISHOPS WALTHAM
(Hampshire)
Bishops Waltham Pottery
decorative earthenwares
only from 1866–7 in
Greek revival form

BISHOPS
WALTHAM
printed

BOVEY TRACEY (Devon)
Bovey Tracey Pottery Co.
earthenwares, 1842–94
Bovey Pottery Co. Ltd.
1894–1957
also
'Blue Waters Pottery'
*c*. 1954–57

B.T.P. CO.
printed or impressed

*c*. 1937–49     1949–56

Devonshire Potteries Ltd.
earthenwares. 1947–
also
'Trentham Art Wares'
1959–

TRENTHAM
ART WARE

Ehlers, A. W. G.
Lowerdown Cross, 1946–55
studio-potter

incised or painted

22

Leach, David, 1956–
(also at St. Ives *c.* 1932–56)
   'LD' for Lowerdown
   Pottery

impressed

BOW (London)
(Stratford High St., Essex)
*c.* 1747– *c.* 1776
soft-paste porcelain
   early marks, *c.* 1750

incised

   presumably 'repairers'
   marks 1750–60

incised

impressed   *B*

probably mark of
'repairer'
Mr. Tebo (Thibaud?)
   marks on blue-painted
   wares 1750–70

T•   T

impressed

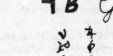

underglaze blue

on figures and other late pieces
and
'anchor and dagger'
period, *c.* 1762–76

in red

in underglaze
blue and red

in red

in underglaze blue

in underglaze    in underglaze
blue and red    blue

on blue-and-white
cups, in underglaze
blue

in underglaze blue

BRADFORD (W. Yorkshire)      F.B.
   Booth, Frederick, *c.* 1881
   earthenware


BRAMPTON (Derbyshire)      KNOWLES
   Knowles & Son, Matthew
   stonewares, *c.* 1835–1911

   Oldfield & Co., *c.* 1838–88     J. OLDFIELD
   earthenware

                     OLDFIELD & CO.
                       impressed
   Pearson Ltd., James      J.P. LTD.
   Oldfield and London     impressed or printed
   Potteries. stonewares     from 1907
   19th century—1939
   1920–

*Bramfield Ware*

24

BRAUNTON (N. Devon)
  Braunton Pottery Co. Ltd.
  earthenwares, 1910–
      mark of *c.* 1947–
  (moved or finished by 1972)

BRAUNTON
POTTERY
DEVON
printed or impressed

BRISTOL (Avon)
  (Lund & Miller's factory)
  soft-paste (soapstone)
  porcelain 1748–52, then
  transferred to Worcester

BRISTOL
BRISTOLL
in relief

(Cookworthy & Champion's factory)
hard-past porcelain
1770–81, transferred
from Plymouth

2

underglaze blue,
blue enamel, red or
gold

    early mark during
    Cookworthy's
    ownership (also used
    at Plymouth)

X    6
        x

in blue enamel

    underglaze blue
    and blue enamel

+X    xB

blue
enamel

tin-glazed earthenware
(delftware) *c.* 1650–

mark of John Bowen,
painter, apprenticed
1734

*yf. 1st: Sept.r*
*1761*
*Bowen - fecit,*

in blue

25

initials of Michael Edkins, delft-painter and his wife on plate dated 1760

M<sup>E</sup>·B
J760
in blue

Bristol Pottery
c. 1785–1825
earthenwares

BRISTOL POTTERY
impressed or painted

Coombes, a china-mender
c. 1775–1805
  in pale brown lustre

Coombes
Queen St
Bristol

Fifield, William (*b.* 1777,
*d.* 1857) painter on
Bristol pottery
c. 1810–55

W.F.
W.F.B.
W. FIFIELD

Pardoe, Thomas (*d.* 1823)
painter at Derby,
Worcester, Cambrian
Pottery, Swansea,
factories, independent
decorator of pottery and
porcelain in Bristol
c. 1809–20

Pardoe
28 Bath St.,
Bristol
Warranted

Pardoe, Bristol
painted

Pardoe, William Henry
(son), decorator at
Cardiff and elsewhere
c. 1820–35

PARDOE, CARDIFF

Patience, Thomas
18th century stoneware

PATIENCE
impressed

| | |
|---|---|
| Pountney & Allies<br>Bristol Pottery *c.* 1816–<br>35, earthenware | P.<br>P. & A.  P.A.<br>B.P. |
| printed, impressed or<br>painted | P.A.<br>BRISTOL POTTERY |
| impressed |  |
| Pountney & Goldney<br>Bristol Pottery, 1836–49 | POUNTNEY & GOLDNEY<br>(or as above) |
| impressed | BRISTOL POTTERY |
| Pountney & Co., 1849–<br>Bristol Victoria Pottery | P. & CO. |
| 1849–89 | POUNTNEY & CO. |
| 1889– | POUNTNEY & CO. LTD. |
| *c.* 1954–<br>now Cauldon Bristol<br>Potteries Ltd. | Bristol<br>founded ✕ in 1652<br>✕✕<br>England |
| Powell, William (& Sons)<br>Temple Gate Pottery<br>*c.* 1830–1906, stoneware | POWELL<br>BRISTOL |
| impressed *c.* 1830– | BRISTOL TEMPLE<br>GATE POTTERY |

27

Ring, Joseph 1785–
(*d.* 1788), cream
coloured earthenware
continued by partners
until 1812

RING & CO.
impressed

BROSELEY (Salop)
Maw & Co. Ltd., 1850–
tiles and art pottery
from *c.* 1875
   *c.* 1880–

MAW & CO.

FLOREAT MAW
SALOPIA

BURTON-ON-TRENT (Derbyshire)
Bretby Art Pottery, Woodville
Tooth & Ault 1883–87
Tooth & Co. 1887–
earthenwares
   Henry Tooth *c.* 1883–1900

   *c.* 1914–

CLANTA
WARE

Woodward, James
Swadlincote Pottery
'Majolica' earthenware
1859–88

printed or impressed

CASTLE HEDINGHAM (Essex)
Hedingham Art Pottery
Bingham, Edward
1864–1901
reproduction of medieval
and Tudor type wares

applied in relief

28

incised signature
1864–1901

E. BINGHAM
CASTLE HEDINGAM
ESSEX

early 20th century

ROYAL ESSEX ART
POTTERY WORKS

CASTLEFORD (W. Yorkshire)
Clokie & Masterson
earthenware, 1872–81

C. & M.
CLOKIE &
MASTERMAN
printed or impressed

Clokie & Co., 1888–1961
earthenware
(Ltd. after 1940)
   printed

Dunderdale & Co., David
Castleford Pottery,
*c.* 1790–1820
earthenware and
stoneware

D.D. & CO.

D.D. & CO.
CASTLEFORD

Gill, William (& Sons)
Providence Pottery
1880–1932

printed

Hartley's (Castleford)
Ltd., Phillips Pottery
*c.* 1898–1960
stoneware and earthenware;
decorative art wares
from 1953

HARTROX

29

| | |
|---|---|
| Nicholson & Co., Thomas earthenware, *c.* 1854–71 | T.N. & CO. printed with name of pattern |
| Robinson Bros. Castleford & Allerton Potteries stoneware, 1897–1904 | R.B. printed or impressed |
| Robinson & Son, John stoneware, 1905–33 | J.R. & S. impressed |

CAUGHLEY (Salop)
Turner, Thomas
*c.* 1772–1799 (then taken over by John Rose
of Coalport factory)
soft-paste porcelain and      SALOPIAN
black basaltes             Salopian
(*see also* 'Benthall')       impressed

printed or painted in
underglaze blue *c.* 1772–95

printed or painted
*c.* 1772–95

printed mark usually
Worcester
open printed crescent
also on Coalport           printed

Chinese type mark

CHEAM (Surrey)
Clark, Henry, 1869–80
earthenware

HENRY CLARK
CHEAM POTTERY
impressed or incised

CHELSEA (London)
c. 1745–1784 soft-paste porcelain
(1770–84 known as 'Chelsea-Derby'
period under William Duesbury)

rare incised mark on
'triangle' period
1745–c. 1749

usual triangle mark

incised

rare mark of 'crown
and trident', 1745–c.
1750 in underglaze blue

'raised-anchor' mark
c. 1749–52, latterly
picked out in red

in applied relief

'red-anchor' mark
1752–c. 1758
occasionally painted in
blue or purple

painted in red

31

*c.* 1750–56
painted in underglaze blue

'gold anchor' mark
*c.* 1756–69
(also seen on Chelsea-
Derby wares as late
as 1775)

in gold

rare 'repairers' mark
(not Roubiliac)

impressed

Chelsea Pottery, 1952–       CHELSEA POTTERY
(Rawnsley Academy Ltd.)     incised
impressed or
incised, 1952–

Vyse, Charles, 1919–*c.* 63     C.V.   C.V.
studio-potter                    CHELSEA

painted mark with
year-date added

19 Ⅴ 34

CHELSEA

CHESTERFIELD                  P. & CO.
(Derbyshire)
Pearson & Co., 1805–       PEARSON & CO.
Whittington Moor            WHITTINGTON
Potteries                        MOOR
1805–*c.* 1880               impressed

32

1880–

from *c.* 1925 renamed as
Pearson & Co. (Chesterfield) Ltd.

Barker Pottery Co.
1887–1957
stoneware
   printed or impressed
   mark 1928–1957

CHURCH GRESLEY (Derbyshire)
   Green & Co. Ltd., T.G.
   *c.* 1864– earthenware
and stoneware
   printed mark *c.* 1888–

GRESLEY

   mark of *c.* 1930, numerous
   other late marks all
   include 'T. G. Green
   & Co., Ltd.'

CLEVEDON (Avon)                  1879–1920
   Elton, Sir Edmund
   Sunflower Pottery
   1879–1930         1920–30    *Elton*

Holland, William Fishley
studio-potter, 1921–
earthenware

incised

33

Holland, Isabel Fishley
pottery figures, 1929–42

I. HOLLAND

Holland, George Fishley
earthenware, 1955–

CLIFTON JUNCTION
(nr. Manchester)
Pilkington Tile & Pottery
Co. Ltd., earthenwares
and tiles, (decorative
pottery, 1897–1938,
1948–57)

P
early incised mark

factory mark, VIII for
1908

*c.* 1914–38

'ROYAL LANCASTRIAN'

marks of notable designers:

Lewis F. Day   Walter Crane   C. E. Cundall   R. Joyce

Jessie Jones   G. M. Forsyth   Gladys Rodgers   W. Mycock

COALPORT (Salop)
  John Rose, *c.* 1796–
  (transferred to Stoke-on-Trent
  *c.* 1926)
    rare early mark in red          COALBROOKDALE

    1815–25 on many wares
    decorated in Swansea
    style                           impressed

    *c.* 1810–25, in underglaze    *Coalport*
    blue

underglaze blue mark
*c.* 1810–20

C. B. DALE

marks used from *c.* 1820

1830–50

JOHN ROSE & CO.
COALBROOKDALE
SHROPSHIRE
35

c. 1851–61, painted or gilt

c. 1861–75, 'c'
Coalport, 's',
Swansea, 'N', Nantgarw

painted or gilt

printed mark c. 1870–80
incorporating Patent
Office Registration
mark

c. 1875–81, printed or
painted
late marks c. 1881–
'England' added 1891
'Made in England'
c. 1920

COALPORT A.D. 1750

wares made for London
dealer A. B. & R. P.
Daniell c. 1860–1917

large size anchor mark
on Coalport copies of
Chelsea, also on
Continental wares
without 'c'

CODNOR PARK
(Derbyshire)
  Burton, William,
  *c.* 1821–32, stoneware

W. BURTON
CODNOR PARK
impressed

CROWBOROUGH (Sussex) & REDHILL (Surrey)
  Walford, J. F., 1948–
  studio-potter

DARTINGTON (S. Devon)
  Trey, Marianne de
  studio-potter, 1947–
  Shinners Bridge Pottery

incised or painted

  Haile, T. S., *c.* 1936–43,
  1945–8, studio-potter

impressed

DENBY (Derbyshire)
  Bourne & Son Ltd.,
  Joseph, *c.* 1809–
  stoneware

BOURNES
WARRANTED

  Joseph Bourne, 1833–60
  'Son' added 1850

J. BOURNE & SON
PATENTEES
DENBY POTTERY
NEAR DERBY
impressed

DENHOLME (W. Yorkshire)
  Taylor, Nicholas
  1893–1909
  earthenware

N. Taylor
Denholme
incised

37

DERBY (Derbyshire)
  *c.* 1750–1848
soft-paste porcelain
  early marks of Planché
  period *c.* 1750–56

*Derby*          incised

Derby Porcelain Works
1756–1848
  'William Duesbury &
  Co.' *c.* 1760

incised

  'N' seen on dishes, etc.
  *c.* 1770–80

incised

  'Chelsea-Derby' marks
  *c.* 1770–84

in gold

  *c.* 1770–82, in blue or
  purple

incised model numbers
on figures, *c.* 1775–
early 19th century

common Derby mark
1782–, incised, purple,
blue or black
*c.* 1800–25 in red
enamel

38

mark of Isaac
Farnsworth 'repairer'

mark of Joseph Hill
'repairer'

'size' mark

'Duesbury & Kean',
c. 1795
in blue, crimson or purple

blue-painted mark in
imitation of Meissen
c. 1785–1825

*Robert Bloor Period*

printed in red
c. 1820–40

printed in red
c. 1830–48

mark in imitation of
Sèvres, c. 1825–48
in blue enamel

Locker & Co., King Street factory
*c.* 1849–59

similar marks used also
by:
Stevenson Sharp & Co.
1859–61
'Courtney late Bloor'
1849–63

Stevenson & Hancock
1861–1935, this mark
also used after 1935
when King St. factory
was taken over by Royal Crown Derby
Porcelain Co. Ltd.

Derby Crown Porcelain Co. Ltd. Est. 1876
*c.* 1878–90, together
  with year mark as
  shown in table on next
  page
printed

Derby

impressed

Royal Crown Derby Porcelain Co. Ltd.
1890–
  printed mark of *c.* 1890
  'England' from 1891
  'Made in England'
  added from *c.* 1920
  together with year
  mark

(Part of Royal Doulton Tableware Ltd. from 1973)

## TABLE OF DERBY YEAR-MARKS,
1882–

| 1882 | 1883 | 1884 | 1885 | 1886 | 1887 | 1888 |
|------|------|------|------|------|------|------|

| 1889 | 1890 | 1891 | 1892 | 1893 | 1894 | 1895 |
|------|------|------|------|------|------|------|

| 1896 | 1897 | 1898 | 1899 | 1900 | 1901 | 1902 |
|------|------|------|------|------|------|------|

| 1903 | 1904 | 1905 | 1906 | 1907 | 1908 | 1909 |
|------|------|------|------|------|------|------|

| 1910 | 1911 | 1912 | 1913 | 1914 | 1915 | 1916 |
|------|------|------|------|------|------|------|

| 1917 | 1918 | 1919 | 1920 | 1921 | 1922 | 1923 |
|------|------|------|------|------|------|------|

| 1924 | 1925 | 1926 | 1927 | 1928 | 1929 | 1930 |
|------|------|------|------|------|------|------|

| 1931 | 1932 | 1933 | 1934 | 1935 | 1936 | 1937 |
|------|------|------|------|------|------|------|

| 1938 | 1939 | 1940 | 1941 | 1942 | 1943 | 1944 |
|------|------|------|------|------|------|------|
| I | II | III | IV | V | VI | VII |

| 1945 | 1946 | 1947 | 1948 | 1949 | 1950 | 1951 |
|------|------|------|------|------|------|------|
| VIII | IX | X | XI | XII | XIII | etc. |

| | |
|---|---|
| Derby Pot Works creamwares, *c.* 1750–80 | T. RADFORD SC. DERBY |
| Thomas Radford, engraver of prints found on some Cockpit Hill wares | RADFORD fecit DERBY POT WORKS |
| Potts, W. W. St. George's Works, *c.* 1831–, earthenware (also at Burslem) | marks indicating patent printing processes, 1831 & 1835 |

DONYATT (Somerset)
Rogers, James, 19th century
(with descendants)
*sgraffiato* slipwares

Jas Rogers
Maker Octr 10th
1848

impressed on jug
dated 1864

ROGERS & SONS
CROCK STRETT
POTTERY

EAST HENDRED (Oxfordshire)
Thompson, Pauline
studio-potter, 1950–

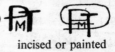

incised or painted

EAST HORSLEY (Surrey)
Moore, Denis & Michael
Buckland
Green Dene Pottery
1953–
(initials also used)

impressed or painted

FARNHAM (Surrey)
Hammond, Henry
studio-potter, 1934–40,
1946–

incised   impressed

Barron, Paul
studio-potter, 1948–

B

impressed

FELIXSTOWE (Suffolk)
Kemp, Dorothy, 1939–
studio-potter

incised or impressed

FERRYBRIDGE (Yorkshire)
Ferrybridge Pottery, 1792–
known as Knottingley Pottery, 1792–1804

| | |
|---|---|
| 1792–6, *c.* 1801–34 | TOMLINSON & CO. |
| | impressed or printed |
| Wedgwood, Ralph, *c.* 1796–1801 | WEDGWOOD & CO. |
| *c.* 1804– | FERRYBRIDGE |
| | impressed |

| | | |
|---|---|---|
| Reed & Taylor, *c.* 1843–56 | R. & T. | R.T. & CO. |
| Woolf & Sons, L., *c.* 1856–83 | L.W. | L.W. & S. |
| Poulson, Bros., Ltd. 1884–97 | P.B. | P.BROS |
| Sefton & Brown, *c.* 1897–1919 | S.B. | |
| Brown & Sons, T., *c.* 1919– | T.B & S. | |

43

FREMINGTON (Devon)
  Fishley, Edwin Beer
  1861–1906, earthenware

E. B. FISHLEY
FREMINGTON
N. DEVON
  incised

FULHAM (London)
  Dwight, John, 1671–
  salt-glazed stoneware

no certain
marks

De Morgan, William
  c. 1872–1907
  decorator of earthenwares made to order
  from other factories, and own wares
    impressed mark, 1882–
    '& Co.' added after 1888

marks used at Merton Abbey, 1882–88
made own tiles from c.
1879, and wares from 1882

    impressed or painted
    1882–

Sands End Pottery, 1888–97
(period of partnership with
Halsey Ricardo)

1898–1907, partnership with
Frank Iles, Charles & Fred
Passenger at Fulham

decoration continued
until 1911, four years
after De Morgan retired

all impressed

earthenwares were decorated
in De Morgan style at
Mrs. Ida Perrin's studio,
Bushey Heath, 1921–33
by Fred Passenger

Fulham Pottery & Cheavin Filter Co. Ltd.
vases & commercial pottery
1889–present

FULHAM POTTERY
LONDON

1948–

impressed

GATESHEAD (Tyne and Wear)
Durham China Co. Ltd.
general ceramics, 1947–57

printed or impressed

HENLEY-ON-THAMES
(Berkshire)
Hawkins, John & Son
china and glass dealers
closed about 1935

'FAMOUS HENLEY CHINA'
EST. 1867
HAWKINS
HENLEY-ON-THAMES

HEREFORD
    Godwin & Hewitt, tiles
    1889–1910, mark printed
    or impressed

HONITON (Devon)
    Honiton Art Potteries      THE HONITON
    Ltd., earthenware, *c.*     LACE ART POTTERY
    1881–, printed or           CO.
    impressed *c.* 1915

    Collard, C., 1918–1947    COLLARD HONITON
    printed or impressed        ENGLAND

    Hull, N. T. S., 1947–1955     N.T.S. HULL

    1947–               HONITON POTTERY
                        DEVON

    Hull, Norman          NORMAN HULL
    Norman Hull Pottery      POTTERY
    1947–55

HORNSEA (Humberside)
    Hornsea Pottery Co. Ltd.
    earthenware, *c.* 1951
        printed or impressed, 1962–

HULL (Humberside)          S.L.
    Longbottom, Samuel    impressed
    earthenware, late 19th
    century, closed 1899

IPSWICH (Suffolk)
  Balaam, W., 1870–81
  Rope Lane Pottery
  slipwares

W. BALAAM
ROPE LANE POTTERY
IPSWICH
impressed

ISLEWORTH (London)
  earthenware, *c.* 1760–
  1825, Shore, J.
  Shore & Co.
  Shore & Goulding

SHORE & CO.
S. & CO.
S. & G.
ISLEWORTH

  (*Note:* S. & G. seen on Wedgwood type wares
  are Schiller & Gerbing, Bodenbach, Bohemia.
  *See Pocket-Book of German Ceramic Marks*)

JACKFIELD (Salop)
  Craven Dunnill & Co.
  Ltd., tiles, 1872–1951

CRAVEN & CO.

JACKFIELD

KEW (Surrey)
  Duckworth, Ruth
  studio-potter, 1956–

painted or incised

KILMINGTON MANOR (Wiltshire)
  Pleydell-Bouverie, Katharine
  stoneware, 1925–
  studio-potter
  (also at other addresses)

incised or stamped

LAMBETH (London)　　　　'Coade Lambeth'
　　Coade & Sealy, 1769–
　　1811, artificial stoneware

Doulton & Watts
stoneware and earthenware
　c. 1815–1858

　　c. 1826–1838
　　on early brown salt-
　　glazed wares

　　c. 1826–1858

all marks impressed
moulded or incised

Doulton & Co.
Lambeth, c. 1858–1956
Burslem, c. 1882–

　　c. 1869–77, decorated
　　coloured wares, year often
　　appears in centre after 1872

'4D' mark on decorated
salt-glaze

*Note:* 'England' added
after 1891　　　　　　c. 1877–80　　c. 1880–1902

mark on mural tiles
c. 1879–1900

on wares decorated with
coloured clays
*c.* 1887–1900

underglaze decorated
earthenware

*c.* 1872–73

*c.* 1873–1908

underglaze decorated
earthenware, *c.* 1881–1910

'Carrara' ware, stoneware
covered with translucent
crystalline enamel
*c.* 1888–1898

'Silicon' ware, unglazed
stoneware, *c.* 1882–1912

fine earthenware and china,
made at Burslem
*c.* 1882–1902

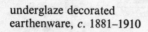

standard impressed mark
*c.* 1902–22
*c.* 1927–36

Lambeth stoneware
*c.* 1922–

Burslem factory marks          DOULTON
*c.* 1882–1902

          DOULTON
                                                 &SLATERS
                                                   PATENT

*c.* 1900–          ROYAL          ROYAL
                            DOULTON          DOULTON
                            FLAMBE          KALON

*c.* 1960–          ENGLISH
                            TRANSLUCENT
                                CHINA

selection of initials used
by Doulton decorators:
Atkins, Elizabeth, *c.* 1876–82     *EA*
Banks, Eliza, *c.* 1876–84                         *E/B*
Barlow, Arthur B., 1871–8     *AB 3*
Barlow, Florence E., *c.* 1873–1909          *FEB*

Barlow, Hannah B., *c.* 1872–1906     *HB*

Barnard, Harry, *c.* 1880–90                    *B*

Butler, Frank A., *c.* 1872–1911

Butterton, Mary, *c.* 1874–94

Capes, Mary, *c.* 1876–83

Dewsberry, David, 1889–1919 D.Dewsberry

Dunn, William, E., *c.* 1883–95

Lee, Frances E., *c.* 1875–90 FƐL

Marshall, Mark V., 1879–
  1912 M·V·M

Pope, Frank C., 1880–1923 F·C·P

Raby, Edward J., 1892–1911 E·Raby

Rowe, William, 1883–1939 WR

Simeon, Henry, 1894–1936 HS

Simmance, Eliza, *c.* 1873–1928 S

Tinworth, George, 1886–1913 T

A full-list of painters, modellers and designers are
shown in *Royal Doulton* 1815–1965 by Desmond
Eyles, London, 1965, together with full guides,
etc. to precise dating

Green, Stephen
Imperial Pottery
stoneware, *c.* 1820–58

impressed marks

STEPHEN GREEN
IMPERIAL
POTTERIES
LAMBETH

Stiff, James                    J. STIFF
London Pottery, *c.* 1840–
1913 stonewares
      *c.* 1863             J. STIFF & SONS
                            impressed

LANGLEY MILL (Nottingham)
   Lovatt & Lovatt, 1895–
   stoneware and earthenware
   printed or impressed marks
                    *c.* 1900–

        now Langley
   Pottery Ltd. (1967)   *c.* 1900–   *c.* 1931–62

LEEDS (W. Yorkshire)
   *c.* 1770–1881
   creamware, earthenware and stoneware

   Green Bros., 1770–        LEEDS *POTTERY
                              impressed

   Humble, Green & Co., 1774–76
                    52

Humble, Hartley, Greens
& Co., 1776–1780

LEEDS POTTERY

LEEDS *POTTERY

Hartley, Greens & Co.
1781–1830

LEEDS * POTTERY

1800–1830

LEEDS.POTTERY

HARTLEY GREENS & Co.
LEEDS * POTTERY

all marks impressed

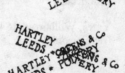

1780–1810
impressed or enamelled

LP

Britton & Son, Richard
1872–8, earthenware
    initials found on variety
    of transfer-printed wares

R.B. & S.
printed

Rainforth & Co. 1800–17
Petty's Pottery, 1817–46
earthenware & creamware

RAINFORTH & CO.
PETTYS & CO. LEEDS

printed or impressed

| | |
|---|---|
| Burmantofts | BURMANTOFTS |
| art-pottery, 1882–1904 | FAIENCE |
| marks impressed | |

| | |
|---|---|
| Leeds Fireclay Co. Ltd. | L. |
| earthenware, *c*. 1904–14 | F.C. |
| | |
| decorative wares, made | LEFICO |
| up until 1914, after | |
| which only commercial | GRANITOFTS |
| & utility wares were | |
| produced | |
| | |
| Yates, William, *c*. 1840–76 | YATES |
| (retailer only) | LEEDS |
| | printed or painted |

LETCHWORTH | ICENI WARE
(Hertfordshire) | impressed
    Cowlishaw, W. H.
    1908–14, earthenwares

LIVERPOOL (Merseyside)
    Chaffers, Richard, 1743–65
    tin-glazed earthenware
    and soft-paste porcelain
        dated example referring
        to son:

| | |
|---|---|
| Christian, Philip | 'CHRISTIAN' |
| *c*. 1765–1776 | impressed |
| | |
| Billinge, Thomas | *Billinge Sculp* |
| engraver, *c*. 1760–80 | *Liverpool* |

| | |
|---|---|
| Sadler, John & Green, Guy, printers only, their work seen on tiles, Wedgwood's creamware, Longton Hall, etc., 1756–1799 | *J. Sadler, Liverpool*<br><br>*Green, Liverpool* |
| Abbey, Richard engraver and printer 1773–80, potter from 1790 | ABBEY<br>LIVERPOOL<br><br>*R. Abbey, sculp.* |
| Johnson, Joseph engraver, second half 18th century | 'I. JOHNSON, LIVERPOOL' |

Herculaneum Pottery          HERCULANEUM
earthenware and procelain
*c.* 1793–1841
Worthington, Humble
& Holland, 1794–1806

impressed or printed marks, *c.* 1796–1833

1822–41          HERCULANEUM POTTERY
impressed or printed
in blue

55

Case, Thomas & Mort,
John, 1833–1836

printed, usually in red

Mort & Simpson

'Liver' bird printed or
impressed, *c.* 1836–41

Gibson, John &
Solomon, earthenware,
early 19th century

JOHN GIBSON
LIVERPOOL
1813

LONDON
## VARIOUS RETAILERS OF POTTERY & PORCELAIN

Allsup, John, 1832–58
  printed

JOHN ALLSUP
ST. PAUL'S CHURCH-
YARD, LONDON

Blades, John
*c.* 1800–30

BLADES LONDON

Bradley & Co., J.
decorators and retailers
*c.* 1813–20

J. BRADLEY & CO.

Brameld, J. W.
*c.* 1830–50
partner of
Rockingham Works

I. W. BRAMELD

at various
London addresses

56

Daniell, A. B. & R. P.
*c.* 1825–1917
   printed mark on wares
   of Coalport, etc. made
   to order for Daniell's

Dreydel & Co., Henry
late 19th century
   mark of wares made
   to order both in England
   and on Continent

Goode & Co. (Ltd.), Thomas
*c.* 1860–present
'Ltd' from 1918
now in South Audley St.

Green & Co., J.
1834–42 at St. Paul's
Churchyard, elsewhere
until *c.* 1874

Haines, Batchelor & Co.
1880–90

H.B.
printed

Hales, Hancock &
Goodwin, Ltd., 1922–60
(Hales, Hancock & Co.
Ltd., and Hales Bros.)

H.H. & G. LTD.
printed

| | |
|---|---|
| Hart & Son<br>1826–69 | H. & S.<br>printed |
| Howell & James<br>c. 1820–1922 (also<br>retailers of materials<br>for amateur decorators) | HOWELL & JAMES |
| Mortlock, J.<br>1746–c. 1930<br>   many marks used<br>   including name of such<br>   manufacturers as<br>   Mintons | MORTLOCK<br><br>MORTLOCKS<br>OXFORD STREET |
| Pearce, Alfred B.<br>1866–1940 | ALFRED B. PEARCE<br>39 LUDGATE HILL<br>LONDON |
| Pellatt & Co., Apsley<br>c. 1789–<br>(also glass retailers) | APSLEY PELLATT<br>& CO. |
| Pellatt & Green<br>c. 1805–30 | PELLATT & GREEN<br>LONDON |
| Pellatt & Wood<br>c. 1870–90 | PELLATT & WOOD |

Phillips, c. 1799–1929

| | |
|---|---|
| c. 1858–97 | W. P. & G. PHILLIPS |
| c. 1897–1906 | PHILLIPS & CO. |
| c. 1908–29 | PHILLIPS LTD. |

Walker, William      WALKER MINORIES
*c.* 1795–1800

## MINOR FACTORIES AND STUDIO-POTTERS
## IN LONDON

Benham, Tony, 1958
   mark written or incised
   with year, studio-potter
(now at Wateringbury, Kent),
Billington, Dora
studio-potter, 1912–     incised or painted

Briglin Pottery Ltd.      BRIGLIN
earthenware, 1948–      impressed

Dalton, William B.
stoneware and porcelain
studio-potter, 1900–     incised or painted
*c.* 1955
(In U.S.A. from 1941)

Eeles, David      D.E.
studio-potter, 1955
Shepherd's Well Pottery
London, then in 1962
to Mosterton, Dorset

Fine Arts Porcelain Ltd.
earthenwares, 1948–52

printed

Fry, Roger, Omega
Workshops *c.* 1913–19,
studio-potter

Groves, Lavender
studio-potter, 1952–

*Groves*

Leach, Jeremy     J.L.   J.L.
studio-potter, *c.* 1959     D.S.

Martin Bros. (Robert Wallace, Walter, Edwin
and Charles), studio-potters, stoneware,
1873–1914

    1873–5          R. W. Martin fecit

    1873–4    *R W Martin Fulham*

    1874–8         *R W Martin London*

    1878–9    *RW Martin Southall*

      SOUTHALL          MARTIN
      MARTIN            SOUTHALL
      POTTERY           POTTERY

    1879–82    *R W Martin London & Southall*

    1882–       *R W Martin & Brothers London & Southall*

all marks either incised or impressed together
with month and year

Mills, Donald
studio-potter, 1946–55

Murray, William Staite
studio-potter, 1919–62
in S. Rhodesia from 1940

W. S. MURRAY
(date)
LONDON

Northen & Co., W.
Union Potteries,
Lambeth, stoneware,
1847–92, '& Co.'
added 1887

W. NORTHEN
POTTER
VAUXHALL
LAMBETH

O'Malley, Peter
studio-potter, 1953–

Parnell, Gwendolen
studio-potter, 1916–36

CHELSEA CHEYNE
(date)
G.P.

Parr, Harry
studio-potter, *c.* 1919–
*c.* 1948

HY PARR
CHELSEA (date)

Powell, Alfred & Louise
decorators of Wedgwood
earthenwares, *c.* 1904–39

Powell, John
painter and retailer
*c.* 1810–30

Powell
91, Wimpole St.

Richards, Frances E.
studio-potter, 1922–31
  mark incised

Rie, Lucie
studio-potter, *c.* 1938–
  mark impressed

Samuel, Audrey
studio-potter, 1949–

A·S

Smith & Co., Thomas
stonewares, 1879–93

T. SMITH & CO.
OLD KENT ROAD
LONDON

Stabler, Harold &
Phoebe, earthenware
designers and potters
*b.* 1872–*d.* 1945 (wife
*d.* 1955)

Phoebe Stabler
(date)

Stabler (date)

Vergette, Nicholas
studio-potter, 1946–58

Walters, Helen
studio-potter, 1945–
(now Helen Swain,
mark 'HWS')

1945–53     1953–

White, William J.
Fulham Pottery
stoneware, *c.* 1750–1850

W.W.
(date)

W. J. WHITE
incised dated marks
(date)

LOWER DICKER (Sussex)
U. Clark & Nephews,
1843–1946, earthenware
1933–
Dicker Potteries Ltd. 1946–59

U.C. & N.
THE DICKER
SUSSEX
DICKER WARE

LOWESBY (Leicestershire)
Lowesby Pottery
Fowke, Sir Frederick
*c.* 1835–40
earthenwares

LOWESBY

LOWESTOFT (Suffolk)
soft-paste porcelain
*c.* 1757– *c.* 1800
decorators numbers,
to approx. 17, painted
on inner wall of foot-
rim, *c.* 1760–75
copies of Worcester

*1 3 5*

*7 9 13*

and Meissen marks
*c.* 1775–1790

Allen, Robert, *b.* 1744, *d.* 1835
decorator at Lowestoft factory
and independent enameller
from *c.* 1800

painted

MADELEY (Salop)
Randall, Thomas M.
*c.* 1825–40, decorator of
English and Sèvres porcelain;
with factory at Madeley
for production of soft-paste
imitations of Sèvres

painted

MALVERN (Worcestershire)
Woods, Richard, *c.* 1850–
retailer only

R. WOODS
printed

MANCHESTER
Sutcliffe & Co., *c.* 1885–1901
decorative tiles

printed or impressed

MANSFIELD
(Nottinghamshire)
Billingsley, William
1799–1802
painter and gilder

BILLINGSLEY
MANFIELD
painted

MEXBOROUGH
(S. Yorkshire)
Emery, James
earthenware, 1837–61

J. EMERY
MEXBRO

incised

Rock Pottery  \*REED\*
Reed, James, *c.* 1839–49  impressed

Mexbro Pottery
Reed, John, *c.* 1849–73

Sowter & Co., *c.* 1795–  SOWTER & CO.
1804, Mexborough Old  MEXBRO
Pottery
  marks impressed  S. & CO.

Wilkinson & Wardle
Denaby Pottery, 1864–6
earthenware

Wardle & Co., John,
Denaby Pottery
earthenwares (including creamware)
1866–70
  printed mark  JOHN WARDLE & CO.

MIDDLESBROUGH  LINTHORPE
(Cleveland)  impressed
  Linthorpe Pottery, 1879–90
  earthenware (art pottery type)

    incised, impressed or  Chr. Dresser
    painted signature of Dresser

    Tooth, Henry, manager  Ħ  HT
    1879–1882

Middlesbrough Pottery Co.  M.P. CO.
1834–44
earthenware and  MIDDLESBRO'
creamware  POTTERY CO.

65

Middlesbrough  M.E. & CO.
Earthenware Co.
1844–52, earthenware
 initials used with various
 printed or impressed marks

MIDDLESBRO POTTERY
(with anchor)
Wilson & Co., Isaac  I.W. & CO.
Middlesbrough Pottery  MIDDLESBRO'
1852–87  impressed

MORTLAKE (London)  KISHERE
 Mortlake Pottery, *c.*
 1800–43, Kishere,  I.K.
 Joseph  impressed
 salt-glazed stoneware

NEW BARNET (Hertfordshire)  D.A.
 Arbeid, Dan, 1956–
 Abbey Art Centre  ARBEID
 studio-potter  painted or impressed
 (now at Saffron Walden, Essex)

NEWCASTLE UPON TYNE  DAVIES & CO.
(Tyne and Wear)  impressed
 Davies & Co., 1833–51
 Tyne Main Pottery
 earthenware

 Fell, Thomas, 1817–90  FELL
 St. Peter's Pottery  impressed
 earthenware and creamware
 1817–30

impressed

| | |
|---|---|
| Fell & Co., *c.* 1830–90 | F. & CO. |
| initials used with | T.F. & CO. |
| various marks: | T. FELL & CO. |
| | |
| Ford & Patterson | FORD & PATTERSON |
| Sheriff Hill Pottery | Sheriff Hill |
| *c.* 1820–*c.* 1830 | Pottery |
| earthenware | impressed |
| Jackson & Patterson | J. & P. |
| 1830–45 | |
| Maling, Robert | MALING |
| Ouseburn Pottery | M |
| 1817–59, earthenware | impressed |
| | |
| Maling, C. T. | MALING |
| Ford Pottery, 1859–90 | C. T. MALING |
| earthenware, often | C.T.M. |
| with lustre decoration | |

Maling & Sons, Ltd.
1890–1963
earthenwares, mark of
  *c.* 1875–1908

1890–      *c.* 1908      *c.* 1949–63

Patterson & Co.                 PATTERSON & CO.
Sheriff Hill Pottery,              printed or
1830–1904, earthenware        impressed


Sewell, 1804– *c.* 28              SEWELL
St. Anthony's Pottery, *c.* 1780–1878
earthenware (including creamwares)
1780–1820                      ST. ANTHONY'S
Sewell & Donkin              SEWELL & DONKIN
1828–52
Sewell & Co., 1852–78         SEWELL & CO.
                        all impressed or printed


Taylor & Co., *c.* 1820–5        TAYLOR & CO.
Tyne Pottery                     printed
earthenware


Wallace & Co., J.              WALLACE & CO.
Newcastle or Forth Bank          impressed
Pottery, 1838–93, earthenware


Warburton, John, &            J. WARBURTON
family, Carr's Hill              N. ON TYNE
Pottery, earthenware, *c.* 1750–1817


NEWTON ABBOT (Devon)          ₣ⅠΛΕΩ ⅡⅎⅠⅎOΝ
Phillips & Co., John
Aller Pottery, 1868–87        printed or impressed


Aller Vale Art Potteries         ALLER VALE
earthenware, 1887–1901         impressed


68

Royal Aller Vale &
Watcombe Pottery Co.
(Torquay) *c.* 1901–62
  impressed or printed
  1901–

ROYAL ALLER VALE

ROYAL   DEVON
TORQUAY  MOTTO
POTTERY  WARE

Candy & Co. Ltd.
Great Western Potteries
earthenwares, 1882–

CANDY WARE
C
N A

NORTH SHIELDS
(Tyne and Wear)
  Carr, John
  earthenware, *c.* 1845–1900

J. CARR & CO.

NOTTINGHAM
  (Nottinghamshire)
  Lockett, William
  stoneware, *c.* 1740–80

'Wm. and Ann Lockett,
1755'

OXFORD (Oxfordshire)
  Blackman, Audrey
  studio-potter, 1949–
  'Astbury-type' figures

A. BLACKMAN

OXSHOTT (Surrey)
  Oxshott Pottery, 1919
  Wren, Henry, *c.* 1919–47

HW   hw

Wren, Denise, *c.* 1919–

DKW

Wren, Rosemary, *c.* 1945–

PINXTON (Derbyshire)
　Pinxton Works, *c.* 1796–1813
　John Coke, William Billingsley
　soft-paste porcelain
　(Billingsley, *c.* 1796–93)
　(Cutts, *c.* 1803–1813)

in red　　in purple
from arms of Coke

　　marks found on late
　　pieces

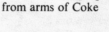

PLYMOUTH (Devon)
　Plymouth Porcelain Works
　Cookworthy, William
　hard-paste porcelain, 1768–70
　(transferred to Bristol in 1770)
　　workman's mark also seen
　　on Bow, Worcester, Bristol
　　and Wedgwood

underglaze-blue,
blue enamel,
red or gold

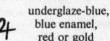

　Plymouth Pottery Co. Ltd.
　earthenware, 1856–63

P.P. COY.L
STONE CHINA

POOLE (Dorset)
　Carter & Co.
　earthenware, 1873–1921

CARTER & CO.
CARTER POOLE

　Carter, Stabler & Adams
　1921–
　　'Ltd.' added 1925
　　1956–
　1963– Poole Pottery Ltd.

POOLE
ENGLAND

printed

70

PRAZE (Cornwall)
    Crowan Pottery, 1946–62
    Davis, Harry & May
    studio-potters

impressed

PRESTBURY (Cheshire)
    Nowell, C. D., *c.* 1946–59
    studio-potter
    (at Disley *c.* 1946–51)

PRESTBURY

PRESTWOOD (Buckinghamshire)
    Newland, William
    studio-potter, 1948–

WN

(date)

    Casson, Michael & Sheila
    studio-potters, 1953–
        Sheila Casson, 1951–59

w
s

RAINHAM (Kent)
    Upchurch Pottery, 1913–61
    Baker, W. & J.
      'Seeby', name of agent
      1945–61

UPCHURCH

UPCHURCH
SEEBY

    Rainham Pottery Ltd.
    earthenware, 1948–
    Wilson, Alfred, now
    E. J. Baker

Rainham
impressed or painted

RAMSBURY (Wiltshire)
    Holdsworth Potteries
    Holdsworth, Peter, 1945–

READING (Berkshire)
Collier Ltd., S. & E.
terra-cotta, *c.* 1848–1957

RICHMOND (Surrey)      Steven Sykes
Sykes, Steven, 1948–55     (signature)
studio-potter

ROCKINGHAM (Yorkshire)
Rockingham Works
(nr. Swinton) earthenware
*c.* 1750–1842 (porcelain
also made from about 1826)     BINGLEY
*c.* 1778–87             impressed

Brameld & Co., 1806–42      BRAMELD
                       impressed

  *c.* 1826–30     ROCKINGHAM   ROCKINHGAM
                   WORKS,       BRAMELD
                   BRAMELD

  *c.* 1830–42          ROYAL
                ROCKINGHAM
                   WORKS
                 BRAMELD

  'griffin-mark', *c.* 1826–30
from crest of Earl Fitzwilliam,
Marquis of Rockingham

from *c.* 1830–42
  'Royal' added to title
of factory
mark in red *c.* 1826–30, puce 1830–42
'Manufacturer to the King' added to mark
in 1830–37 (William IV)

72

Baguley, Alfred & Isaac          'Griffin mark'
Rockingham Works                 with
decorator only of                'Baguley'
porcelain in Rockingham
style, *c.* 1842–65 (Mexborough)
   *c.* 1865–91          printed


ROLVENDEN (Kent)
  Watson, Dorothy
  Bridge Pottery 1921–

                        impressed or printed


ROTHERHAM (S. Yorkshire)          J.J. & CO.
  Holmes Pottery, 1870–87
  Jackson & Co., J.                J. & CO.
  earthenware
  Shaw & Sons, Ltd., G.           G.S. & S.
  1887–1948                        printed


  Northfield Pottery               W. & G. HAWLEY
  earthenware
  Hawley, W. & G., 1863–8,
  Hawley Bros Ltd.,                       H.B.
  1868–1903, 'Ltd'. added 1897     HAWLEY BROS.


  Northfield Hawley Pottery Co. Ltd.
  earthenware, 1903–19

    impressed or printed
    mark introduced about
    1898 by Hawley Bros.

Walker & Son                          WALKER
earthenware, *c.* 1772–

RUSTINGTON (Sussex)
Champion, G. H. & E. E.
studio-potters, 1947–


RYE (Sussex)                          SUSSEX WARE
1869– mark of *c.* 1900
pottery (including tin-glaze)
*c.* 1869–1920
(Sussex Rustic Ware)
's.A.W.' Sussex Art Ware
*c.* 1920–39
J. C. Cole & W. V.                    RYE
Cole, 1947–
    various marks including
    name 'RYE'
Walter V. Cole, 1957–

Cadborough Pottery,                   OLD SUSSEX WARE
1807–71, earthenware                  RYE


Mitchell, William, *c.*               MITCHELL
1840–, W. Mitchell &                  M
Sons, 1859–69,
Mitchell, F. & H., 1869–71


Iden Pottery, 1961–
Townsend, D. & Wood, J. H.
studio-potters
(moved from Iden to Rye
in 1963)

74

Everett, Raymond, 1963–
studio-potter

ST. IVES (Cornwall)
Leach, Bernard, 1921–
  Leach Pottery marks
studio-pottery
  personal marks of B. Leach

Hamada, Shoji
1920–23, 1929–*c*. 30

Leach, Janet, 1956–

Leach, John, *c*. 1950–8
(at Langport, Somerset since 1964)
Marshall, William, 1954–

      impressed

incised

Mc. Kenzie, Warren, 1950–2

(at Dartington from 1963–)
  mark used at Dartington

Quick, Kenneth, 1945–63
(at St. Ives 1945–*c*. 55 and
1960–63)
  mark used at Tregenna Hill Pottery
  *c*. 1955–60

75

ST. MARY CHURCH (Devon) WATCOMBE
   Watcombe Pottery Co.   TORQUAY
   1867–1901                WATCOMBE
                                 POTTERY

   printed mark, 1875–1901

   Royal Aller Vale &             ROYAL
   Watcombe Pottery Co.       TORQUAY
   *c.* 1901–62                POTTERY

SALISBURY (Wiltshire)     PAYNE SARUM
   Payne, retailer only     printed
   *c.* 1834–41

SMETHWICK              TAYLOR
(nr. Birmingham)        impressed
   Ruskin Pottery, 1898–1935
   earthenware
   Taylor, W. Howson, *c.* 1898–

   painted or incised

   impressed mark, *c.* 1904–15
   with added date

STANMORE (London)     E.C./(date)
   Collyer, Ernest & Pamela
   studio-potters, 1950–

   Collyer-Nash        P.N. (Pamela Nash)

STEDHAM (Sussex)        Ray Marshall
   Marshall, Ray      (date)
   studio-potter, 1945–
   impressed mark          signature

STOCKTON-ON-TEES (Cleveland)
Ainsworth, W. H. & J. H.
1865–1901, earthenware

impressed

Harwood, J.
Clarence Pottery, 19th
century earthenware
  impressed mark, *c.* 1849–77

HARWOOD
STOCKTON

Skinner & Co., George
Stafford Pottery
earthenware, *c.* 1855–70

G.S. & CO.
printed

Skinner & Walker
1870–80

S. & W.
QUEEN'S WARE
STOCKTON

Smith & Co.,          W.S. & CO.          W.S. & CO.
William, *c.* 1825–55                           STAFFORD
Stafford Pottery       W.S. & CO'S          POTTERY
                      WEDGWOOD

Smith, George F.        G.F.S.
North Shore Pottery
*c.* 1855–60, earthenware

Smith (Junr), William        W. S. JUNR. & CO.
*c.* 1845–84          all printed or impressed

STOURBRIDGE (West Midlands)
Sunfield Pottery, 1937–
earthenware and stoneware

77

SUNDERLAND
(Tyne and Wear)
Southwick Pottery,
1788–99, Atkinson & Co., earthenware

ATKINSON & CO.
impressed or
printed

Deptford Pottery,
1857–1918
Ball, William,
earthenware, Ball Bros., 1884–

COPYRIGHT BALL
BROS.
SUNDERLAND

Wear Pottery
Brunton, John,
1796–1803, earthenware

J. BRUNTON
printed

South Hylton &
Ford Potteries
Dawson, John, c. 1799–1864
c. 1799–1848, earthenware
Thomas Dawson & Co.,
c. 1837–48, earthenware
   printed marks

DAWSON      I. DAWSON

DAWSON & CO.

FORD POTTERY   J. DAWSON
                SOUTH HYLTON

Garrison or
Sunderland Pottery
earthenware, c. 1807–65
   c. 1807–12

J. PHILLIPS
SUNDERLAND
POTTERY

c. 1813–19

PHILLIPS & CO. DIXON & CO.
                DIXON, AUSTIN

c. 1820–26

& CO.
DIXON, AUSTIN

c. 1827–40

PHILLIPS & CO.

c. 1840–65

DIXON, PHILLIPS
& CO.

Wear Pottery, 1803–74     MOORE & CO.
Moore & Co., Samuel     SUNDERLAND
earthenware

North Hylton       MALING
Pottery, 1762–67,       impressed
earthenware, Maling, William, 1762–, continued
by family until 1815

Phillips & Co.,      JOHN PHILLIPS
John, 1815–67      HYLTON POT
(Phillips &         WORKS
Maling, 1780–1815)

Southwick Pottery, *c.* 1800–97
    *c.* 1800–29     A. SCOTT & CO.
                            SCOTT, SOUTHWICK
    *c.* 1829–44     A. SCOTT & SONS
                                   S. & SONS
    *c.* 1844–54     S.B. & CO.
                           SCOTT BROTHERS
    *c.* 1854–97     A. SCOTT & SON
                                   S. & S.

Union Pottery,      UNION POTTERY
*c.* 1802          printed

SWADLINCOTE (S. Derbyshire)
Ault, William, 1887–1923
earthenware
    The wares of this
    pottery sometimes
    bear the signature
    of the designer
    Christopher Dresser
    and date from    printed or     printed
    1891–6         impressed

Ault & Tunnicliffe Ltd.
1923–37
(*see* Ashby Potter's Guild)

Ault Potteries Ltd., 1937–
(now Pearson & Co., Group)
  marks impressed or printed

SWINTON (Yorkshire)
Don Pottery, earthenware
1790–1893
  1800–34

  1820–34, impressed or
  printed

DON POTTERY

GREEN
DON POTTERY

Barker, Samuel, 1834–93

  '& Son' or '& Sons'
  added 1851–93

BARKER
DON POTTERY

Bingley & Co., Thomas
earthenware, 1778–87

BINGLEY
impressed

Twigg, Joseph & brothers
Kilnhurst Pottery & Newhill Pottery, *c.* 1822–81
earthenware
  impressed or
  printed, *c.* 1822–
  impressed, *c.*
  1822–66
  impressed, *c.*
  1839–81

J.T.

TWIGG
NEWHILL

TWIGG
K.P.

TONBRIDGE (Kent)
  Slack & Brownlow
  earthenware, *c.* 1928–34

TONBRIDGE WARE
printed or impressed

TORQUAY (Devon)
  Torquay Terra-Cotta Co. Ltd.
  Dr. Gillow, 1875–1909
  earthenware figures, busts, etc.

impressed or printed

TRING (Hertfordshire)
  Pendley Pottery, 1949–
  Fieldhouse, Murray
  studio-potter (now at
  Northfields Studio)

incised or printed

TRURO (Cornwall)
  Chapel Hill Pottery,
  1872–, Lake & Son Ltd.,
  W. H., earthenware

LAKE'S CORNISH
POTTERY TRURO
printed or impressed

WAREHAM (Dorset)
  Sibley Pottery Ltd., 1922–
  62, earthenware and
  stoneware

SIBLEY POTTERY LTD
DORSET
ENGLAND
impressed or printed

WATTISFIELD (Suffolk)
  Watson Potteries Ltd., Henry
  earthenware and stoneware
  *c.* 1800–; mark of about
    1948, early wares unmarked

WELWYN GARDEN CITY (Hertfordshire)
  Coper, Hans, 1947–
  studio-potter

WENFORD BRIDGE (nr. Bodmin, Cornwall)
Wenford Bridge Pottery
*c.* 1939–42; 1949–
impressed mark
(*see also* WINCHCOMBE)

WESTON-SUPER-MARE (Avon)
Matthews, John
terra-cotta, 1870–88
impressed mark with
Royal Arms

JOHN MATTHEWS
LATE PHILLIPS
ROYAL POTTERY
WESTON-SUPER-MARE

WHITTINGTON (Derbyshire)
Walton Pottery Co. Ltd.
1946–56
Gordon, William
salt-glazed stoneware

WINCANTON Somerset)
Ireson, Nathaniel
*c.* 1730–50
tin-glazed earthenware

IRESON
WINCANTON

WINCHCOMBE (Gloucestershire)
*c.* 1926–39
Cardew, Michael A.
also at Wenford Bridge
*c.* 1939–42
studio-potter

mark impressed

Finch, Raymond, 1939–
studio-potter, impressed
mark used from *c.* 1926

WITHERNSEA (Humberside)
Eastgate Potteries, Ltd.
earthenware, 1955–

EASTGATE
ENGLAND
(on a gate)

WOODVILLE (Derbyshire)
Ashby Potters' Guild
earthenware, 1909–22

impressed

Mansfield Bros., Ltd.
Art Pottery Works, *c.* 1890–
1957

M.B.
impressed

WORCESTER (Worcestershire)
Worcester Porcelain Factory
1751 (Lund & Miller's Bristol factory
est. 1748, taken over in 1752)
soft-paste porcelain (soapstone)

workmen's marks
in underglaze blue

'open' crescent on painted
wares, 1755–83

83

crescent-mark with
crossed-hatched lines
on printed wares          ☾

in underglaze blue

any crescents in gilt or enamel colour
probably indicate outside decorator or
reproduction
on painted and printed
wares          $w$  $W$

painted in blue

marks on wares decorated
with 'Japan patterns'
*c.* 1760–75

in blue

'fretted square' mark
usually on heavily decorated
wares with scale-blue ground
*c.* 1755–75 (frequently seen
on reproductions)          in blue

Worcester imitation of Meissen
crossed-swords mark
*c.* 1760–70

in blue

printed numerals disguised as Chinese
characters, numbers 1–9, until recent
excavations at Worcester factory site these were
thought to be marks of Caughley (Salop)

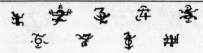

'Flight' period, 1783–92
  'small crescent', 1783–92

  mark in blue, 1783–92

  mark in blue, 1788–92

**'Flight & Barr' period**
**1792–1807**

'Barr', *c.* 1792–1807

incised

'Barr Flight & Barr' period
1807–13

impressed

Barr, Flight & Barr    BARR, FLIGHT
Worcester    & BARR
Flight & Barr    ROYAL PORCELAIN
Coventry Street,    WORKS
London    WORCESTER
Manufacturers to their    LONDON HOUSE
Majesties and    NO. 1
Royal Family    COVENTRY STREET

85

'Flight, Barr & Barr' period
1813–40

impressed

(factory taken over by Chamberlains, 1840–52)

Kerr & Binns, 1852–62

Kerr & Binns, '54' = 1854
   mark on outstanding
   examples, including decorator's
   initials (bottom left)

standard mark, printed or
impressed, *c.* 1852–62
*Note:* crown added
in 1862

'Worcester Royal Porcelain Company Ltd.'
(Royal Worcester) 1862–present

standard mark, 1862–present
early version, with 'C'
in centre replacing crescent
in Kerr & Binn's version
numbers below = last 2 years
of date

From 1867 a letter indicating the year of
manufacture was printed under the factory mark
according to the following table:

86

| *Worcester* | | **England** | | *Worcester* |
|---|---|---|---|---|
| A 1867 | G 1872 | M 1877 | T 1882 | Y 1887 |
| B '1868 | H 1873 | N 1878 | U 1883 | Z 1888 |
| C 1869 | I 1874 | P 1879 | V 1884 | O 1889 |
| D 1870 | K 1875 | R 1880 | W 1885 | |
| E 1871 | L 1876 | S 1881 | X 1886 | |

'a' in Old English script in 1890; date letter
omitted in 1891.
'Royal Worcester England' written around mark
from 1891, after which, dots, stars and other
letters and forms were added to the mark each
year as listed below until 1963 when the year in
full is added.

1892, dot to left of crown, 1893 dot either side of
crown; dots were then added to either side of
crown until 1915, thus:

| | | | | |
|---|---|---|---|---|
| 1894 3 dots | 1900  9 dots | 1906 15 dots | 1912 21 dots |
| 1895 4 dots | 1901 10 dots | 1907 16 dots | 1913 22 dots |
| 1896 5 dots | 1902 11 dots | 1908 17 dots | 1914 23 dots |
| 1897 6 dots | 1903 12 dots | 1909 18 dots | 1915 24 dots |
| 1898 7 dots | 1904 13 dots | 1910 19 dots | |
| 1899 8 dots | 1905 14 dots | 1911 20 dots | |

In 1916 the dots alongside the crown were
replaced by a star under the mark, dots were then
added to either side of this star until 1927:

| | |
|---|---|
| 1916 1 star | 1922 star & 6 dots |
| 1917 star & 1 dot | 1923 star & 7 dots |
| 1918 star & 2 dots | 1924 star & 8 dots |
| 1919 star & 3 dots | 1925 star & 9 dots |
| 1920 star & 4 dots | 1926 star & 10 dots |
| 1921 star & 5 dots | 1927 star & 11 dots |

then as follows:

1928 ▭    1929 ◇    1930 ÷

1931 ∞    1932 ∞∞    1933 ∞∞ ·

further dots were then added to three interlaced circles as follows:

| | |
|---|---|
| 1934 circles & 2 dots | 1938 circles & 6 dots |
| 1935 circles & 3 dots | 1939 circles & 7 dots |
| 1936 circles & 4 dots | 1940 circles & 8 dots |
| 1937 circles & 5 dots | 1941 circles & 9 dots |

from 1941 to 1948 inclusive there were no changes in the year-mark

| | |
|---|---|
| 1949 V | 1953 W and 3 dots |
| 1950 W | 1954 W and 4 dots |
| 1951 W and 1 dot | 1955 W and 5 dots |
| 1952 W and 2 dots | |

| | |
|---|---|
| 1956 R in place of W with 6 dots | 1960 R and 10 dots |
| | 1961 R and 11 dots |
| 1957 R and 7 dots | 1962 R and 12 dots |
| 1958 R and 8 dots | 1963 R and 13 dots |
| 1959 R and 9 dots | |

From 1963 all new patterns have the year in full.

(*By courtesy of the Worcester Royal Porcelain Co. Ltd.*)

Hancock, Robert, *b.* 1730, *d.* 1817
engraver of transfer-prints
*c.* 1756–65

*Rf . Worcester*

(Hancock associated with
Turner of Caughley in
1776)

initials of Hancock
and rebus of Richard
Holdship on prints

Chamberlain, *c.* 1786–1852
decorators from *c.* 1786–*c.* 1790, then
manufacturers of soft-paste porcelain
　*c.* 1790–1810

*Chamberlains
Worcs No 276*

in red

written or printed
*c.* 1811–40
(under crown)

*Chamberlain's
Worcester,
& 155
New Bond Street
London,
Royal Porcelain
Manufactory*

*c.* 1814–16

*Chamberlain's
Worcester,
& 63 Piccadilly,
London*

written or printed

89

| | |
|---|---|
| incised, *c*. 1815–25 | CHAMBERLAINS<br>ROYAL PORCELAIN<br>WORCESTER |
| printed mark under<br>crown, *c*. 1840–5<br>('& Co.' from this<br>date) | CHAMBERLAIN & CO.<br>WORCESTER<br>155 New Bond St.<br>& No. 1<br>COVENTRY ST.<br>LONDON |
| written or printed<br>*c*. 1846–50 | CHAMBERLAIN & CO.<br>WORCESTER |
| impressed or printed<br>*c*. 1847–50 | CHAMBERLAINS |
| printed *c*. 1850–52 |  |

(then Kerr & Binns, p. 86)

| | |
|---|---|
| Doe and Rogers,<br>*c*. 1820–40<br>porcelain decorators | Doe & Rogers<br>Worcester |
| Grainger, Wood & Co.<br>*c*. 1801–12, porcelain<br>rare mark | Grainger Wood & Co.<br>Worcester, Warranted |
| Grainger, Lee & Co.<br>*c*. 1812–*c*. 39<br>porcelain | Grainger, Lee & Co.<br>Worcester<br>painted |

| | |
|---|---|
| *c*. 1820–30 painted | New China Works Worcester |
| *c*. 1812–30 painted | Royal China Works Worcester |

| | |
|---|---|
| Grainger, George *c*. 1839–1902 porcelain | GEO. GRAINGER CHINA WORKS WORCESTER |
| painted or printed mark *c*. 1839–60 | |
| '& Co.' added *c*. 1850 | G. GRAINGER & CO. WORCESTER |

's.p.' for 'Semi-Porcelain', *c*. 1850–
initials included in printed marks, 1850–60
1850–89

G.G. & CO.      S.P.
     S.P.      G.G.W.
impressed or printed
G.W.

G. & CO. W.

printed mark on copies of 'Dr. Wall' period wares
*c*. 1860–80
printed or impressed
*c*. 1870–89

GRAINGER & CO.
WORCESTER

*c*. 1889–1902 ('England' added in 1891)

letters added under mark to indicate year of
manufacture from 1891–1902:

| A 1891 | D 1894 | G 1897 | J 1900 |
| B 1892 | E 1895 | H 1898 | K 1901 |
| C 1893 | F 1896 | I 1899 | L 1902 |

George Grainger & Co. was taken over by
Worcester Royal Porcelain Co. Ltd. in 1889 and
closed down in 1902.

Hadley & Sons, James
porcelain and earthenware
1896–1905

*Hadley*

signature on work
modelled by Hadley for
Worcester Royal Porcelain Co.

incised or impressed

*c.* 1875–94
printed or impressed
1896–97

1897–1902,
impressed

FINE ART
HADLEY'S
TERRA-COTTA

printed mark 1897–1902
(centre ribbon omitted
from 1900)

printed mark, 1902–5

Locke & Co., porcelain
1895–1904

LOCKE & CO.
WORCESTER

'globe-mark', *c*. 1895–1904
'Ltd,' added in *c*. 1900

Sparks, George, *c*.    Sparks Worcester
1836–54, decorator of    written mark
Worcester and Coalport porcelain

WROTHAM (Kent)          I.G.
Greene, John
slipware potter, *c*. 1670

Hubble, Nicholas         N.H.
slipware potter, second
half of 17th century

Ifield, Thomas, Henry       T.I.
& John           H.I.     I.I.
slipware potters whose
   initials are found on wares
   dating from *c*. 1620–75

Livermore, John          I.L.
(*d*. 1658) slipware potter,
wares dated from 1612–49

Richardson, George       G.R.
slipware potter, wares
dated from 1642–77    all above slip-trailed

Wells, Reginald,        WELLS
(1877–1951)           incised
studio-potter

| | | |
|---|---|---|
| *c.* 1909 | | COLDRUM |
| | | WROTHAM |
| *c.* 1910–24 (at | | COLDRUM |
| Chelsea) | | CHELSEA |
| *c.* 1910 | | R. F. WELLS |
| *c.* 1918–51 | | SOON |
| (at Storrington, | | impressed or incised |
| Sussex, *c.* 1925–51) | | |

YARMOUTH (Norfolk)
Absolon, William, 1784–1815
independent enameller of
the wares of various
earthenwares and glass        painted in brown

## STAFFORDSHIRE

Since the early seventeenth century the area in,
and around, Stoke in Staffordshire has been the
centre of the English ceramic industry.
Manufacture was first confined to earthenwares,
but later included salt-glazed stonewares,
jasperwares, bone-china and the mass of various
hybrid pottery and porcelain bodies introduced
about 1800 and later. The smaller pottery towns
are today grouped together to form
Stoke-on-Trent.

In this section of the book, the various

94

Staffordshire potters are listed alphabetically under the names of the towns in which they potted.

Many of the more recent factories have often changed their mark many times and the following general aids to dating are often sufficient enough as a guide.

Few serious collectors seek pieces which include 'ENGLAND' in the mark, for this implies the piece was made in, or after, 1891 in order to comply with the American McKinley Tariff, which called for the country of origin to be marked on imported wares. The term 'MADE IN ENGLAND' suggests a date of about 1920.

The mass of blue-printed earthenwares are difficult to attribute if unmarked. Many have just a Royal Arms as a mark; this is a sure indication of a 19th-century date, whereas often similar marks, or 'back-stamps', include the name of the design and the initials of the potter. These initials may well be included in the index at end of the book. Versions of the Royal Arms used after 1837 lack the small inescutcheon on the quartered shield which is present on arms previous to this date.

In addition to factory marks, many wares will be found to bear the well-known 'diamond' or 'lozenge'-mark (see Appendix A, page 284). This mark was applied by either printing, impressing, or applying as a relief medallion and indicates that the design of the form or decoration had been registered with the London Patent Office and was protected against 'piracy'

for a period of three years. If the numbers and
letters in the four corners of this 'diamond-mark'
can be accurately read, the reader should consult
the key diagrams and tables on pages 284–7 to
check the day, month and year the design was
initially registered between 1842 and 1883. After
this year wares bear only a registered number
(e.g. Rd. 12345), which can be dated to the year, up
until 1909.

Appendix B in this book is an abbreviated copy
of the Class IV (pottery, porcelain, etc.) Index,
giving the name and whereabouts of the firms
registering ceramic designs between 1842 and
1883. This list is reproduced with the kind
permission of the Public Record Office.

BILSTON (Staffs., now West Midlands)
Myatt Pottery Co., *c.* 1850–94
earthenware, mark of 1880    MYATT

BURSLEM (Staffs, now West Midlands.)
Albert Potteries Ltd.
earthenware, 1946–54        printed or impressed

Allman, Broughton & Co.,       A.B. & CO.
earthenware, 1861–8        printed or impressed

Baggaley, Jacob                 J.B.
earthenware, 1880–6           impressed

Bagshaw & Meir                 B. & M.
earthenware, 1802–8        printed or impressed

Ball, Izaac                     I.B.
slipware, *c.* 1700

Bancroft & Bennett
earthenware, 1846–50

Barker & Son                   B. & S.
earthenware, *c.* 1850–60        printed
                           BARKER & SON
                        printed or impressed

Barker, Sutton & Till          B.S. & T.
earthenware, 1834–43

Bates, Elliott & Co.    B.E. & CO.
general ceramics, 1870–5
97

Bates, Gildea & Walker,
general ceramics, 1878–81

B.G. & W.
printed

Bates, Walker & Co.
general ceramics, 1875–78

B.W. & CO.
printed

Bathwell & Goodfellow
earthenware, 1818–23
(also Tunstall 1820–2)

BATHWELL &
GOODFELLOW
impressed

Beech, James
earthenware, 1877–89
Swan Bank Works (also
at Tunstall)

J.B.
printed

Blackhurst & Bourne
earthenware, 1880–92

B. & B.
printed

Blackhurst & Tunnicliffe
earthenware, *c.* 1879

B. & T.
printed

Bodley & Co.
earthenware, 1865

Bodley & Co., E. F.
earthenware, *c.* 1862–81

E.F.B. & CO.

SCOTIA POTTERY

BODLEY

Bodley & Son
bone-china, 1874–5

B. & SON
printed

Bodley, E. J. D.
general ceramics, 1875–92

E.J.D.B.
printed,
impressed or as
monogram

Bodley & Harrold
Scotia Pottery
1863–5, earthenware

B. & H.
Bodley & Harrold
printed

Boote, Ltd., T. & R.
Waterloo Pottery
general ceramics and
tiles, 1842–*c.* 1966

T. & R.B.    T.B. & S.

T. & R. BOOTE
printed or impressed

printed mark
1890–1906
'England' added
from 1891

Booth & Co., Thomas
(also at Tunstall)
earthenware, 1868–72

T.B. & CO.
printed

Bridgwood & Clarke
(also at Tunstall)
earthenware, 1857–64

BRIDGWOOD &
CLARKE
impressed
B. & C.    B. & C.
BURSLEM
printed

| | |
|---|---|
| Brown & Steventon, Ltd.<br>earthenware, 1900–23 | B. & S.<br>printed<br>'sun-face' mark<br>from 1920– |

Buckley, Heath & Co.
earthenware, 1885–90

printed or impressed

Buckley, Wood & Co.
earthenware, 1875–85

B.W. & CO.
printed or impressed

Burgess, Henry
earthenware, 1864–92

H.B.
impressed or printed
under Royal Arms

Burgess & Leigh
earthenware, *c.* 1862–

B. & L.
impressed or printed

'Ltd.' added to marks
from *c.* 1919, large
variety of printed
marks from 1880,
'England' added from
1891

printed

monogram mark
1862–

impressed or printed

100

Burslem Pottery Co. Ltd.
earthenware, 1894–1933

   printed

ENGLAND

Burslem School of Art
earthenware, figures, etc.
in 'Astbury' style
1935–41

impressed

Clarke & Co., Edward
earthenware, *c.* 1880–87
(also at Tunstall, *c.* 1865–
77, and Longport, *c.*
1878–80)

EDWARD CLARKE

EDWARD CLARKE &
CO.
printed

Clowes, William
general ceramics
*c.* 1783–96

W. CLOWES
impressed

Collinson & Co.,
Charles, earthenware,
1851–73

C. COLLINSON & CO.
printed

Cooper & Co., J.
earthenware, 1922–5
printed or impressed
   in circle
Cooper Pottery, Susie
('Ltd.' from *c.* 1961)
general ceramics
   *c.* 1930–

J. COOPER & CO.
ENGLAND
DUCAL WORKS

*Susie Cooper*

CROWN WORKS
BURSLEM
ENGLAND

101

printed mark, 1932–

Cooper China Ltd., Susie
(also at Longton, *c.* 1950–9)
china, *c.* 1959–
Member of the
Wedgwood Group

Cork & Edge　　　　　C. & E.
earthenware,　　　printed with a
1846–60　　　variety of designs

Cork, Edge & Malkin　　C.E. & M.
earthenware, 1860–71　printed with varying
'backstamps' often
including pattern-name

Dale, John　　　J. DALE　　　I. DALE
'Staffordshire　　BURSLEM　　BURSLEM
figures', early 19th century

Daniel & Cork　　　DANIEL & CORK
earthenware, 1867–9　　　printed

Davison & Son, Ltd.
earthenware,
*c.* 1898–1952

mark of 1948–　　　　printed

Dean, S. W.
earthenware, 1904–10

printed mark

Deans (1910) Ltd.     DEANS (1910) LTD.
earthenware, 1910–19     BURSLEM
printed mark     ENGLAND

Doulton & Co.     *see under*
earthenware and     LAMBETH
porcelain, *c.* 1882     for major
(Doulton Fine China Ltd.     marks
from 1955 and Royal
Doulton Tableware Ltd., 1973–)
impressed name of     ENGLISH
new material from     TRANSLUCENT
1960     CHINA

Duke & Nephews, Sir James
various hybrid porcelains
*c.* 1860–3

impressed hand

Dunn, Bennett & Co.
earthenware, 1875–
('Ltd.' added from 1907–)
(now Royal Doulton Group)
marks 1875–1907

D.B. & CO.
printed

---

printed mark, 1937–　DUNN BENNETT & CO. LTD.
*BURSLEM*
ENGLAND

added to mark on
'Ironstone' from 1955–　'Vitreous Ironstone'

Edge, Malkin & Co.　　E.M. & CO.
earthenware, 1871–1903

　　　　　　　　　　　E.M. & CO.
'LTD.' added from 1899　　B
　　　　　　　　　　　printed

Edwards & Son, James　　J.E. & S.
various pottery, 1851–82

　　　　　　　　　　　EDWARDS
'Dale Hall', Burslem　　D.H.
　　　　　　　printed or impressed
Edwards, James & Thomas　J. & T.E.
earthenware, 1839–41

printed or impressed　　J. & T. EDWARDS
　　　　　　　　　　　B

Ellgreave Pottery Co. Ltd.　'Lottie Rhead Ware'
earthenware, 1921–
(Wood & Sons Ltd.)
　and other fully　　'Heatmaster'
　named marks

Elton & Co. Ltd., J. F.　　J.F.E. CO. LTD.
earthenware, 1901–1910　　BURSLEM
(also in monogram)　printed or impressed

104

---

Emery, Francis J.
earthenware, *c.* 1878–93

F. J. EMERY
printed

Evans & Booth
earthenware, 1856–69

E. & B.
printed

Ford & Co., Samuel
earthenware, 1898–1939
(*see* Smith & Ford)

　'F. & CO.' alternative to
　'S. & F.'

S & F.
printed

　*c.* 1936–9

'Samford Ware'

Ford & Riley
earthenware, 1882–93

F. & R.
B

Ford & Sons ('Ltd.'
added 1908),
earthenware, *c.* 1893–1938

F. & S.
B

　also 'CROWN
FORD', 'NEWCRAFT'

F. & SONS, LTD.
printed

Ford & Sons (Crownford)
earthenware, 1938–

　printed, 1961–

Gibson & Sons, Ltd.
earthenware, 1885–

G. & S. LTD.
B

105

Gibson & Sons, Ltd.
'Harvey Pottery'
  printed, *c.* 1904–9

'Royal Harvey', *c.* 1950–5
  large variety of fully named marks, 1909–

Gildea & Walker, 1881–5     G. & W.
earthenware

  *c.* 1881–5:
$$\frac{4}{82} = \text{APRIL, 1882}$$

Gildea, James
earthenware, 1885–8

  printed mark includes
  a pattern-name

Godwin, B. C.     B.C.G.
earthenware, *c.* 1851–     printed

Godwin, Thomas &     T. & B.G.
Benjamin, general     T.B.G.
ceramics, *c.* 1809–34     printed

Godwin, Thomas     THOS GODWIN
earthenware, 1834–54     BURSLEM
                    STONE CHINA

| | |
|---|---|
| Godwin, Rowley & Co. earthenware, 1828–31 | G.R. & CO. printed |
| Hall & Sons, John earthenware, 1814–32 | I. HALL     HALL |
| c. 1822–32 | I. HALL & SONS impressed or printed |
| Hammersley & Son, Ralph, earthenware, 1860–1905 | R.H. |
| '& Son' added 1884– | R.H. & S. printed |
| Hancock, Whittingham & Co., earthenware, 1863–72 | H.W. & CO. printed |
| Harding, Joseph earthenware, 1850–1 | J. HARDING printed |
| Harrison & Phillips earthenware, 1914–15 | H. & P. BURSLEM printed |
| Heath & Son earthenware, c. 1800 | HEATH & SON impressed |
| Heath, John general ceramics, 1809–23 | HEATH impressed |
| Heath, Thomas earthenware, 1812–35 | T. HEATH impressed or printed |

Heath & Blackhurst & Co.,           H. & B.
earthenware, 1859–77               H.B. & CO.

Heath & Greatbatch                  H. & G.
earthenware, 1891–3                   B
                                   printed or impressed

Hill Pottery Co. Ltd.               J.S.H.
general ceramics, *c.* 1861–7      printed
                                   (also as monogram)

Hobson, Charles                     C.H.
earthenware, 1865–80               C.H. & S.
  's' added 1873–5               impressed or printed

Hobson, G. & J.                    HOBSON'S
earthenware, 1883–1901             printed

Hobson, George
earthenware, 1901–23
  printed or impressed

Holdcroft & Co., Peter             P.H. & CO.
earthenware, 1846–52               printed

Holdcroft, Hill & Mellor,          H.H. & M.
earthenware,                       printed
1860–70

Hollinshead & Griffiths       CHELSEA ART POTTERY
earthenware, 1890–1909             H. & G.
                                   BURSLEM
     mark includes lion and crown

108

Holmes, Plant & Maydew
earthenware, 1876–85

H.P. & M.
printed

Hope & Carter
earthenware, 1862–80

H. & C.
printed

Hughes, Thomas
earthenware, 1860–94

THOMAS HUGHES
IRONSTONE CHINA
impressed

Hughes & Son Ltd., Thomas,
general ceramics,
1895–1957

THOS. HUGHES &
SON
ENGLAND

Hulme & Sons, Henry
earthenware, 1906–32
(mark previously used
by Wood & Hulme)

W. & H.
B

Hulme, William
earthenware, 1891–1941

printed
1891–1936

printed or impressed,
1936–41

ALPHA WARE
H
ENGLAND

Jackson, Job & John
earthenware, 1831–5

J. & J. JACKSON
JACKSON'S
WARRANTED
impressed or printed

---

Johnson, Ltd., Samuel      S.J.
earthenware, 1887–1931                 S.J.B.
   'Ltd.' 1912–
   'BRITANNIA POTTERY',      S.J. LTD.
   1916–31      printed

Jones, George      GEORGE JONES
earthenware, *c.* 1854

Keeling & Co. Ltd.      K. & CO.
earthenware, 1886–1936
                     K. & CO. B.

   'England' usually added
   from 1891
   'Losol Ware', *c.* 1912–      all
                  printed

Kennedy, William Sadler      W. S. KENNEDY
earthenware, 1843–54      impressed or printed

Kennedy & Macintyre      W. S. KENNEDY
earthenware, 1854–60      & J. MACINTYRE
                impressed or printed

Kensington Pottery Ltd.
*c.* 1937–
(also at Hanley 1922–37)
now Price & Kensington Potteries Ltd.

Kent (Porcelains) Ltd., William
earthenware 1944–62

| | |
|---|---|
| King & Barrett, Ltd.<br>general pottery, 1898–40 | K. & B.<br>impressed or printed |
| Lakin & Poole<br>pottery and figures, *c.* 1791–5 | LAKIN & POOLE<br><br>L. & P.<br>BURSLEM<br>impressed |
| Leighton Pottery Ltd.<br>earthenware, 1940–54 | 'ROYAL LEIGHTON WARE' |
| Machin & Potts<br>general ceramics<br>1833–7<br>colour-print patent 1835 | MACHIN & POTTS<br><br>MACHIN & POTTS<br>PATENT |
| Machin & Thomas<br>earthenware, *c.* 1831–2 | M. & T.<br>printed |
| Macintyre & Co. Ltd.,<br>James, earthenware, *c.*<br>1860–1928, '& Co.' from<br>　　1867– (continued with<br>　　industrial wares only) | MACINTYRE<br>J. MACINTYRE<br>J.M. & CO.<br>printed or impressed |
| Maddock & Seddon<br>earthenware, *c.* 1839–42 | M. & S. |
| Maddock, John<br>earthenware, 1842–55<br>　　(not to be confused with<br>　　'M' for Minton) | M<br>printed |

111

Maddock & Sons (Ltd.)
general pottery, 1855–
specialist hotel-ware
'Ltd.' added 1896–

various fully named
marks, and
'ROYAL VITREOUS'
'ROYAL IVORY'
'IVORY WARE'
'EMBASSY'

Malkin, Frederick
earthenware, 1891–1905

printed, *c.* 1900–5

Malkin, Samuel
slip-wares, early 18th century

S.M.
moulded in
relief

Mayer, Thomas, John
& Joseph, general
ceramics, 1843–55

T. J. & J. MAYER
printed

Mellor, Taylor & Co.
earthenware, *c.* 1880–1904

'ROYAL IRONSTONE CHINA'

printed or impressed
with name of firm

'SEMI PORCELAIN'

Mellor, Venables & Co.
general ceramics, 1834–51

MELLOR, VENABLES
& CO.

M.V. & CO.
printed or impressed

Midwinter Ltd., W. R.
earthenwares, 1910–
   added numbers indicate
   month and year
(*now Wedgwood Group*)

various fully-named
marks with:
'PORCELON'
'STYLECRAFT'

Moorcroft Ltd., W.
earthenware, 1913–

MOORCROFT
BURSLEM

signature of William
Moorcroft (*d.* 1945)

mark of Walter Moorcroft
(son)

Morgan, Wood & Co.
earthenware, 1860–70

M.W. & CO.
printed
(at times with bee)

Mountford, A. J.
earthenware, 1897–1901

BURSLEM
printed

New Wharf Pottery Co.
earthenware, 1878–94

N.W.P.C.O.
B
printed

Newport Pottery Co. Ltd.
earthenware, 1920–
(now Wedgwood group)

various fully named
marks

*c.* 1938–66

'Clarice Cliff'

113

Parrott & Co. Ltd.
earthenware, 1921
(manufacture ceased *c.* 1962)

Phillips & Son, Thomas    T. PHILLIPS & SON
earthenware, *c.* 1845–6    BURSLEM
printed or impressed

Pinder, Thomas    PINDER BURSLEM
earthenware, 1849–51    printed or impressed

Pinder, Bourne & Hope    P.B. & H.
earthenware, 1851–62    printed

Pinder, Bourne & Co.    P.B. & CO.
earthenware, 1862–82
(taken over by Doultons
in 1878, but name unchanged
until 1882)

Plant Bros. Crown Pottery
porcelain, 1889–1906
(at Longton from 1898)

Plant, Enoch
earthenware, 1898–1905
    (such crowns are a
    common form of mark)    printed or impressed

Poole, J. E.    POOLE
earthenware, *c.* 1796–    impressed
early 19th century

Price Bros.
earthenware, 1896–1903

Price Bros. (Burslem) Ltd.            printed
earthenware, 1903–61         'star-mark', as above
                                    until 1910

  trade-names:
  'PALM ATHLO'
  'ATHLO WARE'
  'MATTONA WARE'

Price & Kensington                  PRICE
Potteries Ltd.                    KENSINGTON
earthenware, 1962–         printed within wreath

Radford Handcraft                G. RADFORD
Pottery, earthenware,             BURSLEM
1933–48                     printed signature

Riley, John & Richard          J. & R. RILEY
general ceramics, 1802–28

  marks painted,                 RILEY'S
  printed or impressed         SEMI-CHINA

Robinson, Joseph                    J.R.
earthenware, 1876–98                 B
                            printed or impressed

Roddy & Co., E.               STAFFORDSHIRE
earthenware, 1925–8               RODDY
                                   WARE

115

| | |
|---|---|
| Sadler & Sons, Ltd.,<br>James, earthenware,<br>1899–<br>   impressed or printed<br>   from 1937– | ENGLAND<br>J.S.S.B.<br>impressed<br><br>SADLER<br>BURSLEM<br>ENGLAND |
| Simpson, Ralph<br>slip-wares, 1651–*c.* 1724<br>   name slip-trailed on front<br>   of large chargers | RALPH SIMPSON<br>slip-trailed |
| Simpson, John<br>slip wares, first half of<br>18th century | JOHN SIMPSON<br>I.S.<br>slip-trailed |
| Smith & Co., Ambrose<br>earthenware, *c.* 1784–6 | A.S. & CO.<br>impressed or printed |
| Smith & Ford<br>earthenware, 1895–8<br>   printed (*see also*<br>   Samuel Ford) | <br>S & F |
| Stanyer, A.<br>earthenware, *c.* 1916–41 | A.S.       A.S.<br>B         ENG.<br>ENG.      B<br>impressed |
| Steel, Daniel,<br>   1790–1824<br>earthenwares and<br>'Wedgwood-type' stonewares | STEEL<br>impressed |

| | |
|---|---|
| Stubbs, Joseph earthenwares, *c.* 1822–35 | JOSEPH STUBBS LONGPORT impressed or printed |
| Stubbs & Kent earthenware, *c.* 1828–30 mark impressed or printed | |
| Sudlow & Sons, Ltd., R. earthenware, 1893– (Part of Howard Pottery Co. Shelton from 1965) | full-name marks impressed or printed from *c.* 1920– |
| Till & Sons, Thomas earthenware, *c.* 1850–1928 | |
| 1861– | |
| 'Globe-mark' from 1880 'Tillson' ware, *c.* 1922–8 | |
| Tundley, Rhodes & Proctor, earthenware, 1873–83, then: | T.R. & P. printed |
| Rhodes & Proctor, 1883–5, earthenware | R. & P. printed |
| Venables & Baines earthenware, *c.* 1851–3 | VENABLES & BAINES |
| Venables & Co. earthenware, *c.* 1853–5 | J. VENABLES & CO. printed or impressed |

Vernon & Son, James      J.V.
earthenware, 1860–80
    1875–                     J.V. & Son
                J.V. & S.              J.V. junr.


Wade & Son, Ltd.,      WADE
George, earthenware    Figures
    1922–,
    1936–

    1947–

Wade & Co.             WADES
earthenware, 1887–1927
                                    W. & CO.
                                      B


Wade, Heath & Co., Ltd.,    WADES
earthenware,                (with lion)
    1927–


    c. 1934–              WADEHEATH
                          ORCADIA
                          WARE


    c. 1934–              WADEHEATH
                          (with lion)
    Trade-names: 'Flaxman Ware', 'ROYAL
    VICTORIA'


Walley, John             J. WALLEY
earthenware, 1850–67     J. WALLEY'S
                          WARE
                     printed or impressed

118

Walton, John
earthenware groups and
figures, *c.* 1818–35

impressed on raised
scroll

Wedgwood & Sons, Ltd.
Josiah, general ceramics, 1759–
very rare incised initials or  'J.W.'
signature, *c.* 1760
rare, *c.* 1759–69
*c.* 1759  WEDGWOOD

Wedgwood & Bentley  WEDGWOOD
partnership, 1769–80  & BENTLEY
concerned only with
the manufacture of  WEDGWOOD
ornamental neo-classical  & BENTLEY
wares  ETRURIA

impressed on cameos, etc.  W. & B.
impressed or raised mark

*c.* 1780–98  Wedgwood

rare impressed mark  WEDGWOOD & SONS
*c.* 1790
printed on bone-china  WEDGWOOD
*c.* 1812–22  red, blue or gold

| | |
|---|---|
| rare printed mark on stone china, *c.* 1827–61 | WEDGWOOD'S STONE CHINA |
| impressed mark *c.* 1840–5 | WEDGWOOD ETRURIA |
| impressed on 'pearlware' *c.* 1840–68 | PEARL |
| as above, post–1868 | P |

From 1860 the Wedgwood factory in addition to their usual name-mark, adopted a system of date-marking consisting of three letters side by side: the first indicates the month, the second a potter's mark and the third the year of manufacture. As from 1907 the first letter, which had hitherto denoted the month of manufacture, was replaced by a number indicating the cycle of year marks in use; previously there was no indication whether the piece was made in the first second, or third cycle.

This system was further changed in 1930 when the cycle number was replaced by the chronological number of the month, e.g.: January = 1, February = 2, etc., and the initial which had previously indicated the year was now replaced by the last two years of the actual date of manufacture.

| **Examples:** | Month | Potter | Year | |
|---|---|---|---|---|
| | Y | O | R | May, 1863 |
| | L | O | E | July, 1902 |
| | Cycle | Potter | Year | |
| | 3 | O | N | 1911 |
| | 4 | O | A | 1924 |

| Month | Potter | Year | |
|-------|--------|------|--|
| 3 | O | 32 | March, 1932 |
| 11 | O | 48 | November, 1948 |

*Monthly marks indicated by the first letter from*
1860–1864:

| | | | | | | | |
|--|--|--|--|--|--|--|--|
| January | J | April | A | July | V | October | O |
| February | F | May | Y | August | W | November | N |
| March | M | June | T | September | S | December | D |

1865–1907:

| | | | | | | | |
|--|--|--|--|--|--|--|--|
| January | J | April | A | July | L | October | O |
| February | F | May | M | August | W | November | N |
| March | R | June | T | September | S | December | D |

*First cycle of year marks:*

| | | | | | | | |
|--|--|--|--|--|--|--|--|
| O | 1860 | R | 1863 | U | 1866 | X | 1869 |
| P | 1861 | S | 1864 | V | 1867 | Y | 1870 |
| Q | 1862 | T | 1865 | W | 1868 | Z | 1871 |

*Second cycle of year marks:*

| | | | | | | | |
|--|--|--|--|--|--|--|--|
| A | 1872 | H | 1879 | O | 1886 | V | 1893 |
| B | 1873 | I | 1880 | P | 1887 | W | 1894 |
| C | 1874 | J | 1881 | Q | 1888 | X | 1895 |
| D | 1875 | K | 1882 | R | 1889 | Y | 1896 |
| E | 1876 | L | 1883 | S | 1890 | Z | 1897 |
| F | 1877 | M | 1884 | T | 1891 | | |
| G | 1878 | N | 1885 | U | 1892 | | |

Note: 'ENGLAND' added to mark from 1891

*Third cycle of year marks:*

| | | | |
|---|---|---|---|
| A 1898 | H 1905 | O 1912 | V 1919 |
| B 1899 | I 1906 | P 1913 | W 1920 |
| C 1900 | J 1907 | Q 1914 | X 1921 |
| D 1901 | K 1908 | R 1915 | Y 1922 |
| E 1902 | L 1909 | S 1916 | Z 1923 |
| F 1903 | M 1910 | T 1917 | |
| G 1904 | N 1911 | U 1918 | |

*Fourth cycle of year marks:*

| | | |
|---|---|---|
| A 1924 | C 1926 | E 1928 |
| B 1925 | D 1927 | F 1929 |

the last two years of the date then appear in full.

'Portland Vase' mark printed
on bone-china from *c.* 1878
occasionally seen impressed
on earthenware, *c.* 1891–1900
*Note:* 'ENGLAND' added
  after 1891 'MADE IN
ENGLAND' from about 1910
'*Bone China*' added *c.* 1920

printed on creamwares
from *c.* 1940

Lessore, Emile, decorator
*c.* 1858–76

122

Thomson, E. G.,
decorator, *c.* 1870

E. G. Thomson

Barnard, Harry, decorator
*c.* 1900

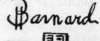

marks on red stonewares,
probably Wedgwood
second-half of
18th century

impressed

Whittingham, Ford & Co.,
1868–73,
earthenware

W.F. & CO.
printed

Whittingham, Ford & Riley,
earthenware, 1876–82

W.F. & R.
printed

Wilkinson, Arthur J.,
1885–*c.* 1970, earthenwares
'ROYAL SEMI-PORCELAIN', *c.* 1891–
'ROYAL IRONSTONE CHINA', *c.* 1896–
'IRONSTONE CHINA', *c.* 1910
'Clarice Cliff', *c.* 1930
'Honeyglaze', *c.* 1947
(merged with W. R. Midwinter Ltd., 1964)

many fully-named
marks including:

Withinshaw, W. E.,
1873–8, general ceramics

W.E.W.
W. E. WITHINSHAW
printed or impressed

Wood, Enoch
*c.* 1784–*c.* 1790 general
ceramics

WOOD          E. WOOD
W (***)
E.W.                    W.

Enoch Wood's marks
can be seen impressed,
moulded or incised

ENOCH WOOD
SCULPSIT

E. WOOD
SCULPSIT

ENOCH WOOD

Wood & Caldwell
1790–1818, earthenware
especially figures, etc.

WOOD & CALDWELL
impressed

Wood & Sons, Enoch
1818–1846, earthenware
  blue-printed wares made
  for U.S.A. include the
  American eagle in mark

ENOCH WOOD
& SONS
BURSLEM
STAFFORDSHIRE

E.W. & S.

E. WOOD & SONS
E. & E. WOOD
BURSLEM

E. & E. WOOD
E. & E.W.
all printed

Wood, H. J.
1884–, earthenware
  many various fully-named marks including:
  'Bursley-Ware' *c.* 1930–
  'E. Radford' *c.* 1935–
  'CHINESE ROSE' *c.* 1960–, etc.

Wood, Isaiah
1710–15, earthenware

ISA WOOD
1712
incised

| | |
|---|---|
| Wood, John Wedge | W.W. |
| 1841–4 (also at Tunstall | impressed |
| 1845–60) | J. WEDGWOOD |
| | printed |

Wood, Ralph (Snr.)   R. WOOD   Ra. WOOD
(1715–72), son of same   Ra. WOOD
name (1748–95)   BURSLEM
grandson (1781–1801)   Ralph Wood
   impressed or incised marks
   *c.* 1770–1801

   rebus of trees (rare)
   *c.* 1770–90

Wood & Son   various fully-named
1865–, earthenware, etc.   marks from *c.* 1890–
   '& Sons', from 1907
   'Ltd.' added *c.* 1910

Wood & Co., Thomas   T.W. & CO.
1885–96, earthenwares   printed or impressed

Wood & Sons, Thomas   T.W. & S.
*c.* 1896–7, earthenware   printed

Wood & Co., W.   W.W. & CO.
1873–1932, earthenware   printed or impressed
   mark of initials printed in 'Staffordshire
   knot', 1880–1915, with crown, 1915–32

| | |
|---|---|
| Wood & Baggaley<br>1870–80, earthenware | w.. & b.<br>printed |
| Wood & Barker, Ltd.<br>1897–1903, earthenware | w. & b. Ltd.<br>printed |
| Wood & Bowers<br>1839, earthenware | w. & b.<br>(can be confused<br>with Wood & Baggaley) |
| Wood & Clarke<br>c. 1871–2, earthenware | w. & c.<br>printed with 'lion<br>rampant' |
| Wood & Hulme<br>1882–1905, earthenware | w. & h.<br>b<br>printed or impressed |
| Wooldridge & Walley<br>1898–1901, earthenware | w. & w.<br>b<br>printed |

COBRIDGE (Staffordshire)

J. & G.A.

| | |
|---|---|
| Alcock, John & George<br>1839–46, earthenware and<br>'INDIAN IRONSTONE' | J. & G. ALCOCK<br>COBRIDGE<br>impressed or printed |
| Alcock, Junior, John &<br>Samuel, c. 1848–50<br>earthenware | J. & S. ALCOCK JR.<br>printed or impressed |

Alcock, John  
1853–61, earthenware

JOHN ALCOCK  
COBRIDGE  
printed

Alcock & Co., Henry  
1861–1910, earthenware  
  fully-named mark from  
  1880, 'Ltd.' from 1900

H.A. & CO.  
printed

Alcock Pottery, The Henry  
1910–35, earthenware

fully named  
'coat of arms' mark  
printed

Alcock & Co., Samuel  
*c.* 1828–53, general ceramics  
  (Also at Burslem  
  *c.* 1830–59)  
  printed, painted or  
  impressed, sometimes  
  with Royal Arms or  
  bee-hive

SAMUEL ALCOCK & CO.  
COBRIDGE  
printed or impressed  
S.A. & CO.  
S. ALCOCK & CO.

Bates & Bennett  
1868–95, earthenware

B. & B.  
printed or impressed

Birks Brothers & Seddon  
1877–86, earthenware

IMPERIAL IRONSTONE  
CHINA  
BIRKS BROS. & SEDDON  
printed below Royal Arms

Blackhurst & Co. Ltd., John  
1951–9, earthenware

J. BLACKHURST  
ENGLAND

Brownfield, William
1850–91, earthenware (also
porcelain after 1871) much
'parian ware'

W.B.

printed, impressed
or moulded

impressed, often with
crown, from 1860–      BROWNFIELD
'S' or '& Son', added 1871
'& Sons', added 1876
printed 'double-globe' mark, 1871–91

Brownfields Guild Pottery     B.G.P. CO.
Society Ltd., 1891–1900,     impressed
general ceramics
(Brownfield's Pottery Ltd.,
*c.* 1898–1900)

printed monogram

printed within circular
strap device     BROWNFIELDS

Cartledge, John     JOHN CARTLEDGE
*c.* 1800, earthenware     rare incised mark
figures

Clews, James & Ralph     CLEWS WARRANTED
1818–34, pottery and porcelain   STAFFORDSHIRE
    impressed under
    crown

impressed mark on
blue-printed wares

Cockson & Chetwynd
1867–75, earthenware

C.C. & CO.

COCKSON &
CHETWYND
printed

Cockson & Seddon
1875–7, earthenware

IMPERIAL IRONSTONE
CHINA
COCKSON & SEDDON
printed under Royal
Arms

Crystal Porcelain Pottery
Co. Ltd., 1882–6,
pottery and porcelain
　(dove sometimes
　included in mark)

C.P.P. CO.
printed or impressed

Daniel, John
*c.* 1770–*c.* 86, earthenware

JOHN DANIEL
incised

Dillon, Francis
1834–43, earthenware

DILLON
impressed

F.D.
printed with various
back-stamps

Furnival & Co., Jacob
*c.* 1845–70, earthenware

J.F. & CO.
printed

Furnival & Sons, Thomas
1871–90, earthenware
  various 'T. F. & Sons'
  monograms

Furnivals (Ltd.)
1890–1968, earthenware
  'Ltd.' added *c.* 1895

FURNIVALS
ENGLAND

*c.* 1905–13
(Taken over by Barratt's
of Staffordshire in 1967,
closed 1968)

1913 date included in
marks from that year

FURNIVALS
(1913)
ENGLAND

Globe Pottery Co. Ltd.
1914–, earthenware (now
Royal Doulton Group)

fully-named
printed 'globe' marks

Godwin, Benjamin E.
1834–41, earthenware

B.G.
printed with back-
stamp

Godwin, John & Robert
1834–66, earthenware

J. & R.G.
printed

Harding & Cockson      COBRIDGE
1834–60, earthenware      H. & C.
         printed

Hughes & Co., Elijah      E. HUGHES & CO.
1853–67, earthenware      impressed

Hulme, William
1948–54, earthenware

printed mark

Jones, Elijah      fully named
1831–9, earthenware      impressed mark
         or
         E.J. printed

Jones & Walley      fully named
1841–3, earthenware      impressed or
         moulded mark
         or
         printed J. & W.

Meakin, Henry      IRONSTONE CHINA
1873–6, earthenware      H. MEAKIN
         printed with Royal
         Arms

North Staffordshire Pottery Co. Ltd.
1940–52, earthenware

trade-mark registered
in 1944

Portland Pottery Ltd.
1946–53, earthenware
　('P.P.C.' monogram,
　　Portland Pottery, Cobridge)

Regal Pottery Co. Ltd.
1925–31, earthenware

Richardson, Albert G.　　REGAL WARE
*c.* 1920–21　　　　　　　A.G.R.
　　　　　　　　　　　　printed

Richardsons (Cobridge) Ltd.,　REGAL WARE
1921–25　　　　　　　　　R(C) LTD.
　　　　　　　　　　　　printed

Robinson, Wood &　　　R.W. & B.
Brownfield, 1838–41,
earthenware, printed

Sant & Vodrey　　　　　S. & V.
1887–93, earthenware　　COBRIDGE
　　　　　　　printed or impressed

Shaw, Ralph　　　　　Made by Ralph Shaw
*c.* 1740–, earthenware　October 31, Cobridge
　　　　　　　　　　　gate

Simpsons (Potters) Ltd.　fully-named marks
1944–, earthenware
　including various trade-names:
　　'Ambassador Ware', 'Solian Ware', 'Loh
　　Yueh Mei Kuei', 'Vogue', 'Chinastyle',
　　'Marlborough Old English Ironstone',
　　'Chanticleer'

132

Stevenson, Andrew
*c.* 1816–30, earthenware

STEVENSON

A. STEVENSON

impressed 'ship'
mark could also refer to
following potter

Stevenson, Ralph
*c.* 1810–32, earthenware

R. STEVENSON

marks impressed

R.S.

Stevenson & Son, Ralph
*c.* 1832–35, earthenware
marks printed

R.S. & S.

R. STEVENSON
& SON

Stevenson, Alcock &
Williams, earthenware *c.* 1825,
marks printed

STEVENSON
ALCOCK &
WILLIAMS

Stevenson & Williams
*c.* 1825, earthenware

R.S.W.

marks printed

STEVENSON & WILLIAMS

Viking Pottery Co.
1950–63, general ceramics

Walley, Edward
1845–56, general ceramics
marks impressed or printed

E. WALLEY

W.

133

| | |
|---|---|
| Warburton, John<br>*c.* 1802–25, earthenwares<br>and stonewares | WARBURTON<br>impressed |
| Warburton, Peter<br>*c.* 1802–12, general ceramics<br><br>*c.* 1810–12 | WARBURTON'S<br>PATENT<br>printed or written<br>under crown |
| Warburton, Peter & Francis<br>1795–1802, earthenware<br><br>marks impressed | P. & F.W.<br><br>P. & F.<br>WARBURTON |
| Wood, Son & Co.<br>1869–79, earthenware | WOOD, SON & CO.<br>printed under<br>Royal Arms |
| Wood & Brownfield<br>*c.* 1838–50, earthenware | W. & B.<br>impressed or printed |
| Wood & Hawthorne<br>1882–7, earthenware | WOOD &<br>HAWTHORNE<br>printed under Royal<br>Arms |

FENTON (Staffordshire)

| | |
|---|---|
| Bailey Potteries, Ltd.<br>1935–40, earthenware | BEWLEY POTTERY<br>MADE IN ENGLAND<br>printed |
| Baker & Co., W.<br>1839–1932, earthenware | W. BAKER & CO.<br>printed or impressed |

printed or impressed
'Ltd.' added 1893

BAKER & CO.

Barkers & Kent
1889–1941, earthenware
  'Ltd.' added 1898

B. & K.

B. & K.L.

printed or impressed

Beardmore & Co., Frank
1903–14, earthenware
  impressed on printed mark

F.B. & CO.

F

printed mark

Bourne, Charles
1817–30, porcelain

C.B.

(pattern no.)

Bowker, Arthur
1948–58, porcelain

STAFFORDSHIRE
FINE BONE CHINA
OF

mark printed under crown

ARTHUR BOWKER

Brain & Co. Ltd.
1903–67
porcelain

HARJIAN
ENGLAND

  1905–
(now Coalport
a division of
the Wedgwood
Group at
Foley Works)

E.B. & CO.

F.

impressed or
printed within
Staffordshire
knot

(Coalport China Ltd., taken over by
E. Brain & Co. Ltd. in 1958)

British Art Pottery Co. (Fenton) Ltd.
1920–6, porcelain

　　mark printed or impressed

Broadhurst & Sons, James
*c.* 1862–, earthenware
　　printed in mark, 1862–70　　　　　　J.B.

　　printed in mark, 1870–1922　　　J.B. & S.
　　'Ltd.' added 1922

Challinor & Co., E.　　　　E. CHALLINOR & CO.
1853–62, earthenware　　　　　　printed

Challinor, E. & C.　　　　　　E. & C.C.
1862–91, earthenware

　　　　　　　　　　　　E. & C. CHALLINOR
　　　　　　　　　　　　　　FENTON
　　　　　　　　　　　　　　printed

Challinor, C. & Co.　　　　C. CHALLINOR & CO.
1892–6, earthenware　　　　　　ENGLAND

Clulow & Co.　　　　　　　CLULOW & CO.
*c.* 1802, earthenware　　　　　　FENTON

Crown Staffordshire Porcelain Co. Ltd.
1889–, porcelain
(renamed Crown Staffordshire China Co. Ltd. in
1948)

printed 1889–1912
(Wedgwood China Div.
from 1973)
   printed marks of from
1906, this firm makes
bone-china reproductions
of Chelsea 'raised-
anchor' birds

'STAFFORDSHIRE'
with a crown within
wreath

Edge, Barker & Co.
1835–6, earthenware

E.B. & CO.
printed

Edge, Barker & Barker
1836–40, earthenware

E.B. & B.
printed

Edwards, John
1847–1900, general ceramics
   '& Co.' added *c.* 1873–9
   named marks including
'PORCELAINE DE TERRE' or
'WARRANTED IRONSTONE CHINA'
from *c.* 1880–1900

J.E.

J.E. & CO.
PORCELAINE
IRONSTONE

Elkin, Knight & Co.
1822–6, earthenware
   marks impressed or
   printed

E.K. & CO.

ELKIN KNIGHT
& CO.

Elkin, Knight & Bridgwood
*c.* 1827–40, earthenware
and porcelain

E.K.B.
printed

137

Forester & Sons, Thomas     T.F. & S.
1883–1959, earthenware

 'Ltd.' added, 1891–
 'Phoenix China', 1912–

Forester & Hulme      F. & H.
1887–93, earthenware   printed under bee

Hulme & Christie      H. & C.
1893–1902, earthenware      F
  mark printed with a dove

Garner, Robert      R.G.
late 18th century, earthenware   moulded

Gimson & Co., Wallis   WALLIS GIMSON &
1884–90, earthenware     CO.
     printed under beehive

Ginder & Co., Samuel   S. Ginder & Co.
1811–43, earthenware     printed

Greatbatch, William     GREATBATCH
*c.* 1760– *c,* 1780, modeller   printed
potter and engraver of
transfer-prints

Green, Thomas      T. GREEN
1847–59, general   FENTON POTTERIES
ceramics     printed

138

Green, Thomas

Green & Co., M.                        M. GREEN & CO.
1859–76, general ceramics              printed

Green, T. A. & S.                      T.A. & S.G.
1876–89, china                         initials printed in
                                       'Staffordshire knot'
From 1889 this firm became known as
'Crown Staffordshire Porcelain Co.'

Greenwood, S.                          S. GREENWOOD
late 18th century                      rare impressed mark
black basaltes

Hines Bros.                            H.B.
1886–1907, earthenware                 impressed

                                       HINES BROS.
                                       printed

Hoods, Ltd.                            H. LTD.
*c.* 1919–, earthenware                printed
(firm now closed)

Hughes & Co., E.                       H
1889–1953, porcelain
    impressed mark, 1889–98

    impressed or printed              H.F.
    1898–1905

printed mark
*c.* 1908–12

HUGHES

FENTON

various 'globe' marks
from 1912–41
1940 firm retitled Hughes (Fenton) Ltd.

Hulme & Christie     H. & C.
1893–1902, earthenware     F
(Christie & Beardmore     printed with dove
1902–3)

Jones, A. G., Harley-     H.J.
1907–34, earthenware
and porcelain
    initials printed with     A.G.H.J.
    various trade-names:
    'FENTONIA WARE', 'PARAMOUNT',
    'WILTON WARE'

Kirkby & Co., William     W.K. & CO.
1879–85, general ceramics
    'K. & Co.', also used in     K. & CO.
    monogram form     printed or impressed

Knight, Elkin & Co.     K.E. & CO.
1826–46, earthenware

    KNIGHT ELKIN
    printed initials with     & CO.
    variously designed
    backstamps     K. & E.

Knight, John King     J. K. KNIGHT
1846–53, earthenware     printed

| | |
|---|---|
| Knight, Elkin & Bridgwood | K.E. & B. |
| *c.* 1829–40, earthenware | |
| 　marks printed | K.E.B. |

| | |
|---|---|
| Knight, Elkin & Knight | K.E. & K. |
| 1841–4, earthenware | printed |

| | |
|---|---|
| Malkin, Ralph | R.M. |
| 1863–81, earthenware | printed |

| | |
|---|---|
| Malkin & Sons, Ralph | R.M. & S. |
| 1882–92, earthenware | printed |

| | |
|---|---|
| Moore & Co. | M. & CO. |
| 1872–92, earthenware | impressed or printed |

| | |
|---|---|
| Moore, Leason & Co. | M.L. & CO. |
| 1892–6, earthenware | printed in shield |
| | under crown |
| | or initials alone |
| | impressed or printed |

| | |
|---|---|
| Morley, Fox & Co. Ltd. | M.F. & CO. |
| 1906–44, earthenware | printed |

　*c.* 1906–

'HOMELEIGHWARE', 1929–

Morley & Co. Ltd., William
1944–57, earthenware

141

| | |
|---|---|
| Pratt & Co. (Ltd.), F. & R. | F. & R.P. |
| *c.* 1818–, earthenware | |
| | PRATT |
| 'Co.' added 1840 | F. & R.P. CO. |
| *c.* 1847–60 | F. & R. PRATT & CO. |
| | FENTON |
| this firm is known | MANUFACTURER'S |
| to have made a great | TO H.R.H. PRINCE ALBERT |
| number of the popular | |
| printed pot-lids and | |
| similarly printed jugs, | |
| etc. *c.* 1850 | |

the firm was taken over in *c.* 1925
by Cauldon Potteries Ltd., who continue
original name together with their own

| | |
|---|---|
| Pratt & Co., John | J.P. & CO. (L.) |
| 1872–8, earthenware | printed |
| Pratt, Hassall & Gerrard | P.H.G |
| 1822–34, general ceramics | P.H. & G. |
| | printed |
| Pratt & Simpson | P. & S. |
| 1878–83, earthenware | printed |

Radford (Ltd.), Samuel
1879–1957, porcelain
 'R.S.' monogram from
 about 1880, 'England'
 added 1891

142

various 'S.R.' monograms
used during this century

Rainbow Pottery Co.
1931–41, earthenware

RAINBOW POTTERY
FENTON
MADE IN ENGLAND
printed or impressed

Reeves, James
1870–1948, earthenware
printed or impressed

J.R.

J.R.

F

J. REEVES

Rubian Art Pottery Ltd.
1906–33, earthenware
impressed or printed
*c.* 1926–33

L.S. & G.

RUBAY ART WARE

Sterling Pottery Ltd.
1947–53, earthenware

other marks include:
'RIDGWAY'

printed

Stubbs Bros.
1899–1904, bone-china
printed

Victoria Porcelain (Fenton) Ltd.
1949–57, earthenware
printed

Victoria & Trentham Potteries Ltd.
1957–60, general ceramics
   lion mark as above but includes new name

| | |
|---|---|
| Wathen & Lichfield | W. & L. |
| 1862–4, earthenware | FENTON |

| | |
|---|---|
| Wathen, James, B. | J.B.W. |
| 1864–9, earthenware | J.B.W. |
| | F |
| | printed |

| | |
|---|---|
| Wileman, James & Charles | J. & C.W. |
| 1864–9, general ceramics | J.F. & C.W. |
| | C.J.W. |
|    'J. Wileman & Co.' | J.W. & CO. |

| | |
|---|---|
| Wileman, James F. | J.F.W. |
| 1869–92 | J. F. WILEMAN |

Wileman & Co.
1892–1925
   'SHELLEY' mark used
   from *c*. 1911

Wilson & Sons, J.
1898–1926, bone-china

printed

FOLEY (Staffordshire)
   Hawley & Co.                    HAWLEY
   1842–87, earthenware      HAWLEY & CO.
                                          impressed

   Mayer, John                       J.M.
   1833–41, earthenware          F
                                          printed

HANLEY (Staffordshire)
   Adams & Co., John          J. ADAMS & CO.
   1864–73, earthenwares and   ADAMS & CO.
   stonewares, etc.                 impressed

   Adams & Bromley     A. & B.          A. & B.
   1873–86, earthenware                   SHELTON
   stonewares, etc.          ADAMS & BROMLEY
                                  printed or impressed

   Alcock, Lindley & Bloore (Ltd.)
   1919, earthenware
   (now Allied English Potteries)
      printed or impressed

   Art Pottery Co.               ART POTTERY CO.
   1900–11, earthenware          ENGLAND
      printed mark                 (with crown)

   Ashworth & Bros. (Ltd.)
   1862–1970, earthenware        ASHWORTH
      1862–80                       impressed
   (now Mason's Ironstone
   China Co. Ltd.)                  A. BROS.
   Wedgwood Group from 1973

Ashworth & Bros.
 printed *c*. 1862–90
 with designs including
 pattern names
 From 1862 Ashworths used mark similar
 to that of Mason's 'Patent Ironstone'
(Mason's Ironstone China
Ltd. from 1968)
 'England' added 1891

G.L.A. & BROS.

 printed mark from
 about 1880

 'LUSTROSA' trade-name
 1932–

 printed on ironstone
 *c*. 1957–

Baddeley, Thomas
1800–34, engraver of
plates for transfer-prints

T. BADDELEY
HANLEY
printed

Baddeley, William
1802–22, 'Wedgwood-
type' ware

EASTWOOD
impressed

Bakewell Bros. Ltd.
1927-43, earthenware

BAKEWELL BROS.
LTD.
printed

146

Bates, Brown-Westhead     B.B.W. & M.
& Moore     printed or impressed
1859–61, general ceramics

Baxter, John Denton     I.D.B.
1823–7, earthenware     J.D.B.
    printed
Bednall & Heath     B. & H.
1879–99, earthenware     printed

Bennett & Co., J.     J.B. & CO.
1896–1900, earthenware     printed or impressed

Bennett (Hanley) Ltd., William     W.B.
1882–1937     H
earthenwares     printed or impressed

Bevington, James & Thomas     J. & T.B.
1865–78, porcelains     impressed

Bevington & Co., John     J.B. & CO.
1869–71, earthenware     H
printed in backstamp

Bevington, John
1872–92, porcelains

      This mark was     underglaze-blue
      obviously adopted to
      imitate that of Meissen on pieces made in
      'Dresden' style

Bevington, Thomas
1877–91, general ceramics

T.B.

printed

Birch & Whitehead
*c.* 1796, 'Wedgwood type'
wares

B. & W.
impressed

Bishop & Stonier
1891–1939, general
ceramics

B. & S.
printed or impressed

printed marks
1891–
'England' added
on fully named
marks from *c.* 1899–

1936–9

BISHOP
ENGLAND

Blue John Pottery Ltd.
1939, earthenware

various 'Blue John'
printed marks

Booth, G. R.   PUBLISHED BY
1829–44, earthenware   G. R. BOOTH & CO.
 '& Co.' added *c.* 1839   HANLEY
 impressed mark   STAFFORDSHIRE

Booth & Colcloughs Ltd.   various marks
1948–54, general ceramics   including
(see Ridgway Potteries Ltd.)   name
 also trade-names:
 'Blue Mist', 'Malvern Chinaware'
 and 'Royal Swan'

Bourne, Samuel   S. BOURNE
early 18th century   impressed
pottery figures

Bournemouth Pottery Co.   BOURNEMOUTH
(Bournemouth, 1945–52)   POTTERY
Hanley 1952–, earthenware   ENGLAND

Boyle, Zachariah   BOYLE
1823–50, general
ceramics
 '& S.' added from   Z.B.   Z.B. & S.
 1828

Brown-Westhead, Moore & Co.   B.W.M.
1862–1904
general ceramics   B.W.M. & CO.

printed or impressed

149

impressed

T. C. BROWN
WESTHEAD-MOORE
& CO.

printed or impressed
1891–

later marks include
initials & 'CAULDON'

Bullers Ltd.
*c.* 1937–55, earthenware

BULLERS MADE
IN ENGLAND
painted

Bullock & Co., A.
1895–1915, earthenware

A.B. & CO. H.
A.B. & CO.
printed or impressed

Burgess, Thomas
1903–17, earthenware
(mark of Harrop & Burgess
was continued)

printed or impressed

Burton, Samuel & John
1832–45, earthenware

S. & J.B.
impressed on
applied tablet

Cauldon Ltd.
1905–20, general ceramics

CAULDON
ENGLAND
printed under crown

marks previously used by Ridgway
and Brown—Westhead, Moore & Co., used
with addition of 'CAULDON'

150

Cauldon Potteries, Ltd.     ROYAL CAULDON
1920–62, general ceramics     ENGLAND
                            EST. 1774
  similar printed marks used from 1930–62,
  when factory was taken over by
Pountney & Co. Ltd. of Bristol (now
Cauldon Bristol Potteries Ltd., Redruth, Cornwall)


Ceramic Art Co. Ltd.     THE CERAMIC ART
1892–1903, decorators     CO. LTD. HANLEY
                        STAFFORDSHIRE
                          ENGLAND
                          printed


Clementson, Joseph     J.C.
*c.* 1839–64, earthenware     J. CLEMENTSON
                          printed


Clementson Bros.     CLEMENTSON BROS.
1865–1916, earthenware     with Royal Arms
and stoneware
  printed 1867–80
  various fully named printed marks with
  phoenix from 1870–
  'Ltd.' added 1910

                        CLEMENTSON BROS.
  printed, 1913–16     ENGLAND
                        under crown
Clementson, Young & Jameson     C.Y. & J.
1844, earthenware

Clementson & Young     CLEMENTSON &
1845–7, earthenware     YOUNG
                  impressed or printed

151

| | |
|---|---|
| Coalbrook Potteries<br>1937–, decorative wares<br>printed– | COALBROOK<br>MADE IN<br>ENGLAND |
| Coopers Art Pottery Co.<br>*c.* 1912–58, earthenware | ART POTTERY CO.<br>ENGLAND<br>with crown |
| Cotton, Ltd., Elijah<br>1880–, earthenware | various fully-<br>named marks |

Trade-names: 'NELSON WARE', *c.* 1913–;
'LORD NELSON WARE', 1956–

Creyke & Sons, G. M.
1920–48, earthenware
initials also used in
monogram form
Trade-name 'BROADWAY'
*c.* 1935–

G.M.C.
printed or impressed

| | |
|---|---|
| Davenport, Banks & Co.<br>1860–73, earthenware | D.B. & CO. |
| impressed or printed<br>marks | DAVENPORT<br>BANKS & CO.<br>ETRURIA |
| Davenport, Beck & Co.<br>1873–80, earthenware | D.B. & CO. |
| Davis, J. Heath<br>1881–91, earthenware | J. H. DAVIS<br>HANLEY |

Diamond Pottery Co. Ltd.    D.P. CO.
1908–35, earthenware    D.P. CO. LTD.
    printed

Dimmock (Junr.) & Co., Thomas    D.
1828–59, earthenware

   impressed or printed
   'double D' monogram

Dimmock & Co., J.    J.D. & CO.
1862–1904, earthenware

firm taken over by

W. D. Cliff in *c.* 1878–
   'Cliff' used in varying    CLIFF
   forms *c.* 1878–1904    ENGLAND

   written on ribbon    ALBION WORKS
   under 'lion rampant'    printed

Dudson, James    DUDSON
1838–88, earthenware    impressed
(this firm made many
'Spaniels' and 'Rockingham-type' dogs)

Dudson, J. T.    J. DUDSON
1888–98, earthenwares
and stonewares    J. DUDSON
   'England' added 1891    ENGLAND
    impressed

153

Dudson Bros., Ltd.
1898–, earthenwares and
stonewares

DUDSON ENGLAND

printed mark, 1936–45

Dudson, Wilcox & Till, Ltd.
1902–26, earthenware
 printed or impressed,
 figure of Britannia also
 used within double-ring
 with full name of firm

Dura Porcelain Co. Ltd.
1919–21, porcelain

printed mark

Ellis, Unwin & Mountford      E.U. & M.
1860–61, earthenware         printed

Fancies Fayre Pottery        STAFFORDSHIRE
*c.* 1946, earthenware            F.F.
 Trade-name 'KNICK            ENGLAND
  KNACKS'            printed or impressed
(now Bairstow & Co.)

Fenton & Sons, Alfred          A.F. & S.
1887–1901, general         impressed or printed
 ceramics                (also written within
                     circular crowned strap)

Fletcher, Thomas
*c.* 1786–1810, printer and
decorator

T. FLETCHER
SHELTON

Ford, Charles
1874–1904, porcelain

impressed
or printed

'Swan' mark, impressed
or printed, *c.* 1900–4

Ford, T. & C.
1854–71, earthenware
impressed or printed
marks

T. & C.F.

Ford, Thomas
1871–4, porcelain

numerals indicate
month and year, e.g.
JULY, 1872

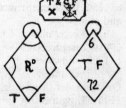

impressed or printed

Ford & Pointon Ltd.
1917–36, porcelain
(absorbed by Cauldon
*c.* 1921)

Furnival, Jacob & Thomas
*c.* 1843, earthenware

J. & T.F.
printed under
Royal Arms

155

Furnival & Co., Thomas     T.F. & CO.
*c.* 1844–6, earthenware     printed

Futura Art Pottery Ltd.     FUTURA
1947–56, earthenware     ART POTTERY LTD.
    printed

Gelson Bros.     GELSON BROS.
1867–76, earthenware     HANLEY
    printed

Glass, John     GLASS HANLEY
*c.* 1784–1838, earthenware     J. GLASS HANLEY
and stoneware     impressed

Glass, Joseph     JOSEPH GLASS
*c.* 1700, slipwares

Goldscheider (Staffordshire) Pottery Ltd.
1946–59, figures in
pottery and porcelain     *Goldscheider*
    printed

Gray & Co. Ltd., A. E.     various printed marks
1912–61, earthenware     depicting ships with
(known as 'Portmeirion     factory name
Potteries Ltd.' from 1962)
moved to Stoke in 1934

    printed mark
    1934–61

Grimwade Bros.
1886–1900, earthenware

G. Bros.
on star within
circle

Grimwades Ltd.
1900–, earthenware
  printed mark, *c.* 1900–

STOKE POTTERY

many various fully named marks including
name or trade-name:
'WINTON' *c.* 1906, 'RUBIAN ART' *c.* 1906–,
'VITRO HOTEL WARE' *c.* 1930, 'ROYAL
WINTON IVORY' *c.* 1930, 'ATLAS' *c.* 1934–9

Hackwood & Co.
1807–27, earthenware and
stoneware

H. & CO.
HACKWOOD & CO.
impressed

Hackwood, William
1827–43, earthenware
  impressed or printed

W.H.
HACKWOOD
printed or impressed

Hackwood & Keeling
1835–6, earthenware

H. & K.
printed

Hall, Samuel
*c.* 1840–56, earthenware

HALL
impressed

Hall & Read
1883–8, earthenware
  'H. & R.' also probably
  used

HALL & READ
HANLEY
printed

Hammersley, J. & R.
1877–1917, general ceramics

J.R.H.
printed

Hanley Porcelain Co.
1892–99, porcelain

printed

Hanley China Co.
1899–1901, porcelain
  printed

H
C C°.
in knot

Harrop & Burgess
1894–1903, earthenware

printed

Heath, J.
*c.* 1770–1800, earthenware

I.H.

HEATH
impressed

Heath, Joshua
*c.* 1740, earthenware

JOSHUA HEATH
incised

Hollins, T. J. & R.
*c.* 1818–22, earthenware

T.J. & R. HOLLINS
impressed

Johnson Bros. (Hanley) Ltd.
1883–, earthenware
  impressed or printed
  name with various
  coat-of-arms, crowns,
  etc.
(now part of Wedgwood Group)

JOHNSON BROS.
ENGLAND

Johnson Bros
England.

Jones & Son     JONES & SON
*c.* 1826–8, earthenware     printed

Keeling, Joseph     JOSEPH KEELING
*c.* 1802–8, earthenware and     impressed
stoneware

Keeling & Co., Samuel     S.K. & CO.
1840–50, earthenware

S. KEELING & CO.
printed

Keeling, Toft & Co.     KEELING & TOFT
1805–26, stonewares
in Wedgwood style     KEELING, TOFT & CO.
impressed

Kensington Fine Art Pottery Co.
1892–9, earthenware

printed or impressed

Lancaster & Sons     L. & SONS LTD.
1900–44, earthenware     HANLEY. ENG.
  '& Sons' & 'Ltd.' added
  *c.* 1906
  *c.* 1920–

'ROYALL & LANSAN' 1930–
'BRITISH CROWN WARE', *c.* 1935–
'CROWN DRESDEN WARE', *c.* 1935–

*c.* 1934–44     LANCASTERS LTD.
HANLEY. ENGLAND

| | |
|---|---|
| Lancaster & Sandland Ltd. 1944–1968, earthenware | BRITISH CROWN WARE |
| many various printed marks including name 'SANDLAND' | CROWN DRESDEN WARE<br><br>SANDLAND STAFFORDSHIRE ENGLAND |
| Langdale Pottery Co. Ltd. 1947–58, earthenware printed | Langdale MADE IN ENGLAND |
| Lear, Samuel 1877–86, general ceramics | LEAR impressed |
| Livesley, Powell & Co. 1851–66, earthenware and stoneware | LIVESLEY POWELL & CO.<br>L.P. & CO. impressed or printed |
| Powell & Bishop 1867–1878, general ceramics | P. & B. POWELL & BISHOP printed or impressed |
| Powell, Bishop & Stonier 1878–91, general ceramics | P.B. & S. printed or impressed |
| 'Chinaman' mark first registered 1880, but continued by Bishop & Stonier |  |

Bishop & Stonier      B. & S.
1891–1939, general ceramics
   full name printed in    BISHOP & STONIER
   various designs, 1899–1936
   'Bishop' only used 1936–9

Lloyd, J. & R.      LLOYD SHELTON
*c.* 1834–52, 'Staffordshire    impressed
figures'

Lockett, Baguley &    LOCKETT BAGULEY
Cooper, 1855–60, porcelain    & COOPER

Lockitt, William H.      W.H.L.
1901–19, earthenware      H
   'DURA-WARE' 1913–19   printed in crescent

Mann & Co.      MANN & CO.
1858–60, general ceramics    HANLEY
             printed

Manzoni, Carlo
*c.* 1895–8, studio pottery

  incised mark including
  date

Mayer, Elijah      E. MAYER
*c.* 1790–1804, various    impressed
Wedgwood-type wares

Mayer & Son, Elijah
1805–34
Wedgwood-type wares

E. MAYER & SON
impressed or printed

Mayer & Co., Joseph
*c.* 1822–33, earthenware

JOSEPH MAYER & CO.
HANLEY

MAYER & CO.

Meakin, Charles
1883–9, earthenware

CHARLES MEAKIN
HANLEY
under Royal Arms

Meakin (Ltd.), J. & G.
1851–, earthenwares
(now part of Wedgwood
Group)
    1890–

J. & G. MEAKIN
impressed or printed

    'ENGLAND' added from
    1891
    'Sun-face' marks from
    1912–
    'PASTEL VITRESOL'
    'STUDIO WARE' and 'SOUTH
    SEAS' recent trade-names

printed

Meigh, Job
*c.* 1805–34, earthenware
    'Son' added *c.* 1812

MEIGH
impressed
OLD HALL
impressed or printed
J.M. & S.

Meigh, Charles         CHARLES MEIGH
1835–49, earthenware and     impressed
stonewares                G.M.
               printed with device
               and pattern name

printed or impressed marks of various
bodies and styles of decoration include:
'Indian Stone China', 'French China',
'Improved Stone China', 'Enamel Porcelain'

Meigh, Son & Pankhurst,     C.M.S. & P.
Charles, 1850–51, earthenware    printed

Meigh & Son, Charles       C.M. & S.
1851–61, earthenware

   many of the marks       M. & S.
   used by this firm
   include the Royal     C. MEIGH & SON
   Arms

                  MEIGH'S
                  CHINA

   printed or impressed      OPAQUE
                  PORCELAIN
Old Hall Earthenware Co Ltd.
1861–86

                  O.H.E.C.
   printed           O.H.E.C.(L.)

printed or impressed

mark registered in 1884 and
continued by Old Hall
Porcelain Works Ltd.
printed

Old Hall Porcelain Works          (as above)
Ltd., 1886–1902, general
ceramics

Mills, Henry                          H. MILLS
*c.* 1892, earthenware                printed

Moore & Co.                           M. & CO.
1898–1903, earthenware           printed with name
                                         of pattern

Morley & Co., Francis                 F.M.
1845–58, earthenware

late form of Masons'              F.M. & CO.
Ironstone mark used
from 1845                        F. MORLEY & CO.
                                   printed with many
                                   various backstamps

Morley & Ashworth                     M. & A.
1859–62, earthenware               MORLEY &
   impressed or printed              ASHWORTH
   with pattern name                   HANLEY

164

| | |
|---|---|
| Neale & Co., James<br>*c.* 1776–*c.* 86, all manner<br>of wares in Wedgwood<br>style | N          NEALE<br>I. NEALE<br>I. NEALE. HANLEY |
| '& Co.' added *c.* 1778 | NEALE & CO.<br>impressed |
| Neale & Bailey<br>*c.* 1790–1814, earthenware | NEALE & BAILEY<br>printed or impressed |
| Neale, Harrison & Co.<br>1875–85, general ceramics | N.H. & CO.<br>printed |
| Neale & Palmer<br>*c.* 1769–76, earthenwares<br>in Wedgwood style | NEALE & PALMER<br>impressed |
| Neale & Wilson<br>*c.* 1784–95, earthenware<br>and Wedgwood-type wares | NEALE & WILSON<br><br>NEALE & CO.<br>impressed |

New Hall Porcelain Works
1781–1835, hard-paste
porcelain 1781–*c.* 1812
bone-china, *c.* 1812–35

printed on bone-china

New Hall Pottery Co. Ltd.
1899–1956, earthenware

printed, *c.* 1930–51

| | |
|---|---|
| New Pearl Pottery Co. Ltd. 1936–41, earthenware, 'Royal Bourbon Ware' | PEARL POTTERY CO. printed |
| Palmer, Humphrey *c.* 1760–78, earthenware and Wedgwood-type stonewares | PALMER  impressed |
| Pankhurst & Co., J. W. 1850–82, earthenware '& Co.' added *c.* 1852 | J.W.P. J. W. PANKHURST |
| Pearl Pottery Co. Ltd. 1894–1936, earthenware 1894–1912 |  printed or impressed |
| printed in various forms, 1912–36 | P.P. CO. LTD. |
| Physick & Cooper 1899–1900, earthenware | P. & C. over crown |
| Art Pottery Co. 1900–11, earthenware | ART POTTERY CO. over crown |
| Coopers Art Pottery Co. *c.* 1912–58, earthenware | printed as above |

| | |
|---|---|
| Podmore China Co.<br>1921–41, porcelain | 'P.C. CO.' monogram<br>under crown |
| Pointon & Co. Ltd.<br>1883–1916, porcelain | POINTONS<br>STOKE-ON-TRENT<br>printed with coat-<br>of-arms |
| Poole, Richard<br>1790–5, earthenware | R. POOLE<br>impressed |
| Ratcliffe, William<br>*c.* 1831–40, earthenware | R<br>HACKWOOD<br>printed or impressed |

printed in underglaze blue

| | |
|---|---|
| Ridgway, Job<br>*c.* 1802–8, earthenware | R       J.R.<br>printed<br>(J.R. also used by<br>John Ridgway) |
| Ridgway & Sons, Job<br>*c.* 1808–14, earthenware | RIDGWAY & SONS<br>impressed or printed |
| Ridgway, John & William<br>1814–*c.* 1830 | J.W.R.   J. & W.R.<br>J. & W. RIDGWAY<br>printed or impressed |

| | |
|---|---|
| Ridgway & Co., John<br>c. 1830–55, general ceramics | JOHN RIDGWAY<br>J.R.<br>JHN RIDGWAY |
| printed or impressed<br>marks usually including<br>name of pattern | I. RIDGWAY<br>'& CO.'<br>added c. 1841 |
| Ridgway, Bates & Co., J.<br>1856–58, general ceramics | J.R.B. & CO.<br>printed |
| Bates, Brown-Westhead<br>& Moore, 1859–61,<br>general ceramics | B.B.W. & M.<br>printed or impressed |
| Brown-Westhead, Moore & Co.<br>1862–1904, general ceramics | *see p.* 149 |
| Cauldon Ltd.<br>1905–20, general ceramics | *see p.* 150 |
| Cauldon Potteries Ltd.<br>1920–62, general ceramics | *see p.* 151 |
| Ridgway & Robey<br>c. 1837–9, figures<br>marks very rare | RIDGWAY & ROBEY<br>HANLEY<br>STAFFORDSHIRE<br>POTTERIES |
| Ridgway, Morley, Wear<br>& Co., 1836–42<br>earthenware | R.M.W. & CO.<br>RIDGWAY, MORLEY<br>WEAR & CO.<br>printed |

*see p.* 149

*see p.* 150

*see p.* 151

Ridgway & Morley     R. & M.
1842–44, earthenware     RIDGWAY & MORLEY
             printed

Ridgway & Abington     E. RIDGWAY & ABINGTON
*c.* 1835–60, earthenware     HANLEY
             impressed

Ridgway, Son & Co.,     W.R.S. & CO.
William, *c.* 1838–48     W. RIDGWAY, SON
             & CO. HANLEY
             printed

Ridgway, Sparks & Ridgway     R.S.R.
1873–79, earthenware     also printed in
             'Staffordshire knot'

Ridgways
1879–20
    mark of 1880–

'RIDGWAYS' and 'ENGLAND' in various
marks from *c.* 1905–20
RIDGWAYS (BEDFORD WORKS) LTD.
1920–52, earthenware
'RIDGWAYS' and/or 'BEDFORD' in variety
of marks used from 1920–52
This firm became 'Ridgway & Adderley Ltd.'
in 1952, Ridgway, Adderley, Booths &
Colcloughs Ltd.' from 1955 and in same year
'Ridgway Potteries Ltd.'
(part of Allied English Potteries, Ltd.
from 1952, now Royal Doulton Group)

| | |
|---|---|
| name of American firm, John R. Roth & Co. seen on some Ridgway exports, *c.* 1930–56 | JONROTH<br>J.H.R. & CO. monogram<br>printed |
| Rigby & Stevenson 1894–1954, earthenware | R. & S.<br>printed |
| Rivers, William *c.* 1818–22, earthenware | RIVERS<br>impressed |
| Robinson & Wood 1832–6, earthenware | R. & W.<br>printed |
| Salt, Ralph *c.* 1820–46, earthenware | 'SALT'<br>impressed on scroll |
| Sandlands & Colley, Ltd. 1907–1910, general ceramics | full name &<br>'S.C.' monogram<br>printed under crown |
| Scrivener & Co., R. G. 1870–83, general ceramics | R.G.S. |
| printed or impressed | R.G.S.<br>& CO. |
| Sherwin & Cotton 1877–30, tiles impressed |  |
| Shorthose & Co. *c.* 1817–1822 | SHORTHOSE & CO.<br>written<br>impressed or printed |

| | |
|---|---|
| Shorthose & Heath<br>*c.* 1795–1815, earthenware | SHORTHOSE &<br>HEATH<br>impressed or printed |
| Shorthose, John<br>1807–23, earthenware | S |
| impressed marks | SHORTHOSE |
| Sneyd & Hill<br>*c.* 1845, earthenware<br>printed | SNEYD & HILL<br>HANLEY<br>STAFFORDSHIRE<br>POTTERIES |
| Sneyd, Thomas<br>1846–7, earthenware | T. SNEYD<br>HANLEY<br>impressed |
| Stevenson, William<br>*c.* 1802, earthenware<br>rare impressed mark | W. STEVENSON<br>HANLEY |

Swinnertons Ltd.
1906–71, earthenware
(Allied English Potteries)
Ltd.), mark printed
  *c.* 1906–17, later marks all include
  full-name of firm

Sylvan Pottery Ltd.
1946–, earthenware

  'B' included in mark
  prior to 1948

SWINNERTONS
HANLEY

171

Studio Szeiler, Ltd.
*c.* 1951–, earthenware

                            printed or impressed

Taylor, George             G. TAYLOR
*c.* 1784–1811, earthenware    GEO. TAYLOR

                          impressed or incised

Taylor, Tunnicliffe & Co.        T.T.
1868–, general ceramics       T.T. & CO.
(now electrical &              printed
industrial wares only)

Thomas & Co., Uriah
1888–1905, earthenware

                      printed or impressed

Toft, James (*b.* 1673)      James Toft
Ralph (*b.* 1638),           Ralph Toft
Thomas (*d.* 1689), slipware   Thomas Toft

Unwin, Mountford &       U.M. & T.
Taylor, *c.* 1864, earthenware    printed

Unwin, Holmes &          U.H. & W.
Worthington, *c.* 1865–8      printed
earthenware

Upper Hanley Pottery Co.     U.H.P. CO.
*c.* 1895–1902, then at        ENGLAND
Cobridge until 1910
earthenware         impressed or printed
   'Ltd.' from 1900

Wardle & Co.
1871–1910, earthenware
Wardle Art Pottery Co. Ltd.
1910–1935, earthenware

WARDLE
impressed

printed, *c.* 1885–90

printed, *c.* 1890–1935

Wardle & Ash
1859–62, earthenware

W. & A.
impressed

Weatherby & Sons, Ltd.
1891–, earthenware
    *c.* 1925–

J.H.W. & SONS

FALCON WARE

    *c.* 1936–, (trade-name)

WEATHERBY WARE
printed

Wellington Pottery Co.
1899–1901, earthenware

printed or impressed

Westminster Pottery Ltd.
1948–56, earthenware

    1952–, (trade-name)

CASTLECLIFFE WARE

Whittaker & Co.      W. & CO.
1886–92, earthenware      printed

Whittaker, Heath & Co.      W.H. & CO.
1892–8, earthenware      printed

Wilson, Robert      WILSON
1795–1801, earthenware

impressed marks

Wilson, David      WILSON
*c.* 1802–18, general ceramics      impressed

Winkle & Wood
1885–90, earthenware

printed

Worthington & Harrop      W. & H.
1856–73, earthenware      printed

Wulstan Pottery Co. Ltd.
*c.* 1940–58, earthenware

printed

Yates, John      J.Y.
*c.* 1784–1835, earthenware

printed or impressed

LANE DELPH (Staffordshire)
Edge, William & Samuel
1841–8, earthenware

W. & S.E.
printed

Harrison, George
*c.* 1790–5, earthenware

G. Harrison
impressed

Mason, William
*c.* 1811–24, earthenware

W. MASON
printed

Mason, Miles
*c.* 1792–1816, porcelain
marks impressed *c.* 1800–16

M. MASON
MILES MASON

printed mark on
chinoiserie patterns

Mason, G. M. & C. J.
1813–29, earthenware
(ironstone)

G.M. & C.J. MASON

G. & C.J.M.

impressed marks
*c.* 1813–25

MASON'S PATENT
IRONSTONE CHINA

patented in 1813

PATENT IRONSTONE
CHINA

standard mark of
*c.* 1820, continued by
Ashworth (*c.* 1862)
'Mason's Ironstone China
Ltd.' from 1968–
(a Division of Josiah
Wedgwood & Sons Ltd., 1974)

printed mark with
pattern number *c.* 1825–

Mason & Co., Charles
James, 1829–45,
earthenware, (ironstone)
  printed

FENTON
STONE WORKS
C.J.M. & CO.
GRANITE CHINA

  printed

C.J. MASON & CO.
LANE DELPH

  *c.* 1840–

'MASON'S CAMBRIAN ARGIL',
'MASON'S BANDANA WARE'
impressed or printed
*c.* 1825–40

Mason, Charles James
*c.* 1845–8, earthenware
(ironstone), also at
Longton, 1851–4

printed

Morley & Co., Francis
1845–58, earthenware
(Hanley)

F.M.
F.M. & CO.
F. MORLEY & CO.

Morley & Ashworth
1859–62, earthenware
(Hanley)

M. & A.
impressed or printed

176

Myatt, late 18th- early
19th centuries,
earthenware

MYATT
impressed

Pratt, William
*c.* 1780–99, earthenware

PRATT

LANE END (Staffordshire)
Abbott, Andrew
*c.* 1781–3, earthenware

ABBOTT POTTER
impressed

Abbott & Mist
1787–1810, earthenware

ABBOTT & MIST
impressed or painted

Aynsley, John
1780–1809, engraver of
prints for earthenwares

'*J. Aynsley Lane End*'
printed

Barker, John, Richard &
William, *c.* 1800
earthenware

BARKER
impressed

Batkin, Walker & Broadhurst,
1840–5, earthenware

B.W. & B.
printed

Booth & Sons
1830–5, earthenware

BOOTH & SONS
impressed

Bott & Co.
*c.* 1810–11, earthenware

BOTT & CO.
impressed

177

| | |
|---|---|
| Carey, Thomas & John<br>*c.* 1823–42, earthenware | CAREYS<br>impressed or<br>printed with anchor |
| Chesworth & Robinson<br>1825–40, earthenware | C. & R.<br>printed |
| Chetham & Woolley<br>1796–1810, earthenware | CHETHAM &<br>WOOLLEY<br>LANE END<br>incised |
| Cyples, Joseph<br>*c.* 1784–1840<br>　(initials of various<br>　potters in this family<br>　rarely used) | CYPLES<br><br>I. CYPLES<br>impressed |
| Deakin & Son<br>1833–41, earthenware<br>printed mark |  |
| Everard, Glover &<br>Colclough, *c.* 1847–<br>general ceramics | E.G. & C.<br>printed |
| Floyd, Benjamin<br>*c.* 1843, earthenware | B.F.<br>printed |
| Goodwin, Bridgwood &<br>Orton, 1827–9<br>earthenware | G.B.O.<br>G.B. & O. |

178

Goodwin, Bridgwood & Harris
1829–31, earthenware

G.B.H.

Goodwins & Harris
*c.* 1831–8, earthenware

GOODWINS &
HARRIS
printed

Griffiths, Beardmore &
Birks, 1830, earthenware

G.B. & B.
printed

Harley, Thomas
1802–8, earthenware

HARLEY
T. HARLEY
impressed

printed or written

T. HARLEY
LANE END

Harvey, Bailey & Co.
1833–5, earthenware

H.B. & CO.
printed

Heathcote & Co., Charles
1818–24, earthenware

C. HEATHCOTE & CO.
printed

Hilditch & Son
1822–30, general ceramics

printed in various
surrounds

Hulme & Sons, John
*c.* 1828–30, earthenware

HULME & SONS
printed

179

| | |
|---|---|
| Lockett, J. & G.<br>*c.* 1802–5, earthenware | J. & G. LOCKETT<br>impressed |
| Lockett, John<br>1821–58, earthenware | J. LOCKETT<br>impressed |
| Lockett & Co., J.<br>*c.* 1812–89, earthenware<br>(also at Longton 1882–<br>1960, and 1960– Burslem) | J. LOCKETT & CO.<br>impressed<br>or<br>printed |
| Lockett & Hulme<br>1822–6, earthenware | L. & H.<br>L.E.<br>printed |
| Mayer & Newbold<br>*c.* 1817–33, general ceramics | M. & N. |
| marks painted or<br>printed | MAY<sup>R</sup> & NEWB<sup>D</sup> |

MAY^R & NEWB^D

| | |
|---|---|
| Plant, Benjamin<br>*c.* 1780–1820, earthenware<br>marks incised | |

| | |
|---|---|
| Plant, Thomas<br>1825–50, earthenware | T P |

painted

| | |
|---|---|
| Ray, George, modeller<br>early 19th century | G. RAY<br>Lane End |

Turner, John (also
entered under Longton)
*c.* 1762–1806, earthenware
and porcelain
　early impressed marks

TURNER
I. TURNER

printed or impressed
from 1784 after Turner
was potter to the
Prince of Wales

**TURNER**

impressed, *c.* 1780–6
1803–6

TURNER & CO.

painted on earthenwares
1800–5

*Turner's Patent*

Turner & Abbott
*c.* 1783–7 (Abbott
probably only agent)
earthenwares and
stoneware in Wedgwood
style

TURNER & ABBOTT
impressed

LONGPORT (Staffordshire)

Bodley & Son, E. F.
1881–98, earthenware

E.F.B. & SON

　trade-mark, 1883–98

Bourne, Edward                    E. BOURNE
1790–1811, earthenware            impressed

Corn, W. & E.                     W. & E.C.
1864–1904, earthenware
(also at Burslem *c.* 1864–       W.E.C.
1904, nearly all marks
    are late and include 'ENGLAND' (post-1891)

Davenport & Co., W.
*c.* 1793–1887, general
ceramics; 1798–1815              Davenport

*c.* 1815–60                      DAVENPORT
    'Davenport' or 'DAVENPORT'
    is impressed with or
    without anchor

marks on 'Stone-China'
*c.* 1815–30

19th century mark to
about 1860, including
last two numerals of
year
    anchor mark alone *c.* 1820–40

many printed wares of 1820–60 bear
name of pattern and 'DAVENPORT'

| | |
|---|---|
| printed on porcelain | DAVENPORT |
| *c.* 1815– | LONGPORT |

three numerals denote month and last
two numerals of year made
'Manufacturers of China to His Majesty
and the Royal Family' on porcelain
*c.* 1830–37

| | |
|---|---|
| | DAVENPORT |
| impressed *c.* 1850–70 | PATENT |

printed in underglaze-blue
*c.* 1850–70
(sometimes in enamel
colours prior to 1830)

| | |
|---|---|
| This mark was used | DAVENPORT |
| from *c.* 1830–45 in puce | LONGPORT |
| and from *c.* 1870–87 | STAFFORDSHIRE |
| in red | printed under crown |

printed on earthenware   DAVENPORTS LTD.
*c.* 1881–7

| | |
|---|---|
| Liddle, Elliott & Son | L.E. & S. |
| 1862–71, general | impressed or printed |
| ceramics | |

Mayer & Elliott
1858–61, earthenware
  number of month and
  last two numerals of year

printed

impressed, e.g. $\dfrac{6}{59}$ = June, 1859

Phillips, Edward & George       PHILLIPS
1822–34, earthenware            LONGPORT

  printed marks                 E. & G.P.

Phillips, George                PHILLIPS
1834–48, earthenware
  name with or without knot,
  sometimes 'Longport' also

Rogers, John & George           ROGERS
*c.* 1784–1814, earthenware
                                J.R.
  impressed marks               L.

Rogers & Son, John              as above and
*c.* 1814–36, earthenware
                                J.R.S.
                                ROGERS & SON

Smith, Ltd., W. T. H.           W.T.H. SMITH & CO.
1898–1905, earthenware          LONGPORT
                                printed with 'globe'

Wood & Son (Longport)           ARTHUR WOOD
Ltd., 1928–, earthenware        full name printed in
  'ROYAL BRADWELL               variety of marks
  ART WARE' trade-name

Wood, Arthur                    A.W.
1904–28, earthenware            L
  mark impressed or             ENGLAND
  printed

LONGTON HALL (Staffordshire)
  *c.* 1749–60, porcelain
    rare marks painted in
    underglaze blue

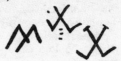

LONGTON (Staffordshire)

Adams & Co. Harvey
1870–85, general ceramics

H.A. & CO.
over crown
printed

Adams & Cooper
1850–77, porcelain

A. & C.
printed

Adderleys Ltd.
1906–, general ceramics

  printed mark 1906–26
  many other marks all
  including full name of firm

Adderley, J. Fellows
1901–5, porcelain

J.F.A.

  printed marks

Adderley, William Alsager
1876–1905

W.A.A.

W.A.A. & CO.

  and 'sailing-ship' trade-
  mark as above

Adderley Floral China Works
1945– bone-china
decorative wares
  printed mark
(Royal Doulton Group
from 1973)

Aldridge & Co.　　ALDRIDGE & CO.
1919–49, earthenware　　LONGTON
impressed

Allerton & Sons, Charles　　C.A. & SONS
1859–1942, general
ceramics
  printed or impressed　　CHAS. ALLERTON &
  marks, *c.* 1890–1942　　SONS
  Many other fully named　　ENGLAND
  marks also used

Alton China Co. Ltd.　　ALTON
1950–7, bone-china　　BONE CHINA
printed

Amison, Charles　　C.A.
1889–1962, porcelain　　L.
  impressed initials, 1889–

  printed mark of 1906–30
  '& Co.' added 1916
  '& Co. Ltd.', 1930

  further late marks include
  'Stanley' and 'Staffordshire
  Floral Bone China'

Anchor Porcelain Co. Ltd.
1901–18, porcelain
  impressed marks

A.P. CO.

A.P. CO. L.

  impressed or printed
'anchor-mark', 1901–15
'ROYAL WESTMINSTER CHINA' printed
with 'A.P. CO. L.', 1915–18

Aristocrat Florals & Fancies
1958–, bone-china decorative
wares (Wedgwood Group
from 1973)

ENGLISH
*Aristocrat*
*Florals*
BONE
CHINA

Asbury & Co.
1875–1925, general ceramics
  printed marks

ASBURY
LONGTON

A. & CO.

Avon Art Pottery
1930–69, earthenware
  recent mark, printed
(seemingly merged with
Elektra Porcelain Co., 1962)

MADE IN
*AvonWare*
ENGLAND

Aynsley & Co., H.
1873–, earthenware
  'Ltd.' added 1932
  late marks include
  name in full

H.A. & CO.
L.

187

Aynsley & Sons, John       AYNSLEY
1864–, porcelain       impressed
  various later marks include full name and
  'ENGLAND' added from 1891
(now Aynsley China Ltd.–Waterford Glass Co.
Ltd.)

Baddeley, William       EASTWOOD
1802–22, earthenware       impressed
(Wedgwood-type)

Baggerley & Ball       B. & B.
1822–36, earthenware       L.
             printed in blue
             within oval frame

Bailey & Sons, William
1912–14, earthenware
  printed mark

Bailey & Batkin       BAILEY & BATKIN
1814–*c.* 27, earthenware
including lustreware
  marks impressed or moulded    B. & B.

Bailey & Harvey       BAILEY & HARVEY
1834–5, earthenware       impressed
including lustre

Balfour China Co. Ltd.       BALFOUR
1947–52, bone-china       ROYAL CROWN
(then known as:       POTTERY
Trentham Bone China    printed with crown
Ltd.)

Barker Bros. Ltd.       B.B.
1876–, general ceramics    impressed
   large variety of other printed marks
   including such trade names as:
   MEIR CHINA, MEIR WARE, TUDOR WARE
   and ROYAL TUDOR WARE
(Alfred Clough Ltd.)

Barlow & Son Ltd., T. W.    B. B. & S.
1882–1940, earthenware    rare impressed
                         marks
   marks used from about 1928 include
   'CORONATION WARE'

Barlow, Thomas       B.
1849–1882, general ceramics    impressed

Barlows (Longton) Ltd.    B. Ltd.
1920–52, earthenware    impressed
   later marks include 'MELBAR WARE'

Baxter, Rowley & Tams    B.R. & T.
1882–5, porcelain    impressed

Beardmore & Edwards    B. & E.
1856–8, earthenware    printed

Bentley & Co. Ltd., G. L.    G.L.B. & CO.
1898–1912, porcelain    LONGTON
   'Ltd.' added from 1904

Beswick & Son　　　　　　B. & S.
1916–30, porcelain　　printed or impressed
　'ALDWYCH CHINA', trade-name also used by
　Bridgett & Bates, former prop's.

Beswick Ltd., John　　　　BESWICK
1936–, earthenware　　　　ENGLAND
(Royal Doulton Group 1973)　printed

Blackhurst & Hulme　　　　B. & H.
1890–1932, porcelain
　early mark of printed
　initials, later full　　　THE BELGRAVE
　mark used from *c.* 1914　　CHINA
　　　　　　　　　　　　　B. & H.
　　　　　　　　　　　　　L
　　　　　　　　　　　ENGLAND

Blair & Co.
1880–1930, porcelain
　'Ltd.' added *c.* 1912
　(LONGTON) added *c.* 1923
　early impressed 'B'
　up until about 1900
　'BLAIRS CHINA, ENGLAND'
　impressed or printed
　*c.* 1900–
　printed mark of *c.* 1900–

Blyth Porcelain Co. Ltd.　　B.P. CO. LTD.
*c.* 1905–35, porcelain　　printed in
　'DIAMOND CHINA'　　varying forms
　also used from *c.* 1913

Boulton & Co.          B . & CO .   B . & CO .
1892–1902, porcelain                    L
                       printed or impressed

Bradbury, Anderson & Bettany   B.A. & B.
1844–52, general ceramics      printed

Bradley, F. D.                 BRADLEY
1876–96, porcelain             impressed

Bradleys (Longton) Ltd.        BRADLEYS
1922–41, porcelain             LONGTON
    mark printed with crown    MADE IN
                               ENGLAND

Bridgett & Bates               B. & B.
1882–1915, porcelain      impressed or printed
    'ALDWYCH CHINA' trade-name from *c.* 1912

Bridgett, Bates & Beech
1875–82
    printed or impressed mark

Bridgwood & Son Ltd.,     BRIDGWOOD & SON
Sampson, 1805–, earthenware
(porcelain until *c.* 1887)

                          S. BRIDGWOOD &
    impressed or printed marks   SON
    from *c.* 1850–

                               S.B. & S.

other various printed marks include
full name of firm or initials

'Parisian Granite' mark
*c.* 1870–, printed

Britannia China Company
1895–1906, porcelain

B.C. CO.
impressed

other fully-named marks
also used
1904–6

printed or impressed

British Anchor Pottery Co. Ltd.
1884–, earthenware
(from 1971, Hostess Tableware Ltd.)
    printed or impressed
    1884–*c.* 1913

other various marks include full
names and such trade names as:
REGENCY, MONTMARTRE, RICHMOND,
HOSTESS and TRIANON

British Pottery Ltd.
*c.* 1930–, agents only

B.P. LTD.
printed

Brough & Blackhurst
1872–95, earthenware

BROUGH &
BLACKHURST
printed or impressed

Burgess Bros.  "BURCRAFT"
1922–39, earthenware  BURGESS BROS.
'Burgess Ware' also  MADE IN ENGLAND
used  printed

Capper & Wood  C. & W.
1895–1904, earthenware  printed or impressed

Cara China Co.  CARA CHINA
1945–, porcelain  printed

Cartlidge & Co., F.  F.C.
1889–1904, porcelain  F.C. & CO.
'& Co.' added *c.* 1892  printed or impressed

Cartwright & Edwards, Ltd.  C. & E.
*c.* 1857–  printed or impressed
(Alfred Clough Ltd.)
  printed mark of 1912–
  'Ltd.' added *c.* 1926–
  trade names of 'Norville'
  & 'Baronian' ware used
  with 'C. & E.' from *c.* 1930–

Chapman & Sons, David
1889–1906, porcelain
  'Atlas' mark of 1889–1906

Chapmans Longton Ltd.  STANDARD CHINA
1916–*c.* '67 porcelain  crown
  printed 1916–30  ENGLAND
(now Paragon China Ltd.)

193

various other marks including trade-names of:
'ROYAL STANDARD' and 'ROYAL
MAYFAIR', (from 1973 part of Royal Doulton
Group)

| | |
|---|---|
| Chetham | CHETHAM |
| 1810–34, earthenware | impressed |
| '& Son' added 1818 | |

| | |
|---|---|
| Chetham, Jonathan Lowe | J.L.C. |
| 1841–62, earthenware | printed |

| | |
|---|---|
| Chetham, J. R. & F. | J.R. & F.C. |
| 1846–69, earthenware | printed |

| | |
|---|---|
| Chetham & Robinson | C. & R. |
| 1822–37, earthenware | printed |

| | |
|---|---|
| Chew, John | J.C. |
| 1903–4, porcelain | L |
| | impressed |

| | |
|---|---|
| Clare China Co. Ltd. | BONE CHINA |
| 1951–, decorators | CLARE |
| printed mark, possibly | MADE IN ENGLAND |
| taken over by Taylor & | with crown |
| Kent | |

| | |
|---|---|
| Clough's Royal Art | 'ROYAL ART POTTERY' |
| Pottery, 1961–69, | ENGLAND |
| earthenware | with crown |
| mark also used by | printed |
| Alfred Clough Ltd. | |
| (Royal Art Pottery), 1951–61 | |

Transferred to Alfred Clough, Ltd., Longton
under name of Barker Bros. Ltd. in 1968

Coggins & Hill　　　　　　c. & h.
1892–8, porcelain　　　printed or impressed

Colclough & Co.　　　　r.s. monogram
1887–1928, general ceramics
　printed marks　　　'ROYAL STANLEY WARE'

Colclough, H. J.　　　　　h.j.c.
1897–1937, general ceramics　　l
　various marks including 'h.j.c.' and/or
　'VALE CHINA'

Colclough China Ltd.　　　　Colclough
1937–48, porcelain　　　　GENUINE
　　　　　　　　　　　BONE CHINA
　late printed marks　　MADE IN ENGLAND

Collingwood Bros. Ltd.　　COLLINGWOOD
1887–1957, porcelain　　early impressed mark

　initials used with crown　　c.b.
　*c.* 1887–1912　　　　　l
　later marks fully named

Collingwood & Greatbatch
1870–1887, porcelain

　printed or impressed
　(crown also used　　　c. & g.
　alone)

| | | |
|---|---|---|
| Cone Ltd., Thomas | T.C. | T.C. |
| 1892–*c.* 1967 | L | LONGTON |

earthenware     printed or impressed
    mark of 1892–1912
(moved to Meir in 1964)
    printed 1912–35     T.C. monogram
    'Alma Ware' 1935–
    'ROYAL ALMA' 1946–68


Conway Pottery Co. Ltd.     CONWAY
1930–, earthenware     POTTERY
    mark printed from 1945–     ENGLAND


Cooke & Hulse     COOKE & HULSE
1835–55, porcelain     printed


Cooper & Dethick     C. & D.
1876–88, earthenware     printed


Co-operative Wholesale Society Ltd.
1922, porcelain and
from 1946 also earthenware
    printed mark on porcelain
    from *c.* 1946, also
    'Clarence Bone-China'

    'Crown Clarence'
    earthenware from 1946–
    also 'Balmoral'
(from 1971–, Jon Anton Ltd.)


J. H. Cope & Co. Ltd.     C. & CO.
1887–1947, porcelain     impressed or printed

printed with 'back-stamps'  J.H.C. & CO.
from *c.* 1900
'WELLINGTON CHINA' with crown *c.* 1906–
'WELLINGTON CHINA' and profile of Duke
*c.* 1924–1947

Cotton & Barlow          C. & B.
1850–5, earthenware      printed

Cyples & Barker          CYPLES & BARKER
1846–7, earthenware      impressed

Day, George              STAFFORDSHIRE
1882–9, earthenware
  printed mark

Day & Pratt              DAY & PRATT
1887–8, porcelain     printed or impressed

Decoro Pottery Co.       TUSCAN
1933–49, earthenware     DECORO
  various fully-named     POTTERY
  printed marks

Denton China (Longton) Ltd.  DENTON
1945–, porcelain             CHINA
(Aynsley China Ltd.)

Dewes & Copestake        D. & C.
1894–1915, earthenware      L
  various printed marks
  including initials

Diane Pottery Co.  DIANE
1960–, now closed,  POTTERY
porcelain  LONGTON
   various printed marks  STAFFORDSHIRE
   with full name

Dinky Art Pottery Co. Ltd.  MADE IN
1931–47, earthenware  DINKY WARE
   printed mark  ENGLAND

Dixon & Co., R. F.  various marks
1916–29, ceramic retailers  include 'D.C.'
and importers  for Dixon & Co.

Dresden Floral Porcelain Co. Ltd.
1945–56, porcelain
   printed mark

Dresden Porcelain Co.  D.P. CO.  D.P. CO.
1896–1904, porcelain  L
   printed or impressed

printed mark 1896–1903

Edwards & Brown  E. & B.
1882–1933, porcelain  L
   impressed or printed mark 1882–1933
   'E. & B.L.' with 'DUCHESS CHINA', 1910–33

198

Elektra Porcelain Co Ltd.
1924–71, earthenware
  printed mark of 1924–
(now Allied English Potteries)
  similar mark 'VULCAN WARE' *c.* 1940–

Elkin, Samuel        S.E.
1856–64, earthenware     printed

Elkin & Newbon       E. & N.
*c.* 1844–5, earthenware

Fell & Co., J. T.     EMBOSA WARE
1923–57, earthenware

              MADE BY CYPLES
  printed or impressed    OLD POTTERY
                    1793

Finney & Sons Ltd., A. T.    DUCHESS
1947, porcelain       BONE CHINA
  trade-name in a variety    printed
  of styles

Flacket, Toft & Robinson    F.T. & R.
1857–8, earthenware      printed

Floral China Co. Ltd.
1940–51, porcelain
  printed mark

Forester & Co., Thomas
1888–, earthenware
  printed mark

Forester & Sons, Thomas    T.F. & S.
1883–1959, general ceramics
  'Ltd.' added 1891
  printed, 1891–1912
  later marks include
  'PHOENIX CHINA'

Gallimore, Robert      R.G.
1831–40, earthenware    impressed

Gallimore & Co. Ltd.,    G. & CO.
1906–34, earthenware      L
  mark impressed or printed

Gladstone China (Longton)    GLADSTONE
Ltd., 1939–1952,      BONE       CHINA
porcelain
  printed mark until    MADE IN ENGLAND
  1961 after firm became:   various marks with
Gladstone China     'Gladstone Bone China'
1952–, porcelain

Green & Clay
1888–91, earthenware
  printed or impressed

Grove & Stark      G. & S.
1871–85, earthenware    printed
  printed or impressed
  'G.S.' impressed     GROVE & STARK
  monogram also used    LONGTON

Hallam & Day                    H. & D.
1880–85, earthenware            printed, often with
                                Royal Arms

Hammersley & Co.                H. & C.    H. & CO.
1887–1932, porcelain
(Hammersley & Co., Longton) Ltd.
from 1932–present
    crown mark used without
    initials, 1887–1912
    many various fully-named marks from 1912–
(now Carborundum Group)

Hammersley & Asbury             H. & A.
1872–5, earthenware             printed, sometimes
                                with 'Prince of Wales'
                                feathers

Hampson & Broadhurst            H. & B.
1847–53, earthenware            printed

Harvey, C. & W. K.              C. & W.K.H.
1835–53, general ceramics
    name also printed with          HARVEY
    Royal Arms and 'REAL            printed
    IRONSTONE CHINA'

Hawley, Webberley & Co.
1895–1902, earthenware
    printed mark

Hewitt & Leadbeater
1907–19, porcelain
then Hewitt Bros. until
c. 1926                      printed

Hibbert & Boughey                    H. & B.
1889, general ceramics          printed with crown

Hill & Co.                           H. & CO.
1898–1920, porcelain          impressed or printed

Holdcroft, Joseph                       printed or
1865–1940, general ceramics                    impressed
(Holdcrofts Ltd., *c.* 1906–,                   1865–1906
later Cartwright & Edwards Ltd.)
   mark of 'H.J.' monogram on globe from
   1890–1939

Holland & Green                      H. & G.
1853–82, earthenware            LATE HARVEY
                              printed or impressed

Holmes & Son                         H. & S.
1898–1903, earthenware            LONGTON
   other marks include      impressed or printed
   full name

Hudden, John Thomas                  J.T.H.
1859–1885, earthenware          J.T. HUDDEN
                                   printed

Hudson, William                      W.H.
   1889–1941, porcelain            printed
   printed mark 1892–1912
   other later marks
   include 'SUTHERLAND
   CHINA'

Hudson & Middleton, Ltd.
1941–, porcelain
   various late marks
   include 'SUTHERLAND'
   and 'H.M.' with lion

Hulse & Adderley
1869–75, general
ceramics
   printed mark as
   used later by
   W. A. Adderley & Co.

H. & A.

Hulse, Nixon & Adderley     H.N. & A.
1853–68, earthenware     printed

Jackson & Gosling     J. & G.     J. & G.
1866–1968, porcelain                   L
   'Ltd.' added *c.* 1930     impressed or printed
variety of marks including trade-name of
'Grosvenor China'

Jones (Longton) Ltd., A. E.
1905–46, earthenware
   printed or impressed
   *c.* 1908–36     ENGLAND
other 'Palissy' mark continued by
Palissy Pottery, Ltd., now a subsidiary of
Royal Worcester, Ltd.

PALISSY

Jones & Co., Frederick   F. JONES LONGTON
1865–86, earthenware   impressed or printed


Jones & Sons, A. B.    A.B.J. & S.
1900–, porcelain    A.B.J. & SONS
(A. B. Jones from 1876)   A.B. JONES & SONS
  large variety of marks including
  initials, full name and/or trade-name of
  'GRAFTON' or 'ROYAL GRAFTON'
(acquired in 1966 by Crown House Glass Ltd.)


Jones, Shepherd & Co.    J.S. & CO.
1867–8, earthenware    printed


Jones, Josiah Ellis     J.E.J.
1868–72, earthenware    or full name
         printed


Kent, James     JAMES KENT
1897–, general ceramics   ENGLAND
  'Ltd.' added 1913   with Royal Arms &
  printed mark of   'ROYAL SEMI CHINA'
  1897–1915
  various shield or 'globe' marks with full name
  or J.K.L. or J.K., from 1897–present, when
  'Old Foley' is used


Lawrence (Longton) Ltd., Thomas
1892–1964, earthenware
  printed or impressed
  marks include name
  'Falcon Ware'

Leadbeater, Edwin
1920–24, porcelain
  printed or impressed mark

Ledgar, Thomas P.
1900–5, general ceramics
  impressed or printed mark

T.P.L.

Lockett & Sons, John
1828–35, earthenware

J. LOCKETT & SONS
impressed

Longton New Art Pottery Co.
Ltd., 1932–66, earthenware
  various printed marks

KELSBORO'
WARE

Longton Porcelain Co. Ltd.
1892–1908, porcelains

L.P. CO.
monogram

Longton Pottery Co. Ltd.
1946–55, earthenware

L.P. CO. LTD.
printed

Lowe, William
1874–1930, porcelain

               printed or impressed
  also full name or initials with trade-names
  'ROYAL SYDNEY WARE', 'COURT CHINA'

Lowe, Ratcliffe & Co.
1882–92, earthenware
  printed or impressed

Mackee, Andrew  A.M.
1892–1906, general ceramics  L.
                     impressed or printed

Malkin, Walker & Hulse  M.W. & H.
1858–64, earthenware  printed

Martin, Shaw & Cope  MARTIN SHAW
*c.* 1815–24, general ceramics  & COPE
                  IMPROVED CHINA
                      printed

Mason, Holt & Co.  M.H. & CO.
1857–84, porcelain  printed or impressed

Massey, Wildblood & Co.  M.W. & CO.
1887–9, porcelain  printed

Matthews & Clark  M. & C.
*c.* 1902–6, general ceramics  L.
   printed mark in frame

Mayer & Sherratt  M. & S.
1906–41, porcelain  L.
                 under crown
   also other printed marks including trade-name
   of 'MELBA CHINA'

McNeal & Co. Ltd.
1894–1906, earthenware
   printed

Middleton & Co., J. H.
1889–1941, porcelain
   various printed marks
   with trade-name of
   'DELPHINE'

Moore Bros.
1872–1905, porcelain

   'Bros.' added 1872–1905

   printed from *c.* 1880

   printed mark, 1902–5
Bernard Moore
continued at Stoke
until 1915

MOORE
printed or impressed

MOORE BROS.

MOORE (with globe)

Morris, Thomas
1892–1941, porcelain

   early printed mark, from
   *c.* 1912 trade-name of
   'CROWN CHELSEA CHINA' used

New Chelsea Porcelain Co. Ltd.
   from 1913 many marks used
   including anchor and
   'Chelsea', 'New Chelsea'
   or 'Royal Chelsea'

New Chelsea China Co. Ltd.
1951–61, porcelain

New Park Potteries Ltd.          N.P.P. LTD.
1935–57, earthenware             NEW PARK
  initials or factory-      POTTERIES
  name printed in          LONGTON
  varying frames           NEW PARK

Osborne China Co. Ltd.          'Osborne China'
1909–40, porcelain               with torch

Palissy Pottery Ltd.
1946–, earthenware
(subsidiary of Royal
Worcester Ltd.)

  variety of printed marks include,
  'Palissy Pottery' or 'Palissy Ware', etc.

Paragon China Ltd.
1920–, porcelain
  large variety of marks
  include 'Royal Arms'
  and 'Paragon'
(now an Allied English
Potteries Ltd. company)

Pattison, J.                     JOHN PATTISON
*c.* 1818–30, earthenware        incised

Plant, Benjamin
c. 1780–1820, earthenware

incised

Plant & Co., R. H.
1881–98, porcelain

'R.H.P. & CO.'
in knot under a
winged crown

Plant, Ltd., R. H. & S. L.
c. 1898–1970, porcelain
 numerals under
 mark indicate last
 two numerals of year
 made. From 1973:

'TUSCAN CHINA'
trade-name in
many various
forms
'WEDGWOOD–ROYAL
TUSCAN DIVISION'

Plant & Sons, R.
1895–1901, earthenware

P. & S.
L
printed

Poole, Thomas
1880–1952, general ceramics

impressed or printed
crown, 1880–1912
(common mark)
early form of 'ROYAL
STAFFORD CHINA' used
from 1912–

Poole & Unwin
1871–6, earthenware

P. & U.
printed or impressed

209

Proctor & Co., J. H.
1857–84, earthenware

WARRANTED
P
printed or impressed
under crown

Procter, John
1843–6, earthenware

J.P.
L
printed or impressed

Procter & Co. Ltd., G.
1891–1940, porcelain
  with or without 'L'
  for Longton
  'GLADSTONE CHINA'
  from 1924–40

G.P. & CO.
L
printed

trade-name

Ratcliffe & Co.
1891–1914, earthenware

printed

Redfern & Drakeford Ltd.
1892–1933, porcelain
  printed or impressed
  mark, 'BALMORAL
  CHINA' added in
  1909–33

Regency China Ltd.
1953–, porcelain

Reid & Co.
1913–46, porcelain

   'PARK PLACE CHINA'
   *c.* 1913–24

   'ROSLYN CHINA'
   *c.* 1924–46
   (SEE ROSLYN CHINA)  all printed

Riddle & Bryan  RIDDLE & BRYAN
*c.* 1835–40, earthenware  Longton
   printed

Robinson, W. H.  W.H. ROBINSON
1901–4, porcelain  LONGTON
   printed mark in  BALTIMORE CHINA
   circle under crown

Robinson & Son  R. & S.
1881–1903, porcelain  L.

   'Foley' is a name  FOLEY CHINA
   used by several potters

Roper & Meredith  R. & M.
1913–24, earthenware  LONGTON

Roslyn China
1946–63, porcelain
   printed mark also
   used by Reid & Co.

Rowley & Newton Ltd.            R. & N.
1896–1901, general ceramics   printed or impressed
  'R. & N.' often with lion 'rampant'

Royal Albion China Co.      ROYAL ALBION CHINA
1921–48, porcelain                    L
  printed marks                  ENGLAND
                                with crown

Royal Stafford China         variety of marks
1952–, porcelain                    with
  printed marks            'ROYAL STAFFORD'

Salisbury Crown China Co.
(Salisbury China Co. from
1949)
*c.* 1927–61, porcelain

  printed mark of *c.* 1952

Salt & Nixon, Ltd.               S. & N.
1901–34, porcelain                   L
  various marks with initials
  & 'SALON CHINA'               printed

Shaw & Sons (Longton) Ltd., John
1931–63, general ceramics

  printed mark of *c.* 1949
  various other marks,
  include 'Burlington'

212

Shaw & Copestake
1901–, earthenware
    various printed or impressed
    marks with trade-name of 'SYLVAC'

Shelley Potteries, Ltd.
1925–67, porcelain
(now Royal Albert Ltd.)
    various printed marks
    with 'SHELLEY' (Royal Doulton Group)

Shepherd & Co., Alfred     A. SHEPHERD & CO.
1864–70, earthenware          printed

Shore & Co., J.              J.S. & CO.
1887–1905, porcelain         printed

Shore, Coggins & Holt       S.C.H.
1905–10, general ceramics      L
    initials printed under    *ENGLAND*
    crown

Shore & Coggins
1911–*c.* 67, porcelain
    mark of *c.* 1930, other
    marks include trade-name
    'Bell China' (now Royal Doulton Group)

Smith, Sampson           S.S.
*c.* 1846–1963, general      impressed
ceramics

's.s.' monogram used in a variety of
marks during this century and 'WETLEY
CHINA' or 'OLD ROYAL CHINA'

Stanley & Lambert　　　　　　　S. & L.
*c.* 1850–4, earthenware　　　　　printed

Stanley Pottery Ltd.
1928–31, general ceramics

　同 same printed marks as
　　used by Colclough & Co.

Star China Co.　　　　　　　　　　　S.C. CO.
1900–19, porcelain　　　　printed with crown
　　　　　　　　　　　　　　　or star with
　　　　　　　　　　　　'THE PARAGON CHINA'

Stevenson, Spencer & Co. Ltd.
1948–60, porcelain
　　fully named marks
　　with 'WILLOW' or
　　'ROYAL STUART'

Sutherland & Sons, Danial　　　　S. & S.
1865–75, general　　　　　　　impressed or
ceramics　　　　　　　　　　　　printed

Swift & Elkin　　　　　　　　　　　S. & E.
1840–3, earthenware　　　　　　printed

Tams, John　　　　　　　　J.T.
c. 1875–, earthenware　　(or as monogram)
　printed marks

　　　　　　　　　　　　J. Tams
　'& Son' added 1903–12　J.T. & S.
　'LTD.' from 1912, with trade-marks:
　'NANKIN WARE', 'ELEPHANT BRAND',
　'TAMS REGENT' and 'CHININE'

Tams & Lowe　　　　　　T. & L.
1865–74, earthenware　　printed

Taylor & Kent　　　　　T. & K.
1867–, porcelain　　　　　L
　　　　　　　　　printed or impressed
　variety of named or initialled marks
　with 'KENT' or 'ELIZABETHAN'

Thorley China Ltd.　　THORLEY CHINA
1940–70, decorative　　　LTD.
porcelain　　　　　printed under crown
(last six years in Fenton)

Tomkinson & Billington　T. & B.
1868–70, earthenware　　printed

Townsend, George　　G. TOWNSEND
c. 1850–64, earthenware　printed

Trentham Bone China Ltd.
1952–7, porcelain
　printed

Turner, John
*c.* 1762–1806, Wedgwood-
type earthenwares and
stonewares

TURNER
impressed

TURNER.

    printed or impressed
    from 1784

    impressed *c.* 1780–6,
      1803–6
    painted mark on
    'ironstone' type ware
    1800–5

TURNER & CO.

Turner's-Patent.

Turner & Abbott
*c.* 1783–7, Wedgwood-
type wares

TURNER & ABBOTT
impressed

Universal Pottery (Longton) Ltd.
1949–62, general ceramics
    various printed marks
    with 'Universal Ware'

Unwin, Joseph
1877–1926, earthenware
figures, etc.

UNWIN
moulded in
relief

Wagstaff & Brunt
1880–1927, general
ceramics

W. & B.
LONGTON
printed

Wain & Sons, Ltd., H. A.
1946–, earthenware

Waine & Co., Charles
1891–1920, porcelain
  printed, 1891–1913
  'Ltd.' from 1913

C.W.
or as monogram

Walker & Carter
1866–72, earthenware
(at Stoke 1872–89)

W. & C.
printed

Walton, J. H.
1912–21, porcelain

J. H. W.

LONGTON

  printed or impressed

Warrilow, George
1887–1940, porcelain
  '& S.' or '& Sons'
  and 'Ltd.' added
  from 1928

G.W.

G.W. & S.

G.W. & S. LTD.

Rosina China Co. Ltd.
1941–
  various marks with
  trade-names 'Rosina'
  or 'Queen's' China

ROSINA

CHINA
ENGLAND

Wayte & Ridge
*c.* 1864, general
ceramics & figures

W. & R.
L
printed

Wedgwood & Co. Ltd., H.F.     H.F.W. & CO. LTD.
*c.* 1954–9, general          ISLINGTON
ceramics                printed

Wild Bros.              J.S.W.
1904–27, porcelain     or in monogram
                     W. Bros.

Wild & Co., Thomas C.    T.W. & CO.
1896–1904
   printed or impressed    T.C.W. with crown

Wild, Thomas C.
1905–17, porcelain
   printed mark, 1905–7

Wild & Sons (Ltd.), Thomas C.
1917–*c.* 72, porcelain
   various printed marks
   with trade-name
   'Royal Albert', now Royal Doulton Group

Wild & Adams          W. & A.
1909–27, earthenware   printed or impressed
   'Ltd.' from 1923
   various marks with 'ROYAL CROWN'

Wildblood, Richard Vernon
1887–8, porcelain

   printed

Wildblood & Heath
1889–99, porcelain
   printed

Wildblood, Heath & Sons
1899–1927, porcelain

  'Ltd.' added from 1915

Williamson & Sons, H. M.
*c.* 1879–1941, porcelain

  various marks of 'W. & Sons',
  'H.M.W.' or 'Heathcote
  China'
  printed mark of *c.* 1908–

Winterton Pottery (Longton)   'WINTERTON'
Ltd., 1927–54, earthenware   printed over crown

  'Bluestone Ware'

Wood & Co., J. B.
1897–1926, earthenware

  late printed or impressed
  mark

Woolley, Richard       WOOLLEY
1809–14, earthenware   impressed

Yale & Barker                                    Y. & B.
1841–53, earthenware                        printed


MIDDLEPORT (Staffordshire)       FIVE TOWNS CHINA
Five Towns China Co. Ltd.            CO. LTD.
1957–67, porcelain                       ENGLAND
  name with various
  printed marks


SHELTON (Staffordshire)              ASTBURY
Astbury, mid-18th                incised or impressed
century, earthenware

Astbury, Richard Meir                   R.M.A.
1790–, earthenware                      impressed

Baddeley, John & Edward               B
1784–1806, earthenware             I.E.B.
  impressed initials                         I.E.B.
then:                                          W
Hicks & Meigh                       HICKS & MEIGH
1806–22, earthenware              impressed or
and 'Ironstone'                         printed
then:
Hicks, Meigh & Johnson              H.M.J.
1822–35, earthenware
and 'Ironstone'
                                              H.M. & J.
                                         printed with
                                         Royal Arms

then:


220

Ridgway, Morley, Wear & Co., 1836–42, earthenware — R.M.W. & CO.

RIDGWAY, MORLEY
WEAR & CO.
printed

then:
Ridgway & Morley — R. & M.
1842–44
  various printed marks — RIDGWAY & MORLEY
  (backstamps) with
  names of pattern

Baddeley, Ralph & John — BADDELEY
1750–95, earthenware
  marks impressed — R. & J.
BADDELEY

Bairstow & Co., P. E. — Fancies
1954–. earthenware — Fayre
and porcelain — England

Bentley, Wear & Bourne — BENTLEY, WEAR
1815–23, decorators — & BOURNE
  printed mark
(Bentley & Wear 1823–
  33)

Birch, Edmund John — BIRCH
1796–1814, Wedgwood-
type wares
E.I.B.
impressed

Birch & Whitehead — B. & W.
1796, Wedgwood-type — impressed

| | |
|---|---|
| Cockson & Harding 1856–62, earthenware marks printed or impressed | C. & H. C. & H. LATE HACKWOOD |
| Cutts, James *c.* 1834–70, engraver and designer | J. CUTTS signature on prints |
| Dakin, Thomas early 18th century earthenware | THOMAS DAKIN sliptrailed |
| Hackwood & Son, Wm. 1846–9, earthenware | W.H. HACKWOOD printed |
| Harding, W. J. 1862–72, earthenware | W. & J.H. printed |
| Hicks & Meigh 1806–22, earthenware 'Stone-China' & Royal Arms also used | HICKS & MEIGH impressed or painted |
| Hicks, Meigh & Johnson 1822–35, earthenware 'Stone-China' and Royal Arms also used | H.M.J. H.M. & J. printed |
| Hollins, Samuel *c.* 1784–1813 | S. HOLLINS |

'Wedgwood-type' ware          HOLLINS
                              impressed

Hollins, T. & J.              T. & J. HOLLINS
*c.* 1795–1820, earthenware   impressed

Howard Pottery Co.
1925–, earthenware
  printed mark of 1925–

Keeling, Charles              C.K.
1822–5, earthenware           printed

Meir John                     JOHN MEIR
late 17th – early 18th-       sliptrailed
centuries, slipware

Meir, Richard                 RICHARD MEIR
late 17th – early 18th-       sliptrailed
centuries, slipware

Phillips, Edward              EDWARD PHILLIPS
1855–62, earthenware          SHELTON
  printed mark      STAFFORDSHIRE

Read & Clementson             R. & C.
1833–5, earthenware           printed

Read, Clementson &            R.C. & A.
Anderson                      printed
*c.* 1836, earthenware

| | |
|---|---|
| Ridgway, John & William<br>1814–1830, general<br>ceramics | J.W.R.<br>J. & W.R.<br>J. & W. RIDGWAY<br>printed or impressed |
| Ridgway, William<br>*c.* 1830–54, earthenware<br>(also at Hanley from<br>*c.* 1838–48)<br>　'& Co.' added *c.* 1834<br>　'QUARTZ CHINA' used<br>　from *c.* 1830–50 | W. RIDGWAY<br><br>W.R.<br>printed or impressed<br><br>W.R. & CO. |
| Tittensor, Charles<br>*c.* 1815–23, earthenware<br>including figures | TITTENSOR<br>impressed or<br>printed |
| Twemlow, John<br>1795–7, earthenware<br>and stoneware | J.T.<br><br>rare initials |
| Washington Pottery Ltd.<br>1946–, earthenware<br>(now Washington Pottery<br>(Staffordshire) Ltd.) |  |
| Worthington & Green<br>1844–64, earthenware<br>and Parianware | WORTHINGTON<br>&<br>GREEN<br>impressed |

224

STOKE (Staffordshire)
Alton Towers Handcraft
Pottery (Staffs.) Ltd.
1953–, earthenware

printed or impressed

Arkinstall & Sons (Ltd.)
1904–24, bone-china

A. & S.
printed, 1904–12

   trade marks on
souvenir wares 1904–
24
(under various other
firms from 1908)

ARCADIAN

ARCADIAN CHINA

printed marks

Atlas China Co. Ltd.
1906–10, china
(name revived by
Grimwades Ltd. 1930–6)

'ATLAS CHINA' with
figure supporting
globe
printed

Bennett & Co., George
1894–1902, earthenware

G.B. & CO.
impressed or printed

Bilton (1912) Ltd.
1900–, earthenware
   current mark, printed
(now Biltons Tableware Ltd.)

Birks & Co., L. A.
1896–1900, general
ceramics

BIRKS
impressed

B. & CO.

Birks, Rawlins & Co. (Ltd.)
1900–33, bone-china
  other marks include
  trade-names of:
  SAVOY CHINA
  CARLTON CHINA

printed

Booth & Son, Ephraim    E.B. & S.
*c.* 1795, earthenware    impressed

Booth, Hugh    H. BOOTH
1784–9, earthenware    impressed
including creamware

Carlton Ware Ltd.
1958–, earthenware
(Arthur Wood & Son Group)

modern printed mark

Ceramic Art Co. (1905)    C.A. & CO. LTD.
Ltd., 1905–19, earthenware    printed or impressed

Close & Co.    CLOSE & CO. LATE
1855–64, earthenware    W. ADAMS & SONS
                           STOKE-UPON-TRENT
                           printed or impressed

Copeland & Garrett
Copeland, W. T., etc.
(*see under* Spode)

Coronation Pottery Co.
1903–54, earthenware

   'Ltd.' from 1947

CORONATION POTTERY
COMPANY LTD.

B

MADE IN ENGLAND
printed or impressed

Crown China Crafts Ltd.
1946–58, general ceramics
   printed mark

HAND MADE : HAND PAINTED
IN ENGLAND
CROWN CHINA CRAFTS LTD.

Daniel, H. & R.
1820–41, pottery and
porcelain
   fully named printed
   marks also used

H. & R. Daniel

H. Daniels & Sons

written marks

Empire Porcelain Co.
1896–1967, earthenware
   printed mark, 1896–1912
(1958–67, Qualcast Group)

P
Staffordshire
England

EMPIRE
ENGLAND    *Shelton Ivory*

   late printed or impressed marks

Era Art Pottery Co.
1930–47, earthenware

   printed mark, 1936–

| | |
|---|---|
| Featherstone Potteries 1949–50, earthenware marks impressed or printed | F.P. F.N.P. |
| Fielding & Co., S. 1879–, earthenwares (part of Crown Devon Group) | FIELDING impressed |
| 'Crown Devon' trade-mark from *c.* 1930 | S.F. & CO. (over crown and lion) printed |
| date-mark: 10th March 1954 | FIELDING 10 M 54 |

Floyd & Sons, R.
1907–30, earthenware

printed or impressed

Folch, Stephen
1820–30, earthenware

FOLCH'S GENUINE
STONE CHINA
impressed

Goss, W. H.
1858–1944, pottery and
porcelain

W.H.G.

W.H. GOSS

printed mark from
*c.* 1862

Greta Pottery     G
1938–41, earthenware    P
          printed or painted

Hamilton, Robert    HAMILTON
1811–26, earthenware    STOKE
         impressed or printed

Hancock & Co., F.
1899–1900, earthenware  
 printed mark

Hancock, B. & S.    B. & S.H.
1876–81, earthenware   printed

Hancock & Sons, Sampson  S.H.
1858–1937, earthenware
(at Tunstall prior    S. HANCOCK
to 1870)       printed

 printed 1891–1935   S.H. & S.

         S.H. & SONS

 printed 1900–12
From 1935–37:— 
S. Hancock & Sons
(Potters) Ltd.

Hancock & Whittingham  H. & W.
1873–9, earthenware   printed

Heath, Job
early 18th century
earthenware

JOB HEATH
sliptrailed

Jones, George
1861–1951, general ceramics

'& Sons', added on
crescent from 1873

in relief, impressed
or printed

Keys & Mountford
1850–7, 'Parian' ware

K. & M.

S. KEYS
& MOUNTFORD
impressed

Kirkham, William
1862–92, earthenware

W. KIRKHAM
impressed

Kirkhams Ltd.
1946–61, earthenware
(now Portmeiron
Potteries Ltd.)

KIRKHAM
POTTERY
MADE IN ENGLAND

Mayer, Thomas
1836–8, earthenware
(last three years at
Longport)

T. MAYER
T. MAYER, STOKE
printed

Meigh, W. & R.
1894–9, earthenware
printed mark

Minton
1793–, general ceramics
(Royal Doulton Group from 1973)
   Sèvres type mark used
on porcelain *c.* 1800–30,
sometimes with     in blue enamel
pattern number

printed mark with
'M', 1822–1836

printed 1822–36

'M. & B.' for Minton &
Boyle partnership
1836–41, printed

'M. & Co.' Minton &
Co., 1841–73

'M. & H.', Minton &
Hollins partnership
1845–68

231

1862–71, 's' added
in 1873

MINTON
impressed

printed 1860–*c.* 69

impressed for 'BEST
BODY' mid-19th century

B.B.

'Globe-mark', 1863–72
'S' added to Minton
in 1871

impressed mark with
year 1875, used from
1868–80

18
MINTON
75

printed mark from 1873,
'England' added from
1891, and 'Made in
England' about 1910

impressed or moulded
*c.* 1890–1910

MINTONS
ENGLAND

'Globe-mark', *c.* 1912–50

standard factory-mark
adopted in 1951

'Ermine' mark used
from *c.* 1850 to identify
wares that had been
dipped in a soft-glaze
on which painting was
to be applied

relief mark of *c.* 1847–8
on 'Summerly's Art
Manufacturers' made
by Minton

Solon, Marc Louis, 1870–1904
decorator

signature on 'Henri Deux'    TOFT
reproductions
Mussill, W. (*d.* 1906)    W.  Mussill
decorator in 1870s

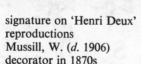

## YEARLY MARKS OF MINTONS LTD., 1842–1942:

| | | | | |
|---|---|---|---|---|
| ✳ | △ | ☐ | ✕ | ⬭ |
| 1842 | 1843 | 1844 | 1845 | 1846 |
| ⌢ | ─ | ⪥ | ♣ | ⋮ |
| 1847 | 1848 | 1849 | 1850 | 1851 |
| ∨ | ⌓ | ∿ | ✳ | ♀ |
| 1852 | 1853 | 1854 | 1855 | 1856 |
| ◇ | ♈ | ⚮ | ⚘ | ⅄ |
| 1857 | 1858 | 1859 | 1860 | 1861 |
| ⯒ | ⬦ | Ƶ | 〰 | Ⴤ |
| 1862 | 1863 | 1864 | 1865 | 1866 |
| ⋈ | Ꮆ | ⊡ | Ⓜ | Ɲ |
| 1867 | 1868 | 1869 | 1870 | 1871 |
| ⊗ | ✳ | ↓ | ℰ | ⊖ |
| 1872 | 1873 | 1874 | 1875 | 1876 |
| ⊡ | ◮ | ◮ | ◭ | ⊞ |
| 1877 | 1878 | 1879 | 1880 | 1881 |
| ⊗ | ⊘ | ⊠ | ⋈ | B |
| 1882 | 1883 | 1884 | 1885 | 1886 |
| ♕ | ⧖ | S | T | ⛉ |
| 1887 | 1888 | 1889 | 1890 | 1891 |

| | | | | |
|---|---|---|---|---|
| 1892 | 1893 | 1894 | 1895 | 1896 |
| 1897 | 1898 | 1899 | 1900 | 1901 |
| 1902 | 1903 | 1904 | 1905 | 1906 |
| 1907 | 1908 | 1909 | 1910 | 1911 |
| 1912 | 1913 | 1914 | 1915 | 1916 |
| 1917 | 1918 | 1919 | 1920 | 1921 |
| 1922 | 1923 | 1924 | 1925 | 1926 |
| 1927 | 1928 | 1929 | 1930 | 1931 |
| 1932 | 1933 | 1934 | 1935 | 1936 |
| 1937 | 1938 | 1939 | 1940 | 1941 |
| | | 1942 | | |

At the commencement of 1943 the system of yearly date-marks that had operated from 1842 was discontinued, being replaced by figures denoting the year of production, preceded by a number allocated to the actual maker of the article, Number one was given to the factory's leading plate-maker, and plates he produces today have stamped in the clay 1–76, the last two digits representing the year.

Moore, Bernard
1905–15, art pottery and
porcelain, with
*flambé* glazes

painted

painted or printed

Mountford, G. T.
1888–98, earthenware

G.T.M.
STOKE
printed

Mountford, John
1857–9, 'Parian' ware

J. MOUNTFORD
STOKE
incised signature

Myott, Son & Co. Ltd.
1898–, earthenware
(now subsidiary of
Interpace Corporation)
(later Cobridge and
Hanley)

1898–1902

late marks fully named

*c.* 1900–

236

Ollivant Potteries Ltd.
1948–54, earthenware

O.P.

O.P.L.

printed marks, usually
together with pattern

OLLIVANT

Plant & Co., J.
1893–1900, earthenware
printed mark

STOKE POTTERY

Portmeirion Potteries Ltd.
1962–, earthenware

PORTMEIRION
POTTERY
STOKE-ON-TRENT

printed mark

MADE IN ENGLAND

Ridgway Potteries Ltd.
1955, earthenware
(an Allied English
Potteries Ltd., company)

contemporary marks (1972)

Robinson & Leadbeater
1864–1924, 'Parian' ware
and bone-china
'Ltd.' added to marks
from *c.* 1905

impressed

237

Ruscoe, William
*c.* 1920– (to Exeter in
1944)
   full year-date added
   to initials from *c.* 1925

incised or painted

Shorter & Son, Ltd.
(member of Crown Devon
Group), 1905–
earthenware

late printed mark

Smith, James
1898–1924, general ceramics

JAMES SMITH

printed or impressed

printed

Spode, Josiah (*b.* 1733–
*d.* 1797) 1770–
earthenware
(Copeland & Garrett
from 1833)

Spode   SPODE
impressed or
in blue

   *c.* 1784–1805

SPODE   S
impressed

| | |
|---|---|
| painted marks with pattern numbers, *c.* 1790–1820 | SPODE 1989<br>2417 Spode |
| *c.* 1805– | SPODE<br>printed |
| mark on stone-china, in black *c.* 1805–15, in blue *c.* 1815–30 | **SPODE**<br>**Stone China**<br>printed |
| painted | 'Spode Stone China' |
| impressed 1810–15 | **SPODES NEW STONE** |
| printed *c.* 1805–33 | N.S.<br>**Spode's Imperial** |
| printed in puce enamel on felspar porcelain *c.* 1815–27 | Spode felspar Porcelain |
| painted, impressed or printed *c.* 1797 to 1816 | SPODE, SON & COPELAND |

| | |
|---|---|
| Copeland & Garrett 1833–47, general ceramics | C. & G. painted or printed |

COPELAND & GARRETT

printed in blue, with name of pattern, *c.* 1833–47

printed *c.* 1833–47

COPELAND & GARRETT
NEW
JAPAN STONE

Copeland & Sons, Ltd., W. T., 1847–
impressed or printed
*c.* 1847–67

COPELAND, LATE
SPODE

printed on Parian figures
*c.* 1847–55

COPELAND'S
PORCELAIN
STATUARY

printed, 1850–67

printed, *c.* 1847–51

printed, 1851–85

impressed on earthenware
1850–67

printed on porcelain
*c.* 1891–

SPODE
COPELANDS CHINA
ENGLAND

printed in various
colours on 'New Stone'
of this century

present-day mark

𝔖𝔭𝔬𝔡𝔢
ENGLAND

Alcock, S., decorator
*c.* 1890–

S. Alcock

Hürten, C. F., designer
1859–1897

C.F.H.

Steele & Wood
1875–1892, tiles

printed or impressed

Tittensor, Jacob
1780–95, earthenware

Jacob Tittensor
signature

241

Turner, Hassall & Peake
1865–9, general ceramics

T.H.P.

printed or impressed

Turner & Wood
1880–8, general ceramics

TURNER & WOOD
STOKE
impressed

Wiltshaw & Robinson Ltd.
1890–1957, general
ceramics
    printed mark, 1894–
    various marks include
    trade-mark 'CARLTON
    WARE'

Winkle & Co., F.
1890–1931, earthenware

F.W. & CO.
ENGLAND

printed or impressed
marks, 1890–1910
'Ltd.' added in 1911

F. WINKLE & CO.

printed, 1890–1925

misleading mark used
by Winkle & Co., 1908–25
(the wares of the
18th century potter,
Thomas Whieldon, were
not marked)

242

| | |
|---|---|
| Wolfe, Thomas<br>1784–1800, earthenware<br>and later, *c.* 1811–18 | WOLFE<br>impressed |
| Wolfe & Hamilton<br>*c.* 1800–11, earthenware | WOLFE & HAMILTON<br>STOKE<br>impressed or painted |

TUNSTALL (Staffordshire)
   Adams & Sons (Potters)
   Ltd., William,

impressed, 1769–1800       ADAMS & CO.
(on creamware)

impressed, 1787–1864       ADAMS

on blue-printed wares
1804–40

impressed on earthenware
1810–25

impressed mark *c.* 1815       W. ADAMS & CO.

W. Adams & Sons       W.A. & S.
1819–64, printed

243

| | |
|---|---|
| impressed on parian-ware, 1845–64 | ADAMS |
| printed, mid-19th century | W. ADAMS |
| printed as 'back-stamp' with name of pattern, 1893–1917. 'ENGLAND' added in 1891 | W.A. & CO. |

printed from 1879–

printed from 1896–
with varying names
of ceramic bodies
used, e.g. TITIAN
WARE, IMPERIAL
STONE WARE, etc.

| | |
|---|---|
| impressed on Wedgwood-type jasperwares 1896 with confusing establishment date | ADAMS ESTBD 1657 TUNSTALL ENGLAND |

printed mark, 1914–40

late impressed or
printed mark

*Calyx Ware*

late printed mark
*c.* 1950–

W. Adams & Sons
England
under crown

Adams, Benjamin
*c.* 1800–20, earthenware
and stoneware

B. ADAMS

impressed

Adams, W. & T.
1866–92, earthenware
printed mark

W. & T. ADAMS
TUNSTALL
under coat-of-arms

Beech & Hancock
1857–76, earthenware

B. & H.
printed

Blackhurst, Jabez
1872–83, earthenware

JABEZ BLACKHURST
printed

Booth & Son, Thomas
1872–6, earthenware

T.B. & S.
printed

Booth, Thomas, G.
1876–83, earthenware
  name of pattern on strap

Booth, T. G. & F.
1883–91, earthenware

T.G. & F.B.
printed

Booth (Limited)
1891–1948, earthenware
printed, 1891–1906

painted or printed on
earthenware reproductions
of Worcester porcelain, 1905–

variety of marks used with 'Silicon China'
from about 1906. 'England' sometimes included

late mark of 1930–48

Boulton, Machin & Tennant
1889–99, earthenware

mark printed or impressed

Bourne, Nixon & Co.          BOURNE NIXON
1828–30, earthenware            & CO.
mark impressed

printed initials included     B.N. & CO.
in backstamp

Bowers & Co., G. F.
1842–68, pottery &
porcelain
other printed or              G.F. B.B.T.
impressed marks               printed
include full name

246

Breeze & Son, John
1805–12, pottery & porcelain
(other potters of this
name were operating from
late 18th century to *c.* 1826)

BREEZE
incised or
painted

British Pottery Ltd.
1920–26, earthenware

mark printed

Brougham & Mayer
1853–5, earthenware

BROUGHAM &
MAYER
printed

Brownhills Pottery Co.
1872–96, earthenware

B.P. CO.
printed or impressed

printed marks of
*c.* 1880–96

Butterfield, W. & J.
1854–61, earthenware

W. & J.B.
printed

Challinor, Edward
1842–67, earthenware

E.C.

E. CHALLINOR
printed

Christie & Beardmore    C.B.      C.B.
1902–3, earthenware             F.

printed initials with
various backstamps

Clews & Co. Ltd., George
1906–61, earthenware
    printed 'globe' mark from
    1906, other marks all
    include full name

Clive, J. H.           CLIVE
1802–11, earthenware     impressed

Clive, Stephen    S.C.     S.C. & CO.
1875–80, earthenware     printed

Colley & Co. Ltd., A.
1909–14, earthenware
    mark printed or impressed

Cumberlidge & Humphreys    C. & M.
1886–9; 1893–5
earthenware            C. & M.
    marks printed or impressed    TUNSTALL

Dean & Sons, Ltd., T.
1879–1947, earthenware
    printed 1896–1947

1937–47

Eardley & Hammersley
1862–6, earthenware

E. & H.
printed

Edge & Grocott
*c.* 1830, earthenware
figures

EDGE & GROCOTT

Elsmore & Forster
1853–71, general ceramics

ELSMORE & FORSTER
printed with
variety of backstamps

Elsmore & Son, T.
1872–87, earthenware

ELSMORE & SON
ENGLAND

Emberton, William
1851–69, earthenware

W.E.
printed

Emberton, T. I. & J.
1869–82, earthenware

T.I. & J.E.
printed

Ford, Challinor & Co.   F.C.
1865–80, earthenware

F.C. & CO.
initials used with
various printed
marks

Gater & Co., Thomas
1885–94 (at Burslem)
earthenware

G.H. & CO.
later printed initials

Gater, Hall & Co.
1895–1943, earthenware
  printed mark of 1914–

printed mark from 1914–
(firm moved to Burslem
in 1907). Taken over
by:
Barratt's of Staffordshire
1943–. Some former
    marks continued:

    other marks include
    full name of Barratt's.
    'Delphatic' from 1957
(Barratt's now member of the manufacturing
division of G.U.S. Ltd.)

Gem Pottery Ltd.
1961–, earthenware
    printed mark

printed

Goodfellow, Thomas
1828–59, earthenware

T. GOODFELLOW
printed

Grenville Pottery Ltd.
1946–, earthenware

Grindley & Co. Ltd., W. H.
1880–, earthenware
    printed mark to 1914
    ('England' included from 1891)

printed from 1914–25
'Ltd.' included from 1925
other marks include full
name of firm

modern printed mark

(W. H. Grindley & Co.
now a subsidiary of
Alfred Clough Ltd.)

Grindley Hotel Ware Co. Ltd.
1908–, earthenware
mark printed from *c.* 1946–

Hall, Ralph
1822–49, earthenware
  printed in backstamp
  1822–41                R. HALL
  *c.* 1836           R. HALL & SON

  1841–49           R. HALL & CO.

                   R.H. & CO.

Heath & Co., Joseph      J. HEATH
1828–41, earthenware    printed

Heath, Joseph        J. HEATH & CO.
1845–53, earthenware    printed
  Note: the letter 'J' is   J.H. & CO.
  often printed as 'I'    printed

251

Holland, John                                J. HOLLAND
1852–4, earthenware                           printed

Hollingshead & Kirkham      H. & K.          H. & K.
1870–1956, earthenware                        TUNSTALL
  1870–1900                   printed or impressed

  mark of 1890 after                    H. & K.
  take-over of Wedgwood            LATE WEDGWOOD
  & Co.                                 impressed

  printed mark, 1900–24

TRADE     MARK

  later marks all include
  name or initials of
  firm                      HOLLINSHEAD & KIRKHAM
                                  TUNSTALL
                                  ENGLAND

Ingleby & Co., Thomas                    T.I. & CO.
*c.* 1834–5, earthenware                  printed

Keele Street Pottery Co.                   K.S.P.
1915–, earthenware
  other later printed marks include full name

Keeling, Anthony & Enoch    A. & E. KEELING
*c.* 1795–1811, general ceramics

                            A.E. KEELING

Kirkland & Co. (Etruria)                 K. & CO.
1892–, earthenware
  printed on various                     K. & CO.
  backstamps                                E

other various printed marks include full name
of Kirkland & Co. or K. & Co./E.

'Kirklands (Etruria Ltd.)'
from *c.* 1938, printed
'Kirklands (Staffordshire)
Ltd.' from *c.* 1947

Knapper & Blackhurst  KNAPPER AND
1867–71, earthenware  BLACKHURST
impressed or printed

(1883–8 at Burslem)
initials also probably used  K. & B.

Lingard Webster & Co. Ltd.
1900–, earthenware

impressed or printed from
*c.* 1946–

Maudesley & Co., J.  STONE WARE
1862–4, earthenware  J.M. & CO.
(J.M. & Co. was also
used by other firms)

Mayer & Maudesley  M. & M.
1837–8, earthenware  printed

Meakin Ltd., Alfred  ALFRED MEAKIN
1875–, earthenware  impressed or printed

'Ltd.' added in 1897
and omitted from *c.* 1930
early mark *c.* 1875–97

ALFRED MEAKIN
LTD.

Firm re-named 'Alfred
Meakin (Tunstall) Ltd.'
in *c.* 1913

printed mark from *c.* 1891
when the word 'ENGLAND'
was added

later marks include 'M. IRONSTONE'
'BLEU DE ROI', 'GLO-WHITE' and
'TRADITIONAL IRONSTONE, LEEDS'

Meir, John
*c.* 1812–36, earthenware

J.M.    I.M.
printed

Meir & Son, John
1837–97, earthenware
    initials used in various
    printed or impressed
    marks
    Date codes sometimes
    used e.g. 9 : Sept. 1875
        $\overline{75}$

J.M. & S.
        I.M. & S.
J.M. & SON

J. MEIR & SON

MEIR & SON

Pitcairns Ltd.
1895–1901, earthenware
    printed mark

Podmore, Walker & Co.              P.W. & CO.
1834–59, earthenware              printed in various
                                  backstamps

Podmore, Walker &                 P.W. & W.
Wedgwood, *c.* 1856–9
    various printed marks         WEDGWOOD
    included the confusing,
    name of 'Wedgwood'            WEDGWOOD & CO.
    Enoch Wedgwood being
    a partner. Name of firm changed to
Wedgwood & Co. in *c.* 1860

Rathbone, Smith & Co.             R.S. & CO.
1883–97, earthenware              printed
then:
Smith & Binnall
1897–1900, earthenware
    printed
then:
Soho Pottery, Ltd.
1901–6, earthenware
(1906–44 at Cobridge)

    other later marks include full name of
    firm and various trade-names, e.g.
    'SOLIAN WARE', 'AMBASSADOR WARE',
    'QUEENS GREEN', 'CHANTICLEER' and
    'HOMESTEAD', etc.
then:
Simpsons (Potters) Ltd.
1944–, earthenware
(at Cobridge)

Simpsons (Potters) Ltd. of Cobridge continue
to use many of the Soho Pottery Ltd.
trade-names plus 'MARLBOROUGH',
'Ironstone' and 'CHINASTYLE'
e.g.

Rathbone & Co., T.          T.R. & CO.
1898–1923, earthenware      TUNSTALL

late printed mark:

Richardson, Albert G.       A.G.R. & Co. Ltd.
1915–34, earthenware        printed
(moved to Cobridge
in *c.* 1934)
various printed marks including trade-
name of 'Crown Ducal'

Salt Bros.                  SALT BROS.
1897–1904, earthenware      TUNSTALL
(then 'taken-over' by       ENGLAND
T. Till & Sons of           printed or impressed
Burslem)

256

Selman, J. & W.                    SELMAN
c. 1864–65, earthenware           impressed
figures

Shaw, Anthony                      ANTHONY SHAW
1851–1900, earthenware

                        A. SHAW              A. SHAW
  '& Son' added to                            BURSLEM
  mark in c. 1882–c. 98

                        SHAWS                SHAW
  '& Son' replaced by                        BURSLEM
  '& Co.' from c. 1898
Shaws taken over by A. J. Wilkinson Ltd.
in c. 1900

Simpson, William                   WILLIAM SIMPSON
late 17th- early 18th-               in slip-trailing
century, slip-trailed earthenware
(this name is also recorded at other
pottery towns in Staffs.)

Smith, Theophilus                  T. SMITH
1790–c. 97, earthenware           impressed

Smith & Binnall                    (*see* Rathbone,
1897–1900, earthenware             Smith & Co.,
                                   Tunstall)

Soho Pottery Ltd.                  (*see* Rathbone,
1901–6, earthenware                Smith & Co.,
                                   Tunstall)

257

Summerbank Pottery Ltd.    SUMMERBANK
1952–, earthenware    printed
(now Summerbank Pottery
(1970) Ltd.)    COOPERCRAFT
    MADE IN
    ENGLAND

Tunnicliff, Michael    TUNNICLIFF
1828–41, earthenware toys    TUNSTALL
and figures

Turner, Goddard & Co.    TURNER, GODDARD
1867–74, earthenware    & CO.
  'ROYAL PATENT    printed
  IRONSTONE'

Turner & Tomkinson    TURNER &
1860–72, earthenware    TOMKINSON

printed in various marks    T. & T.

Turner & Sons, G. W.    TURNERS
1873–95, earthenware
    G.W.T. & SONS
various forms of
initials used in a    G.W.T.S.
variety of backstamps
sometimes in the form    G.W.T. & S.
of a Royal Arms
'England' added in    G.T. & S.
1891

258

Walker, Thomas                    T. WALKER
1845–51, earthenware
  various printed               THOS. WALKER
  backstamps include
  name

Wedgwood & Co.               WEDGWOOD & CO.
(Enoch Wedgwood                impressed
(Tunstall) Ltd. from 1965)
  printed mark from *c.* 1862

'Ltd.' added from 1900

variety of printed marks used with the
following trade-names: 'IMPERIAL
PORCELAIN', 'WACOLWARE', 'WACOL
IMPERIAL', 'EVERWARE', 'ROYAL
TUNSTALL' and 'VITRILAIN'. From 1965
renamed Enoch Wedgwood (Tunstall) Ltd.
also producing former patterns of
Furnivals, 'Quail', 'Old Chelsea' and
'Denmark'

| | |
|---|---|
| Wood & Challinor<br>1828–43, earthenware | w. & c.<br>printed |
| Wood, Challinor & Co.<br>*c.* 1860–64, earthenware | w.c. & co.<br>printed |
| Wood & Pigott<br>1869–71, earthenware | w. & p.<br>printed |
| Wooliscroft, George<br>1851–3 : 1860–4<br>earthenware | G. WOOLISCROFT<br>or<br>G. WOOLLISCROFT |

FRESHWATER (I.o.W.)
  Island Pottery Studio
  Lester, Joe
  earthenware, 1956–
      'Freshwater' sometimes
      added to mark

printed or impressed

WHIPPINGHAM (I.o.W.)
  Isle of Wight Pottery
  Saunders, S. E., *c.* 1930–40
  earthenware
      (same monogram used at
      Carisbrooke Pottery Works, Newport, 1929–32)

## CHANNEL ISLANDS

GUERNSEY (Channel Islands)
  The Guernsey Pottery Ltd.
  red ware, studio pottery
  1961–

JERSEY (Channel Islands)            JERSEY POTTERY
  Jersey Pottery Ltd., 1946–          C.I.
  earthenware                         painted

          1946–
impressed or printed marks                1951

# ISLE OF MAN

Isle of Man Potteries, Ltd.
earthenware, 1963–

Isle of Man
    Pottery
    Handmade

## NORTHERN IRELAND

PORTADOWN (Co. Armagh)
    Wade (Ireland) Ltd., 1947–
    porcelain, industrial
    and artware
    (subsidiary of Wade
    Potteries, Ltd.)

printed

## SCOTLAND

AIRTH (Central Region)
    Dunmore Pottery Co.,
    1903–11, earthenware,
    *c.* 1860–1903
    (Dunmore Pottery)

PETER GARDNER
DUNMORE POTTERY
DUNMORE
impressed

BO'NESS (Central Region)
    McNay & Sons, Charles W.
    earthenware, 1887–1958
    'Dalmeny' trade-name

stick-on labels

Marshall & Co. Ltd., John    JOHN MARSHALL &
earthenware, 1854–99                CO.
'Ltd.' added in 1897         printed


COATBRIDGE (Strathclyde)
Crest Ceramics (Scotland)
earthenware souvenirs,
etc.


DUNOON (Strathclyde)
West Highland Pottery Co. Ltd.
earthenware, 1961–
trade-names: 'Flow' ware,
'Argyll', 'Cowal'
printed


EDINBURGH (Lothian)              JOHN MILLAR
Millar, John, 1840–82             printed
retailer only


GLASGOW (Strathclyde)              B.M. & CO.
Bayley, Murray & Co.         SARACEN POTTERY
earthenware, 1875–          printed or impressed
1900 (Saracen
Pottery Co. from *c.* 1884)

Britannia Pottery Co. Ltd.
earthenware, 1920–35
'HIAWATHA' trade-name
from *c.* 1925                  printed

Campbellfield Pottery Co. Ltd.   C.P. CO.
earthenware, 1850–1905
  'Ltd.' added *c.* 1884

printed or impressed    CAMPBELLFIELD
marks

                  C.P. CO. LTD.

printed mark of *c.* 1884–
*c.* 1905
or,
'SPRINGBURN' with thistle

Cochran & Fleming   C. & F.      C. & F.
earthenware, 1896–                   G
1920               ROYAL
            IRONSTONE CHINA

    printed

PORCELAIN OPAQUE    COCHRAN & FLEMING
GLASGOW. BRITAIN     GLASGOW BRITAIN
FLEMING              printed

Cochran & Co., R.        R.C. & CO.
general ceramics       impressed
1846–1896

Geddes & Son, John
earthenware and porcelain
*c.* 1806–27
   '& Son' added in 1824

JOHN GEDDES
Verreville
Pottery
printed

Govancroft Potteries Ltd.
pottery, 1913–
   trade-names: 'Croft',
   'Hamilton', 'Lunar'
   1913–49

CROWN      GOVAN
printed or impressed

printed 1949–

Grosvenor & Son, F.
pottery, *c.* 1869–1926

printed mark from 1879

Kennedy & Sons Ltd., Henry
stoneware, 1866–1929

Lockhart & Arthur
earthenware, 1855–64
   marks impressed or
   printed

L. & A.

LOCKHART &
ARTHUR

Lockhart & Co., David
earthenware, 1865–98

D.L. & CO.
printed

Lockhart & Sons Ltd., David
earthenware, 1898–1953
  printed in backstamps

D.L. & SONS

Murray & Co. Ltd., W. F.
pottery, 1870–98
  mark impressed or
  printed

Nautilus Porcelain Co.
porcelain, 1896–1913
  printed mark

North British Pottery
earthenware, 1869–75

J.M. CO.

printed marks          J.M. & CO.          I.M. & CO.

Port Dundas Pottery Co. Ltd.
stoneware, *c.* 1850–1932

PORT DUNDAS
GLASGOW POTTERY

  impressed or printed

Possil Pottery Co.
general ceramics,
1898–1901

printed

'Star Pottery'
stoneware and 'majolica'
1880–1907

impressed or printed

Thomson & Sons, John
*c.* 1816– late 19th century
  '& Sons' added *c.* 1866

J.T.
ANNFIELD

J.T. & SONS
GLASGOW

Williamson, John
pottery, 1844–94

WELLINGTON
POTTERY

  marks impressed or
printed

WILLIAMSON
WELLINGTON
POTTERY

GREENOCK (Strathclyde)
Clyde Pottery Co. Ltd.
earthenware, *c.* 1815–
1903
  'Ltd.' used *c.* 1857–63

CLYDE

G.C.P. CO.

GREENOCK
impressed or printed

Greenock Pottery
earthenware, *c.* 1820–
60

GREENOCK
POTTERY

  mark impressed or
printed

267

Shirley & Co., Thomas   T.S. & COY.
earthenware, *c.* 1840–57

T.S. & C.
impressed

INVERDRUIE (Highland Region)
Castlewynd Studios, Ltd.
earthenware and stoneware
trade-names, 'Castlewynd'
'Aviemore'
Started Edinburgh 1950
moved to Gifford 1954
(Castlewynd Studios
(Highland China) 1974
at Fort William)

printed

KIRKCALDY (Lothian)   R.H. & S.
Heron & Son, Robert
earthenware, *c.* 1850–
1929
Date of 1820 in mark
is that of an earlier
pottery taken over by Heron

printed

Methven & Sons, David   D.M. & S.
19th century–*c.* 1930
earthenware

METHVEN

D. METHVEN & SONS

NORTH BERWICK   Tantallon
(Lothian)   Ceramics
Tantallon Ceramics   NORTH BERWICK
earthenware, 1962–

268

PAISLEY (Strathclyde)
  Brown & Co., Robert  BROWN  PAISLEY
  earthenware, 1876–1933

  printed or impressed

PORTOBELLO (nr. Edinburgh, Lothian)
  Buchan & Co. Ltd., A. W.
  stoneware, 1867
    trade-name: 'Thistle'
    printed mark from 1949–

  Gray & Sons, Ltd., W. A.      W.A. GRAY
  pottery, *c.* 1857–1931         printed
    '& Sons' from 1870, 'Ltd.'
    from 1926

  Milne Cornwall & Co.       MILNE CORNWALL
  stoneware, *c.* 1830–40          & CO.
                                 impressed

  Rathbone & Co., Thomas       T.R. & CO.
  earthenware, *c.* 1810–45

    marks printed or          T. RATHBONE
    impressed                       P

  Scott Brothers           SCOTT BROTHERS
  earthenware, *c.* 1786–96

                      SCOTT BROS.        SCOTT
    marks impressed                      P.B.

PRESTONPANS (Lothian)      FOWLER THOMPSON
  Fowler, Thompson & Co.          & CO.
  earthenware, *c.* 1820–40   printed or impressed

| | |
|---|---|
| Gordon's Pottery earthenware, 18th century–1832 | GORDON impressed |
|     initials in printed backstamps | G.G. |
| Watson's Pottery earthenware, *c*. 1750–1840 | WATSON impressed |
|     mark of *c*. 1800–40 | WATSON & CO. printed |

# WALES

| | |
|---|---|
| CARDIFF AND SWANSEA (Glamorgan)     Primavesi & Son, F. retailers of earthenware *c*. 1850–1915 ('& Son' added *c*. 1860) | F. PRIMAVESI & SON CARDIFF Full name in a variety of marks |
| CARDIGAN (Dyfed)     Cardigan Potteries earthenware, *c*. 1875–90     printed mark | CARDIGAN POTTERIES WOODWARD & CO. CARDIGAN |
| CREIGIAU (nr. Cardiff)     Creigiau Pottery, 1947– Southcliffe, R. G. & Co. Ltd. earthenware in copper lustre traditional style | 'Creigiau'  |

LLANDUDNO (Gwynedd)      CAMBRIAN
  Cambrian Ceramic Co. Ltd.    STUDIO
  (formerly Cambrian Pottery    WARE
  Co. Ltd.), earthenware    impressed or printed
  1958–


LLANELLY (Dyfed)      G. & D.L.
  Guest & Dewsbury
  earthenware, 1877–1927      G.D.
    printed initials in        L
    backstamps

  South Wales Pottery      CHAMBERS
  earthenware, *c.* 1839–58      LLANELLY
  Chambers & Co.
  *c.* 1839–54        S.W.P.
  Coombs & Holland
  *c.* 1854–58      printed or impressed


NANTGARW (Glamorgan)
  Nantgarw China Works      **NANT-GARW**
  porcelain, 1813–14; 1817–22      **C.W.**
  Billingsley, William &      impressed
  Walker, Samuel      (painted and stencilled
    'C.W.' stands for 'China    marks used, but
    Works' (transferred to    also found on later
    Swansea in 1814 until        copies)
    1817)


SWANSEA (Glamorgan)
  Swansea Pottery, Cambrian Pottery
  *c.* 1783–1870, earthenwares
                271

*c.* 1783–, mark impressed      SWANSEA

                        CAMBRIAN POTTERY

impressed or printed        CAMBRIA
marks, *c.* 1783–1810

                   *CAMBRIAN.*

impressed or printed        DILLWYN & CO.
marks, *c.* 1811–17          SWANSEA

                     D. & CO.

impressed from *c.* 1817–24   BEVINGTON & CO.

printed from *c.* 1847–50     

impressed, *c.* 1847–50         CYMRO
                    STONE CHINA

impressed, *c.* 1824–50        DILLWYN

Evans, David & Glasson    
pottery, *c.* 1850–62
    impressed or printed

Evans, D. J. & Co.          D.J. EVANS & CO.
pottery, *c.* 1862–70

                   EVANS & CO.

272

printed, *c.* 1862–70

Swansea porcelain      SWANSEA
impressed marks, 1814–22

printed or written in red
enamel
impressed, sometimes      DILLWYN & CO.
with 'SWANSEA'

rare impressed mark      BEVINGTON & CO.
of *c.* 1820

Baker, Bevans & Irwin      BAKER BEVANS
Glamorgan Pottery      & IRWIN
earthenware, 1813–38      printed or impressed

example of printed mark

The name of Pellatt & Green, retailers
of St. Paul's Church Yard, London, is
sometimes seen on Welsh wares of *c.* 1805–30

Calland & Co., John F.
Landore Pottery
earthenware, 1852–56

C. & CO.

CALLAND SWANSEA

YNYSMEDW (nr. Swansea)
Ynysmedw Pottery
earthenware, *c*. 1850–70

Y.M.P.     Y.P.

impressed

# IRELAND

BELLEEK (Co. Fermanagh)
porcelain, 1863–
McBirney, David &
Armstrong, Robert

BELLEEK
CO. FERMANAGH

FERMANAGH
POTTERY
impressed

impressed or printed
mark of 1863–80

early version of usual
mark, 1863–91

post-1891 version
includes 'Ireland'
and 'Co. Fermanagh'
to comply with the
McKinley Tariff Act

printed

274

CORK
Carrigaline Pottery Ltd.
earthenware, 1928–

printed marks

CARRIG WARE
CARRIGALINE
POTTERY

DUBLIN
Chambers, John, *c.* 1730–
*c.* 1745
tin-glazed earthenware
inscription painted on
plate

Delamain, Captain Henry (*d.* 1757)
1752–*c.* 1771

Donovan & Son, John
decorator of English
pottery and porcelain
*c.* 1770–1829

'DONOVAN' impressed on
wares made to order

DONOVAN

*DONOVAN*
*DUBLIN*
painted

Vodrey's Pottery
earthenware, 1872–*c.* 85

VODREY DUBLIN
POTTERY

impressed

LIMERICK
  Stritch, John, *c.* 1760
  tin-glazed earthenware

Made by John Stritch
Limerick, 4th June 1761

inscription on plate

# ADDENDUM OF RECENT MANUFACTURERS, OTHER CHANGES, ETC.

**BOURNEMOUTH** (Dorset)
Purbeck Pottery Ltd.
stoneware, Dec. 1965–

   printed marks

Purbeck
Pottery
England

**BROADSTAIRS** (Kent)
Broadstairs Pottery Ltd.
stoneware, 1966–
printed mark

**BRUTON** (Somerset)
Goddard Ltd., Elaine
earthenware, 1939–

   mark printed label

**CHESTERFIELD** (Derbyshire)
Price, Powell & Co. Ltd.
earthenware, 1740–
(Ltd. from 1961)          No registered
                          trade mark
Now subsidiary of Pearsons of Chesterfield

CHURCH GRESLEY
(Derbyshire)
  Mason, Cash & Co. Ltd.
  Pool Potteries, 1901
  domestic earthenware
  (Ltd. Co. since 1941)

products
unmarked

DARTMOUTH (Devon)
  Britannia Designs, Ltd.
  earthenware, 1959
    mark an applied label
    used from 1971

ELKESLEY (Nottinghamshire)
  Aston, Christopher S.
  stoneware, 1968
  (moved to Elkesley
  from Bawtry in 1971)

applied label

FARNHAM (Surrey)
  Harris & Sons, A.
  earthenware, 1872
  (established in 1864
  at Elstead, Surrey)

No special mark
used

HINDHEAD (Surrey)
  Surrey Ceramic Co. Ltd.
  Kingswood Pottery
  earthenware and
  stoneware, 1956–

LIVERPOOL (Merseyside)
Prince William Pottery Co.
earthenware, 1953–

'PRINCE WILLIAM'

LONDON
Macbride, Kitty
(Brown & Muntzer)
earthenware figures of
mice. Trade-name:
'The Happy Mice of
Berkeley Square'
1960–

*Kitty MacBride*
*England*

PAIGNTON (Devon)
Barn Pottery, Ltd.
earthenware, 1964

Trade-name 'Barn' ware

REDRUTH (Cornwall)
Foster's Pottery Co.
earthenware, 1949–

stamped mark

FOSTER'S
POTTERY
REDRUTH

STOKE D'ABERTON (Surrey)
Everson, Ronald
porcelain and bone-china
1953
mark in the form of
a dated signature

*Ronald Everson*

279

HANLEY (Staffordshire)
  Mason's Ironstone China Ltd.
  earthenware, March 1968
  (from March 1974 name changed
  to: Mason's Ironstone, a Division
  of Josiah Wedgwood & Sons Ltd.)
    printed marks

LONGTON (Staffordshire)
  Anton Potteries, Ltd., Jon
  ironstone, 1974–
  (pottery established
  *c.* 1874, 'Crown Clarence'
  from *c.* 1953–1971
  Jon Anton Potteries
  1971–74)

    mark on bone-china

Blyth Pottery (Longton) Ltd.
earthenware (taken over by John Tams Ltd.
in April, 1973 and no longer trading on own
account)

LONGTON (Staffordshire)
Hostess Tableware
Thomas Poole &
Gladstone China Ltd.
'Royal Stafford' and
'Hostess' bone china
and 'Hostess' ironstone
1971–

Hostess Tableware

FINE BONE CHINA
STAFFS, ENGLAND

& other full marks

Royal Albert Ltd.
(Royal Doulton Tableware
Ltd.) Ltd. added 1970
bone-china
'Royal Albert' previously
used by Thomas C.
Wild & Sons Ltd.

printed

Royal Grafton Bone China
(A. B. Jones & Sons, Ltd.
part of Crown Lynn Potteries
Group, N.Z. from 1971–)
bone-china from 1959–

Royal Tuscan
bone-china, *c.* 1962–
(Division of Wedgwood
Group from 1966)

281

STOKE (Staffordshire)
Baifield Productions Ltd.
(S. Fielding & Co. Ltd., Crown
Devon Group), 1963–

Blakeney Art Pottery
earthenware, 1968–
'Flow Blue Victoria'
printed ware, Kent
Staffordshire figures
and floral art containers.
M. J. Bailey & S. K. Bailey
Note the lion and harp
in coat-of-arms are in
reverse positions to the
authentic version

printed
backstamps in
blue

Similar Royal
Arms mark used,
with 'Romantic'
pattern

Blakeney Art Pottery (*cont.*)

printed backstamp
in brown 'M.J.B.'
(Michael J. Bailey)

IRONSTONE
STAFFORDSHIRE
ENGLAND

similar backstamp
used with:
FLO BLUE
T.M. STAFFORDSHIRE
ENGLAND

FLO BLUE
T.M. STAFFORDSHIRE
ENGLAND

Dorothy Ann Floral China
bone china floral
jewellery, 1946

STOKE ON TRENT
ENGLAND

TUNSTALL (Staffordshire)
Wedgwood (Tunstall) Ltd., Enoch
name changed from Wedgwood & Co. Ltd.
in 1965 (see p. 259)

# APPENDIX A

# Patent Office Registration Mark

From 1842 until 1883 many manufacturers' wares are marked with the following 'diamond-mark', which is an indication that the design was registered with the British Patent Office; ceramics and glass are Classes IV and III, as indicated in the topmost section of the mark, and gave copyright protection for a period of three years (see Appendix B and Preface, page 11).

The date of the 'diamond mark' only indicates the time of registration, but a popular form of decoration was often produced for far longer than the three years. Printed marks usually refer to the applied pattern, whereas impressed or moulded applied versions are more likely to relate to the form of the ware.

When checking date to determine the name of the manufacturer it will sometimes be the case that the design was registered by retailers, wholesalers or even foreign manufacturers.

'Diamond-marks' impressed into bone-china can often be more accurately read when held before a strong artificial light.

Example of ceramic
design registered on
23rd May 1842

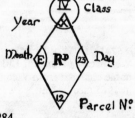

*Index to letters for each year and month from 1842 to 1867:*

Years

| | | | |
|---|---|---|---|
| 1842 X | 1849 S | 1856 L | 1863 G |
| 1843 H | 1850 V | 1857 K | 1864 N |
| 1844 C | 1851 P | 1858 B | 1865 W |
| 1845 A | 1852 D | 1859 M | 1866 Q |
| 1846 I | 1853 Y | 1860 Z | 1867 T |
| 1847 F | 1854 J | 1861 R | |
| 1848 U | 1855 E | 1862 O | |

Months

| | | | | |
|---|---|---|---|---|
| January | C | July | I | |
| February | G | August | R | } For September 1857 |
| March | W | September | D | query letter R used |
| April | H | October | B | from 1st–19th Sept. |
| May | E | November | K | } For December 1860 |
| June | M | December | A | query letter K used. |

*Index to letters for each year and month from 1868 to 1883:*

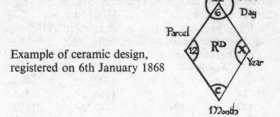

Example of ceramic design,
registered on 6th January 1868

285

*Years*

| 1868 X | 1872 I | 1876 V | 1880 J |
| 1869 H | 1873 F | 1877 P | 1881 E |
| 1870 C | 1874 U | 1878 D | 1882 L |
| 1871 A | 1875 S | 1879 Y | 1883 K |

*Months*

| Jan. C | April H | July I | Oct. B |
| Feb. G | May E | Aug. R | Nov. K |
| Mar. W | June M | Sept. D | Dec. A |

For Registration marks brought in with W for the year, see below:

From 1st to 6th March, 1878, the following Registration Mark was issued:

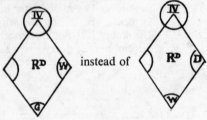

instead of

From 1884 this method of dating registrations ceased and the designs were numbered consecutively in the following manner: 'Rd. 12345' or 'Rd. No. 12345'. The following table gives a guide up until 1910 to the range of numbers used within a year:

| Registered in January | | Registered in January | |
|---|---|---|---|
| 1 | 1884 | 90483 | 1888 |
| 19734 | 1885 | 116648 | 1889 |
| 40480 | 1886 | 141273 | 1890 |
| 64520 | 1887 | 163767 | 1891 |

| | | | |
|---|---|---|---|
| 185713 | 1892 | 368154 | 1901 |
| 205240 | 1893 | 385500 | 1902 |
| 224720 | 1894 | 402500 | 1903 |
| 246975 | 1895 | 420000 | 1904 |
| 268392 | 1896 | 447000 | 1905 |
| 291241 | 1897 | 471000 | 1906 |
| 311658 | 1898 | 494000 | 1907 |
| 331707 | 1899 | 519500 | 1908 |
| 351202 | 1900 | 550000 | 1909 |

Information concerning the work of the full members of the Craftsmen Potters Association (modern studio-potters) is well provided by an excellent directory, *Potters*, where the full particulars, including the mark and an illustration of the ware of 138 potters, are given. This directory may be obtained from the Craftsmen Potters Shop, William Blake House, Marshall Street, London, W.1., price 75p, plus postage.

The part of the Class IV Design Index in the Public Record Office that relates to pottery and porcelain is included in Appendix B, pages 288 to 392.

## APPENDIX B

# Index of Names and Dates of Manufacturers, Retailers, Wholesalers and others who registered designs from 1842 to 1883

**(See Appendix A, page 284, and Preface, page 12)**

| Date | Parcel No. | Patent No. | Factory, Retailer Wholesaler, etc | Place |
|------|------------|------------|-----------------------------------|-------|
| **1842** | | | | |
| Sept 22 | 1 | 1694 | James Dixon & Sons | Sheffield |
| Nov  2 | 1 | 2152 | Joseph Wolstenholme | Sheffield |
|       3 | 1 | 2163 | idem | Sheffield |
|      26 | 3 | 2503–4 | Henry Hunt | London |
| Dec  2 | 3 | 2599–00 | Joseph Clementson | Shelton |
|      30 | 2 | 3346 | James Edwards | Burslem |
| **1843** | | | | |
| Jan 24 | 2 | 4296–7 | John Ridgway & Co. | Shelton |
| Feb  3 | 4 | 4462 | T. Woodfield | London |
|      21 | 1 | 5266–70 | Samuel Alcock & Co. | Burslem |
| Mar 21 | 5 | 5993–4 | Josiah Wedgwood & Sons | Etruria |
|      31 | 6 | 6266 | Samuel Alcock & Co. | Burslem |
| May  2 | 4 | 6978 | Josiah Wedgwood & Sons | Etruria |
|       5 | 1 | 7037 | W. S. Kennedy | Burslem |
|      11 | 2 | 7074 | idem | Burslem |
|      13 | 4 | 7122 | Jones & Walley | Cobridge |
| June 14 | 5 | 7503–5 | Samuel Alcock & Co. | Burslem |
| Aug 30 | 8 | 9678–80 | James Edwards | Burslem |
| Oct  6 | 2 | 10370 | idem | Burslem |
| Nov 10 | 3 | 11292 | Minton & Co. | Stoke |
|      28 | 5 | 11690 | Thos. Dimmock & Co. | Shelton |
| Dec 14 | 10 | 12331 | G. F. Bowers & Co. | Tunstall |

| Date | Parcel No. | Patent No. | Factory, Retailer Wholesaler, etc | Place |
|------|-----------|-----------|-----------------------------------|-------|
| **1844** | | | | |
| Feb 15 | 9 | 16264–5 | Samuel Alcock & Co. | Burslem |
| 20 | 4 | 16374–5 | idem | Burslem |
| Mar 1 | 6 | 16687 | Hamilton & Moore | Longton |
| 5 | 3 | 16831 | Mellor, Venables & Co. | Burslem |
| 7 | 4 | 16871 | J. & T. Lockett | Lane End |
| Apr 3 | 3 | 17566–72 | Thos. Edwards | Burslem |
| 11 | 4 | 17714 | Hilditch & Hopwood | Lane End |
| May 7 | 4 | 18207 | Thos. Dimmock & Co. | Shelton |
| June 29 | 3 | 19182 | idem | Shelton |
| July 20 | 5 | 19977–9 | John Ridgway & Co. | Shelton |
| 30 | 2 | 20332–4 | Herbert Minton & Co. | Stoke |
| Aug 15 | 3 | 20779 | King, Knight & Elkin | Stoke |
| 21 | 7 | 21069–73 | Herbert Minton & Co. | Stoke |
| Sept 9 | 7 | 21450 | Cyples, Barlow & Cyples | Lane End |
| 19 | 4 | 21700–1 | Jn. Ridgeway & Co. | Shelton |
| 21 | 2 | 21715 | Henry Hunt | London |
| 30 | 7 | 21960 | Charles Meigh | Hanley |
| Oct 14 | 4 | 22158 | Copeland & Garrett | Stoke |
| 17 | 3 | 22192 | Clementson, Young & Jameson | Shelton |
| 30 | 4 | 22394–6 | Herbert Minton & Co. | Stoke |
| Nov 6 | 4 | 22424 | idem | Stoke |
| 11 | 5 | 22490 | James Edwards | Burslem |
| 13 | 4 | 22499–500 | John Ridgway & Co. | Shelton |
| 22 | 4 | 22834 | Thos. Dimmock & Co. | Shelton |
| 26 | 3 | 22883 | Ray & Wynne | Longton |
| Dec 2 | 3 | 22919–20 | Copeland & Garrett | Stoke |
| 7 | 4 | 23207–10 | Thos. Edwards | Burslem |
| 16 | 6 | 23593 | Willm. Ridgway, Son & Co. | Hanley |
| 24 | 2 | 23843 | John Meir & Son | Tunstall |
| **1845** | | | | |
| Jan 11 | 6 | 24846 | George Phillips | Longport |

# APPENDIX B

| Date | Parcel No. | Patent No. | Factory, Retailer Wholesaler, etc | Place |
|------|------|------|------|------|
| 15 | 2 | 24996 | Clementson, Young & Jameson | Shelton |
| 21 | 6 | 25199 | T. J. & J. Mayer | Longport |
| 27 | 5 | 25273 | John Rose & Co. | Coalport |
| Feb 26 | 5 | 26532–3 | W. S. Kennedy | Burslem |
| 27 | 3 | 26543 | George Phillips | Longport |
| Mar 5 | 1 | 26608 | Copeland & Garrett | Stoke |
| 6 | 5 | 26617 | Herbert Minton & Co. | Stoke |
| 17 | 10 | 26939 | idem | Stoke |
| 20 | 1 | 26949 | idem | Stoke |
| 31 | 4 | 27034 | Thos. Pearce | London |
| Apr 10 | 1 | 27202 | idem | London |
| 25 | 2 | 27350 | Copeland & Garrett | Stoke |
| 26 | 1 | 27352 | George Pearce | London |
| 26 | 3 | 27354 | T. & R. Boote, Walley & Jones | Burslem, Cobridge and Hanley |
| 30 | 2 | 27383 | Jacob Furnival & Co. | Cobridge |
| May 8 | 2 | 27451 | Herbert Minton & Co. | Stoke |
| 10 | 3 | 27482 | Walley & T. & R. Boote | Cobridge and Burslem |
| 31 | 1 | 27800 | Francis Morley | Shelton |
| June 19 | 1 | 28150 | George Phillips | Longport |
| 26 | 3 | 28296 | Minton & Co. | Stoke |
| July 5 | 1 | 28668–71 | George Phillips | Longport |
| 5 | 2 | 28672 | Enoch Wood | Burslem |
| 26 | 1 | 29173 | William Adams & Sons | Stoke |
| Aug 28 | 3 | 29993 | Joseph Clementson | Shelton |
| Sept 4 | 3 | 30161–3 | Copeland & Garrett | Stoke |
| 11 | 2 | 30286 | Thos. Phillips & Son | Burslem |
| 19 | 1 | 30383 | Minton & Co. | Stoke |
| Oct 6 | 1 | 30543–4 | H. Minton & Co. | Stoke |
| 21 | 1 | 30699 | Copeland & Garrett | Stoke |

# APPENDIX B

| Date | Parcel No. | Patent No. | Factory, Retailer Wholesaler, etc | Place |
|------|------------|------------|-----------------------------------|-------|
| 22 | 2 | 30701 | Clementson & Young | Shelton |
| Nov 15 | 2 | 31128 | Bayley & Ball | Longton |
| 22 | 2 | 31329 | Minton & Co. | Stoke |
| Dec 4 | 4 | 31670–3 | John Ridgway | Shelton |
| 27 | 2 | 32553 | James Edwards | Burslem |
| 29 | 2 | 32555 | Joseph Clementson | Shelton |
| 30 | 3 | 32601 | Furnival & Clark | Hanley |
| **1846** | | | | |
| Jan 7 | 2 | 32698 | Joseph Clementson | Shelton |
| 24 | 2 | 33319 | Jacob Furnival & Co. | Cobridge |
| Feb 26 | 5 | 34031 | T. J. & J. Mayer | Longport |
| Mar 2 | 4 | 34108 | Minton & Co. | Stoke |
| 11 | 2 | 34281–5 | W. S. Kennedy | Burslem |
| Apr 7 | 1 | 34564–66 | idem | Burslem |
| 17 | 3 | 34684 | Copeland & Garrett | Stoke |
| May 21 | 3 | 35030–1 | H. Minton & Co. | Stoke |
| 26 | 2 | 35116–7 | idem | Stoke |
| June 6 | 1 | 35219 | W. Chamberlain & Co. | Worcester |
| 26 | 2 | 35777 | H. Minton & Co. | Stoke |
| 30 | 3 | 35795 | John Goodwin | Longton |
| July 11 | 1 | 36047 | J. K. Knight | Longton |
| 16 | 1 | 36167 | Ridgway, Son & Co. | Hanley |
| 17 | 1 | 36263 | John Ridgway & Co. | Shelton |
| 21 | 1 | 36278 | F. Morley & Co. | Shelton |
| Aug 1 | 2 | 36447–8 | Josiah Wedgwood & Sons | Etruria |
| 3 | 1 | 36450 | idem | Etruria |
| 3 | 2 | 36451–2 | H. Minton & Co. | Stoke |
| Sept 3 | 2 | 37170 | G. Phillips | Longport |
| 3 | 3 | 37171–2 | F. Morley & Co. | Shelton |
| 14 | 4 | 37254 | Copeland & Garrett | Stoke |
| 26 | 2 | 37419–21 | John Ridgway & Co. | Shelton |
| 29 | 3 | 37586 | T. J. & J. Mayer | Longport |
| Oct 26 | 1 | 37806 | F. Morley & Co. | Shelton |
| 26 | 5 | 37864 | J. Edwards | Burslem |

| Date | Parcel No. | Patent No. | Factory, Retailer Wholesaler, etc | Place |
|---|---|---|---|---|
| Nov 3 | 1 | 37935 | Ridgway & Abington | Hanley |
| 5 | 2 | 37986 | G. Phillips | Longport |
| 12 | 3 | 38068 | C. Meigh | Hanley |
| 16 | 2 | 38113 | H. Minton & Co. | Stoke |
| 21 | 2 | 38291–2 | Thos. Furnival & Co. | Hanley |
| Dec 3 | 4 | 38606 | Ridgway & Abington | Hanley |
| 4 | 2 | 38610 | H. Minton & Co. | Stoke |
| 10 | 3 | 38786 | Joseph Clementson | Shelton |
| 14 | 3 | 39480 | James Edwards | Burslem |
| 14 | 4 | 39481 | Minton & Co. | Stoke |
| 16 | 1 | 39519 | John Goodwin | Longton |
| 17 | 2 | 39544–5 | Copeland & Garrett | Stoke |
| 26 | 5 | 39614 | Henry Hunt | London |
| 29 | 2 | 39703 | Edward Challinor | Tunstall |
| 31 | 3 | 39746 | Josiah Wedgwood & Sons | Etruria |
| **1847** | | | | |
| Jan 9 | 4 | 40104–5 | John Ridgway & Co. | Shelton |
| 9 | 7 | 40110 | Copeland & Garrett | Stoke |
| Feb 2 | 7 | 41213 | T. & R. Boote | Burslem |
| 8 | 5 | 41266–7 | T. J. & J. Mayer | Longton |
| 15 | 4 | 41459–60 | Copeland & Garrett | Stoke |
| Mar 17 | 3 | 42044 | John Wedge Wood | Tunstall |
| 17 | 6 | 42047–8 | John Ridgway & Co. | Shelton |
| 22 | 2 | 42233 | Bailey & Ball | Longton |
| 23 | 7 | 42279 | Herbert Minton & Co. | Stoke |
| 30 | 1 | 42363 | James Edwards | Burslem |
| Apr 3 | 6 | 42435 | Samuel Alcock & Co. | Burslem |
| 27 | 1 | 42804 | idem | Burslem |
| May 12 | 4 | 43154 | Copeland & Garrett | Stoke |
| 14 | 1 | 43170–1 | Herbert Minton & Co. | Stoke |
| June 11 | 4 | 43536 | James Edwards | Burslem |
| 11 | 6 | 43557 | Joseph Alexander | Norwich |
| 21 | 5 | 43728 | John Rose & Co. | Coalport |
| 25 | 2 | 43780 | James Edwards | Burslem |

## APPENDIX B

| Date | Parcel No. | Patent No. | Factory, Retailer Wholesaler, etc | Place |
|------|------------|------------|-----------------------------------|-------|
| July 5 | 5 | 43916–7 | Mellor, Venables & Co. | Burslem |
| 15 | 1 | 44014–5 | idem | Burslem |
| 16 | 5 | 44036–9 | James Edwards | Burslem |
| 27 | 3 | 44398 | T. J. & J. Mayer | Longport |
| Aug 3 | 3 | 44872 | John Rose & Co. | Coalport |
| 16 | 2 | 45088 | James Edwards | Burslem |
| 17 | 2 | 45091–2 | W. T. Copeland | Stoke |
| 19 | 3 | 45175 | H. Minton & Co. | Stoke |
| 26 | 2 | 45367 | James Edwards | Burslem |
| Sept 9 | 3 | 45730 | William Taylor Copeland | Stoke |
| 16 | 3 | 45822 | idem | Stoke |
| 25 | 5 | 45992 | John Wedge Wood | Tunstall |
| Oct 1 | 4 | 46130 | Thos. Peake | Tunstall |
| 2 | 5 | 46192–4 | John Ridgway & Co. | Shelton |
| 4 | 3 | 46232 | H. Minton & Co. | Stoke |
| 8 | 4 | 46265 | John Wedge Wood | Tunstall |
| 13 | 1 | 46299 | W. T. Copeland | Stoke |
| 23 | 2 | 46516–8 | H. Minton & Co. | Stoke |
| 27 | 1 | 46529 | John Ridgway & Co. | Shelton |
| Nov 11 | 4 | 46886 | H. Minton & Co. | Stoke |
| 23 | 4 | 47183 | J. Wedgwood & Co. | Etruria |
| Dec 1 | 2 | 47417–20 | John Rose & Co. | Coalport |
| 10 | 3 | 47562–3 | Minton & Co. & John Bell | Stoke |
| 15 | 4 | 48130 | Minton & Co. | Stoke |
| **1848** | | | | |
| Jan 1 | 4 | 48540–2 | Barker & Till | Burslem |
| 6 | 4 | 48717 | Geo. Grainger | Worcester |
| 18 | 2 | 49040 | W. T. Copeland | Stoke |
| Feb 11 | 3 | 49780–1 | H. Minton & Co. | Stoke |
| 29 | 12 | 50473 | Minton & Co. | Stoke |
| Mar 4 | 4 | 50549 | Minton & Co. | Stoke |
| 7 | 1 | 50635–6 | Ridgway & Abington | Hanley |
| 14 | 2 | 50798 | W. T. Copeland | Stoke |
| 15 | 2 | 50803 | idem | Stoke |

| Date | Parcel No. | Patent No. | Factory, Retailer Wholesaler, etc | Place |
|------|-----------|-----------|------------------------------------|-------|
| 20 | 7 | 50994 | Wood & Brownfield | Cobridge |
| 27 | 8 | 51185–91 | J. & S. Alcock Jnr. | Cobridge |
| Apr 15 | 4 | 51542 | John Ridgway & Co. | Shelton |
| 17 | 6 | 51599 | Frederick Harrison | London |
| 22 | 3 | 51661 | Josiah Wedgwood & Sons | Etruria |
| 27 | 4 | 51763 | idem | Etruria |
| 28 | 5 | 51768 | Giovanni Franchi | London |
| May 30 | 3 | 52162 | Thos. Peake | Tunstall |
| June 20 | 4 | 52402 | G. F. Bowers & Co. | Tunstall |
| 30 | 2 | 52529 | W. T. Copeland | Stoke |
| 30 | 3 | 52530 | Ridgway & Abington | Hanley |
| Aug 10 | 3 | 53782 | Geo. Grainger | Worcester |
| 16 | 8 | 53876 | Thos. Pinder | Burslem |
| 23 | 2 | 54018 | John Wedge Wood | Tunstall |
| 26 | 2 | 54067 | John Meir & Son | Tunstall |
| Sept 15 | 3 | 54438 | W. T. Copeland | Stoke |
| 18 | 4 | 54487 | Charles Meigh | Hanley |
| 25 | 4 | 54578–9 | Giovanni Franchi | London |
| 30 | 7 | 54662 | John Ridgway & Co. | Shelton |
| Oct 17 | 3 | 54901 | T. & R. Boote | Burslem |
| Nov 4 | 2 | 55174 | W. T. Copeland | Stoke |
| 13 | 4 | 55337 | idem | Stoke |
| 21 | 5 | 55456–7 | Minton & Co. | Stoke |
| 27 | 2 | 55766 | John Ridgway & Co. | Shelton |
| Dec 16 | 3 | 56631–3 | James Edwards | Burslem |
| 28 | 2 | 56845 | John Ridgway | Shelton |
| **1849** | | | | |
| Jan 3 | 2 | 56978 | William Adams & Sons | Stoke |
| 20 | 2 | 57506–8 | W. Davenport & Co. | Longport |
| Feb 2 | 4 | 58069 | Mellor, Venables & Co. | Burslem |
| 16 | 5 | 58461 | Minton & Co. | Stoke |
| 16 | 11 | 58474 | Ridgway & Abington | Hanley |
| 26 | 2 | 58578 | John Rose & Co. | Coalport |
| Mar 13 | 2 | 58874 | Joseph Clementson | Shelton |

| Date | Parcel No. | Patent No. | Factory, Retailer Wholesaler, etc | Place |
|------|------------|------------|-----------------------------------|-------|
| 26 | 5 | 59232 | Minton & Co. | Stoke |
| 27 | 2 | 59245 | Cope & Edwards | Longton |
| 31 | 2 | 59286 | John Ridgway & Co. | Shelton |
| Apr 2 | 5 | 59308 | Podmore, Walker & Co. | Tunstall |
| 10 | 4 | 59400 | W. T. Copeland | Stoke |
| 16 | 6 | 59571 | C. J. Mason | Longton |
| May 24 | 1 | 60081 | Mr. Wedge Wood | Tunstall |
| June 7 | 3 | 60265 | T. J. & J. Mayer | Longport |
| July 16 | 2 | 61347 | Ridgway & Abington | Hanley |
| Aug 11 | 4 | 61865 | W. T. Copeland | Stoke |
| 15 | 2 | 61986 | H. Minton & Co. | Stoke |
| 17 | 2 | 62003 | W. T. Copeland | Stoke |
| 27 | 5 | 62316 | Mellor, Venables & Co. | Burslem |
| Sept 14 | 6 | 62498 | F. & R. Pratt & Co. | Fenton |
| 28 | 6 | 62690–4 | J. Ridgway | Shelton |
| Oct 10 | 2 | 62883 | idem | Shelton |
| 12 | 4 | 62914 | Minton & Co. | Stoke |
| 26 | 5 | 63267 | J. Hollinshead | Shelton |
| Nov 8 | 6 | 63490 | John Cliff Quince | London |
| 9 | 4 | 63523 | W. T. Copeland | Stoke |
| 17 | 2 | 63718 | Minton & Co. | Stoke |
| 22 | 2 | 64319 | W. T. Copeland | Stoke |
| 30 | 5 | 64627 | John Rose & Co. | Coalport |
| Dec 6 | 3 | 64739 | W. T. Copeland | Stoke |
| 15 | 4 | 64982 | T. J. & J. Mayer | Longport |
| **1850** | | | | |
| Jan 3 | 1 | 65884 | W. Davenport & Co. | Longport |
| 14 | 4 | 66266–7 | J. Ridgway | Shelton |
| 26 | 6 | 66862 | G. Grainger | Worcester |
| Feb 13 | 1 | 67398 | idem | Worcester |
| 13 | 3 | 67413 | J. & M. P. Bell & Co. | Glasgow |
| 27 | 4 | 67783 | G. Grainger | Worcester |
| Mar 9 | 3 | 67987 | W. T. Copeland | Stoke |
| 30 | 9 | 68489 | John Rose & Co. | Coalport |

# APPENDIX B

| Date | Parcel No. | Patent No. | Factory, Retailer Wholesaler, etc | Place |
|------|------|------|------|------|
| Apr 4 | 4 | 68623 | T. J. & J. Mayer | Longport |
| 8 | 1 | 68720 | J. Clementson | Shelton |
| 13 | 7 | 68797 | Minton & Co. | Stoke |
| 18 | 11 | 68959 | John Rose & Co. | Coalport |
| 24 | 3 | 69142 | William Pierce | London |
| 25 | 3 | 69149 | Minton & Co. | Stoke |
| June 4 | 1 | 69679 | J. & M. P. Bell & Co. | Glasgow |
| 5 | 3 | 69685 | Barker & Son | Burslem |
| 21 | 4 | 69884 | E. Walley | Cobridge |
| July 2 | 2 | 70088 | T. J. & J. Mayer | Longport |
| 16 | 5 | 70364 | C. & W. K. Harvey | Longton |
| Sept 9 | 5 | 71843 | Thomas Till | Burslem |
| 16 | 8 | 71952 | J. & M. P. Bell & Co. | Glasgow |
| 16 | 9 | 71953–4 | J. Ridgway | Shelton |
| 19 | 2 | 71989 | W. T. Copeland | Stoke |
| 21 | 1 | 72057 | Mellor, Venables & Co. | Burslem |
| Oct 9 | 2 | 72395–6 | Minton & Co. | Stoke |
| 17 | 6 | 72544 | W. T. Copeland | Stoke |
| Nov 4 | 4 | 73327 | J. Wedgwood & Sons | Etruria |
| 20 | 7 | 73693 | F. Morley & Co. | Shelton |
| 22 | 3 | 73719 | John Rose & Co. | Coalport |
| Dec 5 | 3 | 74138 | F. Morley & Co. | Shelton |
| 19 | 5 | 74785 | John Rose & Co. | Coalport |
| 19 | 6 | 74786 | T. J. & J. Mayer | Longport |
| 20 | 6 | 75148 | W. T. Copeland | Stoke |
| **1851** | | | | |
| Jan 20 | 4 | 75883–4 | James Green | London |
| Feb 10 | 9 | 76664 | William Brownfield | Cobridge |
| Mar 17 | 13 | 77481–91 | J. Ridgway & Co. | Shelton |
| 31 | 4 | 77986 | J. & M. P. Bell & Co. | Glasgow |
| Apr 9 | 2 | 78268 | Thos. Till & Son | Burslem |
| 11 | 4 | 78309–10 | J. & M. P. Bell & Co. | Glasgow |
| 11 | 6 | 78312 | W. S. Kennedy | Burslem |
| 14 | 7 | 78398–401 | J. & M. P. Bell & Co. | Glasgow |

# APPENDIX B

| Date | Parcel No. | Patent No. | Factory, Retailer Wholesaler, etc | Place |
|------|-----------|-----------|-----------------------------------|-------|
| 26 | 3 | 78634 | E. Walley | Cobridge |
| May 30 | 4 | 79085 | W. T. Copeland | Stoke |
| June 7 | 4 | 79164 | J. Ridgway & Co. | Shelton |
| 11 | 2 | 79183 | W. T. Copeland | Stoke |
| 11 | 3 | 79184 | Ralph Scragg | Hanley |
| 19 | 5 | 79300 | W. T. Copeland | Stoke |
| July 10 | 3 | 79588 | R. Britton & Co. | Leeds |
| 14 | 3 | 79684 | W. T. Copeland | Stoke |
| 21 | 7 | 79750–3 | T. & R. Boote | Burslem |
| 24 | 2 | 79782 | Thos. Till & Son | Burslem |
| 26 | 3 | 79802 | C. Collinson & Co. | Burslem |
| Aug 16 | 2 | 80184 | Ridgway & Abington | Hanley |
| Sept 2 | 4 | 80365 | T. J. & J. Mayer | Longport |
| 19 | 3 | 80629–30 | T. & R. Boote | Burslem |
| 29 | 4 | 80815–16 | James Edwards | Burslem |
| 30 | 3 | 80826 | idem | Burslem |
| Oct 1 | 1 | 80827 | W. T. Copeland | Stoke |
| 7 | 3 | 80887 | Chamberlain & Co. | Worcester |
| 10 | 4 | 80910–1 | W. Brownfield | Cobridge |
| 10 | 6 | 80913 | T. & R. Boote | Burslem |
| 14 | 4 | 80980 | Thos. Till & Son | Burslem |
| 16 | 4 | 80989 | W. Brownfield | Cobridge |
| 17 | 3 | 80997 | George Bowden Sander | London |
| 21 | 3 | 81057 | Wm. Ridgway | Shelton |
| Nov 1 | 5 | 81225–6 | Geo. B. Sander | London |
| 10 | 4 | 81492 | Ralph Scragg | Hanley |
| 12 | 6 | 81510–12 | Minton & Co. | Stoke |
| 13 | 2 | 81518 | Charles Meigh & Son | Hanley |
| 14 | 4 | 81558 | Geo. B. Sander | London |
| Dec 2 | 2 | 81815 | T. J. & J. Mayer | Burslem |
| 4 | 3 | 81843–4 | Minton & Co. | Stoke |
| 5 | 5 | 81864 | John Ridgway & Co. | Shelton |
| 8 | 8 | 81960 | W. T. Copeland | Stoke |
| 15 | 6 | 82052 | Geo. B. Sander | London |

# APPENDIX B

| Date | Parcel No. | Patent No. | Factory, Retailer Wholesaler, etc | Place |
|---|---|---|---|---|
| **1852** | | | | |
| Jan 27 | 1 | 83342 | W. & G. Harding | Burslem |
| Feb 17 | 1 | 83826 | Venables & Baines | Burslem |
| Mar 4 | 2 | 84133–4 | Wm. Brownfield | Cobridge |
| 13 | 3 | 84239 | Wm. Ridgway | Shelton |
| 22 | 7 | 84385 | Ralph Scragg | Hanley |
| 24 | 3 | 84406 | James Edwards | Burslem |
| 24 | 4 | 84407 | Minton & Co. | Stoke |
| 25 | 1 | 84410 | John Milner | Cobridge |
| 26 | 3 | 84471 | J. & M. P. Bell & Co. | Glasgow |
| Apr 1 | 1 | 84541 | Thos. Till & Son | Burslem |
| 8 | 4 | 84615 | idem | Burslem |
| 21 | 4 | 84837 | George Ray | Longton |
| May 5 | 5 | 85001–2 | J. M. Blashfield | London |
| 6 | 5 | 85008 | Geo. Bowden Sander | London |
| 7 | 2 | 85010–3 | J. M. Blashfield | London |
| 14 | 5 | 85081 | W. T. Copeland | Stoke |
| 18 | 1 | 85102 | Minton & Co. | Stoke |
| June 1 | 2 | 85224–5 | J. M. Blashfield | London |
| 5 | 5 | 85248 | Minton & Co. | Stoke |
| 14 | 4 | 85354 | W. T. Copeland | Stoke |
| 21 | 2 | 85404 | J. & T. Lockett | Longton |
| July 5 | 3 | 85619 | J. Pankhurst & Co. | Hanley |
| 23 | 3 | 85803–4 | Minton & Co. | Stoke |
| Aug 4 | 3 | 86070–1 | W. T. Copeland | Stoke |
| 13 | 5 | 86126 | Thos. Till & Son | Burslem |
| 25 | 4 | 86318 | Chas. Meigh & Son | Hanley |
| 25 | 5 | 86319 | Geo. Bowden Sander | London |
| Sept 3 | 7 | 86473 | Minton & Co. | Stoke |
| 15 | 5 | 86649 | Thos. Till & Son | Burslem |
| 16 | 1 | 86657 | Minton & Co. | Stoke |
| 24 | 1 | 86815 | idem | Stoke |
| 27 | 3 | 86857 | Warburton & Britton | Leeds |
| Oct 1 | 6 | 86931 | W. T. Copeland | Stoke |
| 7 | 5 | 87040 | Ralph Scragg | Hanley |

| Date | Parcel No. | Patent No. | Factory, Retailer Wholesaler, etc | Place |
|---|---|---|---|---|
| 23 | 4 | 87219 | Davenports & Co. | Longport |
| 25 | 2 | 87228 | Wm. Brownfield | Cobridge |
| 30 | 3 | 87464 | Marple, Turner & Co. | Hanley |
| Nov 4 | 5 | 87541 | John Holland | Tunstall |
| 11 | 3 | 87633 | Minton & Co. | Stoke |
| 22 | 3 | 87883 | J. Pankhurst & J. Dimmock | Hanley |
| 25 | 4 | 88037 | Keys & Mountford | Stoke |
| Dec 16 | 4 | 88350 | John Rose & Co. | Coalport |
| 27 | 1 | 88693 | Warburton & Britton | Leeds |

**1853**

| Date | Parcel No. | Patent No. | Factory, Retailer Wholesaler, etc | Place |
|---|---|---|---|---|
| Jan 3 | 3 | 88808–9 | W. T. Copeland | Stoke |
| 12 | 6 | 88978 | Thos. Goodfellow | Tunstall |
| 14 | 3 | 88987 | Davenports & Co. | Longport |
| 18 | 2 | 89050 | idem | Longport |
| Feb 4 | 9 | 89469 | J. Pankhurst & J. Dimmock | Hanley |
| 10 | 2 | 89626 | Geo. Wooliscroft | Tunstall |
| 11 | 6 | 89646 | Thos. Worthington & J. Green | Shelton |
| 12 | 3 | 89661–3 | Minton & Co. | Stoke |
| 17 | 4 | 89722–3 | W. S. Kennedy & Co. | Burslem |
| 26 | 5 | 89958 | W. T. Copeland | Stoke |
| Mar 10 | 2 | 90253 | J. & M. P. Bell & Co. | Glasgow |
| 17 | 5 | 90360 | J. W. Pankhurst & Co. | Hanley |
| 19 | 2 | 90372 | Minton & Co. | Stoke |
| Apr 4 | 6 | 90610 | John Rose & Co. | Coalport |
| 23 | 2 | 90876 | Wm. Adams & Sons | Stoke |
| May 7 | 5 | 91121–4 | John Alcock | Cobridge |
| June 7 | 3 | 91329 | Geo. Wood & Co. | Shelton |
| 14 | 2 | 91405–6 | Livesley, Powell & Co. | Hanley |
| 22 | 3 | 91469 | Pankhurst & Dimmock | Hanley |
| 24 | 3 | 91487 | Geo. Wooliscroft | Tunstall |
| 24 | 11 | 91512–3 | Ridgway & Co. | Shelton |

| Date | Parcel No. | Patent No. | Factory, Retailer Wholesaler, etc | Place |
|---|---|---|---|---|
| July 18 | 4 | 91737 | John Edwards | Longton |
| 20 | 2 | 91749–50 | J. H. Baddeley | Shelton |
| Aug 8 | 1 | 92001 | Anthony Shaw | Tunstall |
| 10 | 2 | 92018 | Holland & Green | Longton |
| Sept 3 | 2 | 92340 | T. & R. Boote | Burslem |
| 6 | 3 | 92364 | F. Morley & Co. | Shelton |
| 21 | 2 | 92631–2 | James Edwards | Burslem |
| Oct 5 | 2 | 92768–70 | Venables, Mann & Co. | Burslem |
| 10 | 3 | 92859 | Barrow & Co. | Fenton |
| 11 | 5 | 92864 | Ralph Scragg | Hanley |
| 12 | 3 | 92867 | James Edwards | Burslem |
| 12 | 4 | 92868–9 | Livesley, Powell & Co. | Hanley |
| 19 | 4 | 92952 | Minton & Co. | Stoke |
| 22 | 1 | 93008–9 | T. J. & J. Mayer | Longport |
| Nov 24 | 2 | 93438–9 | Thos. Till & Son | Burslem |
| 26 | 2 | 93452 | W. T. Copeland | Stoke |
| 30 | 5 | 93483 | Wm. Adams & Sons | Stoke |
| Dec 6 | 4 | 93536 | J. Alcock | Cobridge |
| 24 | 3 | 93706–7 | Samuel Moore & Co. | Sunderlnd |
| 24 | 4 | 93708 | J. Alcock | Cobridge |
| **1854** | | | | |
| Jan 10 | 4 | 94326 | W. & G. Harding | Burslem |
| 13 | 1 | 94343–4 | Deaville & Baddeley | Hanley |
| 14 | 3 | 94632 | Samuel Moore & Co. | Sunderlnd |
| 21 | 3 | 94727 | J. & M. P. Bell & Co. | Glasgow |
| 30 | 4 | 94815 | Samuel Alcock & Co. | Burslem |
| Feb 23 | 3 | 95163 | W. T. Copeland | Stoke |
| Mar 11 | 4 | 95275 | Samuel Alcock & Co. | Burslem |
| 20 | 1 | 95388 | Thos. Till & Son | Burslem |
| 22 | 2 | 95397 | James Edwards & Son | Longport |
| 24 | 3 | 95420 | Minton & Co. | Stoke |
| 27 | 3 | 95448 | Geo. Baguley | Hanley |
| 27 | 6 | 95451 | J. Deaville | Hanley |
| 31 | 1 | 95469 | Holland & Green | Longton |

# APPENDIX B

| Date | Parcel No. | Patent No. | Factory, Retailer Wholesaler, etc | Place |
|------|-----------|-----------|-----------------------------------|-------|
| Apr 1 | 4 | 95510 | Wm. Brownfield | Cobridge |
| 4 | 3 | 95523 | Woollard & Hattersley | Cambdge |
| 5 | 3 | 95542 | Ralph Scragg | Hanley |
| 6 | 3 | 95553 | Samuel Alcock & Co. | Burslem |
| 10 | 3 | 95575 | J. Deaville | Hanley |
| 10 | 4 | 95576 | Samuel Alcock & Co. | Burslem |
| 11 | 5 | 95587–8 | Pearson, Farrall & Meakin | Shelton |
| 15 | 1 | 95611 | Geo. Baguley | Hanley |
| 21 | 3 | 95646 | Warburton & Britton | Leeds |
| May 4 | 3 | 95733 | John Ridgway & Co. | Shelton |
| 8 | 3 | 95751 | Wm. Brownfield | Cobridge |
| June 3 | 2 | 96003 | Thos. Till & Son | Burslem |
| 9 | 2 | 96039 | Chas. Meigh & Son | Hanley |
| 21 | 5 | 96085–6 | T. & R. Boote | Burslem |
| July 18 | 2 | 96296 | idem | Burslem |
| 18 | 4 | 96298 | Alcock & Co. | Burslem |
| Sept 5 | 3 | 96773 | Samuel Alcock & Co. | Burslem |
| 12 | 2 | 96826 | W. T. Copeland | Stoke |
| Oct 2 | 3 | 96980 | Wm. Brownfield | Cobridge |
| 6 | 4 | 97141 | Davenports & Co. | Longport |
| 9 | 4 | 97160 | T. J. & J. Mayer | Longport |
| 31 | 2 | 97508 | Geo. Ray | Longton |
| Nov 10 | 5 | 97659 | John Ridgway & Co. | Shelton |
| Dec 27 | 3 | 98640 | Samuel Alcock & Co. | Burslem |
| 27 | 4 | 98641 | Pankhurst & Dimmock | Hanley |
| 29 | 1 | 98648 | F. & R. Pratt & Co. | Fenton |
| **1855** | | | | |
| Jan 4 | 2 | 98696 | Worthington & Green | Shelton |
| 6 | 4 | 98786 | Samuel Alcock & Co. | Burslem |
| 15 | 2 | 99042 | Pinder, Bourne & Hope | Burslem |
| 15 | 4 | 99051 | Brougham & Mayer | Tunstall |
| 19 | 3 | 99086 | Pankhurst & Dimmock | Hanley |
| 30 | 1 | 99188 | John Edwards | Longton |

## APPENDIX B

| Date | Parcel No. | Patent No. | Factory, Retailer Wholesaler, etc | Place |
|------|-----------|-----------|-----------------------------------|-------|
| Feb 3 | 4 | 99231 | J. & M. P. Bell & Co. | Glasgow |
| 5 | 7 | 99282 | Coomb(e)s & Holland | Llanelly |
| 7 | 2 | 99310 | John Alcock | Cobridge |
| 17 | 3 | 99394 | Pratt & Co. . | Fenton |
| 26 | 3 | 99488 | Lockett, Baguley & Cooper | Shelton |
| 28 | 4 | 99528 | J. Ridgway & Co. | Shelton |
| Mar 1 | 5 | 99538–40 | Minton & Co. | Stoke |
| 5 | 3 | 99579 | Elsmore & Forster | Tunstall |
| 13 | 4 | 99653 | Warburton & Britton | Leeds |
| 17 | 1 | 99679 | Wm. Baker | Fenton |
| Apr 7 | 7 | 99814 | W. T. Copeland | Stoke |
| 17 | 4 | 99876 | Stephen Hughes & Son | Burslem |
| 26 | 1 | 99972–4 | Wm. Brownfield | Cobridge |
| 28 | 7 | 100008 | Venables, Mann & Co. | Burslem |
| May 10 | 5 | 100094 | Beech, Hancock & Co. | Burslem |
| 14 | 3 | 100116 | Minton & Co. | Stoke |
| June 7 | 4 | 100246–7 | John Alcock | Cobridge |
| 11 | 3 | 100299 | Saml. Alcock & Co. | Burslem |
| July 4 | 5 | 100624 | J. Thompson | Staffs. |
| 24 | 1 | 100816 | Chas. Meigh & Son | Hanley |
| Aug 6 | 1 | 101019 | James Dudson | Shelton |
| 8 | 5 | 101026 | J. Edwards & Son | Longport |
| 11 | 1 | 101082 | Geo. Grainger & Co. | Worcester |
| 20 | 3 | 101127 | Thos. Ford | Shelton |
| 27 | 2 | 101229–31 | Barrow & Co. | Fenton |
| Sept 27 | 4 | 101623–4 | Saml. Bevington & Son | Shelton |
| Oct 3 | 2 | 101681 | Geo. Mayor & Co. | London |
| 3 | 3 | 101682 | Minton & Co. | Stoke |
| 17 | 8 | 101932 | John Williamson | Glasgow |
| 25 | 3 | 102325 | D. Chetwynd | Cobridge |
| 29 | 6 | 102355 | G. W. Reade | Burslem |
| Nov 1 | 3 | 102415 | Josiah Wedgwood & Sons | Etruria |
| 22 | 4 | 102744 | J. & M. P. Bell & Co. | Glasgow |
| 28 | 3 | 102785 | Wm. Brownfield | Cobridge |

| Date | Parcel No. | Patent No. | Factory, Retailer Wholesaler, etc | Place |
|------|------------|------------|-----------------------------------|-------|
| **1856** | | | | |
| Jan 5 | 3 | 103103 | J. Edwards | Longton |
| 15 | 4 | 103404 | James Pankhurst & Co. | Hanley |
| 23 | 3 | 103506 | J. Roberts | Kent (Upnor) |
| 23 | 4 | 103507 | Minton & Co. | Stoke |
| 31 | 4 | 103616 | Josiah Wedgwood & Sons | Etruria |
| Mar 11 | 1 | 104078 | Davenports & Co. | Longport |
| 12 | 3 | 104090 | Pratt & Co. | Fenton |
| Apr 7 | 2 | 104313–16 | A. Shaw | Tunstall |
| 7 | 3 | 104317 | J. & M. P. Bell & Co. | Glasgow |
| 18 | 2 | 104392 | Wm. Beech | Burslem |
| 18 | 3 | 104393 | Ralph Scragg | Hanley |
| 18 | 6 | 104396 | E. Walley | Cobridge |
| 18 | 7 | 104397 | Ridgway & Abington | Hanley |
| 30 | 3 | 104602–3 | Wm. Brownfield | Cobridge |
| May 8 | 2 | 104694 | Minton & Co. | Stoke |
| 22 | 1 | 104762 | idem | Stoke |
| June 13 | 3 | 105059 | Chas. Meigh & Son | Hanley |
| 28 | 3 | 105223 | Worthington & Green | Hanley |
| 30 | 7 | 105258 | J. Clementson | Shelton |
| July 28 | 3 | 105492 | E. Challinor | Tunstall |
| 30 | 5 | 105702 | J. Edwards & Son | Longport |
| Aug 12 | 2 | 105871 | F. & R. Pratt & Co. | Fenton |
| 19 | 5 | 105926 | idem | Fenton |
| 22 | 4 | 105955–9 | T. & R. Boote | Burslem |
| Sept 1 | 3 | 106161 | W. T. Copeland | Stoke |
| Oct 2 | 3 | 106477 | H. Baggaley | Hanley |
| 16 | 2 | 106671–2 | Minton & Co. | Stoke |
| 22 | 3 | 106770 | W. T. Copeland | Stoke |
| Nov 7 | 6 | 106950 | F. & R. Pratt & Co. | Fenton |
| 14 | 9 | 107038 | Davenports & Co. | Longport |
| 27 | 3 | 107708 | idem | Longport |
| 27 | 6 | 107714 | Wm. Brownfield | Cobridge |
| 29 | 1 | 107783–5 | E. Walley | Cobridge |

| Date | Parcel No. | Patent No. | Factory, Retailer Wholesaler, etc | Place |
|------|------|------|------|------|
| Dec 11 | 4 | 107955 | W. T. Copeland | Stoke |
| 18 | 2 | 108052 | Mayer & Elliott | Longport |
| 23 | 4 | 108105 | idem | Longport |
| **1857** | | | | |
| Jan 15 | 5 | 108605 | F. & R. Pratt & Co. | Fenton |
| 26 | 7 | 108785 | J. Edwards | Longport |
| Feb 4 | 5 | 108854–5 | John Meir & Son | Tunstall |
| 9 | 4 | 108930 | Minton & Co. | Stoke |
| 17 | 3 | 109063 | idem | Stoke |
| 23 | 9 | 109180 | Podmore, Walker & Co. | Hanley |
| Mar 20 | 4 | 109427 | John Alcock | Cobridge |
| Apr 16 | 1 | 109738 | John Alcock | Cobridge |
| 29 | 1 | 109810 | W. T. Copeland | Stoke |
| June 5 | 3 | 110096–7 | Wm. Brownfield | Cobridge |
| 19 | 1 | 110160 | W. T. Copeland | Stoke |
| 19 | 2 | 110161 | Wilkinson & Rickhuss | Hanley |
| 25 | 1 | 110247 | J. & M. P. Bell & Co. | Glasgow |
| July 30 | 2 | 110780 | Ridgway, Bates & Co. | Shelton |
| Aug 4 | 5 | 110806 | Taylor, Pears & Co. | Fenton |
| 11 | 3 | 110862 | Kerr & Binns | Worcester |
| Sept 7 | 2 | 111105 | W. T. Copeland | Stoke |
| Oct 3 | 3 | 111495–6 | Doulton & Watts | London |
| 5 | 5 | 111515–6 | idem | London |
| 14 | 1 | 111585 | Ridgway & Abington | Hanley |
| 17 | 1 | 111642 | Mayer Bros. & Elliott | Longport |
| 17 | 2 | 111643–4 | T. & R. Boote | Burslem |
| 22 | 1 | 111677 | Pratt & Co. | Fenton |
| Nov 3 | 3 | 111831–2 | Maw & Co. | Broseley |
| 28 | 2 | 112263 | Kerr & Binns | Worcester |
| Dec 4 | 4 | 112350 | Minton & Co. | Stoke |
| 9 | 2 | 112354 | Wm. Brownfield | Cobridge |

# APPENDIX B

| Date | Parcel No. | Patent No. | Factory, Retailer Wholesaler, etc | Place |
|------|-----------|-----------|-----------------------------------|-------|
| **1858** | | | | |
| Jan 29 | 3 | 112875 | Cockson & Harding | Hanley |
| 29 | 4 | 112876 | E. & W. Walley | Cobridge |
| Mar 25 | 2 | 113290 | Kerr & Binns | Worcester |
| Apr 9 | 2 | 113387 | idem | Worcester |
| 17 | 4 | 113456 | Ridgway & Abington | Hanley |
| 22 | 5 | 113565 | T. & R. Boote | Burslem |
| 30 | 5 | 113631 | Minton & Co. | Stoke |
| May 6 | 4 | 113668 | J. Edwards | Longton |
| 25 | 4 | 113864 | A. Shaw | Burslem |
| 31 | 1 | 113900 | Holland & Green | Longton |
| 31 | 4 | 113903 | Wm. Adams | Tunstall |
| June 2 | 1 | 113905–6 | Wm. Brownfield | Cobridge |
| 23 | 6 | 114048 | Samuel Alcock & Co. | Burslem |
| July 13 | 2 | 114214 | Mayer & Elliott | Longport |
| 29 | 4 | 114532 | Samuel Alcock & Co. | Burslem |
| Aug 24 | 2 | 114763 | Wm. Brownfield | Cobridge |
| Sept 3 | 2 | 115120 | Sharpe Bros. & Co. | Swadlncte |
| 6 | 5 | 115197 | James Edwards | Longport |
| 10 | 3 | 115217 | John Edwards | Longton |
| 10 | 6 | 115343 | Bridgwood & Clarke | Burslem |
| Oct 5 | 2 | 115901 | Minton & Co. | Stoke |
| 5 | 3 | 115902 | Wm. Brownfield | Cobridge |
| 7 | 1 | 115953 | Ridgway & Abington | Hanley |
| 18 | 3 | 116176 | Minton & Co. | Stoke |
| 29 | 2 | 116468 | B. Green | Fenton |
| Nov 3 | 8 | 116585 | James Stiff | London |
| 5 | 5 | 116607 | Wm. Savage | Winchstr |
| 11 | 2 | 116737 | E. & W. Walley | Cobridge |
| Dec 8 | 11 | 117336–8 | T. & R. Boote | Burslem |
| 8 | 12 | 117339 | J. Clementson | Hanley |
| 17 | 6 | 117443 | W. T. Copeland | Stoke |
| 23 | 2 | 117516 | J. Clementson | Hanley |
| 23 | 9 | 117530 | W. T. Copeland | Stoke |
| 27 | 4 | 117559 | J. Clementson | Hanley |

| Date | Parcel No. | Patent No. | Factory, Retailer Wholesaler, etc | Place |
|------|-----------|-----------|-----------------------------------|-------|
| **1859** | | | | |
| Jan 25 | 4 | 118119 | W. T. Copeland | Stoke |
| Feb 2 | 3 | 118294 | T. & R. Boote | Burslem |
| 3 | 2 | 118303–4 | Davenports & Co. | Longport |
| 8 | 6 | 118415 | Leveson Hill (Excrs. of) | Stoke |
| Mar 19 | 1 | 118827 | Alsop, Downes, Spilsbury & Co. | London |
| 21 | 7 | 118891 | T. & R. Boote | Burslem |
| 29 | 7 | 119137 | idem | Burslem |
| May 7 | 1 | 119721–2 | E. & W. Walley | Cobridge |
| 10 | 2 | 119760 | Samuel Alcock & Co. | Burslem |
| 20 | 1 | 119968 | Wm. Brownfield | Cobridge |
| 26 | 1 | 120096 | Lockett, Baguley & Cooper | Hanley |
| July 2 | 2 | 120560 | W. T. Copeland | Stoke |
| Aug 6 | 7 | 121140 | F. & R. Pratt & Co. | Fenton |
| 27 | 6 | 121724 | Samuel Alcock & Co. | Burslem |
| Sept 1 | 3 | 121833 | James Edwards & Son | Longport |
| Oct 12 | 4 | 122959 | Wm. Adams | Tunstall |
| 14 | 4 | 123116 | W. T. Copeland | Stoke |
| 25 | 1 | 123389–91 | Minton & Co. | Stoke |
| 28 | 1 | 123604 | Davenports & Co. | Longport |
| Nov 2 | 3 | 123738–40 | Elsmore & Forster | Tunstall |
| 5 | 4 | 123816 | Wm. Brownfield | Cobridge |
| 17 | 4 | 124140–3 | Minton & Co. | Stoke |
| 23 | 4 | 124274 | idem | Stoke |
| Dec 10 | 5 | 124653 | Josiah Wedgwood & Sons | Etruria |
| 14 | 2 | 124716 | E. & W. Walley | Cobridge |
| 15 | 3 | 124725 | Minton & Co. | Stoke |
| **1860** | | | | |
| Jan 10 | 4 | 125365 | W. T. Copeland | Stoke |
| 23 | 7 | 125863 | Mayer & Elliott | Longport |
| Feb 14 | 9 | 126446–7 | W. T. Copeland | Stoke |

| Date | Parcel No. | Patent No. | Factory, Retailer Wholesaler, etc | Place |
|------|------------|------------|-----------------------------------|-------|
| Mar 1 | 2 | 126950 | Bates, Brown-Westhead & Moore | Hanley |
| 27 | 1 | 127513 | idem | Hanley |
| Apr 5 | 1 | 127766 | Geo. Grainger & Co. | Worcester |
| 12 | 4 | 127965 | Minton & Co. | Stoke |
| May 2 | 2 | 128476 | John Meir & Son | Tunstall |
| 19 | 9 | 129129 | Lockett, Baguley & Cooper | Hanley |
| 30 | 10 | 129578 | Edward Corn | Burslem |
| June 6 | 4 | 129680–2 | Wm. Brownfield | Cobridge |
| 22 | 2 | 130106 | Minton & Co. | Stoke |
| 28 | 2 | 130135 | Minton & Co. | Stoke |
| Aug 21 | 2 | 131943 | John Wedge Wood | Tunstall |
| Sept 24 | 3 | 133411 | Minton & Co. | Stoke |
| 29 | 7 | 133788 | idem | Stoke |
| Oct 13 | 5 | 134204 | B. Green | Fenton |
| 18 | 4 | 134519–20 | Bates, Brown–Westhead & Moore | Hanley |
| 19 | 4 | 134555–7 | J. Clementson | Shelton |
| 19 | 5 | 134558–9 | Holland & Green | Longton |
| 29 | 3 | 134936 | Minton & Co. | Stoke |
| 29 | 9 | 134968 | Wm. Brownfield | Cobridge |
| Nov 23 | 9 | 136032 | T. & R. Boote | Burslem |
| Dec 3 | 3 | 136285–6 | Bates, Brown–Westhead & Moore | Hanley |
| 12 | 3 | 136643 | Bates & Co. | Hanley |
| **1861** | | | | |
| Jan 8 | 6 | 137217 | T. & R. Boote | Burslem |
| 21 | 7 | 137529 | Wedgwood & Co. | Tunstall |
| Feb 15 | 3 | 138356 | J. Furnival & Co. | Cobridge |
| 27 | 5 | 138535 | James Edwards & Son | Longport |
| Mar 7 | 7 | 138861–2 | Turner & Tomkinson | Tunstall |
| 19 | 3 | 139053 | W. T. Copeland | Stoke |
| 19 | 4 | 139054–5 | W. H. Kerr & Co. | Worcester |

# APPENDIX B

| Date | Parcel No. | Patent No. | Factory, Retailer Wholesaler, etc | Place |
|------|------------|------------|-----------------------------------|-------|
| Apr 5 | 3 | 139360 | Pinder, Bourne & Hope | Burslem |
| 6 | 1 | 139369–72 | Minton, Hollins & Co. | Stoke |
| 12 | 3 | 139714–5 | Davenports & Co. | Longport |
| 18 | 5 | 139881 | T. & R. Boote | Burslem |
| 20 | 6 | 139945 | F. & R. Pratt | Fenton |
| 25 | 2 | 140200 | James Dudson | Hanley |
| May 3 | 8 | 140367 | W. T. Copeland | Stoke |
| 6 | 3 | 140478 | The Hill Pottery Co. | Burslem |
| 6 | 5 | 140480–1 | The Old Hall Earthenware Co. | Hanley |
| 9 | 3 | 140578–9 | Bates, Brown–Westhead & Moore | Hanley |
| 13 | 7 | 140679 | Minton & Co. | Stoke |
| 14 | 2 | 140683 | W. H. Kerr & Co. | Worcester |
| 25 | 2 | 141055 | idem | Worcester |
| 31 | 3 | 141114 | Cork, Edge & Malkin | Burslem |
| June 4 | 1 | 141214 | Bates, Brown–Westhead & Moore | Hanley |
| 7 | 5 | 141288 | The Hill Pottery Co. | Burslem |
| 11 | 2 | 141326–7 | W. T. Copeland | Stoke |
| 13 | 6 | 141369 | Minton & Co. | Stoke |
| July 4 | 2 | 141715 | Lockett & Cooper | Hanley |
| 5 | 2 | 141727 | Beech & Hancock | Tunstall |
| 6 | 2 | 141732 | Wm. Brownfield | Cobridge |
| 18 | 4 | 141869–70 | Josiah Wedgwood & Sons | Etruria |
| Aug 19 | 7 | 142755 | T. & R. Boote | Burslem |
| 22 | 7 | 142847 | Wedgwood & Co. | Tunstall |
| 23 | 2 | 142850 | G. W. Reade | Cobridge |
| Sept 6 | 6 | 143313 | Wm. Brownfield | Cobridge |
| 12 | 6 | 143400 | J. & J. Peake | Newcastle |
| 17 | 2 | 143702 | W. T. Copeland | Stoke |
| 18 | 7 | 143769 | Wm. Beech | Burslem |
| 26 | 7 | 144179 | John Cliff & Co. | London |
| Oct 10 | 5 | 144757 | W. H. Kerr & Co. | Worcester |
| 11 | 3 | 144767 | Mountford & Scarratt | Fenton |

| Date | Parcel No. | Patent No. | Factory, Retailer Wholesaler, etc | Place |
|---|---|---|---|---|
| 15 | 3 | 144896 | Leveson Hill (Excrs of) | Stoke |
| 18 | 3 | 145157 | W. T. Copeland | Stoke |
| 24 | 5 | 145499 | Hulse, Nixon & Adderley | Longton |
| 28 | 7 | 145686–7 | Bates, Brown–Westhead & Moore | Hanley |
| Nov 15 | 3 | 146352–4 | J. Clementson | Hanley |
| 29 | 5 | 146924 | Josiah Wedgwood & Sons | Etruria |
| Dec 4 | 7 | 147309–10 | Wm. Brownfield | Cobridge |
| 5 | 5 | 147322 | Till, Bullock & Smith | Hanley |
| 20 | 7 | 147820 | Lockett & Cooper | Hanley |
| 20 | 9 | 147823 | Wedgwood & Co. | Tunstall |

**1862**

| Date | Parcel No. | Patent No. | Factory, Retailer Wholesaler, etc | Place |
|---|---|---|---|---|
| Jan 11 | 5 | 148517 | Wm. Brownfield | Cobridge |
| 25 | 3 | 148870 | idem | Cobridge |
| Feb 1 | 4 | 149090 | Elliot Bros. | Longport |
| 10 | 6 | 149290 | W. H. Kerr & Co. | Worcester |
| 10 | 8 | 149292 | Minton & Co. | Stoke |
| 27 | 4 | 149673–4 | James Dudson | Hanley |
| Mar 1 | 6 | 149716 | T. & R. Boote | Burslem |
| 13 | 6 | 149938 | W. T. Copeland | Stoke |
| 13 | 7 | 149939 | Wm. Adams | Tunstall |
| 14 | 8 | 149955 | J. Knight | Fenton |
| 14 | 9 | 149956 | Wedgwood & Co. | Tunstall |
| 14 | 10 | 149957–8 | Wm. Brownfield | Cobridge |
| 21 | 6 | 150100 | Thompson Bros. | Burton-on-Trent |
| 22 | 9 | 150152 | T. & R. Boote | Burslem |
| 27 | 1 | 150241 | J. & M. P. Bell & Co. | Glasgow |
| 28 | 5 | 150301–3 | idem | Glasgow |
| 29 | 3 | 150322 | Minton & Co. | Stoke |
| Apr 1 | 5 | 150377 | Josiah Wedgwood & Sons | Etruria |
| 4 | 2 | 150455 | Minton & Co. | Stoke |
| 4 | 5 | 150458 | J. & T. Furnival | Cobridge |

# APPENDIX B

| Date | Parcel No. | Patent No. | Factory, Retailer Wholesaler, etc | Place |
|------|-----------|-----------|-----------------------------------|-------|
| 7 | 12 | 150515 | Geo. Grainger & Co. | Worcester |
| 9 | 3 | 150538 | The Old Hall Earthenware Co. (Ltd.) | Hanley |
| 17 | 5 | 151029–30 | Thompson Bros. | Burton |
| 24 | 2 | 151141 | Turner & Tomkinson | Tunstall |
| May 1 | 7 | 151351 | Eardley & Hammersley | Tunstall |
| 3 | 3 | 151378 | G. L. Ashworth Bros. | Hanley |
| 5 | 5 | 151456 | John Cliff | London |
| 9 | 9 | 151568–9 | Brown–Westhead, Moore & Co. | Hanley |
| 14 | 3 | 151672–3 | Geo. Jones & Co. | Stoke |
| 27 | 3 | 151995 | E. Challinor | Tunstall |
| 29 | 5 | 152013 | J. Furnival & Co. | Cobridge |
| June 24 | 5 | 152709 | T. C. Brown–Westhead, Moore & Co. | Hanley |
| July 2 | 4 | 152859 | Minton & Co. | Stoke |
| 4 | 8 | 152963 | J. Clementson | Hanley |
| 12 | 4 | 153112 | idem | Hanley |
| 14 | 2 | 153127 | Beech & Hancock | Tunstall |
| 19 | 6 | 153366 | J. Clementson | Hanley |
| 31 | 3 | 153476 | Jones & Ellis | Longton |
| 31 | 4 | 153477 | Minton & Co. | Stoke |
| Aug 16 | 5 | 153821 | Richard Edwards | Longport |
| 16 | 7 | 153823 | J. H. Baddeley | Hanley |
| 18 | 4 | 153827 | Hulse, Nixon & Adderley | Longton |
| 19 | 4 | 153844 | G. L. Ashworth & Bros. | Hanley |
| 25 | 3 | 154143–4 | E. F. Bodley & Co. | Burslem |
| 30 | 3 | 154220 | Thos. Fell & Co. | Newcastle upon Tyne |
| 30 | 4 | 154221 | T. & R. Boote | Burslem |
| Sept 6 | 2 | 154401 | Malkin, Walker & Hulse | Longton |
| 11 | 3 | 154678 | Minton & Co. | Stoke |
| 12 | 2 | 154693 | Thos. Cooper | Longton |

# APPENDIX B

| Date | Parcel No. | Patent No. | Factory, Retailer Wholesaler, etc | Place |
|---|---|---|---|---|
| 17 | 6 | 154812 | Hope & Carter | Burslem |
| 22 | 7 | 155103 | Minton & Co. | Stoke |
| 26 | 1 | 155220–2 | Hope & Carter | Burslem |
| Oct 1 | 7 | 155263–4 | Thos. Fell & Co. | Newcastle upon Tyne |
| 9 | 3 | 155550 | Hill Pottery | Burslem |
| 15 | 2 | 156190 | Turner & Tomkinson | Tunstall |
| 23 | 8 | 156715–7 | Wm. Baker & Co. | Fenton |
| Nov 11 | 3 | 157274 | E. F. Bodley & Co. | Burslem |
| 19 | 5 | 157547 | Geo. Wooliscroft | Tunstall |
| 28 | 4 | 157907 | Minton & Co. | Stoke |
| Dec 3 | 5 | 158052–3 | T. C. Brown–Westhead Moore & Co. | Hanley |
| 5 | 2 | 158091 | Wm. Brownfield | Cobridge |
| 9 | 5 | 158221 | Thomas Cooper | Hanley |
| 17 | 5 | 158480 | The Old Hall Earthenware Co. (Ltd.) | Hanley |
| 18 | 3 | 158498 | Geo. Jones | Stoke |
| **1863** | | | | |
| Jan 12 | 6 | 159083 | Davenport, Banks & Co. | Etruria |
| 16 | 2 | 159123 | Minton & Co. | Stoke |
| 16 | 8 | 159153 | Liddle, Elliot & Sons | Longport |
| 29 | 1 | 159551 | Josiah Wedgwood & Sons | Etruria |
| 30 | 3 | 159573 | T. & R. Boote | Burslem |
| Feb 2 | 3 | 159613 | Minton & Co. | Stoke |
| 17 | 4 | 159972 | T. & R. Boote | Burslem |
| 24 | 5 | 160110 | James Stiff & Sons | London |
| Mar 6 | 2 | 160319 | G. L. Ashworth & Bros. | Hanley |
| 13 | 2 | 160456 | Hope & Carter | Burslem |
| 13 | 3 | 160457 | Wilkinson & Sons | Hanley |
| 20 | 8 | 160752 | Worthington & Green | Hanley |
| 20 | 9 | 160753–4 | John Pratt & Co. | Fenton |
| 21 | 2 | 160759 | Beech & Hancock | Tunstall |

# APPENDIX B

| Date | Parcel No. | Patent No. | Factory, Retailer Wholesaler, etc | Place |
|---|---|---|---|---|
| 21 | 4 | 160761 | Hulse, Nixon & Adderley | Longton |
| 21 | 5 | 160762 | James Edwards & Son | Burslem |
| 23 | 2 | 160791–2 | Bodley & Harrold | Burslem |
| Apr 11 | 1 | 161404 | J. Macintyre | Burslem |
| 23 | 4 | 161852 | T. C. Brown–Westhead Moore & Co. | Hanley |
| 25 | 1 | 161861 | Beech & Hancock | Tunstall |
| 30 | 3 | 162021 | Wilkinson & Son | Hanley |
| May 4 | 6 | 162122 | Harding & Cotterill | Burton-on-Trent |
| 11 | 3 | 162261–2 | E. Pearson | Cobridge |
| 12 | 1 | 162267 | Bodley & Harrold | Burslem |
| 15 | 10 | 162304 | Harding & Cotterill | Burton-on-Trent |
| 22 | 4 | 162618–9 | W. T. Copeland | Stoke |
| 26 | 9 | 162765 | T. C. Brown–Westhead, Moore & Co. | Hanley |
| June 4 | 5 | 162976 | The Old Hall Earthenware Co. (Ltd.) | Hanley |
| 8 | 15 | 163188 | Minton & Co. | Stoke |
| 8 | 16 | 163189 | Wm. Brownfield | Cobridge |
| July 14 | 2 | 164213 | Turner & Tomkinson | Tunstall |
| 15 | 3 | 164221 | H. Venables | Hanley |
| 20 | 3 | 164353 | Wm. Brownfield | Cobridge |
| 24 | 3 | 164468–9 | W. T. Copeland | Stoke |
| 28 | 6 | 164635 | Minton & Co. | Stoke |
| Aug 11 | 3 | 165045–7 | Turner & Tomkinson | Tunstall |
| 12 | 4 | 165171 | Hancock, Whittingham & Co. | Burslem |
| 21 | 1 | 165317 | J. Clementson | Hanley |
| 28 | 5 | 165448 | H. Venables | Hanley |
| Sept 7 | 6 | 165720 | T. & R. Boote | Burslem |
| 28 | 4 | 166439 | H. Venables | Hanley |
| 28 | 6 | 166441–2 | James Edwards & Son | Longport |

# APPENDIX B

| Date | | Parcel No. | Patent No. | Factory, Retailer Wholesaler, etc | Place |
|------|---|---|---|---|---|
| Oct | 2 | 5 | 166625 | H. Venables | Hanley |
| | 6 | 5 | 166775 | Thompson Bros. | Burton |
| | 14 | 7 | 167289 | Wm. Brownfield | Cobridge |
| | 15 | 2 | 167299 | F. Brewer & Son | Longton |
| | 17 | 1 | 167374 | T. & R. Boote | Burslem |
| | 22 | 5 | 167536 | Eardley & Hammersley | Tunstall |
| | 24 | 5 | 167560 | Josiah Wedgwood & Sons | Etruria |
| | 26 | 7 | 167594–5 | The Old Hall Earthenware Co. (Ltd.) | Hanley |
| | 28 | 8 | 167715 | George Jones & Co. | Stoke |
| | 31 | 3 | 167761–3 | Edmund T. Wood | Tunstall |
| Nov | 3 | 5 | 168132 | John Meir & Son | Tunstall |
| | 4 | 7 | 168188 | T. & R. Boote | Burslem |
| | 6 | 1 | 168234–5 | Geo. Jones & Co. | Stoke |
| | 16 | 10 | 168765 | Wm. Kirkham | Stoke |
| | 26 | 12 | 169553 | Wm. Brownfield | Cobridge |
| | 27 | 3 | 169561 | Bodley & Harrold | Burslem |
| Dec | 2 | 5 | 169774 | J. W. Pankhurst | Hanley |
| | 2 | 6 | 169775 | T. & R. Boote | Burslem |
| | 18 | 4 | 170294 | F. & R. Pratt & Co. | Fenton |
| | 23 | 2 | 170418 | Wm. Brownfield | Cobridge |
| | 30 | 1 | 170590 | T. C. Brown–Westhead Moore & Co. | Hanley |
| **1864** | | | | | |
| Jan | 5 | 2 | 170759 | Wm. Brownfield | Cobridge |
| | 11 | 5 | 170883 | Malkin, Walker & Hulse | Longton |
| Feb | 2 | 5 | 171421 | Josiah Wedgwood & Sons | Etruria |
| | 5 | 5 | 171520 | Hope & Carter | Burslem |
| | 6 | 3 | 171536 | Thos. Goode & Co. | London |
| | 13 | 6 | 171673 | W. T. Copeland | Stoke |
| | 22 | 7 | 171970 | Cork, Edge & Malkin | Burslem |
| | 25 | 6 | 172060 | Liddle, Elliot & Son | Longport |
| | 29 | 6 | 172183 | J. & D. Hampson | Longton |
| Mar | 3 | 4 | 172212 | Geo. L. Ashworth & Bros. | Hanley |

# APPENDIX B

| Date | Parcel No. | Patent No. | Factory, Retailer Wholesaler, etc | Place |
|------|------------|------------|-----------------------------------|-------|
| 12 | 5 | 172559 | Cork, Edge & Malkin | Burslem |
| 18 | 1 | 172648 | T. C. Brown–Westhead, Moore & Co. | Hanley |
| 22 | 3 | 172815–6 | Minton & Co. | Stoke |
| 23 | 4 | 172876 | Burgess & Leigh | Burslem |
| Apr 9 | 4 | 173200 | Josiah Wedgwood & Sons | Etruria |
| 15 | 4 | 173659 | Geo. Jones | Stoke |
| 18 | 5 | 173671 | Minton & Co. | Stoke |
| 21 | 4 | 173785 | T. C. Brown–Westhead Moore & Co. | Hanley |
| 21 | 8 | 173799 | Liddle, Elliot & Son | Longport |
| 23 | 11 | 173996 | Geo. L. Ashworth & Bros. | Hanley |
| 26 | 3 | 174112 | Bodley & Harrold | Burslem |
| 27 | 4 | 174138 | Hope & Carter | Burslem |
| 29 | 2 | 174168 | Wm. Brownfield | Cobridge |
| May 9 | 3 | 174424 | R. T. Boughton & Co. | Burslem |
| 10 | 5 | 174455–8 | Geo. Jones & Co. | Stoke |
| 11 | 3 | 174475 | R. H. Grove | Barlaston |
| 18 | 5 | 174795 | Geo. Ray | Longton |
| 21 | 1 | 174817 | J. & D. Hampson | Longton |
| June 9 | 7 | 175330 | Minton & Co. | Stoke |
| 16 | 3 | 175500 | Hope & Carter | Burslem |
| 30 | 4 | 175927 | Wm. Brownfield | Cobridge |
| 30 | 10 | 175935 | The Worcester Royal Porcelain Co. Ltd. | Worcester |
| July 2 | 3 | 175959 | Wood & Sale | Hanley |
| 9 | 5 | 176164 | Pinder, Bourne & Co. | Burslem |
| 11 | 8 | 176235–6 | idem | Burslem |
| 18 | 6 | 176597 | Bodley & Harrold | Burslem |
| 18 | 7 | 176598 | Evans & Booth | Burslem |
| 19 | 4 | 176701 | Hope & Carter | Burslem |
| 19 | 8 | 176706 | Wood & Sale | Hanley |
| 28 | 4 | 176916 | Holland & Green | Longton |
| Aug 10 | 2 | 177455 | James Fellows | W/hmptn |
| 20 | 10 | 177912 | Geo. Jones & Co. | Stoke |

314

| Date | Parcel No. | Patent No. | Factory, Retailer Wholesaler, etc | Place |
|------|-----------|-----------|----------------------------------|-------|
| 26 | 5 | 178037 | T. C. Brown–Westhead Moore & Co. | Hanley |
| Sept 6 | 5 | 178264 | W. T. Copeland | Stoke |
| 10 | 1 | 178410 | Minton & Co. | Stoke |
| 12 | 2 | 178433 | idem | Stoke |
| 14 | 4 | 178521 | Bodley & Harrold | Burslem |
| 16 | 6 | 178597–8 | Geo. L. Ashworth & Bros. | Hanley |
| 19 | 1 | 178680–1 | Josiah Wedgwood & Sons | Etruria |
| 21 | 1 | 178693–4 | Minton & Co. | Stoke |
| 22 | 6 | 178823–7 | Josiah Wedgwood & Sons | Etruria |
| Oct 4 | 2 | 179445 | Geo. Jones & Co. | Stoke |
| 12 | 4 | 179656 | Wm. Brownfield | Cobridge |
| 27 | 4 | 180444 | Evans & Booth | Burslem |
| 28 | 2 | 180449 | The Worcester Royal Porcelain Co. Ltd. | Worcester |
| 28 | 4 | 180453 | Bodley & Harrold | Burslem |
| 28 | 9 | 180483 | Minton & Co. | Stoke |
| 29 | 2 | 180486 | Chas. Collinson & Co. | Burslem |
| 31 | 3 | 180569 | Cork, Edge & Malkin | Burslem |
| Nov 1 | 7 | 180695 | W. T. Copeland | Stoke |
| 4 | 3 | 180713 | Livesley, Powell & Co. | Hanley |
| 10 | 2 | 181214–5 | Elsmore & Forster | Tunstall |
| 10 | 3 | 181296 | Hope & Carter | Burslem |
| 10 | 10 | 181286 | Geo. Jones & Co. | Stoke |
| 24 | 5 | 181722 | T. C. Brown–Westhead Moore & Co. | Hanley |
| 29 | 1 | 181843 | Hope & Carter | Burslem |
| Dec 9 | 1 | 182203 | Wm. Kirkham | Stoke |
| 10 | 8 | 182249 | Hope & Carter | Burslem |
| 31 | 6 | 182699 | Geo. Jones & Co. | Stoke |
| **1865** | | | | |
| Jan 6 | 3 | 182806 | Hope & Carter | Burslem |
| 6 | 4 | 182807 | Minton & Co. | Stoke |
| 14 | 4 | 183331 | Geo. Jones & Co. | Stoke |

# APPENDIX B

| Date | Parcel No. | Patent No. | Factory, Retailer Wholesaler, etc | Place |
|------|------|------|------|------|
| Feb 1 | 1 | 183650–2 | Minton & Co. | Stoke |
| 2 | 4 | 183706–7 | Geo. L. Ashworth & Bros. | Hanley |
| 13 | 7 | 183940 | F. & R. Pratt & Co. | Fenton |
| 14 | 4 | 183945 | Liddle, Elliot & Son | Longport |
| 27 | 4 | 184220 | Livesley, Powell & Co. | Hanley |
| Mar 31 | 3 | 185473 | Hope & Carter | Burslem |
| Apr 1 | 4 | 185520 | Wm. Brownfield | Cobridge |
| 3 | 4 | 185613 | Minton & Co. | Stoke |
| 22 | 5 | 186266 | Thos. Till & Sons | Burslem |
| 22 | 7 | 186273 | James Edwards & Son | Burslem |
| 26 | 5 | 186325 | idem | Burslem |
| 28 | 4 | 186349 | Hope & Carter | Burslem |
| 28 | 7 | 186354 | Henry Alcock & Co. | Cobridge |
| 29 | 3 | 186361 | The Worcester Royal Porcelain Co. (Ltd.) | Worcester |
| May 2 | 8 | 186477 | Livesley, Powell & Co. | Hanley |
| 15 | 2 | 186841 | J. T. Hudden | Longton |
| 17 | 2 | 186901 | Minton & Co. | Stoke |
| June 6 | 6 | 187358–9 | J. T. Hudden | Longton |
| 9 | 4 | 187403 | The Worcester Royal Porcelain Co. (Ltd.) | Worcester |
| 13 | 5 | 187533 | idem | Worcester |
| 14 | 6 | 187574 | The Hill Pottery Co. Ltd. | Burslem |
| 15 | 2 | 187576 | J. T. Hudden | Longton |
| 16 | 1 | 187583 | Evans & Booth | Burslem |
| 17 | 5 | 187633 | The Worcester Royal Porcelain Co. (Ltd.) | Worcester |
| 29 | 2 | 187847–8 | Ed. F. Bodley & Co. | Burslem |
| 30 | 4 | 187861 | The Hill Pottery Co. Ltd. | Burslem |
| July 3 | 7 | 187972 | T. C. Brown–Westhead, Moore & Co. | Hanley |
| 12 | 3 | 188167 | James Edwards & Son | Burslem |
| Aug 21 | 6 | 189155 | J. Furnival & Co. | Cobridge |
| 23 | 5 | 189283 | Josiah Wedgwood & Sons | Etruria |
| Sept 11 | 4 | 189700 | R. T. Boughton & Co. | Burslem |

| Date | Parcel No. | Patent No. | Factory, Retailer Wholesaler, etc | Place |
|------|-----------|-----------|-----------------------------------|-------|
| 11 | 5 | 189701 | Thos. Cooper (Excrs of) | Hanley |
| 14 | 2 | 189718 | T. C. Brown–Westhead, Moore & Co. | Hanley |
| 18 | 6 | 189782 | Liddle, Elliot & Son | Longport |
| 28 | 4 | 190200 | Minton & Co. | Stoke |
| 30 | 4 | 190656 | S. Barker & Son | Swinton |
| Oct 13 | 8 | 190903 | T. C. Brown–Westhead, Moore & Co. | Hanley |
| 24 | 4 | 191292 | Edward Johns | Staffs. |
| 30 | 4 | 191407–8 | Wm. Brownfield | Cobridge |
| Nov 10 | 4 | 192236 | Pinder Bourne & Co. & Anthony Shaw | Burslem |
| 23 | 10 | 192793 | The Old Hall Earthenware Co. Ltd. | Hanley |
| 29 | 8 | 192963 | James Edwards & Son | Burslem |
| Dec 2 | 3 | 193061 | The Worcester Royal Porcelain Co. (Ltd.) | Worcester |
| 23 | 3 | 193844 | James Dudson | Hanley |
| **1866** | | | | |
| Jan 2 | 4 | 194063 | Pratt & Co. | Fenton |
| 3 | 6 | 194194 | J. T. Close & Co. | Stoke |
| 13 | 2 | 194450 | Ed. F. Bodley & Co. | Burslem |
| 17 | 4 | 194537 | Burgess & Leigh | Burslem |
| 24 | 1 | 194696 | Minton & Co. | Stoke |
| 31 | 5 | 194840 | James Edwards & Son | Burslem |
| Feb 2 | 7 | 194949 | W. T. Copeland | Stoke |
| Mar 2 | 2 | 195644 | Ford, Challinor & Co. | Tunstall |
| 10 | 1 | 195841 | The Old Hall Earthenware Co. (Ltd.) | Hanley |
| Apr 14 | 6 | 196551 | Walker & Carter | Longton |
| 14 | 7 | 196552–4 | Geo. L. Ashworth & Bros. | Hanley |
| 16 | 8 | 196619 | The Old Hall Earthenware Co. (Ltd.) | Hanley |
| 18 | 4 | 196651 | James Edwards & Son | Burslem |

# APPENDIX B

| Date | Parcel No. | Patent No. | Factory, Retailer Wholesaler, etc | Place |
|---|---|---|---|---|
| 20 | 7 | 196672–3 | Wm. Brownfield | Cobridge |
| May 1 | 4 | 196987–8 | J. Furnival & Co. | Cobridge |
| 25 | 1 | 197705–6 | Hope & Carter | Burslem |
| June 4 | 4 | 197857 | James Broadhurst | Longton |
| 12 | 1 | 198135–7 | John Edwards | Fenton |
| 21 | 4 | 198383–4 | Pinder, Bourne & Co. | Burslem |
| 30 | 4 | 198589 | Thos. Minshall | Stoke |
| July 19 | 5 | 199186 | J. T. Hudden | Longton |
| 25 | 3 | 199295 | Geo. Jones | Stoke |
| Aug 17 | 3 | 200006 | Morgan, Wood & Co. | Burslem |
| 29 | 4 | 200324 | Ed. F. Bodley & Co. | Burslem |
| Sept 6 | 4 | 200599 | F. & R. Pratt & Co. | Fenton |
| 13 | 9 | 201040 | T. & C. Ford | Hanley |
| 15 | 8 | 201089 | Geo. L. Ashworth & Bros. | Hanley |
| 20 | 8 | 201495 | Anthony Keeling | Tunstall |
| Oct 8 | 3 | 202103–5 | Minton & Co. | Stoke |
| 13 | 3 | 202493 | Thos. Furnival | Cobridge |
| Nov 3 | 6 | 203173 | Minton & Co. | Stoke |
| 12 | 3 | 203538 | W. T. Copeland | Stoke |
| 14 | 8 | 203817 | T. C. Brown–Westhead, Moore & Co. | Hanley |
| 15 | 4 | 203912 | Geo. Grainger & Co. | Worcester |
| Dec 13 | 4 | 204764 | Liddle, Elliot & Son | Longport |
| 14 | 8 | 204794 | Samuel Barker & Son | Swinton |
| 15 | 5 | 204863 | T. C. Brown–Westhead, Moore & Co. | Hanley |
| 19 | 5 | 205088 | John Meir & Son | Tunstall |
| 24 | 2 | 205201 | J. T. Hudden | Longton |
| **1867** | | | | |
| Jan 8 | 5 | 205372 | James Edwards & Son | Burslem |
| 17 | 3 | 205596 | Ed. F. Bodley & Co. | Burslem |
| 23 | 2 | 205759 | The Worcester Royal Porcelain Co. (Ltd.) | Worcester |
| Feb 9 | 1 | 206033 | Ed. F. Bodley & Co. | Burslem |

318

| Date | Parcel No. | Patent No. | Factory, Retailer Wholesaler, etc | Place |
|---|---|---|---|---|
| 23 | 5 | 206275 | Worthington & Harrop | Hanley |
| Mar 2 | 7 | 206422 | Josiah Wedgwood & Sons | Etruria |
| 4 | 4 | 206497 | T. C. Brown–Westhead, Moore & Co. | Hanley |
| 5 | 6 | 206517 | Powell & Bishop | Hanley |
| 6 | 4 | 206522 | The Old Hall Earthenware Co. (Ltd.) | Hanley |
| 9 | 3 | 206564 | John Edwards | Fenton |
| 11 | 2 | 206662 | Josiah Wedgwood & Sons | Etruria |
| 14 | 1 | 206718 | Davenport Banks & Co. | Etruria |
| 15 | 7 | 206762–6 | Wm. Brownfield | Cobridge |
| 18 | 5 | 206867–8 | Cockson & Chetwynd & Co. | Cobridge |
| 19 | 5 | 206881 | James Edwards & Son | Burslem |
| 20 | 2 | 206887 | Josiah Wedgwood & Sons | Etruria |
| 21 | 10 | 206971 | James Edwards & Son | Burslem |
| 25 | 3 | 206994 | Josiah Wedgwood & Sons | Etruria |
| 26 | 4 | 207024–5 | Minton & Co. | Stoke |
| Apr 3 | 5 | 207163 | idem | Stoke |
| 4 | 2 | 207165 | Josiah Wedgwood & Sons | Etruria |
| 4 | 9 | 207201 | Elsmore & Forster | Tunstall |
| 17 | 1 | 207564 | Chas. Hobson | Burslem |
| 23 | 3 | 207616 | Adams, Scrivener & Co. | Longton |
| 24 | 2 | 207636 | W. T. Copeland | Stoke |
| May 6 | 3 | 207938 | J. & M. P. Bell & Co. | Glasgow |
| 7 | 4 | 207977 | John Meir & Son | Tunstall |
| 8 | 6 | 208002 | T. C. Brown–Westhead Moore & Co. | Hanley |
| 18 | 7 | 208394 | Wm. McAdam | Glasgow |
| 22 | 6 | 208434–5 | Clementson Bros. | Hanley |
| June 6 | 3 | 208750 | Josiah Wedgwood & Sons | Etruria |
| 11 | 6 | 208819 | Clementson Bros. | Hanley |
| 11 | 7 | 208820 | Cockson, Chetwynd & Co. | Cobridge |
| 13 | 3 | 208891 | W. & J. A. Bailey | Alloa |
| 21 | 4 | 209057 | Wm. Brownfield | Cobridge |

# APPENDIX B

| Date | Parcel No. | Patent No. | Factory, Retailer Wholesaler, etc | Place |
|---|---|---|---|---|
| 21 | 8 | 209062 | E. & D. Chetwynd | Hanley |
| 24 | 4 | 209087 | idem | Hanley |
| July 1 | 7 | 209290 | Joseph Ball | Longton |
| 4 | 5 | 209362 | E. J. Ridgway | Hanley |
| 8 | 3 | 209431 | Geo. L. Ashworth & Bros. | Hanley |
| 12 | 5 | 209530 | Geo. Jones | Stoke |
| 15 | 2 | 209556 | Josiah Wedgwood & Sons | Etruria |
| 17 | 2 | 209601 | E. & D. Chetwynd | Hanley |
| 25 | 3 | 209726 | Hope & Carter | Burslem |
| Aug 28 | 10 | 210598 | The Worcester Royal Porcelain Co. Ltd. | Worcester |
| Sept 16 | 7 | 211275 | Thos. Goode & Co. | London |
| 17 | 3 | 211290 | Wedgwood & Co. | Tunstall |
| 21 | 1 | 211536 | Geo. L. Ashworth & Bros. | Hanley |
| 25 | 9 | 211873–4 | Powell & Bishop | Hanley |
| Oct 2 | 1 | 211995 | Minton & Co. | Stoke |
| 3 | 5 | 212054 | Thompson Bros. | Burton-on-Trent |
| 3 | 6 | 212055 | Minton & Co. | Stoke |
| 7 | 4 | 212078 | idem | Stoke |
| 10 | 1 | 212194 | Thos. Booth | Hanley |
| 24 | 5 | 212765 | Ford, Challinor & Co. | Tunstall |
| 26 | 1 | 212881 | W. T. Copeland & Sons | Stoke |
| 28 | 4 | 212956 | idem | Stoke |
| 29 | 3 | 212964 | Josiah Wedgwood & Sons | Etruria |
| 30 | 3 | 212974 | J. T. Hudden | Longton |
| 31 | 7 | 213065 | Powell & Bishop | Hanley |
| Nov 6 | 7 | 213430 | W. & J. A. Bailey | Alloa |
| 7 | 4 | 213436 | James Edwards & Son | Burslem |
| 18 | 9 | 214000 | Ford, Challinor & Co. | Tunstall |
| Dec 3 | 3 | 214618 | W. T. Copeland & Sons | Stoke |
| 12 | 6 | 214981 | F. & R. Pratt & Co. | Fenton |
| 20 | 3 | 215085 | Josiah Wedgwood & Sons | Etruria |
| 27 | 1 | 215314 | J. & J. B. Bebbington | Hanley |

# APPENDIX B

| Date | Parcel No. | Patent No. | Factory, Retailer Wholesaler, etc | Place |
|------|-----------|------------|-----------------------------------|-------|
| **1868** | | | | |
| Jan 3 | 1 | 215481 | Minton & Co. | Stoke |
| 7 | 8 | 215636 | Thompson Bros. | Burton-on-Trent |
| 7 | 11 | 215642 | Cockson, Chetwynd & Co. | Cobridge |
| 8 | 5 | 215674 | T. & R. Boote | Burslem |
| 9 | 7 | 215698 | Taylor, Tunnicliffe & Co. | Hanley |
| 10 | 2 | 215705 | Cork, Edge & Malkin | Burslem |
| 11 | 2 | 215725 | Wm. Brownfield | Cobridge |
| 13 | 2 | 215735 | Geo. L. Ashworth & Bros. | Hanley |
| 16 | 13 | 215879 | The Old Hall Earthenware Co. (Ltd.) | Hanley |
| 25 | 3 | 216186 | Hope & Carter | Burslem |
| 30 | 6 | 216333 | J. Furnival & Co. | Cobridge |
| 31 | 8 | 216347 | Josiah Wedgwood & Sons | Etruria |
| 31 | 14 | 216363 | T. & R. Boote | Burslem |
| Feb 5 | 4 | 216451 | Adams, Scrivener & Co. | Longton |
| 5 | 8 | 216470 | E. Hodgkinson | Hanley |
| 10 | 8 | 216676–8 | Minton & Co. | Stoke |
| 12 | 1 | 216699 | Josiah Wedgwood & Sons | Etruria |
| 14 | 10 | 216821 | John Mortlock | London |
| 18 | 1 | 216895 | Josiah Wedgwood & Sons | Etruria |
| 18 | 2 | 216896–7 | T. C. Brown–Westhead, Moore & Co. | Hanley |
| 20 | 9 | 216988 | Minton & Co. | Stoke |
| 25 | 6 | 217070 | John Rose & Co. | Coalport |
| 27 | 5 | 217100 | Alcock & Digory | Burslem |
| 28 | 7 | 217112 | W. & J. A. Bailey | Alloa |
| Mar 5 | 12 | 217208 | Thos. Goode & Co. | London |
| 5 | 15 | 217212 | Minton & Co. | Stoke |
| 25 | 7 | 217615 | W. T. Copeland & Sons | Stoke |
| 25 | 8 | 217616–7 | The Worcester Royal Porcelain Co. (Ltd.) | Worcester |
| 26 | 3 | 217630 | Walker & Carter | Longton |
| Apr 1 | 6 | 217727 | Minton & Co. | Stoke |

# APPENDIX B

| Date | Parcel No. | Patent No. | Factory, Retailer Wholesaler, etc | Place |
|------|------------|------------|-----------------------------------|-------|
| 6 | 6 | 217938–9 | Pinder, Bourne & Co. | Burslem |
| 16 | 7 | 218139 | Geo. L. Ashworth & Bros. | Hanley |
| 21 | 6 | 218285 | Beech & Hancock | Tunstall |
| 23 | 8 | 218387 | R. Hammersley | Tunstall |
| 28 | 7 | 218466 | T. G. Green | Burton-on-Trent |
| May 13 | 1 | 218664 | Adams, Scrivener & Co. | Longton |
| 14 | 2 | 218764 | Hope & Carter | Burslem |
| 14 | 6 | 218773 | Philip Brookes | Fenton |
| 26 | 5 | 218951 | T. C. Brown–Westhead Moore & Co. | Hanley |
| 26 | 6 | 218952 | Pinder, Bourne & Co. | Burslem |
| 28 | 3 | 218967 | Holdcroft & Wood | Tunstall |
| 28 | 5 | 218969–71 | Minton & Co. | Stoke |
| 28 | 7 | 218973 | J. & T. Bevington | Hanley |
| 30 | 4 | 219042 | T. & R. Boote | Burslem |
| June 8 | 4 | 219174 | Burgess & Leigh | Burslem |
| 12 | 5 | 219316–7 | Wm. Brownfield | Cobridge |
| 16 | 4 | 219344 | W. P. & G. Phillips | London |
| 22 | 5 | 219484 | Minton & Co. | Stoke |
| July 10 | 3 | 219756 | Josiah Wedgwood & Sons | Etruria |
| 16 | 3 | 219833 | Hackney & Co. | Longton |
| 20 | 2 | 219942–3 | Hope & Carter | Burslem |
| 24 | 4 | 219997 | W. T. Copeland & Sons | Stoke |
| 30 | 6 | 220183 | Adams, Scrivener & Co. | Longton |
| Aug 1 | 5 | 220236–7 | T. & R. Boote | Burslem |
| 13 | 1 | 220772 | Josiah Wedgwood & Sons | Etruria |
| 15 | 8 | 220821–4 | James Edwards & Son | Burslem |
| 17 | 2 | 220828 | Ed. F. Bodley & Co. | Burslem |
| 21 | 2 | 220906 | Ralph Malkin | Fenton |
| 31 | 7 | 221124 | T. & R. Boote | Burslem |
| Sept 1 | 1 | 221125–6 | James Wardle | Hanley |
| 4 | 6 | 221203–4 | Gelson Bros. | Hanley |
| 5 | 3 | 221214 | T. C. Brown–Westhead, Moore & Co. | Hanley |

322

# APPENDIX B

| Date | Parcel No. | Patent No. | Factory, Retailer Wholesaler, etc | Place |
|------|------|------|------|------|
|     | 5 | 6 | 221217–9 | McBirney & Armstrong | Belleek |
|     | 9 | 4 | 221311 | Hope & Carter | Burslem |
|     | 9 | 5 | 221312 | F. Jones & Co. | Longton |
|     | 9 | 6 | 221313 | Wedgwood & Co. | Tunstall |
|     | 9 | 9 | 221316 | J. & T. Bevington | Hanley |
|     | 12 | 3 | 221521–2 | Minton & Co. | Stoke |
|     | 14 | 4 | 221548 | Thos. Booth & Co. | Burslem |
|     | 17 | 4 | 221688 | T. C. Sambrook & Co. | Burslem |
|     | 21 | 4 | 221814–7 | George Ash | Hanley |
|     | 25 | 4 | 221881–2 | Minton & Co. | Stoke |
|     | 25 | 13 | 222083–4 | T. C. Brown–Westhead, Moore & Co. | Hanley |
| Oct | 8 | 7 | 222460 | Minton & Co. | Stoke |
|     | 9 | 2 | 222476 | J. Holdcroft | Stoke |
|     | 9 | 3 | 222477 | Hope & Carter | Burslem |
|     | 9 | 5 | 222482–4 | Davenports & Co. | Longport |
|     | 14 | 8 | 222736 | Geo. Jones | Stoke |
|     | 17 | 4 | 223063 | Minton & Co. | Stoke |
|     | 21 | 8 | 223308 | W. P. & G. Phillips | London |
|     | 22 | 1 | 223309 | McBirney & Armstrong | Belleek |
|     | 22 | 5 | 223314–5 | James Edwards & Son | Burslem |
| Nov | 3 | 5 | 223817–8 | Minton & Co. | Stoke |
|     | 3 | 6 | 223819 | T. C. Brown–Westhead, Moore & Co. | Hanley |
|     | 6 | 13 | 224090 | Powell & Bishop | Hanley |
|     | 9 | 5 | 224172 | Josiah Wedgwood & Sons | Etruria |
|     | 16 | 3 | 224382 | Knapper & Blackhurst | Tunstall |
|     | 17 | 1 | 224389 | Moore Bros. | Cobridge |
|     | 21 | 5 | 224539 | Minton & Co. | Stoke |
|     | 24 | 5 | 224645 | T. C. Brown–Westhead Moore & Co. | Hanley |
|     | 25 | 4 | 224724 | Cork, Edge & Malkin | Burslem |
| Dec | 1 | 4 | 224953 | T. C. Brown–Westhead, Moore & Co. | Hanley |

323

# APPENDIX B

| Date | | Parcel No. | Patent No. | Factory, Retailer Wholesaler, etc | Place |
|---|---|---|---|---|---|
| | 3 | 5 | 225073–4 | The Worcester Royal Porcelain Co. (Ltd.) | Worcester |
| | 11 | 5 | 225410 | Ed. T. Bodley & Co. | Burslem |
| | 12 | 4 | 225425 | Wm. Brownfield | Cobridge |
| | 14 | 7 | 225441 | Cockson, Chetwynd & Co. | Cobridge |
| | 23 | 5 | 225734 | Minton & Co. | Stoke |
| | 23 | 6 | 225735 | The Worcester Royal Porcelain Co. (Ltd.) | Worcester |
| | 31 | 6 | 225993 | Geo. L. Ashworth & Bros. | Hanley |
| | 31 | 7 | 225994 | R. Hammersley | Tunstall |
| **1869** | | | | | |
| Jan | 1 | 8 | 226051 | Geo. Jones | Stoke |
| | 4 | 4 | 226098 | Minton & Co. | Stoke |
| | 7 | 6 | 226131 | Thos. Goode & Co. | London |
| | 21 | 6 | 226527–8 | Minton & Co. | Stoke |
| | 22 | 5 | 226570 | Gelson Bros. | Hanley |
| | 22 | 13 | 226581 | T. C. Brown–Westhead, Moore & Co. | Hanley |
| | 25 | 3 | 226625 | Worthington & Son | Hanley |
| | 28 | 5 | 226738 | Minton & Co. | Stoke |
| | 28 | 10 | 226747–8 | George Ash | Hanley |
| Feb | 1 | 7 | 226910 | T. C. Brown–Westhead, Moore & Co. | Hanley |
| | 2 | 4 | 226928 | Geo. Yearsley | Longton |
| | 9 | 5 | 227219 | Minton & Co. | Stoke |
| | 11 | 10 | 227277 | Geo. Jones | Stoke |
| | 15 | 1 | 227307 | Thos. Booth & Co. | Burslem |
| | 19 | 2 | 227345 | Josiah Wedgwood & Sons | Etruria |
| | 22 | 6 | 227403 | idem | Etruria |
| | 22 | 11 | 227409 | McBirney & Armstrong | Belleek |
| | 22 | 13 | 227411 | Pinder, Bourne & Co. | Burslem |
| | 27 | 5 | 227518 | Josiah Wedgwood & Sons | Etruria |
| Mar | 1 | 8 | 227556–8 | Worthington & Son | Hanley |
| | 3 | 8 | 227619 | Thos. Till & Sons | Burslem |

| Date | Parcel No. | Patent No. | Factory, Retailer Wholesaler, etc | Place |
|------|-----------|-----------|-----------------------------------|-------|
| 6 | 8 | 227668 | F. Primavesi | Cardiff |
| 8 | 6 | 227696 | F. & R. Pratt & Co. | Fenton |
| 9 | 1 | 227743–4 | Geo. Jones | Stoke |
| 9 | 3 | 227746 | idem | Stoke |
| 10 | 10 | 227823 | F. Primavesi | Cardiff |
| 24 | 1 | 228141 | J. F. Wileman | Fenton |
| Apr 1 | 1 | 228290 | Wood & Pigott | Tunstall |
| 2 | 6 | 228377 | Wm. Brownfield | Cobridge |
| 2 | 7 | 228378 | Minton & Co. | Stoke |
| 6 | 3 | 228430 | Baker & Chetwynd | Burslem |
| 7 | 2 | 228455 | Minton & Co. | Stoke |
| 7 | 4 | 228457 | The Worcester Royal Porcelain Co. (Ltd.) | Worcester |
| 12 | 4 | 228572 | Taylor, Tunnicliffe & Co. | Hanley |
| 12 | 5 | 228573 | Liddle, Elliot & Son | Longport |
| 20 | 5 | 228764 | idem | Longport |
| 28 | 13 | 228937 | J. & T. Bevington | Hanley |
| May 11 | 1 | 229319 | Adams, Scrivener & Co. | Longton |
| 13 | 16 | 229405 | James Edwards & Son | Burslem |
| 21 | 1 | 229523 | Worthington & Son | Hanley |
| 26 | 4 | 229627 | Thos. Booth | Hanley |
| 27 | 8 | 229642–4 | Davenport & Co. | Longport |
| June 3 | 6 | 229837 | McBirney & Armstrong | Belleek |
| 8 | 7 | 229959 | W. P. & G. Phillips & Pearce | London |
| 19 | 5 | 230183–4 | Wm. Brownfield | Cobridge |
| 25 | 4 | 230429 | James Edwards & Son | Burslem |
| 26 | 9 | 230455 | Minton & Co. | Stoke |
| July 3 | 9 | 230707–8 | Josiah Wedgwood & Sons | Etruria |
| 6 | 3 | 230739 | John Meir & Son | Tunstall |
| 19 | 8 | 231101 | James Wardle | Hanley |
| 20 | 2 | 231124 | Josiah Wedgwood & Sons | Etruria |
| 21 | 6 | 231153–4 | George Ash | Hanley |
| 23 | 6 | 231215 | Minton & Co. | Stoke |
| 24 | 4 | 231222 | W. T. Copeland & Sons | Stoke |

| Date | Parcel No. | Patent No. | Factory, Retailer Wholesaler, etc | Place |
|---|---|---|---|---|
| 26 | 4 | 231241 | Leveson Hill (Excrs of) | Stoke |
| 27 | 4 | 231256 | J. T. Hudden | Longton |
| Aug 2 | 6 | 231504 | W. T. Copeland | Stoke |
| 3 | 5 | 231602 | John Edwards | Fenton |
| 4 | 4 | 231613 | Tomkinson Bros. & Co. | Hanley |
| 11 | 13 | 231812 | W. P. & G. Phillips & Pearce | London |
| 19 | 6 | 232307 | W. T. Copeland & Sons | Stoke |
| 26 | 6 | 232474 | idem | Stoke |
| 31 | 6 | 232586–7 | John Pratt & Co. | Lane Delph |
| 31 | 12 | 232598 | W. T. Copeland & Sons | Stoke |
| Sept 4 | 3 | 232822 | Minton & Co. | Stoke |
| 8 | 5 | 232878 | W. T. Copeland & Sons | Stoke |
| 8 | 6 | 232879 | Pinder, Bourne & Co. | Burslem |
| 9 | 3 | 232890 | John Pratt & Co. | Lane Delph |
| 10 | 4 | 232903 | Minton & Co. | Stoke |
| 21 | 7 | 233411 | Gelson Bros. | Hanley |
| 22 | 10 | 233527 | W. & J. A. Bailey | Alloa |
| 30 | 8 | 233864–6 | T. C. Brown–Westhead Moore & Co. | Hanley |
| Oct 1 | 3 | 233923–4 | Minton & Co. | Stoke |
| 4 | 6 | 234016 | idem | Stoke |
| 14 | 3 | 234465 | McBirney & Armstrong | Belleek |
| 15 | 6 | 234486 | Geo. Jones | Stoke |
| 23 | 4 | 235012 | idem | Stoke |
| 26 | 2 | 235158 | James Ellis & Son | Hanley |
| 27 | 5 | 235168 | McBirney & Armstrong | Belleek |
| 29 | 3 | 235399–400 | Minton & Co. | Stoke |
| 29 | 4 | 235401–2 | Powell & Bishop | Hanley |
| Nov 2 | 12 | 235589 | Ed. Clarke | Tunstall |
| 3 | 12 | 235691 | T. C. Brown–Westhead, Moore & Co. | Hanley |

| Date | | Parcel No. | Patent No. | Factory, Retailer Wholesaler, etc | Place |
|---|---|---|---|---|---|
| | 8 | 1 | 235827–9 | McBirney & Armstrong | Belleek |
| | 8 | 2 | 235830 | T. C. Brown–Westhead, Moore & Co. | Hanley |
| | 9 | 11 | 235966 | Tams & Lowe | Longton |
| | 10 | 3 | 235974 | Wm. Brownfield | Cobridge |
| | 13 | 5 | 236184–5 | McBirney & Armstrong | Belleek |
| | 15 | 8 | 236203–7 | Liddle, Elliot & Son | Longport |
| | 18 | 5 | 236435 | Alcock & Digory | Burslem |
| | 19 | 12 | 236478 | The Worcester Royal Porcelain Co. (Ltd.) | Worcester |
| | 20 | 8 | 236533 | Thos. Goode & Co. | London |
| | 20 | 9 | 236534 | John Mortlock | London |
| | 23 | 1 | 236585 | McBirney & Armstrong | Belleek |
| | 24 | 4 | 236628 | Minton & Co. | Stoke |
| | 26 | 3 | 236653 | idem | Stoke |
| Dec | 1 | 3 | 236756 | Geo. Jones | Stoke |
| | 3 | 9 | 236829 | Wm. Brownfield | Cobridge |
| | 17 | 7 | 237224 | Minton & Co. | Stoke |
| | 18 | 2 | 237229 | Powell & Bishop | Hanley |
| | 18 | 3 | 237230 | McBirney & Armstrong | Belleek |
| | 20 | 8 | 237358 | George Ash | Hanley |
| | 22 | 7 | 237500 | Geo. Jones | Stoke |
| | 24 | 1 | 237552 | Gelson Bros. | Hanley |
| | 28 | 2 | 237565 | John Pratt & Co. | Lane Delph |
| | 31 | 2 | 237644 | Minton & Co. | Stoke |
| **1870** | | | | | |
| Jan | 1 | 5 | 237691 | T. C. Brown–Westhead, Moore & Co. | Hanley |
| | 3 | 4 | 237742 | Geo. Jones | Stoke |
| | 7 | 9 | 237899 | Pellatt & Co. | London |
| | 15 | 12 | 238147–8 | Liddle, Elliot & Son | Longport |
| | 27 | 8 | 238388 | Chas. Hobson | Burslem |
| | 29 | 3 | 238436 | Minton & Co. | Stoke |

| Date | Parcel No. | Patent No. | Factory, Retailer Wholesaler, etc | Place |
|---|---|---|---|---|
| Feb 1 | 6 | 238527–8 | T. C. Brown–Westhead, Moore & Co. | Hanley |
| 3 | 13 | 238595–6 | idem | Hanley |
| 4 | 7 | 238603 | Powell & Bishop | Hanley |
| 7 | 5 | 238627 | Wiltshaw, Wood & Co. | Burslem |
| 7 | 6 | 238628 | W. & J. A. Bailey | Alloa |
| 9 | 2 | 238663 | Josiah Wedgwood & Sons | Etruria |
| 10 | 8 | 238688 | Minton & Co. | Stoke |
| 11 | 12 | 238761–2 | W. P. & G. Phillips & Pearce | London |
| 15 | 6 | 238898–9 | T. C. Brown–Westhead Moore & Co. | Hanley |
| 25 | 2 | 239139 | Minton & Co. | Stoke |
| 28 | 6 | 239239 | idem | Stoke |
| Mar 2 | 4 | 239304 | idem | Stoke |
| 7 | 6 | 239422 | Chas. Hobson | Burslem |
| 8 | 1 | 239424–6 | Geo. Jones | Stoke |
| 10 | 1 | 239474 | idem | Stoke |
| 10 | 9 | 239510 | Powell & Bishop | Hanley |
| 11 | 8 | 239528 | Leveson Hill (Excrs of) | Stoke |
| 14 | 4 | 239548 | T. C. Brown–Westhead, Moore & Co. | Hanley |
| 15 | 6 | 239585 | Thos. Till & Sons | Burslem |
| 16 | 2 | 239590–1 | Minton & Co. | Stoke |
| 17 | 4 | 239610–1 | McBirney & Armstrong | Belleek |
| 17 | 7 | 239622 | The Worcester Royal Porcelain Co. (Ltd.) | Worcester |
| 17 | 9 | 239628 | J. Mortlock | London |
| 18 | 6 | 239642 | Minton & Co. | Stoke |
| 23 | 9 | 239793–4 | J. Blackshaw & Co. | Stoke |
| 25 | 4 | 239968 | Hope & Carter | Burslem |
| 25 | 5 | 239969–70 | Minton & Co. | Stoke |
| 26 | 1 | 240000–1 | idem | Stoke |
| 26 | 2 | 240002 | Worthington & Son | Hanley |

# APPENDIX B

| Date | Parcel No. | Patent No. | Factory, Retailer Wholesaler, etc | Place |
|------|------|------|------|------|
| 28 | 9 | 240079 | The Old Hall Earthenware Co. Ltd. | Hanley |
| Apr 7 | 9 | 240383 | Cork, Edge & Malkin | Burslem |
| 7 | 10 | 240384–5 | Baker & Co. | Fenton |
| 7 | 11 | 240386 | Harvey Adams & Co. | Longton |
| 9 | 1 | 240458 | Minton & Co. | Stoke |
| 11 | 3 | 240493 | The Worcester Royal Porcelain Co. Ltd. | Worcester |
| 13 | 4 | 240516 | Thos. Goode & Co. | London |
| 14 | 7 | 240570 | Minton & Co. | Stoke |
| May 5 | 1 | 241231 | James Oldham & Co. | Hanley |
| 6 | 5 | 241264–5 | McBirney & Armstrong | Belleek |
| 10 | 4 | 241367–8 | George Ash | Hanley |
| 13 | 8 | 241474 | T. C. Brown–Westhead, Moore & Co. | Hanley |
| 17 | 7 | 241544 | idem | Hanley |
| 18 | 6 | 241567–8 | Bates, Elliott & Co. | Longport |
| 21 | 6 | 241649 | The Old Hall Earthenware Co. Ltd. | Hanley |
| 21 | 12 | 241666 | James Edwards & Son | Burslem |
| 25 | 7 | 241754 | idem | Burslem |
| 26 | 5 | 241960 | Minton & Co. | Stoke |
| 30 | 15 | 242077 | Geo. Jones | Stoke |
| June 3 | 8 | 242154 | F. & R. Pratt & Co. | Fenton |
| 7 | 15 | 242233 | Hope & Carter | Burslem |
| 7 | 16 | 242234 | Thos. Booth | Hanley |
| 9 | 3 | 242391 | T. C. Brown–Westhead, Moore & Co. | Hanley |
| 10 | 1 | 242392–4 | Wm. Brownfield | Cobridge |
| 11 | 3 | 242439 | James Edwards & Son | Burslem |
| 17 | 7 | 242503–8 | Minton, Hollins & Co. | Stoke |
| 22 | 1 | 242634–5 | Harvey Adams & Co. | Longton |
| 22 | 3 | 242637–8 | Minton, Hollins & Co. | Stoke |
| 22 | 4 | 242639 | The Worcester Royal Porcelain Co. Ltd. | Worcester |

| Date | Parcel No. | Patent No. | Factory, Retailer Wholesaler, etc | Place |
|---|---|---|---|---|
| 27 | 1 | 242715 | Geo. Jones | Stoke |
| July 5 | 5 | 242859 | Baker & Co. | Fenton |
| 8 | 7 | 243049–50 | James Wardle | Hanley |
| 13 | 8 | 243176 | James Edwards & Son | Burslem |
| 14 | 9 | 243197–9 | Minton, Hollins & Co. | Stoke |
| 14 | 10 | 243200 | The Worcester Royal Porcelain Co. Ltd. | Worcester |
| 15 | 1 | 243207 | W. T. Copeland & Sons | Stoke |
| 16 | 2 | 243235 | James Wardle | Hanley |
| 19 | 6 | 243352 | F. & R. Pratt & Co. | Fenton |
| 20 | 5 | 243368 | Thos. Booth | Hanley |
| 21 | 1 | 243378 | idem | Hanley |
| 22 | 1 | 243385 | Cork, Edge & Malkin | Burslem |
| 27 | 1 | 243480 | Beech, Unwin & Co. | Longton |
| Aug 1 | 2 | 243555 | R. G. Scrivener & Co. | Hanley |
| 4 | 4 | 243646 | James Wardle | Hanley |
| 4 | 5 | 243647–8 | J. Broadhurst | Longton |
| 9 | 2 | 243807 | Wm. Brownfield | Cobridge |
| 22 | 4 | 244137–8 | T. & R. Boote | Burslem |
| 23 | 6 | 244173 | Geo. Jones | Stoke |
| 25 | 5 | 244223 | T. & R. Boote | Burslem |
| Sept 7 | 7 | 244703 | Bailey & Cooke | Hanley |
| 10 | 9 | 244741 | Minton & Co. | Stoke |
| 16 | 5 | 244961 | idem | Stoke |
| 19 | 2 | 244976 | Wm. Brownfield | Cobridge |
| 27 | 4 | 245227 | Elsmore, Forster & Co. | Tunstall |
| 27 | 6 | 245229 | W. P. & G. Phillips & D. Pearce | London |
| 28 | 11 | 245265 | Gelson Bros. | Hanley |
| Oct 4 | 7 | 245463 | Joseph Holdcroft | Longton |
| 4 | 8 | 245464 | Minton & Co. | Stoke |
| 6 | 4 | 245604 | idem | Stoke |
| 6 | 5 | 245605 | James Broadhurst | Longton |
| 7 | 3 | 245620 | Minton & Co. | Stoke |
| 8 | 9 | 245668 | Powell & Bishop | Hanley |

# APPENDIX B

| Date | Parcel No. | Patent No. | Factory, Retailer Wholesaler, etc | Place |
|------|------------|------------|-----------------------------------|-------|
| 19 | 2 | 245985–6 | Geo. Jones | Stoke |
| 22 | 2 | 246149 | Wm. Brownfield | Cobridge |
| 25 | 6 | 246181 | T. C. Brown–Westhead, Moore & Co. | Hanley |
| Nov 4 | 9 | 246927 | idem | Hanley |
| 9 | 8 | 247047 | John Meir & Son | Tunstall |
| 9 | 9 | 247048 | Pellatt & Co. | London |
| 10 | 5 | 247071–3 | Minton & Co. | Stoke |
| 10 | 10 | 247079–80 | Wm. Brownfield | Cobridge |
| 12 | 3 | 247248 | McBirney & Armstrong | Belleek |
| 12 | 8 | 247255 | Minton, Hollins & Co. | Stoke |
| 22 | 3 | 247944 | Geo. Jones | Stoke |
| 24 | 3 | 248041 | Minton & Co. | Stoke |
| 24 | 8 | 248049 | Bates, Elliott & Co. | Longport |
| 25 | 1 | 248051 | Minton & Co. | Stoke |
| 25 | 2 | 248052 | Turner, Goddard & Co. | Tunstall |
| 26 | 9 | 248114–6 | T. & R. Boote | Burslem |
| Dec 1 | 7 | 248242 | Wm. Brownfield | Cobridge |
| 2 | 11 | 248294 | T. C. Brown–Westhead, Moore & Co. | Hanley |
| 5 | 4 | 248309–15 | Minton, Hollins & Co. | Stoke |
| 16 | 5 | 248869 | Bates, Elliott & Co. | Longport |
| 17 | 11 | 248899 | idem | Longport |
| 19 | 9 | 248953 | Harvey, Adams & Co. | Longton |
| 27 | 4 | 249104 | James Edwards & Son | Burslem |
| **1871** | | | | |
| Jan 2 | 2 | 249235 | Gelson Bros. | Hanley |
| 6 | 3 | 249331 | Minton & Co. | Stoke |
| 7 | 8 | 249356 | Bates, Elliott & Co. | Longport |
| 9 | 4 | 249388–93 | McBirney & Armstrong | Belleek |
| 10 | 7 | 249439 | Geo. Jones | Stoke |
| 11 | 4 | 249464 | J. Mortlock | London |
| 12 | 7 | 249479 | McBirney & Armstrong | Belleek |
| 12 | 12 | 249490 | Soane & Smith | London |

| Date | Parcel No. | Patent No. | Factory, Retailer Wholesaler, etc | Place |
|------|-----------|-----------|-----------------------------------|-------|
| 24 | 4 | 249811 | idem | London |
| 26 | 8 | 249903–6 | Minton, Hollins & Co. | Stoke |
| 27 | 9 | 249927 | The Worcester Royal Porcelain Co. Ltd. | Worcester |
| 30 | 2 | 249972 | Gelson Bros. | Hanley |
| Feb 2 | 3 | 250020 | James Edwards & Son | Burslem |
| 6 | 5 | 250168–71 | McBirney & Armstrong | Belleek |
| 8 | 9 | 250231 | James Macintyre & Co. | Burslem |
| 11 | 9 | 250291 | T. C. Brown–Westhead, Moore & Co. | Hanley |
| 13 | 6 | 250366 | Edge, Malkin & Co. | Burslem |
| 13 | 7 | 250367 | Worthington & Son | Hanley |
| 13 | 9 | 250369 | Powell & Bishop | Hanley |
| 13 | 10 | 250370 | Ed. F. Bodley & Co. | Burslem |
| 15 | 7 | 250416–8 | Powell & Bishop | Hanley |
| 17 | 7 | 250440–1 | Thos. Peake | Tunstall |
| 20 | 2 | 250478–9 | Elsmore & Forster | Tunstall |
| 28 | 8 | 250657 | The Watcombe Terra Cotta Clay Co. Ltd. | Devon |
| Mar 9 | 4 | 250865 | J. & T. Bevington | Hanley |
| 14 | 4 | 250954 | John Pratt & Co. | Lane Delph |
| 15 | 10 | 251013 | Bates, Elliott & Co. | Longport |
| 27 | 1 | 251246 | Wm. Brownfield & Son | Cobridge |
| 29 | 1 | 251329 | Thos. Furnival & Son | Cobridge |
| Apr 4 | 4 | 251453 | McBirney & Armstrong | Belleek |
| 22 | 4 | 251966 | John Pratt & Co. | Stoke |
| 24 | 4 | 251988 | Josiah Wedgwood & Sons | Etruria |
| 26 | 12 | 252068 | Minton, Hollins & Co. | Stoke |
| 27 | 7 | 252093–4 | Wood & Clarke | Burslem |
| 27 | 8 | 252095–7 | W. P. & G. Phillips & Pearce | London |
| 28 | 1 | 252128 | Wood & Clarke | Burslem |
| 29 | 6 | 252156 | idem | Burslem |
| 29 | 7 | 252157 | James Edwards & Son | Burslem |

# APPENDIX B

| Date | Parcel No. | Patent No. | Factory, Retailer Wholesaler, etc | Place |
|---|---|---|---|---|
| May 1 | 9 | 252171–3 | T. C. Brown–Westhead, Moore & Co. | Hanley |
| 2 | 3 | 252176 | Ambrose Bevington | Hanley |
| 2 | 4 | 252177–80 | Wm. Brownfield & Son | Cobridge |
| 3 | 4 | 252188 | John Jackson & Co. | Rother'm |
| 6 | 1 | 252258 | W. P. & G. Phillips & Pearce | London |
| 9 | 9 | 252387 | Liddle, Elliott & Co. | Longport |
| 11 | 13 | 252487 | Powell & Bishop | Hanley |
| 13 | 6 | 252503 | Elsmore & Forster | Tunstall |
| 22 | 9 | 252709 | McBirney & Armstrong | Belleek |
| 24 | 10 | 252756 | John Meir & Son | Tunstall |
| June 2 | 4 | 253017 | T. C. Brown–Westhead, Moore & Co. | Hanley |
| 7 | 7 | 253069 | Grove & Stark | Longton |
| 16 | 9 | 253335 | John Twigg | Rother'm |
| 17 | 3 | 253339–40 | Minton & Co. | Stoke |
| 19 | 9 | 253378–9 | Pinder, Bourne & Co. | Burslem |
| 22 | 1 | 253472 | Thos. Till & Sons | Burslem |
| 23 | 9 | 253571 | Bates, Elliott & Co. | Longport |
| July 4 | 8 | 253796–8 | W. T. Copeland | Stoke |
| 14 | 6 | 254013 | Taylor, Tunnicliffe & Co. | Hanley |
| 15 | 2 | 254030 | Thos. Booth | Hanley |
| 19 | 2 | 254074 | Ambrose Bevington | Hanley |
| 22 | 8 | 254130–3 | Haviland & Co. | London and Limoges |
| 25 | 12 | 254239 | Bates, Elliott & Co. | Longport |
| 29 | 6 | 254344 | Hope & Carter | Burslem |
| Aug 2 | 3 | 254429 | Robinson & Leadbeater | Stoke |
| 9 | 7 | 254757 | Bates, Elliott & Co. | Longport |
| 18 | 10 | 254899 | Pratt & Co. | Fenton |
| 28 | 5 | 255267 | James Wardle | Hanley |
| 29 | 2 | 255274 | Geo. Jones | Stoke |
| 30 | 4 | 255320 | Thos. Barlow | Longton |

# APPENDIX B

| Date | Parcel No. | Patent No. | Factory, Retailer Wholesaler, etc | Place |
|---|---|---|---|---|
| 31 | 9 | 255333 | J. H. & J. Davis | Hanley |
| Sept 15 | 7 | 255821 | J. Bevington & Co. | Hanley |
| 15 | 10 | 255825 | Thos. Barlow | Longton |
| 19 | 2 | 255849 | Minton & Co. | Stoke |
| 25 | 8 | 256079 | T. C. Brown–Westhead, Moore & Co. | Hanley |
| 28 | 5 | 256215 | Thos. Booth & Co. | Tunstall |
| Oct 4 | 7 | 256357–60 | Minton & Co. | Stoke |
| 4 | 9 | 256362 | Pinder, Bourne & Co. | Burslem |
| 6 | 6 | 256427–9 | Moore & Son | Longton |
| 9 | 8 | 256538 | E. J. Ridgway & Son | Hanley |
| 10 | 3 | 256582 | J. T. Hudden | Longton |
| 10 | 6 | 256586 | T. C. Brown–Westhead, Moore & Co. | Hanley |
| 11 | 4 | 256598 | McBirney & Armstrong | Belleek |
| 14 | 6 | 256687 | Thos. Booth & Co. | Tunstall |
| 14 | 7 | 256688 | Josiah Wedgwood & Sons | Etruria |
| 14 | 8 | 256689 | McBirney & Armstrong | Belleek |
| 18 | 4 | 256853 | Moore & Son | Longton |
| 19 | 6 | 256907 | W. T. Copeland & Sons | Stoke |
| 24 | 3 | 257126 | Robert Cooke | Hanley |
| 31 | 5 | 257258 | Minton & Co. | Stoke |
| 31 | 6 | 257259 | Edge, Hill & Palmer | Longton |
| Nov 3 | 4 | 257364–5 | R. G. Scrivener & Co. | Hanley |
| 3 | 5 | 257366 | J. F. Wileman | Fenton |
| 15 | 4 | 257728 | John Thomson & Sons | Glasgow |
| 23 | 6 | 257944–6 | Thos. Ford | Hanley |
| Dec 1 | 6 | 258095 | Geo. Jones | Stoke |
| 15 | 5 | 258773 | Robinson & Leadbeater | Stoke |
| 16 | 7 | 258816 | McBirney & Armstrong | Belleek |
| 22 | 6 | 258949 | F. & R. Pratt | Fenton |
| 23 | 3 | 258956–7 | Geo. Jones | Stoke |
| 29 | 10 | 259053 | T. C. Brown–Westhead, Moore & Co. | Hanley |

# APPENDIX B

| Date | Parcel No. | Patent No. | Factory, Retailer Wholesaler, etc | Place |
|---|---|---|---|---|
| **1872** | | | | |
| Jan 1 | 5 | 259076 | Moore & Son | Longton |
| 1 | 6 | 259077 | Edge Malkin & Co. | Burslem |
| 5 | 3 | 259264 | McBirney & Armstrong | Belleek |
| 6 | 1 | 259271 | Minton & Co. | Stoke |
| 18 | 6 | 259801 | The Worcester Royal Porcelain Co. Ltd. | Worcester |
| 20 | 6 | 259854 | Geo. Jones | Stoke |
| 30 | 7 | 260081 | W. T. Copeland & Sons | Stoke |
| Feb 2 | 2 | 260187 | Moore & Son | Longton |
| 2 | 11 | 260240–1 | Turner & Tomkinson | Tunstall |
| 3 | 4 | 260255–6 | Geo. Jones | Stoke |
| 7 | 3 | 260297 | Ambrose Bevington | Hanley |
| 15 | 3 | 260463 | Powell & Bishop | Hanley |
| 16 | 6 | 260503 | McBirney & Armstrong | Belleek |
| 16 | 7 | 260504–6 | Geo. Jones | Stoke |
| 19 | 6 | 260565 | Wm. H. Goss | Stoke |
| 20 | 4 | 260578 | The Worcester Royal Porcelain Co. Ltd. | Worcester |
| 22 | 3 | 260640 | Minton & Co. | Stoke |
| Mar 4 | 3 | 260868 | Geo. Jones | Stoke |
| 4 | 4 | 260869–70 | Minton & Co. | Stoke |
| 4 | 6 | 260872 | Minton, Hollins & Co. | Stoke |
| 7 | 7 | 260992–3 | Harvey, Adams & Co. | Longton |
| 7 | 10 | 260998 | Bates, Elliott & Co. | Burslem |
| 8 | 5 | 261006–8 | Minton, Hollins & Co. | Stoke |
| 9 | 1 | 261016 | McBirney & Armstrong | Belleek |
| 13 | 8 | 261120 | Minton, Hollins & Co. | Stoke |
| 16 | 6 | 261190 | Minton & Co. | Stoke |
| 18 | 6 | 261207 | idem | Stoke |
| 20 | 10 | 261325 | The Worcester Royal Porcelain Co. Ltd. | Worcester |
| 21 | 14 | 261379 | R. M. Taylor | Fenton |
| 22 | 5 | 261391 | J. Holdcroft | Longton |

# APPENDIX B

| Date | Parcel No. | Patent No. | Factory, Retailer Wholesaler, etc | Place |
|------|------------|------------|-----------------------------------|-------|
| 22 | 8 | 261394 | T. C. Brown–Westhead, Moore & Co. | Hanley |
| 26 | 3 | 261453–4 | Robinson & Leadbeater | Stoke |
| 26 | 6 | 261458 | Phillips & Pearce | London |
| Apr 5 | 4 | 261638 | Wedgwood & Co. | Tunstall |
| 5 | 5 | 261639 | Minton & Co. | Stoke |
| 6 | 1 | 261646–7 | J. Holdcroft | Longton |
| 9 | 6 | 261724 | T. C. Brown–Westhead, Moore & Co. | Hanley |
| 10 | 11 | 261749 | Thos. Furnival & Son | Cobridge |
| 17 | 13 | 261976 | E. J. Ridgway & Son | Hanley |
| 19 | 5 | 262013 | Minton, Hollins & Co. | Stoke |
| 24 | 5 | 262203 | John Pratt & Co. Ltd. | Lane Delph |
| 27 | 9 | 262354 | Moore & Son | Longton |
| May 2 | 9 | 262425–6 | Harvey Adams & Co. | Longton |
| 2 | 11 | 262428–9 | Thos. Furnival & Son | Cobridge |
| 3 | 9 | 262471–2 | Minton & Co. | Stoke |
| 3 | 11 | 262474 | Bates, Elliott & Co. | Burslem |
| 6 | 3 | 262483–5 | Moore & Son | Longton |
| 6 | 8 | 262493 | Bates, Elliott & Co. | Burslem |
| 6 | 9 | 262494–5 | Minton, Hollins & Co. | Stoke |
| 10 | 1 | 262651 | Moore & Son | Longton |
| 11 | 4 | 262672 | Thos. Booth & Sons | Hanley |
| 27 | 1 | 262951 | Geo. Jones | Stoke |
| 27 | 3 | 262953 | Minton, Hollins & Co. | Stoke |
| 29 | 2 | 262990 | Geo. Jones | Stoke |
| 29 | 5 | 262993–4 | Geo. Grainger & Co. | Worcester |
| 30 | 1 | 262999–3000 | Minton & Co. | Stoke |
| June 3 | 6 | 263106 | The Watcombe Terra Cotta Clay Co. Ltd. | Devon |
| 5 | 3 | 263134 | Hope & Carter | Burslem |
| 6 | 6 | 263162 | Wm. Brownfield & Son | Cobridge |
| 7 | 4 | 263191 | Minton, Hollins & Co. | Stoke |

# APPENDIX B

| Date | Parcel No. | Patent No. | Factory, Retailer Wholesaler, etc | Place |
|------|-----------|-----------|-----------------------------------|-------|
| 11 | 5 | 263315 | Josiah Wedgwood & Sons | Etruria |
| 11 | 12 | 263348 | W. T. Copeland & Sons | Stoke |
| 18 | 3 | 263496–7 | Geo. L. Ashworth & Bros. | Hanley |
| 18 | 4 | 263498–9 | Minton, Hollins & Co. | Stoke |
| 21 | 7 | 263541–2 | idem | Stoke |
| 22 | 5 | 263561 | Minton & Co. | Stoke |
| 22 | 8 | 263565 | Wm. Brownfield & Son | Cobridge |
| 27 | 1 | 263771 | T. C. Brown–Westhead, Moore & Co. | Hanley |
| July 2 | 2 | 263883–4 | Robinson & Leadbeater | Stoke |
| 2 | 3 | 263885 | Josiah Wedgwood & Sons | Etruria |
| 13 | 5 | 264081 | Gelson Bros. | Hanley |
| 15 | 4 | 264194 | Robinson & Leadbeater | Stoke |
| 16 | 5 | 264206–7 | Minton, Hollins & Co. | Stoke |
| 19 | 5 | 264299–303 | R. M. Taylor | Fenton |
| 20 | 3 | 264306–7 | Geo. Jones | Stoke |
| 24 | 2 | 264490 | W. & T. Adams | Tunstall |
| 29 | 7 | 264613 | J. Dimmock & Co. | Hanley |
| 31 | 3 | 264636–7 | Minton & Co. | Stoke |
| Aug 2 | 1 | 264685–6 | E. J. Ridgway & Son | Stoke |
| 14 | 4 | 265105 | T. Booth & Co. | Tunstall |
| 16 | 1 | 265167–8 | Wm. Brownfield & Sons | Cobridge |
| 19 | 4 | 265254 | W. E. Cartlidge | Hanley |
| 19 | 5 | 265255 | W. & J. A. Bailey | Alloa |
| Sept 2 | 3 | 265666 | McBirney & Armstrong | Belleek |
| 2 | 8 | 265687 | Bates, Elliott & Co. | Burslem |
| 12 | 6 | 265969 | Minton, Hollins & Co. | Stoke |
| 25 | 9 | 266628–31 | Minton, Hollins & Co. | Stoke |
| 26 | 2 | 266633 | F. Jones | Longton |
| 26 | 5 | 266636 | W. E. Cartlidge | Hanley |
| Oct 7 | 7 | 266959 | T. C. Brown–Westhead, Moore & Co. | Hanley |
| 11 | 5 | 267060–4 | Josiah Wedgwood & Sons | Etruria |
| 12 | 10 | 267103–4 | Bates, Elliott & Co. | Burslem |

337

# APPENDIX B

| Date | Parcel No. | Patent No. | Factory, Retailer Wholesaler, etc | Place |
|------|-----------|-----------|-----------------------------------|-------|
| 14 | 4 | 267112 | Minton, Hollins & Co. | Stoke |
| 17 | 8 | 267265 | Josiah Wedgwood & Sons | Etruria |
| 18 | 5 | 267317–9 | Geo. Jones | Stoke |
| 30 | 2 | 267523 | J. F. Wileman | Fenton |
| 30 | 5 | 267527 | The Brownhills Pottery | Tunstall |
| 30 | 9 | 267534 | Maw & Co. | Broseley |
| Nov 2 | 6 | 267588–91 | The Worcester Royal Porcelain Co. Ltd. | Worcester |
| 4 | 3 | 267618 | Geo. Grainger & Co. | Worcester |
| 11 | 2 | 267806 | W. E. Cartlidge | Hanley |
| 12 | 4 | 267839 | Minton & Co. | Stoke |
| 14 | 13 | 267893–5 | Wm. Brownfield & Son | Cobridge |
| 14 | 14 | 267896 | Moore Bros. | Longton |
| 18 | 3 | 267972 | Holland & Green | Longton |
| 30 | 8 | 268309 | Belfield & Co. | Preston-pans |
| Dec 2 | 5 | 268322 | T. C. Brown–Westhead, Moore & Co. | Hanley |
| 4 | 3 | 268388 | John Pratt & Co. Ltd. | Lane Delph |
| 10 | 2 | 268724–5 | Minton & Co. | Stoke |
| 11 | 8 | 268748–9 | The Old Hall Earthenware Co. Ltd. | Hanley |
| 14 | 5 | 268806–7 | Wm. Brownfield & Son | Cobridge |
| 24 | 1 | 269197 | Cockson & Chetwynd | Cobridge |
| 27 | 4 | 269269 | John Adams (Excrs of) | Longton |
| 27 | 5 | 269270 | R. G. Scrivener & Co. | Hanley |
| 27 | 8 | 269275 | John Meir & Son | Tunstall |
| **1873** | | | | |
| Jan 10 | 1 | 269585 | Geo. Jones | Stoke |
| 13 | 4 | 269621 | W. T. Copeland & Sons | Stoke |
| 14 | 8 | 269686 | J. Defries | London |
| 15 | 2 | 269690 | Worthington & Son | Hanley |

| Date | Parcel No. | Patent No. | Factory, Retailer Wholesaler, etc | Place |
|---|---|---|---|---|
| 29 | 1 | 269993–70001 | Minton, Hollins & Co. | Stoke |
| 29 | 2 | 270002–4 | Moore Bros. | Longton |
| Feb 1 | 1 | 270042–50 | Minton, Hollins & Co. | Stoke |
| 10 | 2 | 270298 | W. & J. A. Bailey | Alloa |
| 12 | 4 | 270354 | Bates, Elliott & Co. | Burslem |
| 15 | 1 | 270385 | Minton & Co. | Stoke |
| 19 | 14 | 270600–1 | J. & T. Bevington | Hanley |
| 25 | 6 | 270700 | Geo. Jones | Stoke |
| 27 | 4 | 270751 | Thos. Till & Sons | Burslem |
| 27 | 8 | 270755 | Minton, Hollins & Co. | Stoke |
| Mar 6 | 1 | 271031–2 | Minton & Co. | Stoke |
| 6 | 9 | 271057 | The Brownhills Pottery Co. | Tunstall |
| 26 | 6 | 271561–2 | Geo. Jones | Stoke |
| Apr 3 | 6 | 271851 | Minton & Co. | Stoke |
| 15 | 4 | 272091 | Taylor, Tunnicliffe & Co. | Hanley |
| 19 | 2 | 272206 | Minton & Co. | Stoke |
| 23 | 6 | 272293 | Gelson Bros. | Hanley |
| 28 | 5 | 272364–5 | Powell & Bishop | Hanley |
| 29 | 3 | 272384–5 | Geo. Jones | Stoke |
| May 3 | 2 | 272637 | Thos. Till & Sons | Burslem |
| 3 | 7 | 272642–6 | Wm. Brownfield & Son | Cobridge |
| 3 | 8 | 272647–8 | Minton & Co. | Stoke |
| 6 | 2 | 272662 | idem | Stoke |
| 12 | 8 | 272835 | T. C. Brown–Westhead, Moore & Co. | Hanley |
| 14 | 7 | 272896–7 | Moore Bros. | Longton |
| 16 | 6 | 272983 | Minton, Hollins & Co. | Stoke |
| 17 | 4 | 272988–90 | John L. Johnson & Co. | Longton |
| 22 | 5 | 273089 | Worthington & Son | Hanley |
| 26 | 7 | 273158–9 | Moore Bros. | Longton |
| 26 | 8 | 273160 | Soane & Smith | London |
| 29 | 4 | 273246 | Worthington & Son | Hanley |
| 29 | 8 | 273251 | Thos. Ford | Hanley |

# APPENDIX B

| Date | Parcel No. | Patent No. | Factory, Retailer Wholesaler, etc | Place |
|------|-----------|-----------|-----------------------------------|-------|
| 30 | 15 | 273376 | T. C. Brown–Westhead, Moore & Co. | Hanley |
| June 11 | 4 | 273662–3 | Bates, Elliott & Co. | Burslem |
| 17 | 3 | 273736–7 | Taylor, Tunnicliffe & Co. | Hanley |
| 19 | 3 | 273804 | Pinder & Bourne & Co. | Burslem |
| 28 | 4 | 274047 | Thos. Goode & Co. | London |
| 30 | 3 | 274054–5 | Minton, Hollins & Co. | Stoke |
| July 3 | 9 | 274162 | Minton, Hollins & Co. | Stoke |
| 4 | 7 | 274183 | T. C. Brown–Westhead, Moore & Co. | Hanley |
| 28 | 2 | 274663 | Chas. Hobson | Burslem |
| 28 | 8 | 274701 | John Meir & Sons | Tunstall |
| 29 | 3 | 274704 | McBirney & Armstrong | Belleek |
| 31 | 1 | 274725–6 | Mintons | Stoke |
| Aug 5 | 2 | 274804 | Baker & Chetwynd | Burslem |
| 14 | 10 | 275050 | T. C. Brown–Westhead, Moore & Co. | Hanley |
| 25 | 1 | 275514–5 | Geo. Jones | Stoke |
| 27 | 1 | 275600 | The Worcester Royal Porcelain Co. Ltd. | Worcester |
| 30 | 2 | 275661 | T. C. Brown–Westhead, Moore & Co. | Hanley |
| Sept 2 | 8 | 275755 | Edge, Malkin & Co. | Burslem |
| 4 | 3 | 275816 | Mintons | Stoke |
| 10 | 7 | 275994 | Powell & Bishop | Hanley |
| 15 | 3 | 276151 | T. C. Brown–Westhead, Moore & Co. | Hanley |
| 16 | 4 | 276159 | idem | Hanley |
| 17 | 8 | 276213 | The Worcester Royal Porcelain Co. Ltd. | Worcester |
| 19 | 4 | 276338 | T. C. Brown-Westhead, Moore & Co. | Hanley |
| 25 | 8 | 276517 | Harvey, Adams & Co. | Longton |
| 25 | 10 | 276522 | Jane Beech | Burslem |
| 29 | 2 | 276566 | Wm. Brownfield & Son | Cobridge |

| Date | Parcel No. | Patent No. | Factory, Retailer Wholesaler, etc | Place |
|------|-----------|-----------|-----------------------------------|-------|
| Oct 4 | 3 | 276796–8 | Moore Bros. | Longton |
| 4 | 4 | 276799 | Heath & Blackhurst | Burslem |
| 6 | 6 | 276816–7 | T. C. Brown–Westhead, Moore & Co. | Hanley |
| 11 | 6 | 277136 | Mintons | Stoke |
| 13 | 3 | 277148–9 | Geo. Jones | Stoke |
| 22 | 6 | 277385 | Mintons | Stoke |
| Nov 3 | 3 | 277844 | Hope & Carter | Burslem |
| 3 | 4 | 277845–7 | Geo. Jones | Stoke |
| 6 | 6 | 277969 | Wedgwood & Co. | Tunstall |
| 10 | 7 | 278169 | T. C. Brown-Westhead, Moore & Co. | Hanley |
| 12 | 3 | 278185 | Worthington & Son | Hanley |
| Dec 2 | 6 | 278769–70 | Taylor, Tunnicliffe & Co. | Hanley |
| 4 | 6 | 278821 | The Old Hall Earthenware Co. Ltd. | Hanley |
| 5 | 1 | 278822 | Harvey, Adams & Co. | Longton |
| 5 | 8 | 278867 | Wm. Brownfield & Son | Cobridge |
| 10 | 12 | 279180 | Geo. Jones & Sons | Stoke |
| 27 | 7 | 279437 | idem | Stoke |
| **1874** | | | | |
| Jan 1 | 3 | 279476–7 | Bates, Elliott & Co. | Burslem |
| 10 | 15 | 279655–6 | Davenports & Co. | London (and Longport) |
| 20 | 3 | 279938 | Powell & Bishop | Hanley |
| 21 | 7 | 279964 | W. T. Copeland & Sons | Stoke |
| 23 | 5 | 280010 | John Meir & Son | Tunstall |
| 30 | 4 | 280153–6 | Haviland & Co. | Limoges and London |
| Feb 9 | 4 | 280343 | The Worcester Royal Porcelain Co. Ltd. | Worcester |
| 9 | 5 | 280344 | Bodley & Co. | Burslem |

# APPENDIX B

| Date | Parcel No. | Patent No. | Factory, Retailer Wholesaler, etc | Place |
|------|------------|------------|-----------------------------------|-------|
| 11 | 2 | 280350 | Thos. Booth & Sons | Hanley |
| 14 | 9 | 280492 | Worthington & Son | Hanley |
| 19 | 1 | 280609 | Geo. Jones & Sons | Stoke |
| 25 | 6 | 280785 | Robinson & Leadbeater | Stoke |
| 25 | 7 | 280786 | Geo. Jones & Sons | Stoke |
| 26 | 7 | 280802–4 | Minton, Hollins & Co. | Stoke |
| Mar 2 | 1 | 280853 | McBirney & Armstrong | Belleek |
| 3 | 4 | 280907 | Geo. Jones & Sons | Stoke |
| 4 | 3 | 280919 | Mintons | Stoke |
| 4 | 8 | 280925 | The Worcester Royal Porcelian Co. Ltd. | Worcester |
| 13 | 6 | 281106 | J. Dimmock & Co. | Hanley |
| 14 | 2 | 281129 | Mintons | Stoke |
| 17 | 5 | 281190 | Powell & Bishop | Hanley |
| 21 | 5 | 281301 | idem | Hanley |
| 24 | 4 | 281319 | Mintons | Stoke |
| 27 | 2 | 281404 | Worthington & Son | Hanley |
| 28 | 3 | 281429–30 | Geo. Jones & Sons | Stoke |
| 30 | 1 | 281437 | Worthington & Son | Hanley |
| Apr 7 | 4 | 281639 | The Worcester Royal Porcelain Co. Ltd. | Worcester |
| 14 | 4 | 281776 | A. Bevington | Hanley |
| 15 | 7 | 281822 | Mintons | Stoke |
| 20 | 7 | 281871–80 | Minton, Hollins & Co. | Stoke |
| 21 | 8 | 281899 | Geo. Jones & Sons | Stoke |
| 22 | 1 | 281902 | Wm. Brownfield & Son | Cobridge |
| 23 | 8 | 281954 | T. C. Brown–Westhead, Moore & Co. | Hanley |
| 25 | 2 | 281984 | Geo. Jones & Sons | Stoke |
| 29 | 7 | 282088 | Ridgway, Sparks & Ridgway | Hanley |
| 29 | 9 | 282091 | T. Furnival & Son | Cobridge |
| 30 | 2 | 282098 | Thos. Booth & Sons | Hanley |
| May 5 | 3 | 282134 | Bates, Elliott & Co. | Burslem |
| 9 | 3 | 282218–9 | Geo. Jones & Sons | Stoke |

# APPENDIX B

| Date | Parcel No. | Patent No. | Factory, Retailer Wholesaler, etc | Place |
|---|---|---|---|---|
| 11 | 2 | 282249–51 | Moore Bros. | Longton |
| 11 | 3 | 282252 | J. Thomson & Sons | Glasgow |
| 11 | 4 | 282253 | Holland & Green | Longton |
| 20 | 11 | 282497 | Bates, Elliott & Co. | Burslem |
| 21 | 5 | 282526 | Mintons | Stoke |
| 22 | 8 | 282555 | idem | Stoke |
| 23 | 4 | 282567–8 | Geo. Jones & Sons | Stoke |
| June 1 | 7 | 282662 | The Worcester Royal Porcelain Co. Ltd. | Worcester |
| 6 | 2 | 282799–802 | Wm. Brownfield & Son | Cobridge |
| 6 | 5 | 282806 | Chas. Ford | Hanley |
| 16 | 6 | 282982 | Cockson & Chetwynd | Cobridge |
| 17 | 7 | 283041 | Edge, Malkin & Co. | Burslem |
| 18 | 1 | 283050 | Mintons | Stoke |
| 23 | 3 | 283201 | Williamson & Son | Longton |
| 23 | 7 | 283208 | The Worcester Royal Porcelain Co. Ltd. | Worcester |
| 25 | 5 | 283266–8 | Thos. Ford | Hanley |
| 26 | 4 | 283275 | Pinder, Bourne & Co. | Burslem |
| July 10 | 2 | 283547 | Mintons | Stoke |
| 13 | 6 | 283570–1 | T. C. Brown-Westhead, Moore & Co. | Hanley |
| 27 | 1 | 283980 | Hulse & Adderley | Longton |
| 30 | 5 | 284053 | Minton, Hollins & Co. | Stoke |
| Aug 1 | 8 | 284131–5 | Mintons | Stoke |
| 1 | 9 | 284136 | Cockson & Chetwynd | Cobridge |
| 6 | 7 | 284204 | T. C. Brown-Westhead, Moore & Co. | Hanley |
| 8 | 2 | 284254–5 | Wm. Brownfield & Son | Cobridge |
| 15 | 4 | 284417 | Bates, Elliott & Co. | Burlsem |
| 22 | 6 | 284562 | J. T. Hudden | Longton |
| 28 | 4 | 284699–700 | Geo. Jones & Sons | Stoke |
| 31 | 6 | 284779 | T. J. & J. Emberton | Tunstall |

# APPENDIX B

| Date | | Parcel No. | Patent No. | Factory, Retailer Wholesaler, etc | Place |
|---|---|---|---|---|---|
| Sept | 1 | 3 | 284791 | Thos. Till & Sons | Burslem |
| | 3 | 11 | 284883 | Geo. Adler | Saxony and London |
| | 3 | 12 | 284884–5 | Cockson & Chetwynd | Cobridge |
| | 4 | 3 | 284897 | Mintons | Stoke |
| | 5 | 4 | 284916–7 | The Worcester Royal Porcelain Co. Ltd. | Worcester |
| | 5 | 7 | 284920 | Furnival & Son | Cobridge |
| | 7 | 3 | 284936–7 | Thos. Booth & Sons | Hanley |
| | 10 | 3 | 285013 | Wm. Brownfield & Son | Cobridge |
| | 12 | 1 | 285181 | Mintons | Stoke |
| | 15 | 2 | 285281 | Geo. Jones & Sons | Stoke |
| | 16 | 7 | 285304 | M. Bucholz | London |
| | 17 | 4 | 285322 | R. Britton & Sons | Leeds |
| | 30 | 4 | 285776 | Wm. Brownfield & Son | Cobridge |
| Oct | 2 | 5 | 285826–8 | Geo. Grainger & Co. | Worcester |
| | 3 | 4 | 285841–4 | Moore Bros. | Longton |
| | 6 | 3 | 286000 | Mintons | Stoke |
| | 6 | 4 | 286001 | Grove & Stark | Longton |
| | 10 | 4 | 286134 | Mintons | Stoke |
| | 12 | 2 | 286171 | Powell & Bishop | Hanley |
| | 17 | 8 | 286359–60 | Bates, Elliott & Co. | Burslem |
| | 21 | 8 | 286424 | Geo. Jones & Sons | Stoke |
| | 24 | 3 | 286504–5 | Robinson & Leadbeater | Stoke |
| | 27 | 1 | 286530 | George Ash | Hanley |
| | 28 | 9 | 286563 | Pinder, Bourne & Co. | Burslem |
| Nov | 2 | 3 | 286715 | James Edwards & Son | Burslem |
| | 3 | 4 | 286720–2 | W. & E. Corn | Burslem |
| | 6 | 3 | 286759 | Wm. Brownfield & Son | Cobridge |
| | 7 | 4 | 286774–80 | Thos. Ford | Hanley |
| | 10 | 3 | 286794 | Geo. Jones & Sons | Stoke |
| | 12 | 3 | 286931 | Mintons | Stoke |
| | 12 | 12 | 286942 | Bates, Elliott & Co. | Burslem |
| | 20 | 12 | 287317 | F. & R. Pratt & Co. | Fenton |

| Date | Parcel No. | Patent No. | Factory, Retailer Wholesaler, etc | Place |
|---|---|---|---|---|
| 25 | 7 | 287438–9 | Minton, Hollins & Co. | Stoke |
| Dec 1 | 5 | 287598 | W. T. Copeland & Sons | Stoke |
| 4 | 6 | 287638 | Thos. Barlow | Longton |
| 5 | 4 | 287676 | Holmes & Plant | Burslem |
| 7 | 8 | 287694–7 | T. C. Brown–Westhead, Moore & Co. | Hanley |
| 8 | 2 | 287699 | Geo. Jones & Sons | Stoke |
| 10 | 4 | 287731 | Pinder, Bourne & Co. | Burslem |
| 10 | 11 | 287752–6 | The Worcester Royal Porcelain Co. Ltd. | Worcester |
| 12 | 3 | 287776 | Geo. Jones & Sons | Stoke |
| 12 | 5 | 287785 | Port Dundas Pottery Co. | Port Dundas |
| 18 | 6 | 287982 | Geo. Jones & Sons | Stoke |
| 18 | 7 | 287983 | Ambrose Bevington | Hanley |
| 18 | 9 | 287985 | Geo. Grainger & Co. | Worcester |
| 18 | 11 | 287990–7 | Minton, Hollins & Co. | Stoke |
| **1875** | | | | |
| Jan 2 | 4 | 288241–2 | T. C. Brown–Westhead, Moore & Co. | Hanley |
| 6 | 3 | 288276–8 | Minton, Hollins & Co. | Stoke |
| 12 | 3 | 288366 | The Worcester Royal Porcelain Co. Ltd. | Worcester |
| 16 | 9 | 288502 | The Brownhills Pottery Co. | Tunstall |
| 18 | 8 | 288521 | T. C. Brown–Westhead, Moore & Co. | Hanley |
| 20 | 3 | 288552 | Robinson & Leadbeater | Stoke |
| 20 | 4 | 288553–6 | Wm. Brownfield & Son | Cobridge |
| 21 | 2 | 288682 | Geo. Jones & Sons | Stoke |
| 23 | 9 | 288755–8 | T. C. Brown–Westhead, Moore & Co. | Hanley |
| 28 | 5 | 288830 | Mintons | Stoke |
| 29 | 1 | 288861–2 | Worthington & Son | Hanley |
| Feb 3 | 7 | 288972 | Chas. Ford | Hanley |

# APPENDIX B

| Date | Parcel No. | Patent No. | Factory, Retailer Wholesaler, etc | Place |
|------|------|------|------|------|
| 5 | 5 | 289076 | T. & R. Boote | Burslem |
| 6 | 2 | 289083 | Moore Bros. | Longton |
| 9 | 1 | 289172 | Pinder, Bourne & Co. | Burslem |
| 9 | 2 | 289173 | Geo. Jones & Sons | Stoke |
| 12 | 6 | 289280 | J. Maddock & Sons | Burslem |
| 15 | 2 | 289310 | Moore Bros. | Longton |
| 17 | 7 | 289334 | Mintons | Stoke |
| 23 | 5 | 289503 | J. Maddock & Sons | Burslem |
| 23 | 6 | 289504 | Geo. Jones & Sons | Stoke |
| 23 | 8 | 289507–8 | George Ash | Hanley |
| 24 | 3 | 289535 | Stephen Clive | Tunstall |
| Mar 5 | 2 | 289769 | Wm. Brownfield & Son | Cobridge |
| 12 | 5 | 289874–6 | Geo. Jones & Sons | Stoke |
| 24 | 13 | 290153 | Minton, Hollins & Co. | Stoke |
| 24 | 14 | 290154–5 | T. C. Brown–Westhead, Moore & Co. | Hanley |
| 30 | 1 | 290186 | Thos. Booth & Sons | Hanley |
| 31 | 5 | 290209–10 | Wm. Brownfield & Son | Cobridge |
| Apr 3 | 7 | 290259 | J. Dimmock & Co. | Hanley |
| 3 | 9 | 290261–2 | E. F. Bodley & Son | Burslem |
| 7 | 3 | 290352 | Mintons | Stoke |
| 9 | 6 | 290393–4 | Wm. Brownfield & Son | Cobridge |
| 10 | 7 | 290407–8 | Powell & Bishop | Hanley |
| 15 | 5 | 290500 | R. Malkin | Fenton |
| 17 | 1 | 290738 | Pinder, Bourne & Co. | Burslem |
| 20 | 1 | 290787 | J. Dimmock & Co. | Hanley |
| 20 | 2 | 290788 | Mintons | Stoke |
| 21 | 5 | 290812 | Stephen Clive | Tunstall |
| 22 | 3 | 290841–2 | W. P. & G. Phillips | London |
| 22 | 4 | 290843–6 | Minton, Hollins & Co. | Stoke |
| May 3 | 8 | 290998 | Soane & Smith | London |
| 7 | 7 | 291109 | Geo. Jones & Sons | Stoke |
| 7 | 8 | 291110 | Burgess & Leigh | Burslem |
| 11 | 6 | 291229 | Thos. Goode & Co. | London |
| 20 | 1 | 291440 | Bates, Elliott & Co. | Burslem |

| Date | Parcel No. | Patent No. | Factory, Retailer Wholesaler, etc | Place |
|---|---|---|---|---|
| 20 | 3 | 291444 | J. Dimmock & Co. | Hanley |
| 22 | 1 | 291458 | Holland & Green | Longton |
| 26 | 6 | 291518–20 | T. C. Brown–Westhead, Moore & Co. | Hanley |
| 28 | 10 | 291556 | Campbellfield Pottery Co. | Glasgow |
| 28 | 12 | 291558 | J. Mortlock | London |
| 31 | 8 | 291568 | Geo. Jones & Sons | Stoke |
| 31 | 18 | 291611 | Ridgway, Sparks & Ridgway | Hanley |
| June 2 | 9 | 291749–51 | Minton, Hollins & Co. | Stoke |
| 5 | 7 | 291870–1 | W. P. & G. Phillips | London |
| 7 | 3 | 291882 | W. & T. Adams | Tunstall |
| 8 | 4 | 291911 | The Worcester Royal Porcelain Co. (Ltd.) | Worcester |
| 10 | 6 | 292005 | Wm. Brownfield & Son | Cobridge |
| 12 | 5 | 292034 | Chas. Stevenson | Greenock |
| 12 | 6 | 292035 | Maddock & Gater | Burslem |
| 12 | 10 | 292042 | Thos. Furnival & Son | Stoke |
| 15 | 5 | 292080 | Josiah Wedgwood & Sons | Etruria |
| 19 | 6 | 292184 | Thos. Till & Sons | Burslem |
| 26 | 2 | 292367–70 | Geo. Jones & Sons | Stoke |
| July 5 | 1 | 292542 | Wm. Brownfield & Son | Cobridge |
| 7 | 8 | 292579–80 | Moore Bros. | Longton |
| 8 | 5 | 292620 | idem | Longton |
| 20 | 4 | 292985 | E. J. D. Bodley | Burslem |
| 23 | 10 | 293035 | T. C. Brown–Westhead, Moore & Co. | Hanley |
| 27 | 5 | 293114 | F. W. Grove & J. Stark | Longton |
| 28 | 7 | 293129 | Minton, Hollins & Co. | Stoke |
| Aug 19 | 7 | 293748 | F. W. Grove & J. Stark | Longton |
| 28 | 6 | 294038–9 | W. P. & G. Phillips | London |
| Sept 2 | 3 | 294147 | T. Elsmore & Son | Tunstall |
| 13 | 2 | 294434–5 | Geo. Jones & Sons | Stoke |
| 14 | 9 | 294514 | Minton, Hollins & Co. | Stoke |
| 18 | 2 | 294571–2 | Geo. Jones & Sons | Stoke |

| Date | Parcel No. | Patent No. | Factory, Retailer Wholesaler, etc | Place |
|------|------------|------------|-----------------------------------|-------|
| 21 | 1 | 294595 | R. Cochran & Co. | Glasgow |
| 24 | 2 | 294657 | H. Aynsley & Co. | Longton |
| 25 | 3 | 294662 | F. W. Grove & J. Stark | Longton |
| 28 | 6 | 294768–9 | T. C. Brown–Westhead, Moore & Co. | Hanley |
| 30 | 4 | 294825–7 | John Edwards | Fenton |
| Oct 2 | 6 | 294906 | Josiah Wedgwood & Sons | Etruria |
| 6 | 4 | 294936 | R. Cooke | Hanley |
| 11 | 4 | 295001 | Powell & Bishop | Hanley |
| 11 | 10 | 295014–5 | The Brownhills Pottery Co. | Tunstall |
| 16 | 8 | 295131 | Burgess, Leigh & Co. | Burslem |
| 28 | 3 | 295443 | Minton, Hollins & Co. | Stoke |
| 30 | 9 | 295473–4 | W. P. & G. Phillips | London |
| Nov 5 | 3 | 295551–3 | Geo. Jones & Sons | Stoke |
| 8 | 4 | 295792–8 | Minton, Hollins & Co. | Stoke |
| 8 | 8 | 295803 | W. T. Copeland & Sons | Stoke |
| 12 | 1 | 295908 | Geo. Jones & Sons | Stoke |
| 12 | 2 | 295909 | Burgess, Leigh & Co. | Burslem |
| 13 | 8 | 295933 | The Worcester Royal Porcelain Co. Ltd. | Worcester |
| Dec 1 | 2 | 296475 | Wm. Brownfield & Son | Cobridge |
| 1 | 9 | 296508 | Gelson Bros. | Hanley |
| 3 | 4 | 296531 | Geo. Jones & Sons | Stoke |
| 6 | 8 | 296644 | John Meir & Son | Tunstall |
| 10 | 3 | 296770 | Mintons | Stoke |
| 11 | 5 | 296813 | F. W. Grove & J. Stark | Longton |
| 11 | 8 | 296818 | Soane & Smith | London |
| 13 | 8 | 296834–49 | Minton, Hollins & Co. | Stoke |
| 15 | 2 | 296939–40 | Mintons China Works | Stoke |
| 15 | 3 | 296941–5 | Mintons | Stoke |
| 24 | 4 | 297217–8 | Chas. Ford | Hanley |
| 24 | 6 | 297221 | Bates, Walker & Co. | Burslem |
| 29 | 5 | 297245 | Edge, Malkin & Co. | Burslem |
| 29 | 6 | 297246–7 | T. C. Brown–Westhead, Moore & Co. | Hanley |

348

| Date | Parcel No. | Patent No. | Factory, Retailer Wholesaler, etc | Place |
|---|---|---|---|---|
| 30 | 2 | 297250 | Mintons | Stoke |
| 30 | 8 | 297276 | Mintons, Hollins & Co. | Stoke |
| **1876** | | | | |
| Jan 4 | 4 | 297343 | Mintons | Stoke |
| 6 | 2 | 297471 | Moore Bros. | Longton |
| 11 | 7 | 297587 | E. J. D. Bodley | Burslem |
| 21 | 13 | 297791 | Bale & Co. | Etruria |
| 22 | 6 | 297809–11 | Geo. Jones & Sons | Stoke |
| 22 | 8 | 297813 | Chas. Ford | Hanley |
| 24 | 1 | 297817 | Mintons | Stoke |
| 24 | 4 | 297845 | J. Friedrich | London |
| 24 | 6 | 297863–4 | Bates, Walker & Co. | Burslem |
| 26 | 2 | 297977 | Edge, Malkin & Co. | Burslem |
| 26 | 3 | 297978 | Powell & Bishop | Hanley |
| 28 | 8 | 298018 | James Edwards & Son | Burslem |
| 29 | 3 | 298027–9 | Wm. Brownfield & Son | Cobridge |
| Feb 1 | 2 | 298049 | idem | Cobridge |
| 2 | 7 | 298063 | Josiah Wedgwood & Sons | Etruria |
| 2 | 12 | 298069 | Ridgway, Sparks & Ridgway | Hanley |
| 3 | 5 | 298077 | Powell & Bishop | Hanley |
| 4 | 6 | 298103 | Mintons | Stoke |
| 4 | 12 | 298141–2 | The Worcester Royal Porcelain Co. Ltd. | Worcester |
| 8 | 9 | 298235 | Bates, Walker & Co. | Burslem |
| 19 | 5 | 298458 | Geo. Jones & Sons | Stoke |
| 21 | 4 | 298473 | The Worcester Royal Porcelain Co. Ltd. | Worcester |
| 22 | 3 | 298480–3 | Minton, Hollins & Co. | Stoke |
| 29 | 9 | 298693 | J. Dimmock & Co. | Hanley |
| Mar 2 | 8 | 298821–4 | T. Gelson & Co. | Hanley |
| 2 | 11 | 298832 | The Brownhills Pottery Co. | Tunstall |
| 10 | 8 | 299076–8 | Minton, Hollins & Co. | Stoke |

# APPENDIX B

| Date | Parcel No. | Patent No. | Factory, Retailer Wholesaler, etc | Place |
|---|---|---|---|---|
| 14 | 5 | 299177 | T. C. Brown–Westhead, Moore & Co. | Hanley |
| 17 | 5 | 299236 | Mintons | Stoke |
| 18 | 3 | 299246 | Robinson & Chapman | Longton |
| 23 | 8 | 299366 | E. J. D. Bodley | Burslem |
| 24 | 7 | 299380 | Bates, Walker & Co. | Burslem |
| 28 | 8 | 299474 | W. E. Withinshaw | Burslem |
| 30 | 4 | 299497–9 | Geo. Jones & Sons | Stoke |
| Apr 8 | 6 | 299773 | Bates, Walker & Co. | Burslem |
| 11 | 4 | 299819 | Thos. Gelson & Co. | Hanley |
| 12 | 4 | 299830 | Powell & Bishop | Hanley |
| 12 | 11 | 299852 | J. Dimmock & Co. | Hanley |
| 21 | 7 | 300020 | Minton, Hollins & Co. | Stoke |
| 21 | 10 | 300037–8 | Furnival & Son | Cobridge |
| 22 | 5 | 300105 | The Worcester Royal Porcelain Co. Ltd. | Worcester |
| 27 | 3 | 300260 | Mintons | Stoke |
| May 8 | 7 | 300421–3 | T. C. Brown–Westhead, Moore & Co. | Hanley |
| 10 | 3 | 300463 | Geo. Jones & Sons | Stoke |
| 11 | 9 | 300491 | F. & R. Pratt & Co. | Fenton |
| 16 | 7 | 300603–4 | Mintons | Stoke |
| 22 | 3 | 300682 | Moore Bros. | Longton |
| 22 | 4 | 300683–5 | Josiah Wedgwood & Sons | Etruria |
| 23 | 7 | 300734–7 | Haviland & Co. | Limoges and London |
| 24 | 3 | 300746 | Mintons | Stoke |
| 25 | 6 | 300779 | Moore Bros. | Longton |
| 29 | 8 | 300809–10 | Geo. Jones & Sons | Stoke |
| June 3 | 2 | 301030 | Mintons | Stoke |
| 3 | 5 | 301035–7 | E. J. D. Bodley | Burslem |
| 7 | 1 | 301087 | Thos. Gelson & Co. | Hanley |
| 8 | 4 | 301099 | Mintons | Stoke |
| 9 | 6 | 301164 | W. T. Copeland & Sons | Stoke |

# APPENDIX B

| Date | Parcel No. | Patent No. | Factory, Retailer Wholesaler, etc | Place |
|------|------------|------------|-----------------------------------|-------|
| 15 | 1 | 301254 | Henry Meir & Son | Tunstall |
| 15 | 9 | 301267–9 | Minton, Hollins & Co. | Stoke |
| 19 | 2 | 301302 | Josiah Wedgwood & Sons | Etruria |
| 19 | 9 | 301310 | J. Holdcroft | Longton |
| 21 | 4 | 301330 | Mintons | Stoke |
| 22 | 4 | 301342 | Thos. Gelson & Co. | Hanley |
| 23 | 5 | 301402 | Mintons | Stoke |
| 26 | 6 | 301443–4 | Minton, Hollins & Co. | Stoke |
| 28 | 8 | 301543 | J. Aynsley | Longton |
| July 1 | 3 | 301589–90 | Mintons | Stoke |
| 1 | 4 | 301591 | John Tams | Longton |
| 3 | 2 | 301596 | Ford & Challinor | Tunstall |
| 5 | 1 | 301619 | Thos. Till & Sons | Burslem |
| 5 | 7 | 301641 | W. T. Copeland & Sons | Stoke |
| 10 | 3 | 301877 | Thos. Gelson & Co. | Hanley |
| 12 | 2 | 301926 | E. J. D. Bodley | Burslem |
| 18 | 3 | 301984 | Soane & Smith | London |
| 26 | 3 | 302125 | Geo. Jones & Sons | Stoke |
| 28 | 10 | 302178 | Thos. Gelson & Co. | Hanley |
| 28 | 11 | 302179 | Powell & Bishop | Hanley |
| 31 | 8 | 302220 | G. Grainger & Co. | Worcester |
| Aug 8 | 1 | 302384 | Robinson & Chapman | Longton |
| 25 | 8 | 302901 | F. & R. Pratt & Co. | Fenton |
| Sept 5 | 5 | 303289–90 | Bates & Walker & Co. | Burslem |
| 6 | 9 | 303308 | Pinder & Bourne & Co. | Burslem |
| 6 | 10 | 303309 | Wm. Brownfield & Sons | Cobridge |
| 9 | 8 | 303455 | Worthington & Son | Hanley |
| 9 | 9 | 303456–7 | T. C. Brown–Westhead, Moore & Co. | Hanley |
| 11 | 1 | 303459 | E. J. D. Bodley | Burslem |
| 12 | 6 | 303522–3 | Geo. Jones & Sons | Stoke |
| 18 | 10 | 303677 | G. L. Ashworth & Bros. | Hanley |
| 20 | 3 | 303731–2 | Hollinshead & Kirkham | Burslem |
| 22 | 3 | 303757 | Powell & Bishop | Hanley |
| 26 | 5 | 303853 | Hope & Carter | Burslem |

# APPENDIX B

| Date | Parcel No. | Patent No. | Factory, Retailer Wholesaler, etc | Place |
|------|-----------|-----------|-----------------------------------|-------|
| 26 | 10 | 303918 | T. C. Brown–Westhead, Moore & Co. | Hanley |
| 28 | 2 | 303926–7 | Moore Bros. | Longton |
| 28 | 10 | 303942 | Hope & Carter | Burslem |
| Oct 7 | 2 | 304128 | Wm. Harrop | Hanley |
| 7 | 3 | 304129–31 | Wm. Brownfield & Sons | Cobridge |
| 7 | 4 | 304132–3 | Josiah Wedgwood & Sons | Etruria |
| 7 | 6 | 304144–5 | Wm. Adams | Tunstall |
| 9 | 1 | 304149–50 | Geo. Jones & Sons | Stoke |
| 12 | 8 | 304321 | Ambrose Bevington | Hanley |
| 17 | 4 | 304376 | T. C. Brown–Westhead, Moore & Co. | Hanley |
| 17 | 9 | 304383 | Wardle & Co. | Hanley |
| 19 | 3 | 304428 | Burgess, Leigh & Co. | Burslem |
| 20 | 2 | 304454–66 | Mintons | Stoke |
| 21 | 3 | 304473 | Edge, Malkin & Co. | Burslem |
| 23 | 2 | 304489 | Mintons | Stoke |
| 31 | 2 | 304910–4 | Wm. Brownfield & Sons | Cobridge |
| Nov 1 | 2 | 304926 | Moore Bros. | Longton |
| 7 | 3 | 305065 | Robert Jones | Hanley |
| 8 | 3 | 305080 | Geo. Jones & Sons | Stoke |
| 8 | 9 | 305090 | Wm. Brownfield & Sons | Cobridge |
| 9 | 10 | 305150 | Belfield & Co. | Preston-pans |
| 11 | 9 | 305173 | Moore Bros. | Longton |
| 13 | 3 | 305181 | Mintons | Stoke |
| 14 | 2 | 305189 | Josiah Wedgwood & Sons | Etruria |
| 14 | 8 | 305195 | Clementson Bros. | Hanley |
| 17 | 3 | 305222 | Banks & Thorley | Hanley |
| 18 | 3 | 305233 | Minton, Hollins & Co. | Stoke |
| 18 | 7 | 305264 | Minton, Hollins & Co. | Stoke |
| 18 | 9 | 305266 | The Worcester Royal Porcelain Co. Ltd. | Worcester |
| 23 | 5 | 305312 | Wm. Adams | Tunstall |
| 24 | 15 | 305461–2 | Thos. Furnival & Sons | Cobridge |

| Date | Parcel No. | Patent No. | Factory, Retailer Wholesaler, etc | Place |
|------|-----------|-----------|-----------------------------------|-------|
| 28 | 2 | 305510 | W. Hudson & Son | Longton |
| 29 | 11 | 305568 | Thos. Furnival & Sons | Cobridge |
| Dec 5 | 2 | 305684 | Wedgwood & Co. | Tunstall |
| 11 | 2 | 305829 | John Tams | Longton |
| 12 | 11 | 305885 | The Campbell Brick & Tile Co. | Stoke |
| 14 | 1 | 305934 | Harvey Adams & Co. | Longton |
| 14 | 11 | 305973 | J. Dimmock & Co. | Hanley |
| 18 | 9 | 306100 | James Beech | Longton |
| 20 | 7 | 306184 | J. & T. Bevington | Hanley |
| 21 | 2 | 306202 | F. W. Grove & J. Stark | Longton |
| 23 | 5 | 306282 | Chas. Ford | Hanley |
| 27 | 15 | 306341 | The Campbell Brick & Tile Co. | Stoke |
| 28 | 6 | 306367 | Harvey Adams & Co. | Longton |
| **1877** | | | | |
| Jan 4 | 10 | 306564 | The Campbellfield Pottery Co. | Glasgow |
| 17 | 5 | 306953 | The Worcester Royal Porcelain Co. Ltd. | Worcester |
| 20 | 2 | 307028 | F. W. Grove & J. Stark | Longton |
| 24 | 10 | 307213 | Wm. Brownfield & Sons | Cobridge |
| 25 | 6 | 307236 | Wood & Co. | Burslem |
| 25 | 7 | 307237–9 | Geo. Jones & Sons | Stoke |
| 26 | 3 | 307258 | Mintons | Stoke |
| 26 | 4 | 307259 | Powell & Bishop | Hanley |
| Feb 1 | 6 | 307432 | James Edwards & Son | Burslem |
| 2 | 7 | 307495–7 | The Worcester Royal Porcelain Co. Ltd. | Worcester |
| 3 | 4 | 307506–7 | Minton, Hollins & Co. | Stoke |
| 5 | 2 | 307525–7 | McBirney & Armstrong | Belleek |
| 7 | 3 | 307551 | Holland & Green | Longton |
| 7 | 7 | 307570–2 | Wm. Brownfield & Sons | Cobridge |
| 9 | 7 | 307603 | Robinson & Co. | Longton |

# APPENDIX B

| Date | Parcel No. | Patent No. | Factory, Retailer Wholesaler, etc | Place |
|------|-----------|-----------|-----------------------------------|-------|
| 9 | 11 | 307613 | T. C. Brown–Westhead, Moore & Co. | Hanley |
| 12 | 3 | 307646 | James Beech | Longton |
| 14 | 16 | 307782 | The Worcester Royal Porcelain Co. Ltd. | Worcester |
| 15 | 10 | 307794 | Minton, Hollins & Co. | Stoke |
| 16 | 9 | 307866 | John Rose & Co. | Coalport |
| 19 | 2 | 307877 | Wm. Brownfield & Sons | Cobridge |
| 20 | 8 | 307892 | G. Grainger & Co. | Worcester |
| 21 | 6 | 307906 | Mintons | Stoke |
| 21 | 9 | 307909 | W. T. Copeland & Sons | Stoke |
| 24 | 3 | 307983 | Thos. Hughes | Burslem |
| 27 | 2 | 308010 | Mintons | Stoke |
| Mar 1 | 4 | 308116–21 | Hallam, Johnson & Co. | Longton |
| 8 | 14 | 308329 | W. T. Copeland & Sons | Stoke |
| 10 | 7 | 308357 | Geo. Jones & Sons | Stoke |
| 14 | 9 | 308493 | The Campbell Brick & Tile Co. | Stoke |
| 20 | 3 | 308650–2 | Clementson Bros. | Hanley |
| 20 | 8 | 308662 | J. Dimmock & Co. | Hanley |
| 22 | 14 | 308718 | E. J. D. Bodley | Burslem |
| 24 | 1 | 308781–2 | Powell & Bishop | Hanley |
| 31 | 7 | 308916 | E. F. Bodley & Co. | Burslem |
| Apr 3 | 1 | 308918 | Powell & Bishop | Hanley |
| 4 | 5 | 308932 | J. Mortlock | London |
| 5 | 2 | 308934 | Ford, Challinor & Co. | Tunstall |
| 12 | 11 | 309233 | J. Dimmock & Co. | Hanley |
| 23 | 4 | 309617 | John Tams | Longton |
| 26 | 2 | 309680 | J. & T. Bevington | Hanley |
| 26 | 7 | 309696 | The Worcester Royal Porcelain Co. Ltd. | Worcester |
| 27 | 10 | 309746 | John Rose & Co. | Coalport |
| May 2 | 2 | 309818–21 | Geo. Jones & Sons | Stoke |
| 4 | 13 | 309917 | The Old Hall Earthenware Co. Ltd. | Hanley |

354

# APPENDIX B

| Date | Parcel No. | Patent No. | Factory, Retailer Wholesaler, etc | Place |
|------|-----------|-----------|-----------|-------|
| 5 | 4 | 309922 | Josiah Wedgwood & Sons | Etruria |
| 12 | 7 | 310034 | Thos. Furnival & Sons | Cobridge |
| 16 | 5 | 310175 | Wm. Brownfield & Sons | Cobridge |
| 18 | 6 | 310267 | Josiah Wedgwood & Sons | Etruria |
| 22 | 5 | 310359–61 | Wm. Brownfield & Sons | Cobridge |
| 24 | 8 | 310448 | T. C. Brown–Westhead, Moore & Co. | Hanley |
| 30 | 13 | 310556 | T. Furnival & Sons | Cobridge |
| June 1 | 2 | 310599 | J. & R. Hammersley | Hanley |
| 5 | 6 | 310670 | E. J. D. Bodley | Burslem |
| 7 | 1 | 310709 | idem | Burslem |
| 7 | 2 | 310710 | Joseph Holdcroft | Longton |
| 8 | 7 | 310761–4 | Minton, Hollins & Co. | Stoke |
| 9 | 3 | 310775–6 | Baker & Co. | Fenton |
| 13 | 2 | 310909 | idem | Fenton |
| 15 | 7 | 310972 | Ridgway, Sparks & Ridgway | Hanley |
| 19 | 4 | 311031 | Ford & Challinor | Tunstall |
| 19 | 6 | 311033 | Murray & Co. | Glasgow |
| 22 | 3 | 311141 | Walker & Carter | Stoke |
| 22 | 13 | 311181–6 | Steele & Wood | Stoke |
| 22 | 14 | 311187 | E. F. Bodley & Co. | Burslem |
| 26 | 11 | 311366 | T. Furnival & Sons | Cobridge |
| 28 | 9 | 311423 | idem | Cobridge |
| 29 | 10 | 311448–9 | Sherwin & Cotton | Hanley |
| July 2 | 3 | 311523 | W. T. Copeland & Sons | Stoke |
| 6 | 2 | 311626 | Mintons | Stoke |
| 7 | 4 | 311684 | Ridge, Meigh & Co. | Longton |
| 9 | 2 | 311711 | Minton, Hollins & Co. | Stoke |
| 14 | 2 | 311883–4 | John Tams | Longton |
| 17 | 9 | 312019–21 | James Edwards & Son | Burslem |
| 20 | 7 | 312062–4 | Haviland & Co. | London and Limoges |
| 20 | 15 | 312113 | Taylor, Tunnicliffe & Co. | Hanley |

| Date | Parcel No. | Patent No. | Factory, Retailer Wholesaler, etc | Place |
|------|------|------|------|------|
| 23 | 2 | 312125 | John Edwards | Fenton |
| 25 | 5 | 312187 | Ford, Challinor & Co. | Tunstall |
| 26 | 6 | 312311–4 | Minton, Hollins & Co. | Stoke |
| 31 | 1 | 312421 | McBirney & Armstrong | Belleek |
| 31 | 2 | 312422 | Minton & Hollins & Co. | Stoke |
| Aug 1 | 4 | 312434 | Holmes, Stonier & Hollinshead | Hanley |
| 3 | 14 | 312521 | The Campbell Brick & Tile Co. | Stoke |
| 13 | 5 | 312909 | Haviland & Co. | London and Limoges |
| 15 | 7 | 313009 | The Campbell Brick & Tile Co. | Stoke |
| 17 | 11 | 313080 | Ridgway, Sparks & Ridgway | Stoke |
| 18 | 6 | 313099–101 | Minton, Hollins & Co. | Stoke |
| 18 | 7 | 313102 | Furnival & Son | Cobridge |
| 23 | 6 | 313280 | W. Hudson & Son | Longton |
| 25 | 2 | 313324 | Wm. Wood & Co. | Burslem |
| 25 | 3 | 313325–9 | Minton, Hollins & Co. | Stoke |
| 28 | 9 | 313381 | T. C. Brown–Westhead, Moore & Co. | Hanley |
| Sept 11 | 3 | 314046 | G. W. Turner & Sons | Tunstall |
| 19 | 5 | 314292 | Minton, Hollins & Co. | Stoke |
| 20 | 3 | 314385 | Josiah Wedgwood & Sons | Etruria |
| 22 | 7 | 314470–1 | Mintons | Stoke |
| 22 | 13 | 314480 | Minton, Hollins & Co. | Stoke |
| 25 | 5 | 314548 | Mintons | Stoke |
| 28 | 9 | 314675 | J. Holdcroft | Longton |
| Oct 2 | 7 | 314890 | Bates, Walker & Co. | Burslem |
| 3 | 2 | 314896 | Robinson & Leadbeater | Stoke |
| 4 | 4 | 314906–7 | J. & T. Bevington | Hanley |
| 10 | 3 | 315102 | John Edwards | Fenton |

356

# APPENDIX B

| Date | Parcel No. | Patent No. | Factory, Retailer Wholesaler, etc | Place |
|------|-----------|-----------|-----------------------------------|-------|
| 10 | 5 | 315104–5 | Wm. Brownfield & Sons | Cobridge |
| 15 | 2 | 315271–2 | Geo. Jones & Sons | Stoke |
| 16 | 6 | 315400–1 | Powell & Bishop | Hanley |
| 19 | 8 | 315473 | Minton, Hollins & Co. | Stoke |
| 19 | 13 | 315479 | T. C. Brown–Westhead, Moore & Co. | Hanley |
| 24 | 10 | 315565 | F. W. Grove & J. Stark | Longton |
| 24 | 14 | 315574 | F. & R. Pratt & Co. | Fenton |
| 30 | 7 | 315684 | Wedgwood & Co. | Tunstall |
| 31 | 6 | 315765 | Geo. Jones & Sons | Stoke |
| Nov 5 | 4 | 315918 | Powell & Bishop | Hanley |
| 6 | 11 | 315954–6 | Wm. Brownfield & Sons | Cobridge |
| 7 | 1 | 316087–9 | E. J. D. Bodley | Burslem |
| 7 | 2 | 316090 | Mintons | Stoke |
| 7 | 10 | 316101 | Pinder, Bourne & Co. | Burslem |
| 9 | 8 | 316122 | Taylor, Tunnicliffe & Co. | Hanley |
| 15 | 12 | 316309 | T. C. Brown–Westhead, Moore & Co. | Hanley |
| 20 | 9 | 316502 | James Edwards & Sons | Burslem |
| 21 | 8 | 316526 | Davenports & Co. | Longport |
| 22 | 1 | 316542–3 | The Old Hall Earthenware Co. Ltd. | Hanley |
| 22 | 13 | 316560 | B. & S. Hancock | Stoke |
| 24 | 7 | 316605 | J. Dimmock & Co. | Hanley |
| 29 | 3 | 316723 | J. Holdcroft | Longton |
| Dec 1 | 5 | 316763 | J. Holdcroft | Longton |
| 1 | 6 | 316764 | Oakes, Clare & Chadwick | Burslem |
| 5 | 2 | 316842 | E. J. D. Bodley | Burslem |
| 6 | 4 | 316863 | Mintons | Stoke |
| 7 | 14 | 316912 | J. Unwin | Longton |
| 14 | 1 | 317112 | J. Dimmock & Co. | Hanley |
| 15 | 10 | 317203 | The Worcester Royal Porcelain Co. Ltd. | Worcester |
| 21 | 6 | 317404 | Mintons | Stoke |

| Date | Parcel No. | Patent No. | Factory, Retailer Wholesaler, etc | Place |
|------|-----------|-----------|-----------------------------------|-------|
| 21 | 10 | 317410 | T. Furnival & Sons | Cobridge |
| 22 | 5 | 317427–8 | Wm. Brownfield & Sons | Cobridge |
| 29 | 6 | 317494 | T. C. Brown–Westhead, Moore & Co. | Hanley |
| **1878** | | | | |
| Jan 3 | 4 | 317537–9 | Minton, Hollins & Co. | Stoke |
| 9 | 4 | 317692–4 | The Brownhills Pottery Co. | Tunstall |
| 10 | 12 | 317733 | J. Mortlock & Co. | London |
| 14 | 1 | 317756 | J. Maddock & Sons | Burslem |
| 14 | 2 | 317757 | Cotton & Rigby | Burslem |
| 14 | 3 | 317758 | Wm. Adams | Tunstall |
| 14 | 6 | 317763 | Minton, Hollins & Co. | Stoke |
| 15 | 5 | 317780 | Josiah Wedgwood & Sons | Etruria |
| 18 | 5 | 317826 | Taylor, Tunnicliffe & Co. | Hanley |
| 22 | 6 | 317940 | J. Dimmock & Co. | Hanley |
| 24 | 6 | 318041 | W. T. Copeland & Sons | Stoke |
| 25 | 9 | 318107–8 | Wm. Brownfield & Sons | Cobridge |
| 28 | 11 | 318141 | T. C. Brown–Westhead, Moore & Co. | Hanley |
| 30 | 3 | 318158–9 | Geo. Jones | Stoke |
| 30 | 15 | 318189–90 | The Brownhills Pottery Co. | Tunstall |
| 31 | 1 | 318210 | B. & S. Hancock | Stoke |
| Feb 1 | 4 | 318239 | Geo. Jones & Sons | Stoke |
| 1 | 11 | 318265–6 | Minton, Hollins & Co. | Stoke |
| 1 | 16 | 318275–9 | The Derby Crown Porcelain Co. Ltd. | Derby |
| 5 | 5 | 318397 | The Campbell Brick & Tile Co. | Stoke |
| 9 | 6 | 318469 | J. Dimmock & Co. | Hanley |
| 11 | 5 | 318543–4 | T. C. Brown–Westhead, Moore & Co. | Hanley |
| 12 | 5 | 318556–63 | Derby Crown Porcelain Co. Ltd. | Derby |
| 20 | 6 | 318800 | Minton, Hollins & Co. | Stoke |

# APPENDIX B

| Date | Parcel No. | Patent No. | Factory, Retailer Wholesaler, etc | Place |
|------|------|------|------|------|
| | 20 | 7 | 318801 | The Worcester Royal Porcelain Co. Ltd. | Worcester |
| | 21 | 10 | 318821 | W. E. Cartlidge | Burslem |
| | 22 | 8 | 318843 | The Campbell Brick & Tile Co. | Stoke |
| | 28 | 3 | 319041 | Dunn, Bennett & Co. | Hanley |
| Mar | 5 | 2 | 319190 | F. W. Grove & J. Stark | Longton |
| | 6 | 5 | 319201 | Minton, Hollins & Co. | Stoke |
| | 7 | 4 | 319219 | John Edwards | Fenton |
| | 9 | 1 | 319278–9 | The Brownhills Pottery Co. | Tunstall |
| | 9 | 8 | 319293 | Moore Bros. | Longton |
| | 9 | 11 | 319296 | Powell & Bishop | Hanley |
| | 11 | 1 | 319310–1 | Taylor, Tunnicliffe & Co. | Hanley |
| | 13 | 1 | 319370 | Mintons | Stoke |
| | 13 | 7 | 319387 | J. & T. Bevington | Hanley |
| | 13 | 10 | 319394 | W. T. Copeland & Sons | Stoke |
| | 15 | 10 | 319507 | John Rose & Co. | Coalport |
| | 23 | 8 | 319634–6 | Derby Crown Porcelain Co. Ltd. | Derby |
| | 25 | 9 | 319679 | F. J. Emery | Burslem |
| | 27 | 6 | 319725–6 | G. W. Turner & Sons | Tunstall |
| | 27 | 15 | 319867–72 | Minton, Hollins & Co. | Stoke |
| Apr | 2 | 6 | 320030 | Belfield & Co. | Preston-pans |
| | 10 | 4 | 320281 | Mintons | Stoke |
| | 13 | 9 | 320373 | McBirney & Armstrong | Belleek |
| | 17 | 4 | 320482 | Mintons | Stoke |
| | 17 | 14 | 320568–9 | Ridgway, Sparks & Ridgway | Stoke |
| | 20 | 2 | 320606 | Thos. Furnival & Sons | Cobridge |
| | 20 | 6 | 320616 | The Worcester Royal Porcelain Co. Ltd. | Worcester |
| | 24 | 2 | 320669 | Wm. Brownfield & Sons | Cobridge |
| | 27 | 12 | 320793 | McBirney & Armstrong | Belleek |
| | 30 | 7 | 320874–5 | Josiah Wedgwood & Sons | Etruria |

# APPENDIX B

| Date | Parcel No. | Patent No. | Factory, Retailer Wholesaler, etc | Place |
|------|------------|------------|-----------------------------------|-------|
| May 3 | 2 | 321028 | Josiah Wedgwood & Sons | Etruria |
| 3 | 9 | 321163 | Robinson & Leadbeater | Stoke |
| 8 | 9 | 321231–2 | Bates & Bennett | Cobridge |
| 14 | 6 | 321361 | Elsmore & Son | Tunstall |
| 17 | 12 | 321575 | J. Dimmock & Co. | Hanley |
| 20 | 9 | 321632–4 | Derby Crown Porcelain Co. Ltd. | Derby |
| 21 | 11 | 321693 | Banks & Thorley | Hanley |
| 23 | 3 | 321704 | Josiah Wedgwood & Sons | Etruria |
| 23 | 4 | 321705 | Moore Bros. | Longton |
| 24 | 2 | 321726 | Josiah Wedgwood & Sons | Etruria |
| 27 | 20 | 322007 | E. J. D. Bodley | Burslem |
| 29 | 9 | 322039 | Minton, Hollins & Co. | Stoke |
| June 1 | 5 | 322130 | J. Mortlock & Co. | London |
| 4 | 9 | 322168 | F. Furnival & Sons | Cobridge |
| 5 | 14 | 322223–4 | W. T. Copeland & Sons | Stoke |
| 7 | 1 | 322309 | Geo. Jones & Sons | Stoke |
| 8 | 8 | 322390 | Wm. Wood & Co. | Burslem |
| 12 | 10 | 322471 | Harvey Adams & Co. | Longton |
| 13 | 2 | 322476 | John Tams | Longton |
| 13 | 3 | 322477 | McBirney & Armstrong | Belleek |
| 19 | 7 | 322597–8 | E. F. Bodley & Co. | Burslem |
| 21 | 8 | 322662 | Allen & Green | Fenton |
| 27 | 7 | 322931–2 | Josiah Wedgwood & Sons | Etruria |
| 29 | 1 | 322948 | Wood, Son & Co. | Cobridge |
| July 1 | 1 | 322971 | Burgess & Leigh | Burslem |
| 3 | 2 | 323132 | Mintons | Stoke |
| 6 | 7 | 323315–20 | Joseph Cliff & Sons | Leeds |
| 8 | 6 | 323396 | Josiah Wedgwood & Sons | Etruria |
| 9 | 8 | 323434 | Mintons | Stoke |
| 9 | 9 | 323435 | Josiah Wedgwood & Sons | Etruria |
| 9 | 10 | 323436 | J. Dimmock & Co. | Hanley |
| 10 | 14 | 323508 | Bates & Bennett | Cobridge |
| 11 | 1 | 323521 | Soane & Smith | London |
| 11 | 11 | 323596 | W. & J. A. Bailey | Alloa |

# APPENDIX B

| Date | Parcel No. | Patent. No. | Factory, Retailer Wholesaler, etc | Place |
|------|------------|-------------|-----------------------------------|-------|
| 12 | 4 | 323604 | Josiah Wedgwood & Sons | Etruria |
| 12 | 13 | 323626 | Samuel Lear | Hanley |
| 12 | 15 | 323628 | T. C. Brown–Westhead, Moore & Co. | Hanley |
| 15 | 1 | 323650–1 | Pratt & Simpson | Fenton |
| 17 | 9 | 323774–5 | Wm. Adams | Tunstall |
| 18 | 2 | 323778 | Ambrose Bevington | Hanley |
| 20 | 1 | 323847 | J. Bevington | Hanley |
| 20 | 6 | 323893 | John Meir & Son | Tunstall |
| 20 | 11 | 323910–1 | E. J. D. Bodley | Burslem |
| 26 | 3 | 324177 | Josiah Wedgwood & Sons | Etruria |
| 30 | 2 | 324324 | idem | Etruria |
| 30 | 6 | 324336 | Powell, Bishop & Stonier | Hanley |
| 30 | 12 | 324347 | E. Clarke | Longport |
| 31 | 8 | 324383 | Mintons | Stoke |
| 31 | 13 | 324388 | James Edwards & Son | Burslem |
| Aug 6 | 3 | 324576 | Moore Bros. | Longton |
| 7 | 3 | 324730 | Thos. Hughes | Burslem |
| 9 | 10 | 324848 | Derby Crown Porcelain Co. Ltd. | Derby |
| 9 | 12 | 324870–2 | Craven, Dunnill & Co. Ltd. | Jackfield |
| 14 | 4 | 325029–34 | S. H. Sharp | Leeds |
| 16 | 9 | 325094 | The Campbell Brick & Tile Co. | Stoke |
| 23 | 1 | 325278 | Moore Bros. | Longton |
| 23 | 7 | 325319 | J. Dimmock & Co. | Hanley |
| Sept 3 | 12 | 325612 | G. & L. Wohlauer | Dresden |
| 5 | 3 | 325716 | Moore Bros. | Longton |
| 9 | 5 | 325992–4 | Wm. Brownfield & Sons | Cobridge |
| 10 | 2 | 326006 | Josiah Wedgwood & Sons | Etruria |
| 12 | 6 | 326146 | J. Bevington | Hanley |
| 13 | 5 | 326155 | G. L. Ashworth & Bros. | Hanley |

# APPENDIX B

| Date | Parcel No. | Patent No. | Factory, Retailer Wholesaler, etc | Place |
|------|-----------|-----------|-----------------------------------|-------|
| 13 | 16 | 326198 | The Worcester Royal Porcelain Co. Ltd. | Worcester |
| 20 | 19 | 326482 | R. Wotherspoon & Co. | Glasgow |
| 24 | 3 | 326785 | T. Bevington | Hanley |
| 28 | 5 | 326970–1 | Minton, Hollins & Co. | Stoke |
| 30 | 1 | 327000 | Mintons | Stoke |
| Oct 2 | 2 | 327035 | Mintons | Stoke |
| 3 | 8 | 327110 | J. T. Hudden | Longton |
| 4 | 8 | 327227 | F. & R. Pratt & Co. | Fenton |
| 5 | 4 | 327235 | Jones Bros. & Co. | W/hmptn |
| 5 | 13 | 327271 | The Worcester Royal Porcelain Co. Ltd. | Worcester |
| 8 | 6 | 327359 | Moore Bros. | Longton |
| 8 | 7 | 327360 | Bates, Gildea & Walker | Burslem |
| 9 | 9 | 327392 | Josiah Wedgwood | Etruria |
| 11 | 8 | 327556 | Minton, Hollins & Co. | Stoke |
| 14 | 8 | 327625–6 | W. T. Copeland & Sons | Stoke |
| 23 | 1 | 328018 | The Brownhills Pottery Co. | Tunstall |
| 23 | 11 | 328144–5 | Pinder & Bourne & Co. | Burslem |
| 24 | 1 | 328146 | T. Furnival & Sons | Cobridge |
| 24 | 2 | 328147 | J. Dimmock & Co. | Hanley |
| 24 | 13 | 328274 | The Worcester Royal Porcelain Co. Ltd. | Worcester |
| 26 | 4 | 328320 | Wm. Brownfield & Sons | Cobridge |
| 30 | 3 | 328436–7 | Minton, Hollins & Co. | Stoke |
| 30 | 5 | 328439–40 | Mintons | Stoke |
| Nov 1 | 3 | 328620 | J. Bevington | Hanley |
| 4 | 1 | 328699 | Edge, Malkin & Co. | Burslem |
| 5 | 11 | 328774 | H. Burgess | Burslem |
| 5 | 17 | 328790–2 | E. J. D. Bodley | Burslem |
| 6 | 3 | 328795 | Samuel Lear | Hanley |
| 13 | 13 | 329075 | John Rose & Co. | Coalport |
| 15 | 1 | 329108 | Craven, Dunnill & Co. Ltd. | Jackfield |
| 15 | 11 | 329147 | F. & R. Pratt & Co. | Fenton |
| 16 | 5 | 329157 | J. Dimmock & Co. | Hanley |

# APPENDIX B

| Date | Parcel No. | Patent No. | Factory, Retailer Wholesaler, etc | Place |
|------|------------|------------|-----------------------------------|-------|
| 20 | 13 | 329378 | Cliff & Tomlin | Leeds |
| 23 | 2 | 329456 | E. & C. Challinor | Fenton |
| 26 | 14 | 329673 | T. & R. Boote | Burslem |
| 27 | 9 | 329709 | J. McIntyre & Co. | Burslem |
| 29 | 14 | 329782–3 | W. & E. Corn | Burslem |
| Dec 2 | 7 | 329901 | T. C. Brown–Westhead, Moore & Co. | Hanley |
| 2 | 8 | 329902 | J. F. Meakin | London |
| 3 | 9 | 329922 | J. McIntyre & Co. | Burslem |
| 4 | 2 | 329939 | Wm. Brownfield & Sons | Cobridge |
| 6 | 3 | 330061 | Mintons | Stoke |
| 7 | 2 | 330097 | A. Shaw | Burslem |
| 19 | 8 | 330485 | Thos. Hughes | Burslem |
| 27 | 13 | 330677 | T. & R. Boote | Burslem |
| 28 | 4 | 330687 | J. Gaskell, Son & Co. | Burslem |
| **1879** | | | | |
| Jan 7 | 7 | 330920 | W. T. Copeland & Sons | Stoke |
| 8 | 11 | 330965–6 | Minton, Hollins & Co. | Stoke |
| 9 | 8 | 330997–8 | Wm. Brownfield & Sons | Cobridge |
| 14 | 5 | 331152 | The New Wharf Pottery Co. | Burslem |
| 14 | 6 | 331153 | The Campbell Brick & Tile Co. | Stoke |
| 16 | 3 | 331228 | B. & S. Hancock | Stoke |
| 16 | 13 | 331342 | F. & R. Pratt & Co. | Fenton |
| 20 | 15 | 331418–9 | Derby Crown Porcelain Co. Ltd. | Derby |
| 22 | 4 | 331458 | Dunn, Bennett & Co. | Hanley |
| 28 | 11 | 331597 | W. T. Copeland & Sons | Stoke |
| 29 | 2 | 331600 | T. Furnival & Sons | Cobridge |
| 29 | 3 | 331601 | T. Bevington | Hanley |
| 29 | 15 | 331677 | E. J. D. Bodley | Burslem |
| 1 | 13 | 331775 | Clementson Bros. | Hanley |
| 3 | 1 | 331777 | Josiah Wedgwood & Sons | Etruria |

# APPENDIX B

| Date | Parcel No. | Patent No. | Factory, Retailer Wholesaler, etc | Place |
|------|------------|------------|-----------------------------------|-------|
| 5 | 7 | 331892–3 | Mintons | Stoke |
| 8 | 1 | 332030 | Mintons | Stoke |
| 14 | 4 | 332251 | T. Furnival & Sons | Cobridge |
| 15 | 2 | 332266 | The Campbell Brick & Tile Co. | Stoke |
| 17 | 6 | 332296 | McBirney & Armstrong | Belleek |
| 24 | 2 | 332606 | W. P. Jervis | Stoke |
| 24 | 3 | 332607–9 | W. & T. Adams | Tunstall |
| 25 | 4 | 332642 | Mintons | Stoke |
| 28 | 1 | 332823 | E. Chetwynd | Stoke |
| 28 | 7 | 332831 | Clementson Bros. | Hanley |
| Mar 1 | 1 | 332837 | T. Furnival & Sons | Cobridge |
| 4 | 4 | 332938 | F. W. Grove & J. Stark | Longton |
| 6 | 10 | 333047 | Powell, Bishop & Stonier | Hanley |
| 12 | 4 | 333210 | Edge, Malkin & Co. | Burslem |
| 12 | 12 | 333235–6 | W. T. Copeland & Sons | Stoke |
| 13 | 1 | 333241–4 | Wm. Davenport & Co. | Longport |
| 13 | 14 | 333301 | Clementson Bros. | Hanley |
| 14 | 9 | 333319 | E. Clarke | Longport |
| 17 | 2 | 333368 | Powell, Bishop & Stonier | Hanley |
| 18 | 1 | 333431 | Josiah Wedgwood & Sons | Etruria |
| 19 | 2 | 333485 | J. Hawthorn | Cobridge |
| 26 | 17 | 333751–2 | The Worcester Royal Porcelain Co. Ltd. | Worcester |
| 28 | 6 | 333801 | Clementson Bros. | Hanley |
| 29 | 4 | 333813 | Beck, Blair & Co. | Longton |
| Apr 3 | 9 | 334030 | T. C. Brown–Westhead, Moore & Co. | Hanley |
| 4 | 12 | 334052–3 | Pinder, Bourne & Co. | Burslem |
| 9 | 5 | 334137 | H. Alcock & Co. | Cobridge |
| 10 | 12 | 334200 | T. C. Brown–Westhead, Moore & Co. | Hanley |
| 12 | 1 | 334206 | The Worcester Royal Porcelain Co. Ltd. | Worcester |

# APPENDIX B

| Date | Parcel No. | Patent No. | Factory, Retailer Wholesaler, etc | Place |
|------|-----------|-----------|-----------------------------------|-------|
| 15 | 6 | 334241–2 | T. C. Brown–Westhead, Moore & Co. | Hanley |
| 23 | 8 | 334508 | T. C. Brown–Westhead, Moore & Co. | Hanley |
| 24 | 3 | 334531 | Josiah Wedgwood & Sons | Etruria |
| May 2 | 5 | 334803 | A. Bevington | Hanley |
| 5 | 1 | 334860–1 | T. Furnival & Sons | Cobridge |
| 5 | 6 | 334897 | Bates, Gildea & Walker | Burslem |
| 6 | 7 | 334923–5 | Sampson Bridgwood & Son | Longton |
| 7 | 11 | 334978 | The Worcester Royal Porcelain Co. Ltd. | Worcester |
| 9 | 15 | 335057 | idem | Worcester |
| 13 | 4 | 335148–51 | Pinder & Bourne & Co. | Burslem |
| 13 | 8 | 335167–8 | Clementson Bros. | Hanley |
| 14 | 9 | 335182 | T. C. Brown–Westhead, Moore & Co. | Hanley |
| 14 | 13 | 335187–8 | E. J. D. Bodley | Burslem |
| 19 | 1 | 335308–9 | Wm. Brownfield & Sons | Cobridge |
| 21 | 5 | 335496 | Harvey Adams & Co. | Longton |
| 23 | 2 | 335551–2 | Sampson Bridgwood & Son | Longton |
| 23 | 14 | 335608 | Harvey Adams & Co. | Longton |
| 29 | 2 | 335715 | John Tams | Longton |
| 29 | 12 | 335739–40 | Pinder, Bourne & Co. | Burslem |
| 30 | 3 | 335744 | McBirney & Armstrong | Belleek |
| 30 | 10 | 335791 | J. Dimmock & Co. | Hanley |
| 30 | 12 | 335793 | F. W. Grove & J. Stark | Longton |
| 31 | 4 | 335805 | Minton, Hollins & Co. | Stoke |
| June 10 | 4 | 336030 | T. Furnival & Sons | Cobridge |
| 11 | 8 | 336075 | Thos. Till & Sons | Burslem |
| 13 | 13 | 336132 | T. C. Brown–Westhead, Moore & Co. | Hanley |
| 18 | 4 | 336185 | F. W. Grove & J. Stark | Longton |
| 24 | 11 | 336415 | Josiah Wedgwood & Sons | Etruria |
| 25 | 1 | 336417 | Clementson Bros. | Hanley |

| Date | Parcel No. | Patent No. | Factory, Retailer Wholesaler, etc | Place |
|---|---|---|---|---|
| 26 | 13 | 336471–4 | Haviland & Co. | Limoges and London |
| 27 | 11 | 336496 | Shorter & Boulton | Stoke |
| 30 | 12 | 336586–7 | Birks Bros. & Seddon | Cobridge |
| July 2 | 2 | 336676 | Josiah Wedgwood & Sons | Etruria |
| 7 | 2 | 336917 | J. F. Wileman | Fenton |
| 8 | 1 | 336930 | Mintons | Stoke |
| 8 | 16 | 336967–8 | T. C. Brown–Westhead, Moore & Co. | Hanley |
| 9 | 12 | 337058 | idem | Hanley |
| 10 | 2 | 337060 | T. Bevington | Hanley |
| 10 | 3 | 337061 | Moore Bros. | Longton |
| 16 | 4 | 337157–8 | A. Bevington & Co. | Hanley |
| 16 | 14 | 337177 | T. C. Brown–Westhead, Moore & Co. | Hanley |
| 25 | 4 | 337497 | Mintons | Stoke |
| 26 | 6 | 337536 | Minton, Hollins & Co. | Stoke |
| 31 | 2 | 337660 | Mintons | Stoke |
| Aug 2 | 2 | 337814 | H. M. Williamson & Sons | Longton |
| 5 | 12 | 337945–7 | J. Mortlock & Co. | London |
| 6 | 6 | 337958 | Wardle & Co. | Hanley |
| 13 | 2 | 338135 | F. W. Grove & J. Stark | Longton |
| 22 | 4 | 338559 | McBirney & Armstrong | Belleek |
| 27 | 13 | 338872 | Bates, Gildea & Walker | Burslem |
| Sept 4 | 6 | 339193 | T. C. Brown–Westhead, Moore & Co. | Hanley |
| 10 | 13 | 339373 | idem | Hanley |
| 17 | 4 | 339685–6 | Wm. Brownfield & Sons | Cobridge |
| 18 | 10 | 339979 | T. C. Brown–Westhead, Moore & Co. | Hanley |
| 26 | 4 | 340431 | J. T. Hudden | Longton |
| 29 | 3 | 340569 | Edge, Malkin & Co. | Burslem |
| Oct 9 | 6 | 341137 | Bates, Gildea & Walker | Burslem |

# APPENDIX B

| Date | Parcel No. | Patent No. | Factory, Retailer Wholesaler, etc | Place |
|------|------------|------------|-----------------------------------|-------|
| 10 | 2 | 341151 | T. C. Brown–Westhead, Moore & Co. | Hanley |
| 11 | 5 | 341229–30 | E. J. D. Bodley | Burslem |
| 15 | 1 | 341347 | Mintons | Stoke |
| 16 | 5 | 341466 | J. Roth | London |
| 16 | 16 | 341500 | Minton, Hollins & Co. | Stoke |
| 17 | 2 | 341502 | G. L. Ashworth & Bros. | Hanley |
| 18 | 3 | 341629 | Josiah Wedgwood & Sons | Etruria |
| 23 | 12 | 341864 | C. Pillivuyt & Co. | London |
| 24 | 4 | 341882–3 | The Campbell Brick & Tile Co. | Stoke |
| 27 | 9 | 341997 | E. F. Bodley & Co. | Burslem |
| 29 | 5 | 342098 | Mintons | Stoke |
| 29 | 7 | 342100 | Clementson Bros. | Hanley |
| 29 | 15 | 342152 | F. D. Bradley | Longton |
| 30 | 4 | 342158 | Mintons | Stoke |
| Nov 3 | 12 | 342396 | Minton, Hollins & Co. | Stoke |
| 3 | 14 | 342398 | Tundley, Rhodes & Procter | Burslem |
| 6 | 2 | 342461 | Josiah Wedgwood & Sons | Etruria |
| 6 | 3 | 342462–3 | Moore Bros. | Longton |
| 6 | 4 | 342464–72 | Burmantofts (Wilcock & Co.) | Leeds |
| 12 | 11 | 342769 | The Worcester Royal Porcelain Co. Ltd. | Worcester |
| 15 | 12 | 342921 | C. Ford | Hanley |
| 15 | 16 | 342925–7 | W. T. Copeland & Sons | Stoke |
| 17 | 2 | 342929 | Powell, Bishop & Stonier | Hanley |
| 19 | 5 | 343017 | idem | Hanley |
| 20 | 4 | 343070–1 | Elsmore & Son | Tunstall |
| 21 | 6 | 343148 | Mintons | Stoke |
| 21 | 14 | 343166 | Soane & Smith | London |
| 22 | 7 | 343219 | The Worcester Royal Porcelain Co. Ltd. | Worcester |
| 28 | 5 | 343530 | Wm. Brownfield & Sons | Cobridge |

# APPENDIX B

| Date | | Parcel No. | Patent No. | Factory, Retailer Wholesaler, etc | Place |
|------|---|---|---|---|---|
| | 28 | 6 | 343531 | A. Bevington & Co. | Hanley |
| | 29 | 3 | 343585 | Mintons | Stoke |
| | 29 | 4 | 343586 | T. C. Brown–Westhead, Moore & Co. | Hanley |
| Dec | 1 | 2 | 343618 | J. Holdcroft | Longton |
| | 2 | 4 | 343652–3 | T. C. Brown–Westhead, Moore & Co. | Hanley |
| | 2 | 5 | 343654 | Elsmore & Son | Tunstall |
| | 2 | 17 | 343716 | J. Aynsley & Sons | Longton |
| | 6 | 2 | 343815–6 | T. & R. Boote | Burslem |
| | 10 | 14 | 344077 | Clementson Bros. | Hanley |
| | 11 | 4 | 344082–4 | Moore Bros. | Longton |
| | 17 | 11 | 344387 | Ridgways | Stoke |
| | 19 | 1 | 344452 | Clementson Bros. | Hanley |
| | 19 | 3 | 344454 | Burmantofts (Wilcock & Co.) | Leeds |
| | 20 | 5 | 344478 | Josiah Wedgwood & Sons | Etruria |
| | 22 | 2 | 344503 | Mintons | Stoke |
| | 24 | 2 | 344568 | Sherwin & Cotton | Hanley |
| **1880** | | | | | |
| Jan | 3 | 1 | 344838 | Sherwin & Cotton | Hanley |
| | 7 | 3 | 344961–2 | T. Bevington | Hanley |
| | 7 | 4 | 344963 | T. & R. Boote | Burslem |
| | 7 | 5 | 344964–9 | Soane & Smith | London |
| | 7 | 8 | 344972 | Minton, Hollins & Co. | Stoke |
| | 8 | 9 | 344997 | The Old Hall Earthenware Co. Ltd. | Hanley |
| | 9 | 3 | 345003 | Sherwin & Cotton | Hanley |
| | 9 | 12 | 345045 | T. G. Allen | London |
| | 13 | 1 | 345131 | T. C. Brown–Westhead, Moore & Co. | Hanley |
| | 14 | 11 | 345184–5 | The Worcester Royal Porcelain Co. Ltd. | Worcester |
| | 16 | 8 | 345288 | S. Fielding & Co. | Stoke |

# APPENDIX B

| Date | Parcel No. | Patent No. | Factory, Retailer Wholesaler, etc | Place |
|------|-----------|-----------|-----------------------------------|-------|
| 16 | 14 | 345299 | Brockwell & Son | London |
| 21 | 7 | 345469–71 | Pinder, Bourne & Co. | Burslem |
| 22 | 2 | 345481 | Mintons | Stoke |
| 22 | 8 | 345493–4 | Minton, Hollins & Co. | Stoke |
| 23 | 5 | 345511 | Mintons | Stoke |
| 26 | 11 | 345719 | Wm. Brownfield & Sons | Cobridge |
| 27 | 13 | 345798 | Wardle & Co. | Hanley |
| 28 | 3 | 345801 | T. C. Brown–Westhead, Moore & Co. | Hanley |
| 28 | 4 | 345802 | J. Aynsley & Sons | Longton |
| 28 | 12 | 345833 | Powell, Bishop & Stonier | Hanley |
| 29 | 9 | 345860–1 | E. J. D. Bodley | Burslem |
| 30 | 2 | 345864 | Taylor, Tunnicliffe & Co. | Hanley |
| Feb 3 | 11 | 345952 | Powell, Bishop & Stonier | Hanley |
| 9 | 18 | 346202 | Whittingham, Ford & Riley | Burslem |
| 10 | 4 | 346208–10 | Mintons | Stoke |
| 11 | 10 | 346344 | T. Bevington | Hanley |
| 12 | 4 | 346360 | W. A. Adderley | Longton |
| 12 | 7 | 346363 | Wm. Brownfield & Sons | Cobridge |
| 14 | 14 | 346467 | Bates, Gildea & Walker | Burslem |
| 18 | 12 | 346594 | The Derby Crown Porcelain Co. Ltd. | Derby |
| 24 | 2 | 346832 | Mintons | Stoke |
| 24 | 11 | 346870 | Wm. Harrop & Co. | Hanley |
| 25 | 18 | 346920 | Clementson Bros. | Hanley |
| 25 | 23 | 346945 | Sherwin & Cotton | Hanley |
| 26 | 6 | 346952–3 | Minton, Hollins & Co. | Stoke |
| 26 | 7 | 346954 | Moore Bros. | Longton |
| Mar 3 | 6 | 347138 | J. Holdcroft | Longton |
| 4 | 8 | 347203 | Soane & Smith | London |
| 8 | 4 | 347344 | T. Furnival & Sons | Cobridge |
| 8 | 10 | 347360 | W. Harrop & Co. | Hanley |
| 12 | 4 | 347476 | W. A. Adderley | Longton |
| 16 | 3 | 347599 | J. F. Wileman & Co. | Fenton |
| 16 | 11 | 347645 | Sherwin & Cotton | Hanley |

| Date | Parcel No. | Patent No. | Factory, Retailer Wholesaler, etc | Place |
|---|---|---|---|---|
| 16 | 12 | 347646–7 | J. Macintyre & Co. | Burslem |
| 17 | 6 | 347660 | Josiah Wedgwood & Sons | Etruria |
| 18 | 3 | 347690–6 | Moore Bros. | Longton |
| 22 | 4 | 347838 | Powell, Bishop & Stonier | Hanley |
| 23 | 4 | 347872 | Taylor, Tunnicliffe & Co. | Hanley |
| 25 | 6 | 348018 | Mintons | Stoke |
| 30 | 4 | 348110 | Sherwin & Cotton | Hanley |
| 31 | 3 | 348114 | Thos. Peake | Tunstall |
| Apr 12 | 6 | 348606–8 | Bates, Gildea & Walker | Burslem |
| 15 | 11 | 348761 | Ridgways | Stoke |
| 19 | 11 | 348911–3 | The Worcester Royal Porcelain Co. Ltd. | Worcester |
| 22 | 11 | 349025–6 | Sherwin & Cotton | Hanley |
| 22 | 5 | 349027 | W. H. Grindley & Co. | Tunstall |
| 26 | 1 | 349221 | T. Furnival & Sons | Cobridge |
| 27 | 11 | 349239–41 | Moore Bros. | Longton |
| 27 | 13 | 349318–23 | The Worcester Royal Porcelain Co. Ltd. | Worcester |
| 29 | 4 | 349340–1 | Mintons | Stoke |
| 30 | 6 | 349380 | T. Furnival & Sons | Cobridge |
| May 3 | 3 | 349438–43 | Wm. Brownfield & Sons | Cobridge |
| 5 | 13 | 349528 | S. Fielding & Co. | Stoke |
| 10 | 6 | 349693 | Powell, Bishop & Stonier | Hanley |
| 11 | 15 | 349791 | Soane & Smith | London |
| 13 | 8 | 349852–3 | Mintons | Stoke |
| 13 | 15 | 349869 | Minton, Hollins & Co. | Stoke |
| 14 | 26 | 349939 | Bates, Gildea & Walker | Burslem |
| 25 | 4 | 350098 | Wm. Brownfield & Sons | Cobridge |
| 26 | 6 | 350142 | Mintons | Stoke |
| June 1 | 4 | 350251 | Mintons | Stoke |
| 2 | 3 | 350353 | Sherwin & Cotton | Hanley |
| 7 | 6 | 350476 | J. Dimmock & Co. | Hanley |
| 8 | 1 | 350477 | Geo. Jones & Sons | Stoke |
| 10 | 3 | 350554 | Sherwin & Cotton | Hanley |
| 10 | 4 | 350555 | E. J. D. Bodley | Burslem |

# APPENDIX B

| Date | Parcel No. | Patent No. | Factory, Retailer Wholesaler, etc | Place |
|---|---|---|---|---|
| 10 | 12 | 350613 | J. Dimmock & Co. | Hanley |
| 11 | 3 | 350616 | Josiah Wedgwood & Sons | Etruria |
| 14 | 12 | 350842 | J. Roth | London |
| 15 | 4 | 350848 | Buckley, Wood & Co. | Burslem |
| 16 | 3 | 350972 | Wedgwood & Co. | Tunstall |
| 17 | 4 | 351025 | Samuel Lear | Hanley |
| 17 | 15 | 351058 | Ridgways | Stoke |
| 17 | 16 | 351059 | J. Macintyre & Co. | Burslem |
| 17 | 20 | 351063 | The Crystal Porcelain Co. | Hanley |
| 17 | 21 | 351064 | J. Dimmock & Co. | Hanley |
| 19 | 11 | 351186 | Josiah Wedgwood & Sons | Etruria |
| 19 | 15 | 351190 | J. Roth | London |
| 22 | 1 | 351259 | W. H. Grindley & Co. | Tunstall |
| 26 | 13 | 351496–7 | The Worcester Royal Porcelain Co. Ltd. | Worcester |
| July 5 | 11 | 351866 | Westwood & Moore | Brierley Hill |
| 7 | 4 | 351909 | Sherwin & Cotton | Hanley |
| 7 | 5 | 351910 | Mintons | Stoke |
| 7 | 15 | 351928 | F. J. Emery | Burslem |
| 12 | 4 | 352094 | Mintons | Stoke |
| 13 | 12 | 352138 | Thos. Barlow | Longton |
| 15 | 3 | 352192 | Dunn, Bennett & Co. | Hanley |
| 15 | 4 | 352193 | F. W. Grove & J. Stark | Longton |
| 16 | 9 | 352224 | Sherwin & Cotton | Hanley |
| 16 | 10 | 352225 | Moore Bros. | Longton |
| 16 | 19 | 352278 | S. Fielding & Co. | Stoke |
| 28 | 2 | 352872 | The Brownhills Pottery Co. | Tunstall |
| 31 | 8 | 353079 | The Old Hall Earthenware Co. Ltd. | Hanley |
| Aug 4 | 3 | 353108 | Pinder, Bourne & Co. | Burslem |
| 11 | 14 | 353543 | Clementson Bros. | Hanley |
| 14 | 12 | 353713–4 | Wm. Davenport & Co. | Longport |
| 17 | 6 | 353746 | Sherwin & Cotton | Hanley |
| 18 | 3 | 353818 | Josiah Wedgwood & Sons | Etruria |

371

# APPENDIX B

| Date | Parcel No. | Patent No. | Factory, Retailer Wholesaler, etc | Place |
|------|-----------|-----------|-----------------------------------|-------|
| 21 | 2 | 354026 | Sherwin & Cotton | Hanley |
| 21 | 10 | 354081 | W. A. Adderley | Longton |
| 23 | 5 | 354092 | Jackson & Gosling | Longton |
| 23 | 6 | 354093–4 | T. C. Brown–Westhead, Moore & Co. | Hanley |
| 24 | 10 | 354154 | E. J. D. Bodley | Burslem |
| Sept 3 | 3 | 354639 | T. C. Brown–Westhead, Moore & Co. | Hanley |
| 4 | 7 | 354766–7 | J. Beech & Son | Longton |
| 11 | 3 | 355091–100 | Wm. Brownfield & Sons | Cobridge |
| 14 | 6 | 355169 | Mintons | Stoke |
| 15 | 6 | 355231 | G. L. Ashworth & Bros. | Hanley |
| 15 | 12 | 355255–7 | Minton, Hollins & Co. | Stoke |
| 23 | 3 | 355575 | Ambrose Wood | Hanley |
| 25 | 6 | 355651–4 | Minton, Hollins & Co. | Stoke |
| 27 | 5 | 355745–6 | John Marshall & Co. | Bo'ness, Scotland |
| 29 | 3 | 355947–8 | The Brownhills Pottery Co. | Tunstall |
| 30 | 4 | 355987 | The Worcester Royal Porcelain Co. Ltd. | Worcester |
| Oct 1 | 3 | 356014 | Wade & Colclough | Burslem |
| 6 | 4 | 356163 | Josiah Wedgwood & Sons | Etruria |
| 12 | 4 | 356514 | Mintons | Stoke |
| 13 | 5 | 356532 | Josiah Wedgwood & Sons | Etruria |
| 20 | 10 | 356970 | Burgess & Leigh | Burslem |
| 21 | 13 | 357033–5 | The Worcester Royal Porcelain Co. Ltd. | Worcester |
| 22 | 4 | 357039 | E. F. Bodley & Son | Burslem |
| 22 | 12 | 357088 | J. Aynsley & Sons | Longton |
| 26 | 13 | 357298–9 | Minton, Hollins & Co. | Stoke |
| 27 | 5 | 357305 | Taylor, Tunnicliffe & Co. | Hanley |
| 27 | 20 | 357429 | J. Tams | Longton |
| 27 | 21 | 357430 | G. Woolliscroft & Son | Etruria |
| 28 | 2 | 357466 | Sherwin & Cotton | Hanley |

# APPENDIX B

| Date | Parcel No. | Patent No. | Factory, Retailer Wholesaler, etc | Place |
|------|-----------|-----------|-----------------------------------|-------|
| 30 | 6 | 357560 | Jones & Hopkinson | Hanley |
| Nov 2 | 2 | 357609 | W. H. Grindley & Co. | Tunstall |
| 4 | 4 | 357656–7 | W. & T. Adams | Tunstall |
| 4 | 15 | 357724–5 | Minton, Hollins & Co. | Stoke |
| 9 | 4 | 357954 | Josiah Wedgwood & Sons | Etruria |
| 10 | 2 | 358062–3 | Wilcock & Co. (Burmantofts) | Leeds |
| 10 | 13 | 358141 | Bednall & Heath | Hanley |
| 18 | 3 | 358466 | S. Radford | Longton |
| 18 | 14 | 358500 | Mintons | Stoke |
| 19 | 15 | 358552 | The Crown Derby Porcelain Co. Ltd. | Derby |
| 24 | 4 | 358747 | F. W. Grove & J. Stark | Longton |
| 24 | 5 | 358748 | Bates, Gildea & Walker | Burslem |
| Dec 6 | 2 | 359292 | Powell, Bishop & Stonier | Hanley |
| 7 | 10 | 359321–6 | Pinder, Bourne & Co. | Burslem |
| 8 | 5 | 359342–3 | Wittmann & Roth | London |
| 15 | 15 | 359668–71 | Wm. Brownfield & Sons | Cobridge |
| 18 | 2 | 359784 | Bates, Gildea & Walker | Burslem |
| 24 | 8 | 359997 | T. C. Brown–Westhead, Moore & Co. | Hanley |
| 29 | 7 | 360042–4 | Doulton & Co. | Lambeth |
| 31 | 1 | 360100 | The Old Hall Earthenware Co. Ltd. | Hanley |
| 31 | 4 | 360103–5 | Sherwin & Cotton | Hanley |
| **1881** | | | | |
| Jan 5 | 7 | 360326 | J. Roth | London |
| 6 | 2 | 360331 | B. & S. Hancock | Stoke |
| 6 | 8 | 360355 | F. D. Bradley | Longton |
| 7 | 13 | 360484 | Sherwin & Cotton | Hanley |
| 12 | 5 | 360633 | idem | Hanley |
| 14 | 10 | 360747 | The Worcester Royal Porcelain Co. Ltd. | Worcester |
| 14 | 18 | 360799 | E. J. D. Bodley | Burslem |

# APPENDIX B

| Date | Parcel No. | Patent No. | Factory, Retailer Wholesaler, etc | Place |
|------|-----------|------------|-----------------------------------|-------|
| 15 | 4 | 360806–7 | Holmes, Stonier & Hollinshead | Hanley |
| 20 | 3 | 360900 | Mintons | Stoke |
| 21 | 11 | 360954 | W. & T. Adams | Tunstall |
| 26 | 4 | 361116–7 | Minton, Hollins & Co. | Stoke |
| 27 | 15 | 361151 | The Worcester Royal Porcelain Co. Ltd. | Worcester |
| 28 | 3 | 361170 | G. Woolliscroft & Son | Hanley |
| Feb 8 | 5 | 361537 | F. W. Grove & J. Stark | Longton |
| 8 | 6 | 361538–41 | Wm. Brownfield & Sons | Cobridge |
| 11 | 10 | 361668 | F. J. Emery | Burslem |
| 15 | 6 | 361748 | W. A. Adderley | Longton |
| 16 | 3 | 361784 | F. D. Bradley | Longton |
| 17 | 2 | 361813 | Murray & Co. | Glasgow |
| 18 | 3 | 361868 | S. Radford | Longton |
| 19 | 15 | 361927 | S. S. Bold | Hanley |
| 21 | 4 | 361937 | Taylor, Waine & Bates | Longton |
| 24 | 8 | 362086 | Wm. Harrop & Co. | Hanley |
| 25 | 14 | 362166 | J. Macintyre & Co. | Burslem |
| 28 | 9 | 362242 | E. J. D. Bodley | Burslem |
| Mar 3 | 5 | 362423 | J. Dimmock & Co. | Hanley |
| 7 | 11 | 362545 | J. Aynsley & Sons | Longton |
| 8 | 3 | 362548 | F. W. Grove & J. Stark | Longton |
| 14 | 1 | 362815 | E. J. D. Bodley | Burslem |
| 17 | 9 | 362992 | Shorter & Boulton | Stoke |
| 19 | 4 | 363026–7 | Mintons | Stoke |
| 23 | 4 | 363157 | Mintons | Stoke |
| 24 | 2 | 363206–7 | T. S. Pinder | Burslem |
| 24 | 3 | 363208 | W. A. Adderley | Longton |
| 29 | 6 | 363421 | T. A. Simpson | Hanley |
| 31 | 2 | 363461 | J. T. Hudden | Longton |
| Apr 7 | 2 | 363720 | Sherwin & Cotton | Hanley |
| 7 | 9 | 363732 | The Old Hall Earthenware Co. Ltd. | Hanley |
| 8 | 2 | 363738 | W. Harrop & Co. | Hanley |

# APPENDIX B

| Date | Parcel No. | Patent No. | Factory, Retailer Wholesaler, etc | Place |
|------|------|------|------|------|
| 8 | 3 | 363739 | Wedgwood & Co. | Tunstall |
| 8 | 14 | 363785 | The Worcester Royal Porcelain Co. Ltd. | Worcester |
| 9 | 5 | 363793 | R. H. Plant & Co. | Longton |
| 11 | 1 | 363800 | A. Bevington & Co. | Hanley |
| 12 | 4 | 363849–50 | Mintons | Stoke |
| 14 | 10 | 363975 | Mintons | Stoke |
| 16 | 17 | 364110 | J. Marshall & Co. | Bo'ness, Scotland |
| 19 | 3 | 364116 | Sherwin & Cotton | Hanley |
| 19 | 5 | 364118 | T. & R. Boote | Burslem |
| 21 | 4 | 364172 | Sherwin & Cotton | Hanley |
| 21 | 5 | 364173–4 | E. J. D. Bodley | Burslem |
| 23 | 7 | 364238 | J. F. Wileman | Fenton |
| 28 | 12 | 364488 | W. T. Copeland & Sons | Stoke |
| 30 | 3 | 364528 | Trubshaw, Hand & Co. | Longton |
| 30 | 4 | 364529 | Josiah Wedgwood & Sons | Etruria |
| May 3 | 4 | 364604 | Wm. Wood & Co. | Burslem |
| 3 | 5 | 364605 | Sherwin & Cotton | Hanley |
| 4 | 2 | 364624 | idem | Hanley |
| 4 | 3 | 364625–7 | Wm. Brownfield & Sons | Cobridge |
| 5 | 2 | 364648 | W. & T. Adams | Tunstall |
| 6 | 4 | 364736 | R. H. Plant & Co. | Longton |
| 11 | 3 | 364941 | J. Tams | Longton |
| 13 | 2 | 365005 | Mintons | Stoke |
| 16 | 2 | 365066 | Josiah Wedgwood & Sons | Etruria |
| 17 | 9 | 365134–5 | J. Mortlock & Co. | London |
| 20 | 11 | 365206 | W. A. Adderley | Longton |
| 21 | 3 | 365211 | Powell, Bishop & Stonier | Hanley |
| 24 | 5 | 365391 | G. L. Ashworth & Bros. | Hanley |
| 24 | 6 | 365392–3 | Mintons | Stoke |
| 24 | 7 | 365394 | F. J. Emery | Burslem |
| 25 | 3 | 365424 | Powell, Bishop & Stonier | Hanley |
| 25 | 9 | 365442–4 | The Worcester Royal Porcelain Co. Ltd. | Worcester |

# APPENDIX B

| Date | Parcel No. | Patent No. | Factory, Retailer Wholesaler, etc | Place |
|---|---|---|---|---|
| 25 | 10 | 365445–6 | Josiah Wedgwood & Sons | Etruria |
| 26 | 7 | 365461 | G. Woolliscroft & Son | Hanley |
| 30 | 1 | 365539 | T. Furnival & Sons | Cobridge |
| 30 | 2 | 365540 | The Decorative Art Tile Co. | Hanley |
| June 1 | 3 | 365730 | Mintons | Stoke |
| 1 | 13 | 365793 | J. Mortlock & Co. | London |
| 3 | 4 | 365827 | S. P. Ledward | Cobridge |
| 4 | 3 | 365852 | T. Furnival & Sons | Cobridge |
| 4 | 4 | 365853 | The Decorative Art Tile Co. | Hanley |
| 7 | 3 | 365875 | E. F. Bodley & Son | Burslem |
| 7 | 4 | 365876–7 | The Decorative Art Tile Co. | Hanley |
| 7 | 17 | 365914–6 | The Worcester Royal Porcelain Co. Ltd. | Worcester |
| 8 | 6 | 365955 | The Crystal Porcelain Co. | Hanley |
| 13 | 1 | 366015 | S. Lear | Hanley |
| 16 | 8 | 366078–9 | S. Fielding & Co. | Stoke |
| 18 | 1 | 366093 | Jackson & Gosling | Longton |
| 21 | 13 | 366220–2 | Birks Bros. & Seddon | Cobridge |
| 21 | 20 | 366246 | Gildea & Walker | Burslem |
| July 2 | 1 | 366634 | McBirney & Armstrong | Belleek |
| 2 | 5 | 366643 | T. Furnival & Sons | Cobridge |
| 6 | 7 | 366809 | Josiah Wedgwood & Sons | Etruria |
| 9 | 10 | 366922–3 | Wardle & Co. | Hanley |
| 14 | 6 | 367133–4 | T. C. Brown–Westhead, Moore & Co. | Hanley |
| 15 | 5 | 367150 | Wm. Corbitt & Co. | Rthrham |
| 16 | 3 | 367213 | Trubshaw, Hand & Co. | Longton |
| 18 | 4 | 367249 | G. Hall | Worcester |
| 19 | 2 | 367259 | The Dalehall Brick & Tile Co. | Burslem |
| 25 | 2 | 367418 | J. H. Davis | Hanley |
| 28 | 3 | 367516 | McBirney & Armstrong | Belleek |

| Date | Parcel No. | Patent No. | Factory, Retailer Wholesaler, etc | Place |
|---|---|---|---|---|
| 28 | 4 | 367517 | A. Wood | Hanley |
| 28 | 14 | 367538 | Ridgways | Stoke |
| 29 | 2 | 367542–3 | Sherwin & Cotton | Hanley |
| 29 | 3 | 367544 | Whittmann & Roth | London |
| 30 | 3 | 367549 | Sampson Bridgwood & Son | Longton |
| 30 | 4 | 367550 | Sherwin & Cotton | Hanley |
| 30 | 5 | 367551 | Mintons | Stoke |
| 30 | 15 | 367590 | W. T. Copeland & Sons | Stoke |
| Aug 2 | 1 | 367608 | E. J. D. Bodley | Burslem |
| 5 | 12 | 367892–3 | Pinder, Bourne & Co. | Burslem |
| 10 | 13 | 368044 | The Old Hall Earthenware Co. Ltd. | Hanley |
| 20 | 11 | 368686 | The Worcester Royal Porcelain Co. Ltd. | Worcester |
| 23 | 3 | 368802 | F. W. Grove & J. Stark | Longton |
| 24 | 11 | 368942 | T. & R. Boote | Burslem |
| 27 | 3 | 369202 | S. Lear | Hanley |
| 27 | 9 | 369215–8 | Gildea & Walker | Burslem |
| 29 | 7 | 369248 | W. & T. Adams | Tunstall |
| Sept 2 | 4 | 369389 | Dale, Page & Goodwin | Longton |
| 3 | 11 | 369526 | T. A. Simpson | Hanley |
| 6 | 1 | 369538 | The Derby Crown Porcelain Co. Ltd. | Derby |
| 7 | 10 | 369654 | Adams & Sleigh | Burslem |
| 9 | 11 | 369731 | The Worcester Royal Porcelain Co. Ltd. | Worcester |
| 10 | 12 | 369778–81 | J. Roth | London |
| 16 | 10 | 370093 | Geo. Jones & Sons | Stoke |
| 22 | 9 | 370400 | Bold & Michelson | Hanley |
| 23 | 21 | 370470–2 | Minton, Hollins & Co. | Stoke |
| 27 | 9 | 370611 | Pinder, Bourne & Co. | Burslem |
| 28 | 4 | 370620 | E. J. D. Bodley | Burslem |
| 28 | 13 | 370633 | Gildea & Walker | Burslem |
| 29 | 3 | 370636 | Geo. Jones & Sons | Stoke |
| 30 | 3 | 370702–3 | Davenports Ltd. | Longport |

# APPENDIX B

| Date | Parcel No. | Patent No. | Factory, Retailer Wholesaler, etc | Place |
|------|------------|------------|-----------------------------------|-------|
| 30 | 15 | 370725–8 | Mintons | Stoke |
| Oct 4 | 6 | 370885 | Wm. Brownfield & Sons | Cobridge |
| 6 | 5 | 370998 | J. & R. Boote | Burslem |
| 6 | 7 | 371000 | The Campbell Brick & Tile Co. | Stoke |
| 7 | 27 | 371098 | Mintons | Stoke |
| 8 | 3 | 371102 | Adams & Sleigh | Burslem |
| 11 | 16 | 371247 | The Worcester Royal Porcelain Co. Ltd. | Worcester |
| 12 | 14 | 371330–1 | Mintons | Stoke |
| 13 | 3 | 371337 | Adderley & Lawson | Longton |
| 13 | 5 | 371339 | T. & R. Boote | Burslem |
| 20 | 1 | 371866 | Thos. Begley | Burslem |
| 20 | 2 | 371867 | Robinson & Chapman | Longton |
| 22 | 1 | 371959 | Mintons | Stoke |
| 26 | 8 | 372138 | Mintons | Stoke |
| 26 | 16 | 372171 | T. C. Brown–Westhead, Moore & Co. | Hanley |
| 27 | 1 | 372185 | Robinson & Chapman | Longton |
| 29 | 3 | 372347 | T. & R. Boote | Burslem |
| 29 | 4 | 372348 | Wm. Brownfield & Sons | Cobridge |
| 29 | 11 | 372376 | Wardle & Co. | Hanley |
| 29 | 14 | 372379 | Minton, Hollins & Co. | Stoke |
| 31 | 11 | 372464 | T. A. Simpson | Hanley |
| Nov 2 | 1 | 372489–90 | T. C. Brown–Westhead, Moore & Co. | Hanley |
| 3 | 12 | 372613 | The Worcester Royal Porcelain Co. Ltd. | Worcester |
| 4 | 24 | 372727 | idem | Worcester |
| 8 | 1 | 372918 | T. & R. Boote | Burslem |
| 9 | 6 | 372979 | F. W. Grove & J. Stark | Longton |
| 9 | 7 | 372980–2 | E. J. D. Bodley | Burslem |
| 10 | 2 | 372995 | Brough & Blackhurst | Longton |
| 19 | 3 | 373541 | Sampson Bridgwood & Son | Longton |

# APPENDIX B

| Date | Parcel No. | Patent No. | Factory, Retailer Wholesaler, etc | Place |
|---|---|---|---|---|
| 19 | 12 | 373573 | The Worcester Royal Porcelain Co. Ltd. | Worcester |
| 21 | 1 | 373575 | J. Bevington | Hanley |
| 22 | 9 | 373615 | J. Tams | Longton |
| 22 | 17 | 373647 | Ambrose Wood | Hanley |
| 23 | 13 | 373707 | Shorter & Boulton | Stoke |
| 25 | 1 | 373821 | Adams & Sleigh | Burslem |
| 25 | 15 | 373860 | J. Roth | London |
| 29 | 10 | 374058 | The Worcester Royal Porcelain Co. Ltd. | Worcester |
| Dec 2 | 16 | 374229 | J. Roth | London |
| 5 | 11 | 374376 | John Rose & Co. | Coalport |
| 8 | 9 | 374498 | Adderley & Lawson | Longton |
| 9 | 2 | 374516 | E. J. D. Bodley | Burslem |
| 10 | 7 | 374579 | T. C. Brown–Westhead, Moore & Co. | Hanley |
| 12 | 12 | 374628 | John Fell | Longton |
| 16 | 3 | 374782 | Mintons | Stoke |
| 20 | 9 | 374948 | Bednall & Heath | Hanley |
| 21 | 3 | 374955 | F. Grosvenor | Glasgow |
| 21 | 9 | 374987 | The Worcester Royal Porcelain Co. Ltd. | Worcester |
| 24 | 5 | 375054 | J. Broadhurst | Fenton |

**1882**

| Date | Parcel No. | Patent No. | Factory, Retailer Wholesaler, etc | Place |
|---|---|---|---|---|
| Jan 3 | 6 | 375415 | Holmes, Plant & Maydew | Burslem |
| 4 | 2 | 375426–7 | W. T. Copeland & Sons | Stoke |
| 4 | 7 | 375439 | J. Roth | London |
| 4 | 9 | 375444 | F. & R. Pratt & Co. | Fenton |
| 7 | 2 | 375494 | W. H. Grindley & Co. | Tunstall |
| 7 | 11 | 375580 | Ridgways | Hanley |
| 10 | 5 | 375599 | S. Lear | Hanley |
| 11 | 1 | 375709–12 | Minton, Hollins & Co. | Stoke |
| 13 | 4 | 375815–6 | The Decorative Art Tile Co. | Hanley |

379

# APPENDIX B

| Date | Parcel No. | Patent No. | Factory, Retailer Wholesaler, etc | Place |
|------|-----------|-----------|-----------------------------------|-------|
| 18 | 10 | 376032 | Robinson & Son | Longton |
| 26 | 5 | 376425 | J. T. Hudden | Longton |
| 26 | 16 | 376443 | S. Fielding & Co. | Stoke |
| 27 | 8 | 376461 | Craven, Dunnill & Co. Ltd. | Jackfield |
| 30 | 2 | 376528 | Hollinshead & Kirkham | Tunstall |
| 30 | 3 | 376529 | F. W. Grove & J. Stark | Longton |
| Feb 1 | 1 | 376580 | Edge, Malkin & Co. | Burslem |
| 3 | 4 | 376672–3 | T. C. Brown–Westhead, Moore & Co. | Hanley |
| 4 | 10 | 376754 | Minton, Hollins & Co. | Stoke |
| 6 | 4 | 376764–6 | The Campbell Tile Co. | Stoke |
| 7 | 2 | 376798 | Wm. Mills | Hanley |
| 8 | 7 | 376839 | Wardle & Co. | Hanley |
| 15 | 4 | 377048 | F. W. Grove & J. Stark | Longton |
| 16 | 6 | 377135–7 | Mintons | Stoke |
| 18 | 5 | 377273 | J. F. Wileman & Co. | Fenton |
| 23 | 17 | 377488–9 | Minton, Hollins & Co. | Stoke |
| 24 | 3 | 377492 | Taylor, Tunnicliffe & Co. | Hanley |
| Mar 1 | 11 | 377779 | The Worcester Royal Porcelain Co. Ltd. | Worcester |
| 1 | 12 | 377780 | Minton, Hollins & Co. | Stoke |
| 7 | 7 | 378051 | idem | Stoke |
| 13 | 3 | 378252 | J. T. Hudden | Longton |
| 15 | 3 | 378337 | Powell, Bishop & Stonier | Hanley |
| 15 | 4 | 378338 | Murray & Co. | Glasgow |
| 20 | 5 | 378643 | W. A. Adderley | Longton |
| 23 | 2 | 378739 | W. & T. Adams | Tunstall |
| 23 | 15 | 378823 | T. A. Simpson | Hanley |
| 27 | 3 | 378937 | D. Chapman | Longton |
| 27 | 10 | 378959 | Shorter & Boulton | Stoke |
| 28 | 12 | 378988 | Ambrose Wood | Hanley |
| 28 | 16 | 378993–4 | A. Bevington & Co. | Hanley |
| 30 | 13 | 379076 | John Rose & Co. | Coalport |
| 30 | 17 | 379080 | S. Fielding & Co. | Stoke |
| 31 | 3 | 379088 | A. Bevington & Co. | Hanley |

# APPENDIX B

| Date | Parcel No. | Patent No. | Factory, Retailer Wholesaler, etc | Place |
|------|-----------|-----------|-----------------------------------|-------|
| Apr 4 | 2 | 379212–3 | Wm. Brownfield & Sons | Cobridge |
| 11 | 6 | 379434 | Geo. Jones & Sons | Stoke |
| 11 | 7 | 379435–6 | Minton, Hollins & Co. | Stoke |
| 21 | 7 | 379767 | Sampson Bridgwood & Son | Longton |
| 27 | 14 | 380072 | The New Wharf Pottery Co. | Burslem |
| May 2 | 5 | 380194 | G. L. Ashworth & Bros. | Hanley |
| 3 | 1 | 380199 | S. Radford | Longton |
| 5 | 2 | 380401 | Wood, Hines & Winkle | Hanley |
| 6 | 5 | 380418 | Powell, Bishop & Stonier | Hanley |
| 6 | 6 | 380419–20 | Whittaker, Edge & Co. | Hanley |
| 8 | 18 | 380549–50 | Davenports Ltd. | Longport |
| 9 | 3 | 380553–4 | H. Alcock & Co. | Cobridge |
| 9 | 4 | 380555 | Whittaker, Edge & Co. | Hanley |
| 9 | 7 | 380558 | Wm. Brownfield & Sons | Cobridge |
| 9 | 11 | 380564 | Minton, Hollins & Co. | Stoke |
| 10 | 4 | 380571–2 | John Edwards | Fenton |
| 10 | 14 | 380676 | S. Fielding & Co. | Stoke |
| 13 | 6 | 380789 | Geo. Jones & Sons | Stoke |
| 17 | 2 | 380869–70 | E. J. Bodley | Burslem |
| 24 | 4 | 381376 | Minton, Hollins & Co. | Stoke |
| 24 | 21 | 381434 | Doulton & Co. | Burslem |
| 25 | 11 | 381480 | W. A. Adderley | Longton |
| 27 | 3 | 381568 | Samuel Lear | Hanley |
| 30 | 5 | 381611 | W. H. Grindley & Co. | Tunstall |
| June 5 | 6 | 381805 | Mintons | Stoke |
| 5 | 7 | 381806 | Wood, Hines & Winkle | Hanley |
| 9 | 3 | 381964 | Hall & Read | Burslem |
| 9 | 4 | 381965–6 | W. A. Adderley | Longton |
| 13 | 11 | 382126 | A. Shaw & Son | Burslem |
| 13 | 14 | 382130–1 | Wardle & Co. | Hanley |
| 21 | 4 | 382406 | Wm. Lowe | Longton |
| 21 | 5 | 382407–8 | Sampson Bridgwood & Son | Longton |
| 21 | 11 | 382472 | The Old Hall Earthenware & Co. Ltd | Hanley |

381

| Date | Parcel No. | Patent No. | Factory, Retailer Wholesaler, etc | Place |
|------|-----------|-----------|-----------------------------------|-------|
| 23 | 1 | 382593–4 | Josiah Wedgwood & Sons | Etruria |
| 23 | 5 | 382598 | Burgess & Leigh | Burslem |
| 28 | 2 | 382721 | The Derby Crown Porcelain Co. | Derby |
| July 1 | 8 | 382829 | Taylor, Tunnicliffe & Co. | Hanley |
| 3 | 2 | 382842 | Mintons | Stoke |
| 3 | 3 | 382843 | E. J. D. Bodley | Burslem |
| 4 | 3 | 382859 | Wright & Rigby | Hanley |
| 6 | 4 | 383020–1 | Wm. Brownfield & Sons | Cobridge |
| 14 | 3 | 383436–7 | Geo. Jones & Sons | Stoke |
| 14 | 10 | 383468 | Wardle & Co. | Hanley |
| 14 | 14 | 383482 | Beech & Tellwright | Cobridge |
| 17 | 8 | 383549 | Wood & Son | Burslem |
| 19 | 7 | 383641 | Wardle & Co. | Hanley |
| 20 | 1 | 383694–6 | John Edwards | Fenton |
| 22 | 8 | 383802 | Geo. Jones & Sons | Stoke |
| 25 | 3 | 383855 | F. Grosvenor | Glasgow |
| 25 | 9 | 383869–71 | The Brownhills Pottery Co. Ltd. | Tunstall |
| 26 | 4 | 383893 | Adderley & Lawson | Longton |
| 28 | 3 | 384078 | Hawley & Co. | Longton |
| 31 | 2 | 384160–1 | Sampson Bridgwood & Son | Longton |
| 31 | 9 | 384171–2 | Mintons | Stoke |
| Aug 5 | 4 | 384353–4 | Wm. Brownfield & Sons | Cobridge |
| 10 | 5 | 384464 | Wright & Rigby | Hanley |
| 21 | 2 | 385106 | John Tams | Longton |
| 21 | 8 | 385129 | Adams & Bromley | Hanley |
| 25 | 2 | 385411 | Mintons | Stoke |
| 26 | 4 | 385490 | Wm. Wood & Co. | Burslem |
| 28 | 2 | 385527 | Belfield & Co. | Preston-pans |
| 28 | 9 | 385544 | Mintons | Stoke |
| 29 | 12 | 385623 | Wm. Brownfield & Sons | Cobridge |
| 30 | 14 | 385693 | The Worcester Royal Porcelain Co. Ltd. | Worcester |

# APPENDIX B

| Date | Parcel No. | Patent No. | Factory, Retailer Wholesaler, etc | Place |
|------|------------|------------|-----------------------------------|-------|
| 31 | 3 | 385701 | A. Bevington & Co. | Hanley |
| Sept 6 | 2 | 385954 | Hawley & Co. | Longton |
| 8 | 5 | 386085–6 | Mintons | Stoke |
| 9 | 3 | 386126 | Taylor, Tunnicliffe & Co. | Hanley |
| 11 | 4 | 386178 | Adams & Bromley | Hanley |
| 16 | 2 | 386388–9 | Hulme & Massey | Longton |
| 19 | 2 | 386542 | W. H. Grindley & Co. | Tunstall |
| 28 | 4 | 387147–8 | T. C. Brown–Westhead, Moore & Co. | Hanley |
| 28 | 22 | 387229 | Bridgett & Bates | Longton |
| 29 | 2 | 387231–2 | The Brownhills Pottery Co. | Tunstall |
| Oct 6 | 2 | 387598–603 | Mintons | Stoke |
| 9 | 3 | 387771 | W. T. Copeland & Sons | Stoke |
| 9 | 4 | 387772 | Dean, Capper & Dean | Hanley |
| 11 | 3 | 387958–60 | Sampson Bridgwood & Son | Longton |
| 11 | 4 | 387961 | Wood & Son | Burslem |
| 12 | 17 | 388200 | T. Furnival & Sons | Cobridge |
| 16 | 4 | 388296 | Wood & Son | Burslem |
| 19 | 4 | 388395 | Lowe, Ratcliffe & Co. | Longton |
| 31 | 2 | 389136 | Wm. Lowe | Longton |
| Nov 1 | 14 | 389201 | Stonier, Hollinshead & Oliver | Hanley |
| 4 | 19 | 389390 | The Worcester Royal Porcelain Co. Ltd. | Worcester |
| 8 | 2 | 389554 | Mintons | Stoke |
| 10 | 10 | 389793 | Ridgways | Stoke |
| 10 | 12 | 389795–7 | Pratt & Simpson | Fenton |
| 11 | 2 | 389801 | Powell, Bishop & Stonier | Hanley |
| 13 | 1 | 389893 | Edge, Malkin & Co. | Burslem |
| 13 | 2 | 389894 | Sampson Bridgwood & Son | Longton |
| 14 | 3 | 389911–2 | Ed. Steel | Hanley |
| 15 | 7 | 390004–5 | S. Fielding & Co. | Stoke |
| 16 | 3 | 390023 | Taylor, Tunnicliffe & Co. | Hanley |
| 21 | 4 | 390255 | J. Holdcroft | Longton |

# APPENDIX B

| Date | Parcel No. | Patent No. | Factory, Retailer Wholesaler, etc | Place |
|------|------------|------------|-----------------------------------|-------|
| 21 | 8 | 390264 | Gildea & Walker | Burslem |
| 22 | 11 | 390285 | S. Fielding & Co. | Stoke |
| 24 | 19 | 390588 | Minton, Hollins & Co. | Stoke |
| 27 | 3 | 390617 | H. Alcock & Co. | Cobridge |
| 27 | 4 | 390618 | The Derby Crown Porcelain Co. Ltd. | Derby |
| 27 | 5 | 390619 | J. F. Wileman & Co. | Fenton |
| Dec 2 | 8 | 390976 | Minton, Hollins & Co. | Stoke |
| 4 | 7 | 390985 | A. Bevington & Co. | Hanley |
| 6 | 2 | 391068–9 | T. C. Brown–Westhead, Moore & Co. | Hanley |
| 13 | 4 | 391361–2 | Mintons | Stoke |
| 13 | 5 | 391363–4 | Josiah Wedgwood | Etruria |
| 14 | 6 | 391409 | S. Lear | Hanley |
| 15 | 3 | 391460 | The Old Hall Earthenware Co. Ltd. | Hanley |
| 18 | 9 | 391596 | J. Lockett & Co. | Longton |
| 19 | 3 | 391620 | H. Kennedy | Glasgow |
| 21 | 4 | 391768 | E. J. D. Bodley | Burslem |
| 21 | 5 | 391769 | Wood, Hines & Winkle | Hanley |
| 22 | 2 | 391818 | F. W. Grove & J. Stark | Longton |
| 22 | 14 | 391846 | Lorenz Hutschenreuther | Bavaria |
| 23 | 4 | 391855 | J. F. Wileman | Fenton |
| 23 | 12 | 391917 | The New Wharf Pottery Co. | Burslem |
| 23 | 14 | 391922–7 | The Worcester Royal Porcelain Co. | Worcester |
| 27 | 1 | 391929 | The New Wharf Pottery Co. | Burslem |
| **1883** | | | | |
| Jan 2 | 2 | 392166 | The Derby Crown Porcelain Co. Ltd. | Derby |
| 3 | 1 | 392176 | Wm. Hines | Longton |
| 3 | 14 | 392362 | T. Furnival & Sons | Cobridge |

384

| Date | Parcel No. | Patent No. | Factory, Retailer Wholesaler, etc | Place |
|---|---|---|---|---|
| 3 | 18 | 392388–9 | John Rose & Co. | Coalport |
| 4 | 5 | 392403 | T. C. Brown–Westhead, Moore & Co. | Hanley |
| 8 | 5 | 392590 | W. T. Copeland & Sons | Stoke |
| 8 | 12 | 392621 | The Worcester Royal Porcelain Co. Ltd. | Worcester |
| 9 | 3 | 392626 | Powell, Bishop & Stonier | Hanley |
| 9 | 4 | 392627 | E. F. Bodley & Son | Longport |
| 9 | 5 | 392628–30 | Hall & Read | Hanley |
| 9 | 11 | 392652 | Davenports Ltd. | Longport |
| 10 | 17 | 392693 | Gildea & Walker | Burslem |
| 12 | 3 | 392725 | Holmes, Plant & Maydew | Burslem |
| 13 | 6 | 392760 | Moore & Co. | Longton |
| 13 | 17 | 392809 | T. & R. Boote | Burslem |
| 16 | 1 | 392855 | Blair & Co. | Longton |
| 17 | 3 | 392888 | W. H. Grindley & Co. | Tunstall |
| 23 | 8 | 393099 | E. F. Bodley & Son | Longport |
| 23 | 10 | 393102–3 | W. T. Copeland & Sons | Stoke |
| 24 | 1 | 393107 | Sampson Bridgwood & Son | Longton |
| 24 | 2 | 393108–9 | Wm. Brownfield & Sons | Cobridge |
| 25 | 3 | 393177 | The Brownhills Pottery Co. | Tunstall |
| 26 | 8 | 393258 | Wm. Lowe | Longton |
| 27 | 8 | 393298 | G. W. Turner & Sons | Tunstall |
| 29 | 6 | 393310 | Wm. Brownfield & Sons | Cobridge |
| 29 | 7 | 393311–2 | W. H. Grindley & Co. | Tunstall |
| 30 | 1 | 393323 | E. F. Bodley & Son | Longport |
| 30 | 12 | 393362 | Wedgwood & Co. | Tunstall |
| 31 | 14 | 393413 | Minton, Hollins & Co. | Stoke |
| Feb 1 | 3 | 393418 | Sampson Bridgwood & Son | Longton |
| 1 | 17 | 393474 | E. J. D. Bodley | Burslem |
| 2 | 4 | 393495 | S. Hancock | Stoke |
| 2 | 17 | 393539 | Wedgwood & Co. | Tuhstall |
| 3 | 3 | 393548 | Mintons | Stoke |
| 5 | 2 | 393647 | J. Holdcroft | Longton |
| 6 | 1 | 393668 | Wood, Hines & Winkle | Hanley |

# APPENDIX B

| Date | Parcel No. | Patent No. | Factory, Retailer Wholesaler, etc | Place |
|------|-----------|-----------|-----------------------------------|-------|
| 7 | 4 | 393714 | Hawley & Co. | Longton |
| 7 | 5 | 393715 | Mountford & Thomas | Hanley |
| 9 | 9 | 393979 | E. J. D. Bodley | Burslem |
| 12 | 3 | 394086 | Dunn, Bennett & Co. | Hanley |
| 14 | 3 | 394185 | W. H. Grindley & Co. | Tunstall |
| 15 | 5 | 394215 | J. H. Davis | Hanley |
| 17 | 13 | 394371 | G. W. Turner & Sons | Tunstall |
| 19 | 1 | 394374 | W. A. Adderley | Longton |
| 20 | 13 | 394443 | Davenports Ltd. | Longport |
| 20 | 17 | 394448 | Gildea & Walker | Burslem |
| 21 | 3 | 394452 | Geo. Jones & Sons | Stoke |
| 22 | 6 | 394556–61 | Hall & Read | Hanley |
| 22 | 20 | 394599 | The Worcester Royal Porcelain Co. Ltd. | Worcester |
| 22 | 21 | 394600 | The Old Hall Earthenware Co. | Hanley |
| 24 | 12 | 394676 | Josiah Wedgwood & Sons | Etruria |
| 24 | 13 | 394677 | The Worcester Royal Porcelain Co. Ltd. | Worcester |
| 26 | 6 | 394687 | Williamson & Sons | Longton |
| 28 | 3 | 394765 | Thos. Till & Sons | Burslem |
| Mar 8 | 5 | 395284 | M. Massey | Hanley |
| 8 | 20 | 395316–7 | E. F. Bodley & Son | Longport |
| 14 | 3 | 395560 | The Derby Porcelain Co. Ltd. | Derby |
| 15 | 3 | 395622 | T. Furnival & Sons | Cobridge |
| 16 | 6 | 395688 | J. Broadhurst | Fenton |
| 17 | 8 | 395703 | Mintons | Stoke |
| 20 | 3 | 395818 | E. A. Wood | Hanley |
| 20 | 4 | 395819 | Josiah Wedgwood & Sons | Etruria |
| 24 | 3 | 396056 | Sampson Bridgwood & Son | Longton |
| 30 | 1 | 396200–1 | Mintons | Stoke |
| 30 | 9 | 396245 | Minton, Hollins & Co. | Stoke |
| Apr 2 | 3 | 396313 | T. & E. L. Poulson | Castleford |
| 3 | 3 | 396316 | E. Warburton | Longton |

# APPENDIX B

| Date | Parcel No. | Patent No. | Factory, Retailer Wholesaler, etc | Place |
|------|-----------|-----------|-----------------------------------|-------|
| 6 | 14 | 396576 | G. & J. Hobson | Burslem |
| 10 | 1 | 396648 | Banks & Thorley | Hanley |
| 19 | 3 | 397090 | R. H. Plant & Co. | Longton |
| 21 | 1 | 397227 | J. F. Wileman & Co. | Fenton |
| 24 | 7 | 397311 | G. L. Ashworth & Bros. | Hanley |
| 25 | 14 | 397376 | Pratt & Simpson | Fenton |
| 27 | 17 | 397512 | C. Littler & Co. | Hanley |
| 27 | 18 | 397513 | J. H. Davis | Hanley |
| 27 | 19 | 397514 | Powell, Bishop & Stonier | Hanley |
| May 2 | 4 | 397609–11 | T. C. Brown–Westhead, Moore & Co. | Hanley |
| 5 | 4 | 397751 | Whittaker, Edge & Co. | Hanley |
| 7 | 8 | 397819 | S. Fielding & Co. | Stoke |
| 8 | 6 | 397829–30 | T. G. & F. Booth | Tunstall |
| 11 | 5 | 398059 | R. H. Plant & Co. | Longton |
| 16 | 12 | 398280 | T. A. Simpson | Stoke |
| 22 | 11 | 398425 | Powell, Bishop & Stonier | Hanley |
| 22 | 12 | 398426 | Burns, Oates | London |
| 23 | 7 | 398436 | T. G. & F. Booth | Tunstall |
| 23 | 8 | 398437–8 | E. A. Wood | Hanley |
| 24 | 3 | 398479 | The Brownhills Pottery Co. | Tunstall |
| 25 | 4 | 398519 | W. A. Adderley | Longton |
| 28 | 2 | 398577–80 | O. G. Blunden | Poling |
| 31 | 17 | 398784 | Wardle & Co. | Hanley |
| June 2 | 9 | 398849–55 | Minton, Hollins & Co. | Stoke |
| 4 | 8 | 398877–8 | Clementson Bros. | Hanley |
| 8 | 2 | 399068 | H. Alcock & Co. | Cobridge |
| 9 | 2 | 399135–6 | Sampson Bridgwood & Son | Longton |
| 9 | 6 | 399143 | Mintons | Stoke |
| 11 | 2 | 399147 | F. W. Grove & J. Stark | Longton |
| 11 | 8 | 399161 | J. Matthews | Westons-'-Mare |
| 11 | 9 | 399162 | idem | Westons-'-Mare |

# APPENDIX B

| Date | Parcel No. | Patent No. | Factory, Retailer Wholesaler, etc | Place |
|------|-----------|-----------|-----------------------------------|-------|
| 13 | 3 | 399319 | Belfield & Co. | Preston-pans |
| 13 | 7 | 399336 | Pratt & Simpson | Stoke |
| 14 | 2 | 399367–70 | F. W. Grove & J. Stark | Longton |
| 18 | 11 | 399554 | John Tams | Longton |
| 18 | 12 | 399555–9 | Wm. Brownfield & Sons | Cobridge |
| 20 | 3 | 399640 | T. & R. Boote | Burslem |
| 20 | 4 | 399641 | Mintons | Stoke |
| 20 | 16 | 399675 | W. & E. Corn | Burslem |
| 21 | 22 | 399822 | Wardle & Co. | Hanley |
| 23 | 4 | 399875 | Josiah Wedgwood & Sons | Etruria |
| 25 | 5 | 399891 | Ford & Riley | Burslem |
| 25 | 10 | 399897–8 | Wm. Brownfield & Sons | Cobridge |
| July 2 | 4 | 400146 | Edge, Malkin & Co. | Burslem |
| 3 | 3 | 400176 | J. Aynsley & Sons | Longton |
| 3 | 4 | 400177 | Moore Bros. | Longton |
| 4 | 7 | 400348 | Wm. Brownfield & Sons | Cobridge |
| 5 | 6 | 400367 | F. W. Grove & J. Stark | Longton |
| 5 | 19 | 400462 | T. Furnival & Sons | Cobridge |
| 5 | 21 | 400464 | Owen, Raby & Co. | Longport |
| 6 | 2 | 400467 | Blackhurst & Bourne | Burslem |
| 10 | 9 | 400582 | Ambrose Wood | Hanley |
| 10 | 11 | 400583–4 | J. Macintyre & Co. | Burslem |
| 11 | 1 | 400596 | Josiah Wedgwood & Sons | Etruria |
| 19 | 4 | 400941 | Davenports Ltd. | Longport |
| 19 | 21 | 400994 | Geo. Jones & Sons | Stoke |
| 20 | 11 | 401035 | Hollinshead & Kirkham | Tunstall |
| 21 | 3 | 401040 | Bridgett & Bates | Longton |
| 23 | 3 | 401087 | Josiah Wedgwood & Sons | Etruria |
| 26 | 1 | 401296 | W. A. Adderley | Longton |
| 27 | 4 | 401410 | T. C. Brown–Westhead, Moore & Co. | Hanley |
| 27 | 13 | 401426–7 | Wm. Bennett | Hanley |
| 30 | 10 | 401553 | Wm. Brownfield & Sons | Cobridge |
| 31 | 3 | 401593 | T. & R. Boote | Burslem |

# APPENDIX B

| Date | Parcel No. | Patent No. | Factory, Retailer Wholesaler, etc | Place |
|------|------|------|------|------|
| Aug 1 | 3 | 401623 | Wagstaff & Brunt | Longton |
| 1 | 4 | 401624 | Geo. Jones & Sons | Stoke |
| 1 | 9 | 401653 | T. C. Brown–Westhead, Moore & Co. | Hanley |
| 2 | 3 | 401663–4 | Davenports Ltd. | Longport |
| 3 | 17 | 401769 | E. J. Bodley | Burslem |
| 8 | 9 | 401842 | J. & E. Ridgway | Stoke |
| 9 | 15 | 401897–9 | Haviland & Co. | France and London |
| 17 | 5 | 402346 | E. J. D. Bodley | Burslem |
| 20 | 8 | 402514 | The Worcester Royal Porcelain Co. Ltd. | Worcester |
| 22 | 1 | 402560–1 | The Brownhills Pottery Co. | Tunstall |
| 23 | 2 | 402625–6 | Grove & Cope | Hanley |
| 24 | 12 | 402736 | Mountford & Thomas | Hanley |
| 25 | 11 | 402839 | Wm. Brownfield & Sons | Cobridge |
| 29 | 3 | 402950 | J. Aynsley & Sons | Longton |
| 31 | 6 | 403110 | W. & E. Corn | Burslem |
| 31 | 7 | 403111 | J. F. Wileman & Co. | Fenton |
| Sept 1 | 10 | 403204 | S. Fielding & Co. | Stoke |
| 5 | 3 | 403298–9 | Wm. Brownfield & Sons | Cobridge |
| 7 | 4 | 403486 | The Derby Crown Porcelain Co. Ltd. | Derby |
| 7 | 19 | 403513–4 | Powell, Bishop & Stonier | Hanley |
| 11 | 4 | 403665 | Josiah Wedgwood & Sons | Etruria |
| 13 | 17 | 403802–3 | H. Aynsley & Co. | Longton |
| 14 | 1 | 403805–6 | W. & T. Adams | Tunstall |
| 14 | 2 | 403807–9 | Mintons | Stoke |
| 17 | 14 | 403978 | The Derby Crown Porcelain Co. Ltd. | Derby |
| 20 | 12 | 404171–5 | Hall & Read | Hanley |
| 20 | 13 | 404176 | The Derby Crown Porcelain Co. Ltd. | Derby |

389

| Date | Parcel No. | Patent No. | Factory, Retailer Wholesaler, etc | Place |
|------|-----------|-----------|-----------------------------------|-------|
| 21 | 4 | 404196 | T. C. Brown–Westhead, Moore & Co. | Hanley |
| 24 | 9 | 404317 | Jones & Hopkinson | Hanley |
| 25 | 4 | 404328 | F. W. Grove & J. Stark | Longton |
| 25 | 5 | 404329–30 | Sampson Bridgwood & Son | Longton |
| 27 | 21 | 404466 | Meigh & Forester | Longton |
| 28 | 4 | 404473 | Blair & Co. | Longton |
| 28 | 5 | 404474 | E. J. D. Bodley | Burslem |
| 29 | 4 | 404571 | Sampson Bridgwood & Son | Longton |
| Oct 2 | 15 | 404643 | Mellor, Taylor & Co. | Burslem |
| 2 | 22 | 404652–3 | Meigh & Forester | Longton |
| 4 | 4 | 404745 | Sampson Bridgwood & Son | Longton |
| 4 | 5 | 404746 | Whittaker, Edge & Co. | Hanley |
| 4 | 24 | 404809 | The Worcester Royal Porcelain Co. Ltd. | Worcester |
| 6 | 2 | 404870 | W. H. Grindley & Co. | Tunstall |
| 8 | 1 | 404900 | Hollinson & Goodall | Longton |
| 8 | 2 | 404901–2 | T. G. & F. Booth | Tunstall |
| 8 | 3 | 404903–5 | Hall & Read | Hanley |
| 9 | 9 | 405016–8 | A. Bevington & Co. | Hanley |
| 11 | 2 | 405215 | Wittmann & Roth | London |
| 12 | 13 | 405336 | Bridgetts & Bates | Longton |
| 13 | 3 | 405341 | Wood & Son | Burslem |
| 13 | 11 | 405363–4 | Wm. Brownfield & Sons | Cobridge |
| 17 | 5 | 405466 | The New Wharf Pottery Co. | Burslem |
| 17 | 6 | 405467–8 | Hall & Read | Hanley |
| 20 | 3 | 405724 | W. A. Adderley | Longton |
| 20 | 4 | 405725–9 | Wm. Brownfield & Sons | Cobridge |
| 23 | 6 | 405855 | J. Dimmock & Co. | Hanley |
| 24 | 11 | 405946–8 | Minton, Hollins & Co. | Stoke |
| 25 | 17 | 406032–3 | Taylor, Tunnicliffe & Co. | Hanley |
| 26 | 7 | 406043 | Jones & Hopkinson | Hanley |
| 27 | 1 | 406046 | The Brownhills Pottery Co. | Tunstall |

# APPENDIX B

| Date | Parcel No. | Patent No. | Factory, Retailer Wholesaler, etc | Place |
|------|------------|------------|-----------------------------------|-------|
| 30 | 2 | 406140 | J. Marshall & Co. | Bo'ness, Scotland |
| 30 | 3 | 406141 | The New Wharf Pottery Co. | Burslem |
| 30 | 17 | 406187 | J. Robinson | Burslem |
| Nov 1 | 1 | 406223 | A. Bevington & Co. | Hanley |
| 1 | 25 | 406370 | Wood, Hines & Winkle | Hanley |
| 1 | 26 | 406371 | S. Fielding & Co. | Stoke |
| 1 | 27 | 406372 | Davenports Ltd. | Longport |
| 2 | 19 | 406464–9 | The Worcester Royal Porcelain Co. Ltd. | Worcester |
| 5 | 13 | 406511 | H. Alcock & Co. | Cobridge |
| 6 | 3 | 406516 | E. & C. Challinor | Fenton |
| 7 | 2 | 406561 | W. & E. Corn | Burslem |
| 10 | 9 | 406781 | Taylor, Tunnicliffe & Co. | Hanley |
| 10 | 10 | 406782 | Wm. Brownfield & Sons | Cobridge |
| 13 | 10 | 406875 | T. G. & F. Booth | Tunstall |
| 14 | 3 | 406893 | Stonier, Hollinshead & Oliver | Hanley |
| 15 | 17 | 407063 | T. Furnival & Sons | Cobridge |
| 17 | 2 | 407155 | The Derby Crown Porcelain Co. Ltd. | Derby |
| 21 | 3 | 407333 | F. J. Emery | Burslem |
| 22 | 3 | 407385 | S. Fielding & Co. | Stoke |
| 23 | 7 | 407587–8 | Minton, Hollins & Co. | Stoke |
| 24 | 3 | 407601 | Powell, Bishop & Stonier | Hanley |
| 26 | 2 | 407623 | W. A. Adderley | Longton |
| 26 | 3 | 407624 | Sampson Bridgwood & Son | Longton |
| 28 | 12 | 407805–10 | The Worcester Royal Porcelain Co. Ltd. | Worcester |
| Dec 1 | 3 | 407913 | idem | Worcester |
| 3 | 10 | 407943 | James Wilson | Longton |
| 5 | 2 | 408035 | Malkin, Edge & Co. | Burslem |
| 5 | 3 | 408036 | The Derby Crown Porcelain Co. Ltd. | Derby |

# APPENDIX B

| Date | Parcel No. | Patent No. | Factory, Retailer Wholesaler, etc | Place |
|------|------------|------------|-----------------------------------|-------|
| 8 | 8 | 408136 | J. F. Wileman & Co. | Fenton |
| 14 | 4 | 408288 | The Brownhills Pottery Co. | Tunstall |
| 15 | 13 | 408356 | T. G. & F. Booth | Tunstall |
| 15 | 14 | 408357 | Hollinson & Goodall | Longton |
| 29 | 4 | 408849 | Powell, Bishop & Stonier | Hanley |

# Index

*Some of the firms listed in Appendix B did not use accepted factory-marks and are therefore omitted from the general index.*

394

395

399

401

407

Griffiths, Beardmore & Birks, 179
Grimwade Bros., 157
Grimwades, Ltd., 157
Grindley & Co. Ltd., W.H., 250, 251
Grindley Hotel Ware Co. Ltd., 251
Grosvenor & Son, F., 265
Grosvenor China, 203
Groves, L.A., 20
Groves, Lavender, 60
Grove & Stark, 200
G.S. & Co., 77
G. & S. Ltd./B., 105
G.S. & S., 73
G.T.M., 236
G.T. & S., 258
Guernsey, 261
Guernsey Pottery Ltd., 261
Guest & Dewsbury, 271
G.U.S. Ltd., 250
G.W., 91, 217
G.W. & S., 217
G.W. & S. Ltd., 217
G.W.T.S., 258
G.W.T. & S., 258

*H.*

H., 139
H. Ltd., 139
H. & A., 201, 203
H. & Co., 157, 201, 202
H.A. & Co., 127
H.A. & Co. over crown, 185
H.A. & Co., L., 187
H.A. & Co., L. in knot, 187
Hackwood, 167
Hackwood & Co., 157
Hackwood, William, 157

Hackwood & Keeling, 157
Hackwood & Son, William, 222
Hadley & Sons, J., 92
Haile, T.S., 37
Haines, Batchelor & Co., 57
Hales Bros., 57
Hales, Hancock & Co., 57
Hales, Hancock & Goodwin Ltd., 57
Hall, 157
Hall, I., 107
Hall, R., 251
Hall, Ralph, 251
Hall, Samuel, 157
Hall & Co., R., 251
Hall & Read, 157
Hall & Son, R., 251
Hall & Sons, John, 107
Hallam & Day, 201
Hamada, Shoji, 75
Hamilton, 265
Hamilton, R., 229
Hammersley & Co., 201
Hammersley, J.R., 158
Hammersley & Son, Ralph, 107
Hammersley & Asbury, 201
Hammond, Henry, 43
Hampson & Broadhurst, 201
Hancock, B. & S., 229
Hancock, Robert, 89
Hancock, S., 229
Hancock & Co. F., 229
Hancock & Sons (Potters) Ltd., 229
Hancock & Sons, Sampson, 229
Hancock & Whittingham, 229
Hancock, Whittingham & Co., 107
hands, clasped, 100

409

421

423

424

426

428